Riding Hard

by

J.L. Sheppard

Hell Ryders MC Book 4

This is a work of fiction. Names, characters, places, and incidents are either the product of the author's imagination or are used fictitiously, and any resemblance to actual persons living or dead, business establishments, events, or locales, is entirely coincidental.

Riding Hard

Contact Information: info@thewildrosepress.com

Cover Art by *Diana Carlile*

The Wild Rose Press, Inc.
PO Box 708
Adams Basin, NY 14410-0708

Visit us at www.thewildrosepress.com

Publishing History
First Scarlet Rose Edition, 2019
Print ISBN 978-1-5092-2575-0
Digital ISBN 978-1-5092-2576-7

Published in the United States of America

What's luck got to do with it?

"Fine. I'll go with you."

Going was her best option. When he took her home, she'd tell him why she'd avoided him and why the two of them getting together was a bad idea. Of course, that'd only work if he didn't kiss her. So her plan—she had to keep him away.

He hesitated for a moment then released her.

"I have to say bye."

She spun and made it halfway around when his fingers gripped her wrist. He tugged, turning her to him again.

"You hear what I said before, Lex, or are you deaf?"

She clenched her jaw and fisted her free hand. Then the anger burning inside her spilled. "For an entire month, I sat in my beautiful house alone. That is, in between the times I got house visits from you being a jerk. I'm very angry with you for ruining the first fun night I've had since moving here."

Her face flushed with each word. That heat crept down her neck and chest. "I've agreed to leave with you, but I'm not happy about it. I'm not anyone you can boss or control. I were you, I'd tread very carefully because quite frankly, I've had it with your insults, your cursing, your caveman tactics. Bottom line…"

She tore her wrist from his grasp and shoved a pointed finger in his face. "I've had it with you."

A muscle in his jaw twitched. He grabbed her wrist, pulled her hand away from his face, and squeezed. "I could control you, babe, you'd be sitting on my face."

PRAISE FOR AUTHOR

J.L. Sheppard

RUNNING WILD

"Ready for some hot bikers? J.L. Sheppard has a new series for you!"

~*Night Owl Reviews*

~*~

"A great beginning to a new MC series!"

~*InD'tale Magazine*

RUNNING HOT

"*Running Hot* is impossible to put down! A great read for anytime of the year!"

~*InD'tale Magazine*

~*~

"*Running Hot* is an amazing second book in a must read series!"

~*TBR Pile*

RIDING BLIND

"You won't want to put [*Riding Blind*] down until it's over. And even then, you'll want more…"

~*Sweet & Spicy Reads*

~*~

"J.L. Sheppard has written a beautiful second-chance love story…"

~*Beyond the Covers*

Dedication

For Bryce Daniel Sheppard

Author Acknowledgments

As always, a big thank you to my family and friends for their continued support.

To my editor, Sharon Pickrel, I'm forever thankful for all I've learned and all I continue to learn from you. Thank you also for your hard work and patience.

To my publisher, including everyone who works behind the scenes: Rhonda, RJ, Diana, and Lisa to name a few, thank you for giving me the opportunity to reach countless readers, and especially, for believing in my stories.

Last but not least, to my readers, it's for you I write. I'm forever grateful.

Chapter One

Alexa Millen wiped the sweat beaded on her brow with the sleeve of her shirt and continued unpacking kitchenware from the cardboard box.

Two boxes down, ten thousand to go. At least that's what it felt like. If she spent the next decade unpacking, she wouldn't care because as the proud owner of a three-bedroom bungalow, she'd moved for the last time.

The thought made her giddy all over again. A homeowner! No more moving, ever. She'd been beyond thrilled, more excited than she'd ever been for the last three months, a very, very long three months. The countdown began the minute she closed on her home and started renovations.

Her adorable house needed a lot of work and updating, but she couldn't afford it all at once, so she'd done what anyone else would've and settled on renovating the most important things first: floors, master bathroom, and kitchen, which included knocking down a wall to make her home open concept. She managed to afford this after purchasing the home on a teacher's salary because she'd saved forever and she bid on a foreclosed home in Wadden, a small, quaint, and quiet town about half an hour from Santa Rosa, California. It was perfect, close to the beach and an hour from San Francisco, where her sister lived. Not to mention, she'd been lucky enough to find a job at the elementary school in that cute town. Come Monday morning, she'd be the kindergarten teacher at Wadden Elementary located three blocks from her home.

Her new job so close to her house made her love her home that much more even if just three months ago it'd been a disaster, even if the stress of renovating took about a decade off her life, even if she still had to renovate a full bath, the deck, and pool, which would no doubt take another decade off her life.

The best part about her home? All hers. She didn't need a man, her parents, her sister, or even a roommate. She'd saved every dime on her own. It took a long time, but it made it all the more rewarding.

Smiling, she stopped unpacking for a second to look around her open-concept living room, dining room, and kitchen. The space looked so much bigger than it had before renovating even with the series of boxes piled inside.

Her beige couch faced the accent wall she'd painted navy where her flat screen television would eventually go. An expresso coffee table sat in front of it. Under it, a beautiful rug with a mass of colors. Blues, purples, greens, and browns covered part of her new hardwood floor. The dining room was empty if you didn't count the moving boxes. She'd sold her two-seater dining table intent on buying a bigger one. This would have to wait since the renovation budget flew out the window after several unexpected expenses.

Her kitchen was absolutely gorgeous: same hardwood floors, dark cabinets, a gorgeous backsplash with a pop of blue color, and marble countertops. On the island, she'd installed a thick slab of bamboo. A large window in the kitchen allowed her to see the large backyard including the mess of her deck and pool. Still, that window was panoramic and larger than any she'd ever seen. It'd inevitably be more gorgeous when she fixed her backyard. Beside the kitchen, a sliding glass door led outside.

To the other side of the kitchen, the one-car garage she'd use mostly for storage. Next to the living room, a hallway led into the guest bathroom and bedrooms. Her master suite was the last room, large enough to fit her bedroom furniture and there was still room for a reading nook: a lounge chair of some sort, a bookcase with her favorites, small end table, and lamp. This would also have to wait. Up next, the most important, fixing the guest bathroom. Pink tiles, pink toilet, and pink sink, a pale pink that made her want to puke. Demolition started Monday. She couldn't wait. Looking at the demo mess would be better than that pink bathroom.

Her phone rang drawing her gaze away from the box she'd been unpacking. Checking the caller ID, she smiled and slid her finger across the screen. "Hey, Meg."

"Don't you sound excited to hear from me."

She smirked. "Thrilled."

"Spare me the sarcasm, sis."

Planting a hand on her hip, she shot back, "You started it." Funny how she never got too old to say that to her sibling.

Meg laughed. "Give me a break, okay? We're worried about you."

Alexa hated being the baby. It meant she'd always be the baby even if she'd soon turn thirty. She knew her sister meant well. Meg always meant well, so Alexa kept her temper in check.

She bit her bottom lip and released it. "I know."

"Wish you would've stayed in San Fran, Lex."

Yikes. Her sister sounded sad. Meg let herself believe she'd stay in San Francisco. Just three years apart, they were close. Part of it had to do with the fact that they spent their childhood moving from place to place.

Staying in San Francisco had never been an option. Alexa didn't like big cities. She liked small, quiet towns. After college, she'd moved to San Francisco because of Meg, but she never intended to stay. When she started house hunting, she considered her sister. It was one of the reasons her house in Wadden was perfect.

"I'm an hour away, Meg."

"I know, Lex. It's just…" Meg trailed off. When she spoke again, she sounded choked up. "I always thought when we were grown up, we'd live close, like around-the-corner close, not an-hour-away close."

She swallowed. "We've been grown for a while, Meg."

"You know what I mean…when we settled down, got married. Any day now you're going to meet the guy for you, and then, you'll get married and have kids and—"

Alexa wished it were that easy. She'd come to terms with the possibility of dying an old maid. Fact, she'd grown tired of dating, tired of waiting, tired of men in general.

She released a heavy sigh. "I know Tim's awesome, and I'm glad you have him, but not every guy is Tim. Trust me."

"Oh God, really, this bullshit again?"

Maybe she had been talking about it too much, partially Meg's fault, hers and their mother's. She'd lost count of the many times they'd set her up with Tim's friends, with co-workers, with random freaking strangers. She was done dating and now, officially done talking about it.

"What? Now you're ignoring me?" Meg snapped.

Where'd that come from? She hadn't hesitated but a second.

She furrowed her brows and tilted her head before she carefully asked, "Are you okay?"

"Crap. Yeah…just…I'm pregnant."

Her heart dropped to her stomach, butterflies there making her jittery. "Oh my God. You're pregnant?"

"Yeah."

A wide smile spread across her face. "I'm going to be an auntie!"

"Ugh, yes. You're going to be an aunt, but who knows when this kid will meet you since you live in BFE."

She loved her sister, but Megan was a handful: moody, emotional, and dramatic with a capital D. Now pregnant? Poor Tim.

She laughed. "I'm an hour away. Stop stressing, and congrats. I bet Tim is—"

"Haven't told him yet."

Her jaw dropped. "What? Why?"

"I just found out this morning, and he's working today."

It was Saturday, but Tim was a workaholic and good at his job. It's the reason he'd been promoted to

Chief Accounting Officer of BEX Real Estate, a large, publicly traded company, at the ripe age of thirty-four.

"You need to fill me in when you do."

"You know I will."

"Though I doubt you'll have to. I know he'll be thrilled."

"Yeah, definitely. He's wanted this for a while. All I have to do is think of the perfect way to tell him."

She and Meg discussed the many ways to announce the news to Tim while she unpacked another two boxes. When she got a crick in her neck, she promised her sister she'd call tomorrow and hung up.

She still had a couple of boxes in her car, so she decided to unload those before she continued unpacking. Heading out the front door with her keys in hand, she unlocked her car and opened the passenger side door of her Toyota Camry. She grabbed a box filled with miscellaneous items, shut the door with her hip, then strode inside and placed the box in the dining room. Back outside, she popped her trunk, reached inside, and clutched another box, this one smaller, also labeled miscellaneous. When she turned, her gaze dropped and landed on a boy.

Young, four, maybe five, wearing a black tee, a pair of jeans ripped at the knee, and sneakers. He had a head of beautifully thick, dark-brown, disheveled hair and a set of piercing, large, brown eyes with long, dark lashes. Those striking eyes were deadlocked on her, not just staring but observing *her*. This, she knew from his drawn brows, contemplative expression, and the intelligence that shined through those eyes.

She smiled softly. "Hi, there."

Tearing her stare from his, she looked down the

street both ways and across it. Several kids wandered, a few playing basketball, several others chasing each other, but no adult, no one who could be his parent.

She peered back at him. “I’m Alexa, but everyone calls me Lex. What’s your name?”

He lifted a hand and rubbed his eye with his knuckles.

“Are you lost?”

He shook his head.

She didn’t think so either, but at least now, she knew he understood her. He didn’t share his name, but maybe he was younger than he looked and didn’t know how to pronounce it. Maybe he didn’t speak yet, or maybe he’d been taught not to talk to strangers.

“Do you live nearby?”

He nodded. Then he grinned.

She parted her mouth, but before she managed a word, a shout echoed.

“Cullen!”

She jumped, almost dropping the box she held, and shut her mouth. Her head snapped up, and her stare fell on *him.* Tall, more than six-feet easily, broad shoulders, and a narrow waist. His face, strong, clean lines, stubble covered his chin and cheeks. Lips full, thick, dark-brown, disheveled hair, short on the sides and longer on top, like the boy’s. Also like the boy’s, his eyes were big and a rich brown color.

Beautiful, as in the most attractive man she’d ever seen.

She thought this as her gaze traveled from his face to his torso, legs, and feet. He wore a pair of jeans, boots, and a black T-shirt, and over it, a leather vest with an inscription on one side that read, “Hell Ryders

Motorcycle Club." She knew when he turned she'd see an emblem, a set of angel wings in flames with a skull in the middle. Around it, it'd read, "Hell Ryders Motorcycle Club." Just that morning, she spotted a few bikers wearing those vests and figured they were passing through town.

"What the fuck?" His voice loud and gravelly, jaw clenched. "Didn't I tell you never to cross the street alone?"

The boy, now turned partially away from her, facing the man, didn't appear afraid. He held his head high, shoulders back.

"Why're you bothering—"

"He wasn't bothering me…"

The man's head shot up. His stare landed on her then slowly drifted down the length of her. When he met her eyes again, his narrowed and a muscle in his jaw twitched. There was something else too, something she saw in the deep depths of his eyes that then flashed across his face.

Both men and women looked at her a lot, and usually, they couldn't help it. Not because she was trim or drop-dead gorgeous or anything except the fact that her hair was strawberry blonde and drew a lot of attention. Men's gazes would gravitate to the color then trail down her body. Nothing to write home about there but not bad. Finally, they'd take a closer look at her face. She'd seen men seem thoughtful, intrigued, and even a couple of times, hungry. But a man had never looked at her like that. It hurt because under that anger, she saw disgust; *she* repulsed the beautiful man.

Then again, there was a first time for everything, but it was a nasty blow to her self-esteem, one she didn't need considering her on-again, off-again ex had damaged it to the point of no return.

She fought a wince and held his eyes. The whole time, she ached from her head to her toes and battled the urge to cry her eyes out.

His stare sliced to the boy. "You do this again, Cullen, I'm grounding you for a month, a month with no TV, no playing outside. You understand?"

The boy nodded.

The man turned his head glancing both ways down the street then looked at the boy. "Go home. Inside. No playing outside for the rest of the day."

The boy crossed the street and went into the larger home across from hers, meaning that motorcycle club was most likely local, meaning also that every time she looked across the street, she'd remember the beautiful man she repulsed.

The man's gaze swung to her. "I'd appreciate it if you didn't butt into how I raise my kid, how I discipline *my* kid."

Well, that answered that. He was the father, Cullen's father. She should've figured since they looked alike except the man was part of a motorcycle club. She didn't think they had kids, not purposefully anyway. Maybe that was just a stereotype though.

She didn't respond. She couldn't speak. Even if she could, she wouldn't. The beautiful man had made his point, so she nodded. Then clutching the box tightly against her chest, she turned and walked too quickly toward her house. She made it inside before the first and only tear she allowed trailed down her face.

What a welcome.

Chapter Two

Alexa couldn't complain. Her first week in her new home, new job, new town, went well, if she excluded meeting her unfriendly neighbor.

Monday, her first day at work, had been nerve-wracking and long, only natural. After introductions, the students had questions about their former teacher. She answered as best as she could and then had the class play a game to liven the mood and get everyone more comfortable. Later, she jumped in to her lesson plan.

The entire week, she spent lots of time talking to parents and relatives of her students. They'd wanted to meet her, and she'd wanted to meet them too. By Thursday, Alexa felt somewhat settled, except for the fact that with meeting parents and relatives, she hadn't had much time to review her students' work and ream out her contractor who'd been a no-show Monday morning and hadn't bothered answering her calls until the end of the week.

Now, it was Saturday. Finally. Demolition of her pink bathroom would start. Her contractor had answered her fifth call, a call she made late afternoon Friday. He'd given her a lousy excuse as to why he hadn't shown Monday, an excuse she didn't believe, but in an effort to get him to do the work, she accepted it.

Since her contractor claimed he'd start demo at seven Saturday morning, she'd set her alarm for six. Waking at that time, she drank coffee while she finished her lesson plan for the following week. Then she showered, brushed her teeth, and dressed casually wearing an old tee and shorts. While waiting for a knock on her door, she settled on an armchair beside one of her front windows reviewing students' work.

An hour after her contractor said he'd show and hadn't, she grabbed her phone, dialed his number, and brought it to her ear. When the second call went unanswered, she left a message. Not the second, third, or fourth time her contractor had been unreliable. Before she'd moved in, three delays for various reasons, twice he'd miscalculated costs for her kitchen and master bath remodel, and earlier that week, he hadn't shown or called and hadn't answered her calls. All of it cost her money, time, and unneeded stress. Naturally, by this point, she was so frustrated she put serious thought into demolishing the bathroom herself. A bad idea, so she decided to do something that managed to calm the worst of her moods.

She loved baking and did often, but she didn't let herself eat more than a few cookies. They'd go straight to her butt, which was already rather large. She baked from scratch and always got lost in the process. This time around, she made her favorite, chocolate chip cookies. Done by noon and still her contractor hadn't shown or called, so she grabbed a plate of cookies, a book, strode outside, and sat on her porch swing. It was old and needed to be refinished, but it worked. Angling herself with her back pressed against the armrest, she kicked her feet up, placing the cookies on her lap, parted her book, and read.

She'd read close to fifty pages and ate three of the five cookies when she caught sight of something from the corner of her eye. Turning her head, she spotted the van parking in front of her house. Seeing the man climbing out, her cheeks heated. She threw her legs off, slammed her book shut, set it and the cookies side by side on the swing then walked toward the steps leading onto her porch. Her contractor, Sam, met her there.

"Hey."

She crossed her arms over her chest and quirked a brow. "Hey?" Sparing a glance at her watch, she then met his stare. "You're six hours late, without so much as a call, all the while ignoring my calls and message, and 'hey' is all you have to say?"

His eyes narrowed. "I don't have time for this. Not today."

She had the impression if she were a man, he'd at the very least have the courtesy to explain. Sometimes, she really hated being a woman. Sometimes, she really hated being *her*. Every man, with the exception of her father and Tim, disappointed her.

She dropped her arms to her sides and fisted her hands. "And *I* don't have time to wait around."

He looked her up and down, locked eyes with her. Then his face grew hard. "Probably why you're still single."

That stung. Not as much as the fact that she disgusted her neighbor, but it wounded her enough she felt the color fade from her face. It shouldn't hurt. Sam was in his mid-thirties but looked mid-forties, and he was undependable and most importantly, a jerk. As far as she could tell, he, too, was unattached. Then again, an unmarried man was a bachelor, considered to be single because he wanted to be. An unmarried woman was an old maid, single because no one wanted her. A lot of good women were single because it took a lot more than being nice or pretty or smart to find someone to share your life with. She knew this, and still, she couldn't help the ache that sliced through her chest, so she looked away to compose herself and laid eyes on *him*, the man she thought about for days because of the expression on his face when he'd looked at her.

She hadn't seen him since, but now, he stood just outside his front door wearing a pair of jeans and that leather vest, staring her way.

Fantastic.

She had more to say to her contractor, but no way she'd let Sam continue to insult her, and no way in hell she'd let him step foot inside her house. It meant she'd do something she'd never done before—walk away without having her say.

She blanketed the emotion from her face. "Sam, I appreciate everything you've done so far, but this is where our business relationship ends."

She turned and took a step before she heard his shout.

"Fuck you, you stupid bitch. I gotta fuckin' life. Don't have time for your shit. I wanted someone nagging me, I'd get married."

He kept yelling, making a scene, but she strode inside, closed and locked her door then blasted her music player. She sat on her living room floor and listened to music mindlessly.

When she felt it safe to go outside, she did. On her porch swing, she found her book and an empty plate.

Chapter Three

Piece of work. Dodge knew it. The whole town did.

Dodge didn't know from personal experience. He'd remodeled his home with the help of his brothers and never had use for a contractor, but he heard stories of how that asshole dragged repairs on for weeks, sometimes longer, charging extra for labor and non-existent repairs. He didn't know the magnitude of dick until that afternoon when that asshole said all that shit to her.

The look on that beautiful face of hers tore right through him. Knowing the stories, he figured the guy had probably bilked her out of thousands. She didn't look like she was swimming in it, alone with no man in that house in a new town. He wanted to beat that bastard until the guy was blue in the face, apologized, and gave her what he owed her.

Dodge spotted the contractor working on the property months ago. He'd thought the guy bought it himself and planned to flip it. Never had he imagined the idiot found some unsuspecting woman to dupe.

It made him feel like shit, more so than he felt already. A week ago, he'd been a grade A asshole. He'd been pissed because Cullen shouldn't have been crossing the street by himself and his boy kept doing it. This time, he couldn't blame the kid.

With her hair that strawberry blonde, no one could miss her. Moth to flame, except everyone was a moth and she, the flame.

Never had he seen hair like that. From one look, even the way she had it in a messy knot at the top of her head, he knew it was long and thick. A strange desire came over him, one he never had, not in thirty-three years, but he wanted with every fiber in his body to run his fingers through her hair.

He'd looked at her real good. A mistake he regretted to that day since then he'd realized it wasn't just the hair but all of her.

She stood at about five-foot-five, the perfect height, meaning she could wear the highest heels and he'd still be taller. Her legs long, hips wide, waist tiny, and her chest was a good size, a C easy.

When his gaze landed on her face, he'd been speechless, in utter awe of how a woman could be so flawless. Her eyes clear, ice blue, cheeks rosy, and lips full. The knowledge of just how gorgeous she was cemented when his stare landed on the freckles sprinkled across the bridge of her nose that proved she wore no makeup though she looked ready for a photoshoot.

He thought about calling all the major news agencies to tell them he found the perfect woman, but that was just stupid and fucked. Men from around the world would line up in front of his house, and he wasn't a masochist to make himself watch that shit play out.

Still, in the back of his mind, he knew he'd watch it happen regardless. The men in town, some of them his brothers, would notice her, want her, and do everything and anything to try to have her.

He had no chance. He never got the girl. He was Dodge, the guy women dodged. Besides, he was a single dad to a three-year-old who was his life because his boy needed him to be. He didn't have time for women.

What had he done? He'd been a dick, took himself out of the game, so then he could blame himself instead of her.

None of it made him want to beat that contractor's ass any less.

The front door parted. He knew who it'd be, so he turned and smiled. Cullen walked toward him and wrapped his arms around his thighs.

He dropped his hands to his son's back, holding him against him. "Hey, you have fun?"

Cullen pulled away, nodded, and then looked up at him. A dark smear around his mouth, no doubt chocolate.

"What'd you eat?"

His boy didn't respond. Then again, it was a long shot. Cullen had never said much. It got worse when his mother left. He hardly ever spoke now and seemed withdrawn. Dodge took him to a speech therapist once a week. It hadn't helped yet. He had hope, but honest to God, he was scared shitless.

"Want to watch a movie with your old man, tonight?"

Cullen looked over his shoulder toward the front door and met his gaze.

"Want to play outside?"

He shook his head.

Dodge bent down, draping an arm around his son's back. "Tell me what you want to do, and we'll do it."

Cullen dropped his head. After several moments, he lifted it. "Pretty. Lady."

The first words he heard his son say in more than a week. Thrilling. Even if what his kid wanted presented a problem, he smiled. "You want to see the pretty lady?"

Cullen grinned and nodded.

"Cul, I don't know…"

The smile faded from his son's face.

His chest constricted, a too-familiar ache knotted his stomach. "Okay, bud."

He didn't know how he'd manage this, but he gave in because quite frankly, he'd give his left nut to make his boy happy.

Cullen grinned.

"We'll go welcome her to the neighborhood," he decided on the spot. "Can't go empty-handed though, so we gotta run to the store."

He'd buy her wine. She looked like the type that drank that shit. He'd give it to her and apologize. Maybe then, he wouldn't feel like such a dick.

****

Alexa spent the day reading. She had a lot to do. Namely, she still had boxes to unpack, but her day, starting with waiting all morning for her contractor, had been a bust, so she decided to bury her mind in a book. Forget drowning in alcohol and waking with a hangover, reading was the best medicine. She wouldn't let herself think that by this point in her life she thought she'd be reading baby books. That afternoon further proved she was right to give up that dream.

A knock sounded on the front door. She slammed her book closed and straightened, pulling herself away from the backrest of her blue armchair.

The knock came again.

She set the book aside, got to her bare feet, and headed for the door. Looking through the peephole, she froze. There *he* stood looking more beautiful than she remembered, knocking on *her* door.

God, why was he there? Had she done something else to upset him? He didn't look angry. Brows furrowed, he looked…worried? What the hell was she supposed to do? Answer the door, maybe? She didn't want to. She didn't want to stare at his too handsome face, didn't want to see that repulsion in his eyes.

The knock came again, louder.

Her hand went to her chest taking several steps away. Heart racing, she ran a hand through her hair and thanked her lucky stars she'd put the book aside to shower, not that it mattered anyway.

She threw open the door and immediately realized he wasn't alone. His right hand rested on his son's shoulder.

Cullen, standing in front of his father, looked adorable wearing a pair of boots, jeans, t-shirt, and a skully. He also looked thrilled, smiling wide.

Her gaze locked on him, she grinned. "Good evening, Cullen, right?"

Cullen nodded.

"It's nice to meet you officially, Cullen."

She then managed the strength to tear her stare away and meet his father's. He hadn't looked mad before, but now, he did. A vein in his neck pulsed. Her smile faded.

"I'm Cullen's dad, Dodge."

The most beautiful man's name was Dodge?

Unusual, but she suspected that wasn't his real name.

"Alexa."

"Lex," Cullen murmured.

She caught sight of Dodge's eyes widening. Ignoring that, she tilted her head down. "Yep, that's right. My friends call me Lex."

Dodge cleared his throat and lifted his left arm. A gift bag in his grip, a bottle of wine peeking out, he held it out to her. "We got you something to welcome you to the neighborhood."

"Really?" Taken back, she actually said that aloud.

She'd never expected a biker to welcome her to the neighborhood. A biker's wife? Maybe, though she was almost positive he didn't have a wife. She tried not to look across the street and notice things, but she did and had. One of the things she learned—not a single woman had come and gone from that home.

After last week, she never expected *this* biker to welcome her to the neighborhood. Only natural she'd been shocked to find him at her door handing over a welcoming gift. Still, she shouldn't have sounded surprised because it was rude.

She cringed. "I mean… Sorry, I didn't mean to sound…" She took a deep breath and grabbed the bag. "I meant to say that's nice. Thank you."

Face heating, she looked to Cullen and tried to lighten the mood. "I bet this was your idea, huh?"

The boy's eyes widened just briefly as his cheeks flushed a rosy shade.

"And I know just how to repay you. If it's okay with your dad, I'll give you some chocolate chip cookies. My way of saying thanks. They're fresh. I baked them today."

Cullen angled his head back to his dad, hopeful though she noticed he didn't say anything. She looked up at his father.

Dodge met her gaze. "That'd be nice."

"Great. Come on in." She parted the door wider, moving out of the way.

They walked inside.

She closed the door, led them toward the back end of the house, and placed the bottle of wine on her counter. "Sorry about the mess. Just moved in."

Dodge chuckled. "Can't tell."

"You can have a seat on the couch if you'd like." She strode into her kitchen, grabbed a small platter, and set several cookies on it. "Would you like something to drink?"

"Milk for Cul."

In one hand, she grabbed a glass of wine and a cup of milk. Between her forearm and stomach, she held a beer, and in her other hand, she carried the plated cookies. When she strode into her living room, he spoke.

"Shit. Let me help you with that." He clutched the beer and milk, his fingers grazing her stomach as he did.

Then something that had never happened to her did. With that simple touch, heat spread through her. She shuddered and prayed like hell he hadn't noticed. She took a chance and tilted her head to meet his stare.

His eyes on hers, brows furrowed, chin cocked to the side. At least he didn't look disgusted.

Her cheeks flushed. Being so fair-skinned, he'd be able to tell immediately, so in an attempt to hide it, she looked away.

"Sorry, didn't mean to."

"It's fine," she replied too quickly.

"Didn't ask for a beer, but thanks."

Her mother taught her how to be a good host. Whether he drank the beer or not, she couldn't get Cullen something to drink and not his father.

She set the cookies and wine on the coffee table then sat on her blue armchair, allowing him to sit next to Cullen on her love seat. He did and managed to make it look small. Her gaze shot to his thighs, which looked more like trunks. Her line of sight blocked when Cullen reached for a cookie and bit into it. She watched his reaction. Smiling, he nabbed another.

"You've done a lot of work."

She dragged her stare from Cullen, grabbed her wine, and sipped. "Technically, I didn't do any of the real work."

"You pick the colors?"

She met his eyes. Those eyes, so rich, so dark… That face… Darn, what had he asked?

She nodded. "Why?"

He shrugged and took a pull of his beer. "Looks nice. Just didn't expect a woman to pick blue. It's kind of a masculine color."

What? Was blue designated for men only? Girls liked blue. Wait. Her house was masculine? How? Where? Yes, she had a blue armchair. Her rug had some blue. An accent wall in her living room was blue, and there was a bit of blue on her backsplash in the kitchen.

She didn't think he'd come to her house with a bottle of wine to insult her, but who knew. Further, she didn't know what to say to that, so she said nothing, just focused on Cullen who'd rammed a third cookie into his mouth and looked like he was having the time of his life.

"So are you gonna do more work?"

She snapped her head up.

Dodge leaned forward, grabbed a cookie, and popped it in his mouth. He chewed then muttered, "Damn, this is amazing. You made this?"

She would've been thrilled to hear that except he sounded shocked like he doubted she could've made them.

"Yes, from scratch."

His brows drew together. "Really?"

Why that was unbelievable, she had no clue but couldn't help feel offended. She wanted to tell him where to shove it, but his adorable son sat there smiling, so she held her tongue, took a deep breath, and responded, "Yes, really."

"Fuckin' amazing."

There he went again—cursing in front of his son. Maybe that's why the boy rarely spoke. All he heard were curse words he knew he shouldn't say.

"So what else are you doing here?"

"I teach."

His eyes widened. "You're a teacher? Where?"

Was that so hard to believe? Wearing on her patience, the only thing holding her civility besides his sweet boy, the fact that he was her neighbor and she'd see a lot of him whether she liked it or not.

"Wadden Elementary. I teach kindergarten."

His brows shot up. "Yeah?"

She nodded.

He angled his head to look at his son. "Hear that,

Cul? Lex'll be your teacher in a couple of years."

Lex? Guess he missed when she said that's what her friends called her.

Cullen grabbed another cookie, looked to her, and smiled.

She smiled at Cullen. "So you're three?"

Cullen placed the entire cookie in his mouth and nodded.

"Meant to ask what else you're doing to your house."

She looked to Dodge and realized she'd misunderstood him before. "My guest bathroom is pink."

A smile spread across his lips. Gorgeous. Then again, she expected nothing less from the most beautiful man she'd ever seen.

He ruined that by saying, "And you're Mrs. Blue, so you're getting rid of it."

Had he meant that as a pun? Did he think she was boring and down? "Blue" implied that, didn't it? Why? Because she read books? Because she taught kids for a living? Because she liked masculine blue instead of pink? Not the only problem with what he said. God, how many times could he offend her in one night?

"It's Miss. As Sam pointed out, I'm not married."

His gaze raked her from top to bottom. "Yeah." He said it like he meant to say "duh." Before that insult settled, he asked, "What else?"

"The backyard's a mess."

Cullen hopped off the couch and headed for the sliding glass door. She stood and followed, stopping just beside him, and flipped the back light on. The yard had a pool, no water since it needed resurfacing. The deck needed refinishing, and the grass needed to be mowed.

"Good size."

She jumped. He stood behind Cullen, close to her side.

"Sorry, didn't mean to startle you."

She avoided his eyes. "It's okay."

"Want to go explore, Cul?"

She looked down at Cullen. His father's hand on his shoulder, rubbing it affectionately. Cullen tilted his head back to look at his father. Smile widening, he nodded.

"Be safe. Yeah?"

Cullen nodded again.

She unlocked the door. Before she parted it, Dodge shifted closer. His arm glided in front of her and slid the door open. Cullen rushed out.

It wasn't a good idea for a three-year-old to play in that mess of a backyard. The grass stood tall making it impossible to see well especially in the dark.

"I wanted to apologize for the way I treated you the other day."

Her lips parted. Woodenly, she faced him. "Really?"

Again, she said this aloud. Something about him made her forget her manners. Not her fault. How many times had he offended her?

She cleared her throat. "Sorry…I meant…"

"Cullen keeps crossing the street alone, and it worries the shit out of me. It's not an excuse, so I wanted to say I'm sorry I was a dick. Cul likes you. Besides, we're neighbors, so I think it'd be good if we got along."

He wanted them to get along, so he decided to buy her a bottle of wine and insult her before he apologized for being a jerk last week. Did this mean next time she saw him he'd apologize for offending her this time?

She had no clue. What she did know—she liked his son, and they were neighbors. She should avoid him from now on.

She nodded. "That's a good idea."

He smiled, big. Then she realized very belatedly he stood too close. So close, she felt the heat of his body. God, what she'd give for one night with the most beautiful man she'd ever seen, if only he'd shut up, if only she were that type of woman.

Her phone rang. Thank God. She'd been staring at him a while. He'd been staring back, but no doubt not for the same reason. After all, he was handsome while she'd been too lazy to bother with makeup.

Chapter Four

Dodge shouldn't care. No good would come of it, and still, he cared enough that he stayed up for hours last night worrying, cared enough that first thing that morning, he looked out his window to make sure she was still there. He cared enough he thought about walking to her place to ask if everything was all right.

He didn't know the whole story just what he heard from a one-sided conversation when she picked up that call. Her pregnant sister was in the hospital. Lex had been talking to someone, he guessed her sister's man, and while she talked, she paced, picking up her purse and keys like she planned on taking off. He thought about driving her, but then, whoever she'd been on the phone with convinced her not to. He wanted to stay and keep her company, but she didn't look like she wanted him to, so he grabbed Cullen and they left. He stayed up late peeking out his window, making sure she didn't leave, hoping if she thought about it, he'd catch her in the act so he could offer to drive her.

He fell asleep around one, woke up at six when Cullen came into bed with him, and then he instantly shot out of bed to check if her car was still parked outside. It had been, and still, he had the urge to go there and see for himself how she was.

He shouldn't, so every time he thought about going, he listed all the reasons he shouldn't.

A biker, a single dad to a three-year-old going through a rough time, he didn't have time for a woman. Cullen's mother fucked with him so bad, he didn't think he could ever trust one. Besides, Alexa, the perfect woman, wouldn't be interested in him. He could tell by the way she looked annoyed with him like he was some sort of insect bugging her. Maybe he had been. In his defense, he'd only been trying to make conversation. She was anyone else, he'd tell her to take a hike. He couldn't though, not just because she was his neighbor, but because he knew Cullen liked her and she liked his boy, and especially because Cullen needed women like her around, women who were strong, successful, smart, and nice, to Cullen at least. Cullen especially needed a woman to pay attention to him, listen to him. He didn't have any of that from his mother. Though he had it from a few of his brothers' women, it wasn't the same.

After listing his reasons, he kept going back to the same thought, the same urge—crossing the street to check on her. He kept looking out his windows, must've done that close to twenty times by midmorning. At noon, he peered out his living room window for the last time and caught sight of her.

That beautiful hair loose and swirling in the wind. Her body plastered against a man's, and her lips pressed to his.

Seeing that, his stomach rolled. He dropped his head, stared at his feet, and breathed deep. After a moment, he shut the blinds and walked away.

The rest of the day, he kept busy and fought the urge to look out his windows.

Chapter Five

It had been a long week, and it was only Wednesday. Lex could blame it on her ex, but that wouldn't be fair.

Mitchell was an engineer, smart and good-looking, great on paper but in reality, the worst type of man. He made her fall for him, made her think they wanted the same things, and then four months in, he wanted a break. She gave him his break. A month later, he told her he made a mistake, that he loved her. She forgave him. Everything's great until another three months later when he broke up with her. Again, he came back and made promises he had no intention of keeping. Every time he left her, she said she wouldn't take him back. Every time, she did. She wasn't naïve or stupid. She knew what he did during those breaks, and still, she loved him and took him back time and time again even when he stopped making promises. This went on for years, *three* years.

Five months ago, he broke up with her for the last time. That day, she decided she wouldn't settle anymore. She'd move on with her life, do all the things she put off doing for him, and she had.

It'd been two months longer than he'd ever gone before, but still, she should've figured eventually he'd come back.

Sunday, he showed on the doorstep of *her* new

home. The minute she opened the door, he *kissed* her. Maybe he thought she couldn't say no after a kiss, but that wouldn't work, not ever. She'd moved on, so she shoved him away and told him if he didn't get off *her* property, she'd call the cops.

Mitchell took off, thankfully, but he hadn't given up. He'd be back. Seeing him brought back a lot of painful memories she'd fought tooth and nail to forget over the last five months.

Monday, she went to work and stayed after school redecorating her classroom. When she arrived home, she spent a couple of hours looking up contractors in the area and making calls. It had been after hours by then, so she left messages. Later, she graded papers. Before Lex knew it, dinnertime. She microwaved a frozen meal, ate it as she finished reading a book then showered and headed for bed. Tuesday had been more of the same except instead of making calls to contractors, a couple returned her call. She planned to meet with one Thursday and with another Sunday morning. This time around, she'd check references, lots of them.

Now, the end of her Wednesday, she had no parent-teacher meetings. She planned on going home to unpack more boxes, but when she turned on her car that morning, her check engine light went on. She hadn't had enough to deal with with Mitchell and worrying when he'd be back, because she knew he would, but now, there was a chance depending on how much her car repair cost, she'd have to postpone remodeling and live with her pink bathroom.

She locked up her classroom and drove to a mechanic shop in town she'd looked up online that morning. Huge and busy, the front lot filled with cars, trucks, SUVs, and motorcycles. Five large metal garage doors open revealing a ton more cars, SUVs, trucks, and motorcycles. On the top of the building, a large sign with the name of the shop, *Ryders' Custom Rides.* She climbed out of her car and headed toward a door off to one side. Over it, a small sign signaled it was the office.

She pulled open the door and froze under the scrutiny of five pairs of eyes. Closest to her, a man in his thirties with dark hair wearing a black tank, the length of his arms covered in tattoos. He looked like he'd just come in from a side door that could only lead into the shop. A second man stood at the dark counter that lined the entirety of the office. His hand buried in a paper bag, he had dark hair tied in a ponytail, and a black, sleeveless shirt stretched across his chest. Both men wore black leather vests with the Hell Ryders Motorcycle Club insignia and emblem.

Two bikers with the same vests from the same club, Dodge's club, was not a coincidence. The shop must be run by his club. Just her luck.

Taking a deep breath, she looked behind the counter.

A stunning blonde with hazel eyes, who looked like she belonged on a runway instead of working behind a counter anywhere, stood. Mid-twenties, she wore a pair of jeans and a black tank. Over it, she had a black leather vest like the bikers except hers fit her petite frame and inscribed on one of the sides under the Hell Ryders inscription, it read, "Ripper's Old Lady."

"Miss Millen!"

She shot her stare behind the beautiful blonde and

met Della's, seated at a desk lining the back wall behind the counter. Beside her, another little girl, a blonde with a set of striking, blue-green colored eyes.

Lex approached the counter. "Hi, Della. Nice to see you again so soon."

"Did you come to see me? Am I in trouble?"

She shook her head. "You're one of my best students. You couldn't possibly be in trouble." She smiled and met the blonde woman's eyes. "I came to get my car fixed."

The blonde grinned. "Guessing you're Della's new teacher?"

She nodded.

"She's been raving about you."

Stare sliding to Della, she softened her smile.

The woman extended her hand. "It's nice to meet you. I'm Em."

Lex took it and shook. "Call me Lex."

"And this back here is my Bree." Em angled her body and reached for the blonde girl. "She's in Pre-K. You'll probably have her as a student next year."

"Nice to meet you, Bree. I'll look forward to having you in my class."

Bree smiled.

Em turned away from Lex completely. "All right, girls, back to homework. Then you can go to the playground."

They turned, facing the back desk, and went to work immediately.

Em spun fully to her. "So you're having car trouble?"

She nodded.

"Aren't you goin' to introduce us?" This came

from the man with the ponytail standing next to her.

Em rolled her eyes. "This is Trick, and behind you is Dash." She looked between the two men and lifted a brow. "There. Are you two happy? Now, get out of my office before Bryce comes…"

The door behind Alexa parted. She looked over her shoulder, realizing the door did, in fact, lead into the garage. In strode another biker, he was wide and tall with dirty blonde hair, stubble along his jaw, and the same striking colored eyes as the little blonde girl, Bree. His gaze went from Trick to Dash and then went feral. Body tensing, jaw clenching, hands balled up. Attractive, but that look in his eyes, that stance completely changed him.

"What the *fuck*?"

How Lex didn't pee her pants, she had no idea. The man was scary. That mad, he was chilling. Thank God his anger wasn't directed at her.

"You fuckers listen to anything I say?" His stare shooting from one man to the other. "I said my old lady isn't your fuckin' chef. She isn't your fuckin' secretary. She isn't your fuckin' maid. She isn't your *anything*. She does shit for me and my kid, and that's it."

Pulse spiking at the base of her neck, Lex stood frozen, staring, terrified of moving, yet thinking cursing had to be part of some biker code.

"Bryce. We have company."

Oh God. Why would the blonde shift the attention to herself or *her*? A death wish, maybe?

She stopped breathing.

The scary biker's gaze sliced to Em. "Why you do shit I tell you not to do, *babe*?"

Em lifted her chin. "I offered."

He took a menacing step toward Em, and in doing so, a step closer to her. “Why you do shit I tell you *not* to do, *Em*?”

Em let out a frustrated sigh. “Because I can.”

The scary biker planted one hand on the counter and launched his whole body over it.

Impressive. And terrifying.

He wrapped one arm around Em’s waist, yanked her against him, and kissed her. A short but deep kiss. When he pulled away, he chuckled. “Gonna pay for that, *babe*. Where’s my food? I’m starved.”

Em smiled, drew away, grabbed a paper bag she had on her desk, handed it over then looked to her. “Bryce, this is Alexa, Della’s teacher. More than likely, she’ll be Bree’s next year.”

Scary biker lifted his head and angled it to her. She involuntarily, probably for self-preservation, took a step back.

His lips twitched like he was fighting the urge to smile. Then he placed the bag on the counter. “Only Em calls me Bryce. Name’s Ripper.”

He turned to the girls. “Hey, Della. Bree, baby, you gonna give your dad a hug?”

Bree stood and circled her arms around his waist. He lifted her off her feet, hugging her tightly and pressing a kiss to her cheek and another on her forehead. “Missed you, baby.”

Bree giggled. “Missed you too, Daddy.”

“So you were saying?”

Ripper released Bree, grabbed the bag of food, and pulled out a foot-long sub.

Her gaze shot to Em. What had she been saying? Where was she? An alternate universe? A moment ago, she'd been petrified of the scary biker. Now, she was dumbfounded. How could a man go from livid to affectionate to his woman and daughter in seconds?

She had a new understanding of Em, whom she just met—ballsy, fearless, and definitely biker babe material.

"I…um…my car."

Em's smile widened. "Right, your car."

She swallowed. "The check engine light is on, so I brought it here."

Ripper tore the wrapper off his sub, bit into it, and chewed. "We'll get it checked out for you."

****

"Brother, we got meat. Hot, sexy, librarian meat with red fuckin' hair."

He heard Hash over the music, over the shouting and talking and everything, and his body locked. Simultaneously, his stomach knotted and hollowed out.

No doubt it was her.

After a split second, despite knowing he shouldn't, he moved, fast.

Sliding out from under the Chevy he'd been working on, he stood and spotted Hash immediately. His brother, gaze aimed at Blaze and Bud, stood with a hip pressed against the side of a yellow Camaro.

Dodge closed the distance between him and Hash and glared. "Don't think about it, *brother*. Do *not* even go near her. Else you and me, we're gonna have fuckin' problems."

Hash threw the towel he'd wiped his grease-stained hands on onto the hood of the car, lifted his arms in surrender, and smirked. "Got you, *brother*."

Then he ran, skirting brothers, toolboxes, cars,

bikes until he reached the other end of the garage. He parted the door to the office. His stare involuntarily and helplessly moved from the top of her head to her toes. Not one thing told him librarian; it told him lots of other shit but not librarian.

That strawberry hair, mostly loose, hung three inches past her shoulders. She wore a dress, blue—of course—fitted on the top, cinched in the middle accentuating her tiny waist, and fell around her hips in a way any man within a quarter mile could tell she had a sweet, round ass and a body shaped like a coke bottle. And he hadn't even gotten to her face. He couldn't see the freckles he loved meaning she wore makeup. Eyes ice blue, her lips rosy, plump, and flawless. Fucking perfect, so whether his brothers saw her in shorts and a tee fitted to that beautiful body of hers with no makeup on, they'd *know* just how perfect she was. They'd make their move. Maybe she'd dump her man and start dating one or the lot of them, and he'd be in hell. Living across the street, he had a front seat to watch that shit play out. He couldn't allow it.

He went about that by blurting, "What the fuck are you doing here?"

He hadn't meant to yell, but he walked in, and she stood there looking perfect, talking to Dash, his VP, covered in tats who banged a series of taps every night.

She flinched then sluggishly turned toward him and arched a brow. "I'm at a mechanic shop. What do you think I'm doing here?"

Yeah, stupid question. Again, he hadn't been thinking, or he had but just about getting her away from his brothers.

"You're having car problems?"

Her pretty, blue eyes narrowed. "That's why *I'm* here."

"What's the problem?"

"I don't know. That's why I'm here."

"Could take a while. I'll drive you home."

Her brows drew together. "I don't need a ride home. I can wait here—"

He advanced closing the distance between them quickly, glaring at Dash as he did. "Yeah, you need a ride. I'll take you home."

"I said—"

He met her stare, grasped her elbow, tugged her out of the office, and across the lot to his SUV. Opening the passenger side door, he helped her in all the while she protested. On the driver's side, he jumped in, turned on the ignition, pulled out of his parking spot, and drove in silence for two seconds.

"I can't believe you did that. I can't believe you're doing *this*."

He spared a glance at her. She sat stiffly with her bag on her lap staring daggers straight ahead. Her mouth in a pout, and her arms crossed over her chest. Maybe she had reason to be pissed. He hadn't been smooth. It wasn't his thing, but she was smart and should've figured he'd done what he had for her own good.

"I fuckin' saved you. The least you could do is thank me."

She turned toward him. "Saved me? From what?"

"From my brothers."

"You're what?"

He came to a stop at a red light and shifted her way. "My brothers. The club."

Eyes widening, she stilled. In a small voice, she asked, "What were they going to do to me?"

"Hit on you."

She dropped her gaze from his and exhaled.

What had she thought they'd do to her besides hit on her? The club was clean. His brothers were rowdy, and the ones who weren't attached were always looking for women to fuck, but that was as far as it went.

She tilted her head to the side. "Why would—"

Shit. She'd just offended him and hadn't realized it. Something else she didn't understand—how fucking perfect she was. Fucked, so fucked. A woman like her should *know*. Every man she'd dated should've made it clear. It made him think her man wasn't just a douche but an idiot who took her for granted.

His eyes hardened. "You gotta mirror, babe?"

She lifted a brow. "Why do you need a mirror?"

She was intelligent, a teacher for fuck's sake, and half the time she was home, she sat on her beat-up porch swing reading. But he now knew she could be dense.

Hilarious, he had to fight not to laugh. She wouldn't find it funny. In fact, he'd bet it'd piss her off, and she wasn't pleased with him to begin with.

"Lex, you gotta mirror at home?"

Her eyes narrowed. "Why are you changing the subject?"

He looked forward. The light turned green, so he lifted his foot from the brake and hit the gas. "Answer the fuckin' question."

"Don't curse at me."

Shaking his head, he released a loaded breath. "Answer the question, please."

"Yes, I have a mirror at home. Now, would you like to know how many?" Sarcasm dripped her tone.

Damn, she was funny, fucking hysterical. He'd never met a woman who made him laugh, another reason she was perfect.

This time, he couldn't hold back a chuckle. "Naw, I want to know if you look in those mirrors, ever?"

"Of course. How do you think I apply makeup?"

He spared a glance at her. "Then I don't have to explain why I needed to save you from my brothers, right?"

Her eyes widened. Then her brows drew together. "You're saying they find me attractive?"

Bingo.

Coming to another red light, he stopped and looked at her. "I'm saying a man would have to be blind and stupid not to find you attractive."

Her jaw dropped. She faced forward, straightening in her seat.

He shouldn't have said that. Granted, he also should've because if a woman like her didn't know, she should.

She didn't respond.

He didn't say anything either. He looked forward and stared at the light, willing it to turn. When the silence became uncomfortable, he changed the subject. "I'll let you know what's wrong with your car. Does Em have your number?"

"Yes."

He pulled up to her house, parked, and unbuckled his seat belt.

"What're you doing?"

He turned to her. "Walking you to your door."

She lifted a brow. "You're walking me to my door?"

"Yeah. A man drops a woman off, he walks her to her door, makes sure she gets in, and locks the door behind her."

For some fucked reason, he was rewarded then, the kind of reward that proved God remembered his name. To him, it happened a lot. Having Cullen was a reward every day.

She laughed loud, and he got to watch—her strawberry hair around her smiling face, sounding flawless, looking gorgeous. A beautiful laugh, another thing perfect about her.

Even having no idea what she found amusing, he couldn't help but chuckle.

"You're funny."

He wanted to ask what made her laugh.

He wanted to tell her he liked he'd made her laugh.

He didn't share any of that.

Instead, he climbed out of his SUV, walked her to her door, made sure she locked it, and headed back to work.

Chapter Six

Lex had hallucinated that whole conversation. Days later, she still couldn't believe it.

After she took her car to the mechanic shop that also happened to be where Dodge worked, he saw her and so eloquently asked her, "What the fuck are you doing here?" Then he dragged her out and drove her home. Per his explanation, he did it to save her from getting hit on by his brothers. Then he said something she could, to that day, swear she'd imagined. He said, "I'm saying a man would have to be blind and stupid not to find you attractive."

Implying he'd found *her* attractive? Either that or he'd called himself blind and stupid. Her heart nearly popped out of her chest. Shocking, so she hadn't said anything. When it settled, no denying she'd been flattered and thrilled.

After driving her home, he insisted on walking her to her door like a gentleman. The concept, an ancient one, and not a quality she looked for in a man because *no one* ever did it anymore.

She'd started dating at sixteen and never had a man walked her to her door unless, of course, he thought he'd get a kiss or inside. Finally, she found a man who went the extra mile and expected nothing in return, who also happened to be the most attractive man she'd ever met, and he was a conundrum.

When they'd met, he'd looked at her like she repulsed him, and he'd not so nicely told her to butt out. Later, he showed on her doorstep with a welcoming gift and offended her repeatedly only to apologize for his behavior when they'd met. Their last interaction, he'd hauled her out of a mechanic shop, insisting he drive her home, taking no for an answer. Then he'd complimented her and walked her to her door.

For some inexplicable reason, she thought about him a lot. She thought about Cullen too, who often stopped by her house while she sat outside and read. But she thought about Dodge differently, maybe because she was attracted to him, maybe because he was a puzzle, maybe because she had a feeling there was more to him than met the eye.

He was less than eloquent in his word usage, but she'd seen him with Cullen. He taught his son right from wrong, worried about him crossing the street alone, and showed affection. He was a single father. This, Lex knew. She hadn't been living across the street long, but she hadn't seen Cullen's mother, meaning whoever his mother was, she hadn't even visited her son. Lex didn't know a woman who'd voluntarily go without seeing her child, but she didn't think a woman like that was a good person. Then again, there were other possibilities. For one, the possibility that Cullen's mother wasn't around because she couldn't be.

Thinking on that, she assumed something she should've before then. Dodge could be like her in the sense that he lost hope. He on women like she had on men. Maybe he fell in love with a woman who bore him a beautiful son then abandoned them both, or maybe he fell in love with a woman who bore him a beautiful son who was then taken from the world, from them both too soon. He was hurt and irrationally took it out on women he came into contact with. Not that it gave him an excuse to be a jerk, it didn't, but at least now, she had an idea why. Believing this didn't stop her from wondering what his real name was; she'd pondered it so many times she'd lost count.

Wednesday evening, Em called her and told her how much the car repair cost, which turned out inexpensive. Em also mentioned her car wouldn't be ready until Thursday afternoon. Not ten minutes later, she received another call from the same number, but it hadn't been Em. It'd been Dodge who insisted on driving her to work the following day. She refused. He wouldn't take no for an answer, and she needed to keep her distance, so she lied and told him a friend from work offered her a ride. Allie, Della's aunt, whom Lex met the first week of school, called her an hour later and mentioned she planned to pick up Della the following afternoon and wouldn't mind taking her to the shop to get her car. Lex made it a rule not to make friends with her students' parents or relatives, but Lex also realized that in a small town, in no time, everyone would be related to one of her present or past students. So when during their first meeting Allie offered to show her around town, she'd agreed, and they'd exchanged numbers.

Thursday, Lex walked to work. The day flew by. Before she knew it, Allie stood at her classroom doorway. Lex locked up and rode with Allie and Della to the garage. On her way to the office, she spotted Cullen running toward her.

"Lex! Lex! Lex!" His body collided with hers.

Even though she'd prepared, the impact sent her a couple steps back. Strong. Further proved when his arms went around her and squeezed.

"Lex!"

She wrapped her arms around his back, looked down at him, and smiled. "Hey, Cullen. You miss me?"

He nodded.

"I missed you too. I'm going to make cookies later. Maybe your dad will let you have some?"

He nodded.

"Cul."

Her head snapped up and met his dark gaze. Brows furrowed, sweat beaded there, a moist black tee covered his broad chest, and his legs were encased in a pair of well-worn jeans. Gorgeous.

"Cul?"

Cullen pulled away and turned to look at his father.

"You'll hurt Lex running into her like that."

She'd been about to say Cullen hadn't hurt her when she thought better of it.

Dodge hadn't missed it. His stare met hers, without so much as a hello, and hardened.

She released a breath and ignored it as best as she could, remembering he couldn't help himself.

"Sowy."

She angled her head down. Grinning, she threaded her fingers through Cullen's thick, dark hair. "No apology needed."

Then she met Dodge's gaze. "Hi, Dodge. Hope you're doing well."

Kill him with kindness. She didn't think that'd work, but she wanted to keep the peace. To accomplish that, she'd be nice.

Eyes widening, the hard lines of his face softened. He dropped his head, shoulders slumping. "Yeah…" Dragging a hand through his hair, he met her eyes and mumbled, "Hope you are too."

She smiled at Cullen. "I'll see you soon." Sparing a glance at Dodge, she said, "Bye."

She made it home in time to meet with a contractor. After he left, she baked a batch of oatmeal chocolate chip cookies from scratch. She waited and waited, but Cullen never showed.

The following day, she took the cookies to school and left them in the main office. After work, because it was a nice, cool evening, she sat on her porch swing and read. Past six, she heard footsteps nearing and looked up. Cullen strode up the steps leading to her front porch.

She smiled. "Hey, Cullen."

He grinned. "Lex."

"How are you?"

He shrugged.

"Did you cross the street alone?"

He shook his head.

"Good. I don't want your Dad getting mad at you."

His gaze slid to her book then to her.

"Would you like me to read to you?"

Eyes widening, he smiled and nodded.

She smiled too. "Be right back."

Heading inside, she dug into one of the boxes filled with children's books she'd opened but hadn't unpacked since she needed to take it to her classroom. She grabbed several, strode outside, and found Cullen sitting on her porch swing, his feet dangling off the edge.

She sat beside him. "Which one do you want me to read you?"

He pointed to one with a series of cars painted on the cover. She placed the book between them. With Cullen cuddled close looking at the illustrations and glancing at her every now and then, she read aloud.

****

Reading to his boy. He left Cullen a couple of hours ago at his friend's house. Levi lived next door to Lex. It got late, and Cullen hadn't returned or called, so Dodge headed outside. He'd been about to cross the street when he spotted them, Cul and Lex sitting on her porch swing. Cullen close beside her, her lips moving. Both their heads slanted down. On her lawn, he noticed the book she held between them.

His heart nearly burst.

Cullen's mother had never read to him. Not once.

Cullen had been read to by women before. The workers at the daycare where he dropped him off every morning read to the kids, and the employees were all women. Still, it was different. He paid them to watch his boy. Allie and Tiff worked there. They were the old ladies to two of his brothers, which made dropping Cullen off every morning before work suck less. The other old ladies, Lynn, Em, and Mia looked out for Cul from time to time. They'd probably read to him too. But again, that was different; they were family.

Lex was no one, no one who should care anyway. Just a neighbor, a teacher who no doubt liked kids, but there were plenty of kids in the neighborhood and he didn't see her reading to or baking for any of them.

A Friday night, no less, she should be on a date or getting laid. Instead, she'd spent her time reading to his boy proving how perfect she was.

He supposed having had a date Sunday and another yesterday with two *different* men, she figured she'd take the night off. But why spend time with his kid? Why not go out to a bar and drink or do something, anything not dealing with children? Wouldn't a teacher be tired of dealing with kids all day, every day?

With his heart in his throat, from the steps leading up to Lex's porch, he called out, "Cul. It's dinner time, then bath time then bedtime."

Cullen shifted to Lex, wrapped one arm around her middle, leaned in to her fully then stood and headed for him.

He cupped the back of Cul's head. "Thank Lex for reading to you."

Cullen turned and mumbled, "Lex."

She smiled at his son and spared a glance at him. "Good night."

"Night," he whispered back before he forced himself to turn and walk away.

****

It'd been a week, and she had *another* man. *Three* men at her house in *one* week.

One last Sunday, dark-haired, skinny, tanned, and looked like a douche. He'd seen them kissing and assumed that guy was her man, one of the reasons he'd insisted on taking her home instead of making her wait at the garage.

Another man on Thursday: dark-haired, tall, dressed like he worked construction. Dodge saw them go inside, and that guy stayed for half an hour. What could they have done in a half hour? It wasn't long enough to watch a movie but just enough time for a quick fuck.

That morning, Dodge saw the third. He hadn't been looking out on purpose. He just meant to glance when he saw her wearing jaw-string shorts and a small, tight tank. That hair of hers a mess around her, a big smile on her face, she ran to an SUV parked on her drive. A man hopped out of the car: dark-haired, tall, and built. He saw her hug that guy, and while she did, that smile never left her face. All he could stand to see. The next instant, he closed the blinds, promised himself he wouldn't look outside or go outside, and tried to convince himself he didn't care how long that guy stayed.

But he did care.

He proved it by thinking about her all day. Even as he spent the day with Cullen, even as he got shit done around the house, he thought about her, about the men she dated, and about what it meant.

Three men in seven days meant she dated a lot. Kissing one of those right outside her door meant she didn't care who knew. One of them looking to be in the working class meant she didn't care what they did for a living. All of them being dark-haired meant she liked them that way. The last two meant maybe, just maybe, he had a chance.

Even as he thought it, he hated he had because of what she made too obvious. So many men in so little days, displaying it for anyone to see, meant she looked out for number one—herself. She didn't care about the men. She used them to get off, didn't need them for anything else. She had a career, a home. Men were disposable. She'd use him for something Cullen's mother never used him for, but she'd use him and he didn't need another woman doing that.

He needed to set an example for his boy, and he *shouldn't* be attracted to a woman like that. Knowing this should make him stop thinking about her.

Still, he couldn't.

****

Her week got better. That day, Saturday, her sister and Tim showed. Surprising and thrilling. For one, she got to see her sister, whom she missed a lot, and Tim, who was a desk guy but a guy's guy who set up her flat-screen TVs, one in her bedroom and one in her living room, and Blu-Ray and DVD players. He also helped her hang a couple of her heavier artwork while her sister watched. By the time they left that evening, her house looked like a home, but most importantly, she spent nine hours with her sister, her best friend, and Tim, the brother she never had.

Sitting on the blue armchair in her living room, feet propped up on an ottoman, she stared at her flat screen TV, off at the moment, and thought how perfect everything looked.

A bang sounded on her door.

She flinched, grabbed her cell phone, strode to the door, and looked through the peephole.

Dodge, brows furrowed, jaw clenched, the muscles lining his shoulders bunched.

Fantastic.

If she opened the door, he'd ruin her day, and she'd finish her week on a low. She could walk away and ignore the knock except she had a feeling he'd bang her whole house down until she answered causing a scene, which would end her week at the lowest low. Steeling herself for the onslaught, she unlocked and opened the door.

There, he stood, eyes hard, hands in fists at his sides and still, undoubtedly gorgeous. He wore his usual, a pair of jeans, a black shirt, and the leather vest.

She walked out, closed the door behind her, and waited.

“I came to tell you to stay away from my kid.”

Not what she expected him to say, but she couldn’t say it surprised her. He always delivered a blow. Even the one time he drove her home and complimented her was a blow, a physical one.

She didn’t understand how such a beautiful man could be such a jerk all the time. Though she had ideas about why he acted the way he did, it didn’t make it okay to bang on her door, ever. It didn’t make it right to treat her the way he had several times.

At this point, she should’ve just agreed, strode inside her house, and closed the door, but instead because she cared about Cullen, she snapped, “Why?”

“Just how many men are you fuckin’?”

He had to be kidding.

Her eyes nearly bulged out of their sockets. “W-what?”

“I fuckin’ save you from getting hit on by my brothers ’cause I think you have a man and you’re cheating?”

The man had her confused for someone else. Had to.

“*What*?” Her voice high pitched.

“You fuckin’ heard me.”

She had, but it didn’t make sense. She wasn’t doing anyone, period. Why he thought she had a man, she had no idea.

Gritting her teeth, she shut her eyes for a moment to gather her thoughts. "First, I didn't ask you to *save* me. I don't need to be *saved*. If I did, I don't need a man to save me. I *save* myself. Second, I don't have a *man*, so it'd be impossible to cheat on him."

Livid now, she felt her face flush, felt that heat creep down her neck and chest and knew he noticed when his gaze lingered that way.

His stare hit hers when he cocked his head. "Come again?"

Maddening.

She fisted her hands. "I don't have a man, so I can't cheat on anyone."

"You shittin' me?"

She crossed her arms over her chest. "If you mean am I taking a dump on you, that would be no. If you mean am I lying, I'm not."

His jaw clamped shut, but before it did, she swore he'd been about to laugh, at *her*.

Infuriating.

"I saw you with that guy. You were kissing, right here." He pointed to the ground.

Now at least some of it made sense. He must've seen Mitchell kiss her.

Her lips parted, eyes widened. She dropped her arms to her sides. "So you saw him kiss me, but you didn't see me push him away?"

Brows furrowing, he reared back. It made her a little less angry.

"Not that it's any of your business, but that guy you just so happened to see me kissing and didn't see me push away is my ex. He's been an ex for five months. He showed thinking he could get me back since it's worked for him in the past. I guess he thought if he kissed me, I wouldn't be able to tell him to get lost. Guess what?" She paused for a split second. "I told him to get lost."

He lifted a brow. "So then you're just fuckin' the other two?"

She didn't owe him any explanations! She didn't owe anyone anything.

That heat traveling down her neck and chest suffused her whole body, searing her from the inside out. "You're *so* vulgar, and that's just none of your business."

Eyes hardening, he took a step toward her. "It isn't my business? Two men in three fuckin' days? Why do you make it everyone's business bringing them home?"

"Stop cursing at me on my porch."

He advanced taking two powerful, menacing steps toward her. Eyes widening, she retreated, stumbling until her back hit the door behind her.

"You get tired of what those assholes give you, babe, you come to a real man. I'll give it to you good. I'll fuck you all night, make you come so hard, you'll beg for more."

Her jaw dropped, not because of what he said, but because of how she reacted. Her pulse jackhammered, breath hitched, body shuddered. Yes, she wanted that so much she almost told him to take her right there.

Insane.

He was a rude biker and a jerk, and she was done with men, but she couldn't deny she wanted that, wanted him.

She shut her eyes tightly as if in doing so she'd shut out that thought. When she parted her lids, she expelled a breath. “Stop cursing at me.”

“Not cursing at you, I’m just fuckin’ talking.”

“Are you done?”

His jaw clamped. “Yeah, I’m fuckin’ done, *Alexa*.” Then he spun and stormed off.

That night, she lay in bed awake and thought for the first time, maybe, just maybe, she’d picked the wrong town.

Chapter Seven

Alexa couldn't help but feel a little down since her last encounter with Dodge. The whole point of moving had been to restart her life, make it her own. She had done that, but it seemed she'd done it in the wrong place. Her nasty luck with men, she blamed it on that. No other way to explain the huge coincidence—how she'd managed to buy, remodel, and move across the street from the biggest jerk who she also happened to be insanely attracted to.

Now, she was convinced he had it out for her.

Saturday, the biggest clue of all. He didn't care who she dated. Why would he? He was just finding ways to humiliate her in front of their neighbors and torment her. He wanted her gone and was doing what he could to make that happen.

He didn't like her, he could ignore her. But no, every chance he had, he tried to make her life hell. He offended her, meddled in her business, and made a scene at her front door all the while insinuating she slept around.

Technically, as unmarried, she could sleep with whoever she wanted, whenever she wanted. It wasn't anyone's business, but if that got around, even if a lie, in a small town where word spread faster than wildfires, it'd affect how parents perceived her as a teacher. Unfortunately, people were judgmental. They'd think she lacked morals and wasn't a proper role model. She'd lose her job meaning she couldn't afford to have him sully her name.

Luckily, there hadn't been another big blow up, but she knew anything could potentially tick him off considering she wasn't even dating anyone and he thought she was sleeping around.

To avoid him, over the course of the last four days, she no longer read outside. In fact, the only time she went outside was to grab her mail. Sunday after meeting with the second contractor she interviewed, she organized the garage making enough room to fit her car. She never parked on her drive anymore. Even so, she'd seen him twice, both times while she'd been getting her mail. Though she looked outside before she walked out to make sure he wasn't around, he magically appeared. She blamed that on her rotten luck with men too. She missed seeing Cullen, but his father hated her and didn't want her around, so she didn't have much choice.

Staying indoors meant by mid-week she had gotten a lot done and had officially unpacked, the last box gone. She liked the outdoors though. Her backyard was such a mess, she couldn't stand being out there. That left her sitting by one of the windows facing her front yard. She'd set up one of her chairs, a table, and lamp, angled so she couldn't see *his* house. That way, she could sit and read and every once in a while look out.

Sitting there, legs tucked under herself, nose in a book, she heard a cry. Her stomach rolled. She shot out of her chair, tossing her book on it, and ran to her door and outside.

In the street, Cullen, his butt on the pavement

cradling his knee. She didn't think. She sprinted his way sparing a glance to her left and another to her right. A car headed toward him. The driver's gaze down.

"Stop!" But she didn't stop.

Her heart beating a million miles a minute, she heard it over the horn blaring and the tires screeching. She jumped in front of the car, grabbed Cullen under his arms, and hauled him to her chest. The next second, she threw herself and Cullen out of the way and turned. She intended on landing on the stretch of grass between the road and sidewalk but miscalculated how far she'd been because her back hit the pavement hard knocking the wind out of her.

The weight of Cullen sprawled on top of her, she lifted her head, looked down at him, and tightened her arms around him. His head came up, eyes wide, tears brimming, cheeks wet.

With the pain in the center of her chest shooting down her back making it impossible to take a breath, she managed, "It's okay, Cul. E-everything's fine."

Everything was fine. Cullen was safe. She'd saved him.

Knowing this, she dropped her head. When it hit the pavement, her eyes fluttered closed.

****

The drier had been giving him trouble for months, but now, it was officially fucked and making some racket. It sucked big because that meant he had to blow money on a new one. Every time he started saving for a new TV for the living room, some shit happened.

He made good money at the garage, just not as much as he could make if he went on guard jobs for the club. Those jobs weren't entirely legal, but he'd make good money and he needed money. He lived paycheck to paycheck and hated it, partly since his bitch wife spent more than he made and had accumulated a lot of debt. He took away her credit cards and told her if she didn't cut the shit, he'd leave her, and she had, for once, listened. They'd ended anyway shortly after but for different reasons. Only recently, he'd paid off the debt, but to do it, he'd had to cut back on a lot and emptied his savings.

He slammed the drier shut and headed toward the living room.

"Stop!" A scream, her voice, scared out of her goddamned mind.

He moved, jogging toward his door. When he threw it open, a part of him died.

Cullen sat in the middle of the road, Lex running toward him. A car headed for them.

His heart sank, stomach rolled making bile rise in the back of his throat. He felt this, but he didn't hesitate a second. He sprinted toward them, knowing no way he'd make it on time and that'd be the end of him too.

A horn echoed. Tires screeched.

Lex grabbed Cullen off the ground, hauled him to her chest then threw herself and Cullen out of the way. Mid-air, she shifted angling her back toward the ground. Dodge extended his arms like he could reach them, save them. Then a loud thump—the sound of her body, *her* landing on her back with Cullen sprawled over her.

Gut-wrenching.

Horrifying.

She lifted her head, looked at Cullen then dropped it.

A second later, he made it to them.

Lex moved, her arms spasmed.

Cullen raised his head. “Lex! Lex! Lex!” He screamed at the top of his lungs, the sound almost more dreadful than witnessing the scene.

Dodge knelt, circled an arm around Cullen, tugged him off her, and scanned his boy. His knee busted bad, blue bruise showing, scraped and bleeding. “You okay, Cul?”

Cullen wrapped his arms around his waist, nodded, and wailed. “Lex!”

He shifted and cradled the back of her head. With his other hand, he tugged her hair away from her face and cupped her cheek. “Lex.”

She didn’t move.

He straightened and looked around them. Maggie, his next-door neighbor, stood a few feet behind them.

“Call an ambulance.”

She stood frozen.

“Mags, now!” She moved then, so he redirected his attention to Lex. “Talk to me, baby.” Heart beating too loud, he barely heard his own voice. It didn’t stop him from talking. “Come on. Speak. Say something, Lex.”

Her ice blue eyes cracked open. “Sorry…” Her voice low, broken.

Cullen, at his side, clutched his cut and cried loud, gut-wrenching sobs.

Turning to Cullen, he released Lex’s cheek to wrap his arm around him. “She’s awake, Cul. Gotta calm down so we hear her.”

His boy went silent.

He faced Lex. Her eyes now closed. “Lex? Lex?”

Her lids parted. She groaned. “I hear you. Stop

screaming."

"Lex!" Cullen lunged.

Acting quickly, he snaked an arm around his son's waist and tugged him back beside him, stopping him from slamming in to her. Locking eyes with his boy, he explained, "Cul, you'll hurt her. Gotta take it easy."

The minute he released Cul, his boy moved to the opposite side of Lex, leaned down, draped his arms around her waist, and rested his face against her stomach.

Instantly, she circled an arm around Cullen's back and threaded the other hand through his hair. "You okay, sweetheart?"

As Cullen drew away, her arms fell from him. His boy then grabbed her hand and nodded.

Smiling at Cul, she brought her free hand to her forehead, took a breath, and with a whimper, sat up. "It's okay, honey. I'm good."

Dodge hooked an arm around her back helping her sit.

Her left hand came to rest on his chest. "I can do it."

Yeah. He knew from one look she didn't need a hero. She was her own. She didn't need a man. She made her own dreams come true. Right then and there, things were different, but he knew if she needed help, she wouldn't want it from him, and he had no one to blame but himself.

"I know you don't need anyone, but I wanna help you. Every once in a while, you should let a man help. It makes us feel useful."

Her gaze flew to his. Out of nowhere, she laughed softly. She probably didn't have the energy for anything else, but the beautiful sound, a little something that gave him hope. He kept his arm around her back when her hand left his chest and went to her stomach.

"Oh, gosh…"

"Where does it hurt?"

"I think…" She closed her eyes. "Everywhere…"

He looked over his shoulder and spotted Maggie. "How long?"

A second later, sirens blared. He tightened his arm around her waist. "You're gonna be okay."

Not long after, the paramedics arrived. He moved aside, giving them room to examine her. Cullen refused to leave her; he stayed beside her holding her hand. Dodge didn't argue the point. As he stood there watching them with his hands fisted at his sides, he felt eyes on him, looked over his shoulder, and noticed what he hadn't before. The sedan parked on the street in front of his house, the car he'd seen almost run over Lex and Cullen. Outside the car stood a man in his early twenties. Dodge didn't let himself look at that guy too long, whether or not the guy had done the right thing and stopped. Because if Dodge did, he'd remember that guy could've killed Lex and Cullen both, and that would make him lose his cool and do something that'd mean he'd spend time in jail. Instead, he looked in front of the man at the cop who stood there speaking to the guy.

"It's okay, sweetheart."

Hearing her voice, he shifted and peered back at Lex and Cul. She now had an arm around him, tucking him close to her side.

"Can you walk to the ambulance?" One of the medics asked.

She nodded. He took two long strides, squatted beside her, snaked an arm around her waist, and helped her to her feet. Cullen didn't release her, not as they strode to the ambulance, not when the paramedics had her sit on the gurney, not while they continued to examine her. His boy wouldn't let her go. Lex didn't seem to mind, so Dodge grabbed Cul under his arms and hefted him up, setting him beside her and stepping away, again giving the medics room to check her.

From the corner of his eye, he caught sight of a blue pick-up truck, one he'd seen before, pull into Lex's drive. A guy hopped out of the car. Dodge got a good look at him, the same man who'd been at her house last Thursday. He was dressed again like he got off his construction job, dark-haired and tall but not as tall as him, and the guy was an idiot. A chance with Lex, he would've at least showered before heading to her place, put on some cologne, bought her flowers, or some shit like that.

He headed for him, stopped a few feet away, and said tersely, "Lex's not here."

The guy cocked a brow.

"She's getting checked by the medics. Had an accident."

"Who?"

Fucking idiot. Who the hell would he be talking about?

He took a step toward him. "Lex, the woman whose drive you just parked in."

"Oh, shit. Yeah? She'll probably want to reschedule."

Worthless. What about asking how she was? Was this the type of man she liked? Why didn't she find herself someone who gave a fuck something happened to her?

He turned and walked away. If he looked at the idiot for longer, he may actually punch him. The guy deserved it, but still.

Reaching the ambulance, Lex sat on the stretcher, Cul beside her, his hand still in hers. The idiot followed Dodge and now stood next to him.

"Alexa?"

Her head snapped up, gaze went from him to the idiot. "Oh, I can't believe…"

"You okay?" The idiot finally asked.

Cullen, his boy, leaned in to Lex, pressing his face against her arm.

She released Cullen's hand to wrap her arm around him and cup the back of his head, holding him against her. She spared a glance at Cullen and then met the idiot's stare again. "Fine. Yes, we should reschedule."

"Gotta check my schedule. Call you tomorrow?"

She nodded.

The guy left, *left her* sitting on a gurney.

While the medics cleared Lex and patched Cullen's knee, the cop neared and told them he'd ticketed the driver of the vehicle who admitted being distracted. After, she went to stand. Dodge pushed the medics aside to get to her. Wrapping his arm around her waist, he lifted her. As he set her on her feet, her body slid down the length of his.

"Um…" She looked away, but before she did, her cheeks heated.

A woman did not flush like that for just anyone. A man she was into, yeah. Could it be? He shook his head. No. Not like it mattered, not anymore, she was dating. He got jealous, acted like a dick, and forever ruined his chances by making her hate him. Still, she'd saved his kid.

Facing Cullen, he grabbed his hand. "Come on, Cul. Hop off."

Cullen jumped, holding on to his hand and Lex's. He made sure Cullen landed on his feet. Then his boy let go of his hand only to grab Lex's again. With his other arm still around Lex, he nudged her toward her house.

"I'm fine, really. You don't have to—"

Turning his head slightly, he looked down at her. "Yeah, I do." She seemed to accept this, didn't fight. Still, he added, "'Sides I want to."

He helped her up the steps to her porch coming to a stop at her front door. He wanted to stay more than anything, make sure she was okay, but he knew she didn't want him there, so he turned to his boy. "Cul, thank Lex, then say bye."

His son peered at Lex with his big, dark eyes and whispered, "Hanks, Lex." He released her hand to wrap both arms around her waist. Cul held her for a while before he drew away, meeting her eyes again. "Bye."

Smiling, she cupped Cul's cheek and slid her hand, threading her fingers through his hair. "Bye, honey. I'll see you around."

Watching that small action, knowing Cul's mother had never touched him like that, made an ache slice up his chest. He fought to ignore the burn as he looked at his boy. "Wait for me on the lawn. I gotta talk to Lex. Then you and me gotta talk, but we'll do it at home."

Tough kid, Cullen knew what would come, and he didn't pout. He lifted his chin, nodded, and did as he was told.

He faced Lex and caught her pulling her hair behind her. Almost getting run over by a car and she looked beautiful, wearing a yellow blouse, a pair of cut off shorts, and flats. Ice blue eyes soft, cheeks rosy, strawberry hair parted in half, loose around her.

"Saturday."

She stiffened.

"I was outta line. Who you're seeing has nothing to do with Cul. He likes when you read to him, likes spending time with you. Honest, he probably has a crush. You saved him today, and I can't thank you enough for that."

"You don't need to thank me—"

"Yeah, I do. I need to thank you and apologize for being a dick, so I'm thanking you and apologizing for being a dick. You want to read to Cul, bake him cookies, you go ahead and knock yourself out. He needs women like you around."

She held his stare for a moment before she nodded.

"And I said it's none of my business, but I gotta say this. You deserve better than a man who doesn't stay around to make sure you're okay."

She giggled and made no attempt to hide it.

"Serious here, Lex."

Bringing a hand to her mouth, she laughed and shook her head. "He cared more about me, I'd be worried. He's just a contractor."

A contractor?

Fuck.

She laughed a little harder.

Right. So that meant what? That she was only seeing one guy?

"Sam was right. There's a reason I'm single. Haven't figured it out yet." She shrugged. "Maybe one day."

"What about that guy, the one who was here Saturday?"

He hadn't meant to ask. Again, none of his business, and she didn't owe him shit.

She lifted a brow. "Tim?" A smile played at her lips. "For the last five years, he's been happily married to my sister. They live in San Francisco and came to visit."

Single, not as in just not married but as in not seeing anyone. He scanned her from top to bottom. Perfect and single. How the fuck was that possible? He'd been an ass for no reason. It made it all the worse.

His throat went dry, but he managed to say, "Thanks, again."

Her brows creased, eyes saddened, shoulders slumped, for some reason looking devastated. Before he did anything about it, she mumbled, "Bye," then turned, strode into her house, and closed the door.

Chapter Eight

Her last encounter with Dodge left her shaken. Not because she jumped in front of a car to save Cullen, not because Dodge had been nice and thanked her, but because of the way he looked at her right before she left. She hadn't been able to forget that look since, the same he'd given her the first time he laid eyes on her—disgust, which meant either she'd imagined hearing him say that a man had to be blind and stupid not to find her attractive or he'd just said it to be nice.

That look, she thought about all night, barely slept, and had been a zombie at school the next day. After school, she stayed inside, graded papers, and then headed to bed. Friday morning, a surprise, she found a bouquet of white and yellow roses on her doorstep. The note said:

Lex,

Thank you.

Cullen.

Sweet. How Cul convinced his father to buy roses for her, she didn't know. Dodge didn't seem like the type who'd buy them, not for a wife or girlfriend and especially not for a neighbor. Then again, if she were the wife or girlfriend of the hottest man on the face of the earth, maybe she didn't need flowers. No denying though Dodge must've bought them, but it was nothing more than a thank you for saving Cullen.

Friday evening, she baked a batch of peanut butter cookies, hoping Cullen wasn't allergic. She sat outside with several cookies and read. Within an hour, Cul showed. She read him several books and made sure he wasn't allergic before giving him some cookies. When she heard Dodge call out for Cullen from her yard, she said goodnight. Without looking at Dodge, she strode inside. She hadn't meant to be rude, but she'd decided to change tactics. Being nice hadn't worked, and so, she'd avoid him unless impossible.

That night, she made dinner, had a glass of wine, and watched a movie, alone. For some reason, she felt the loneliness more than usual. The prospect of spending an entire weekend alone, not comforting at all. She decided to drive to San Francisco the next day.

Saturday morning, she woke early, showered, and drank her coffee while she applied makeup and dressed in a pair of skinny jeans, cute olive top, and matching sandals. She styled her hair in soft curls and packed an overnight bag just in case she decided to stay.

Walking out of her bedroom, down the hall, and into her living room, the doorbell rang. She dropped her duffle, placed her empty coffee mug in the dishwasher, and headed for the door.

Looking through the peephole, she released a frustrated sigh. Mitchell, of course. He had perfect timing. Thinking back, one of the reasons she always took him back had to do with the fact that he came when she felt the loneliest and caved.

"Not this time," she mumbled under her breath.

She put serious thought into not answering her door. Yesterday evening, she parked in her garage, so she hoped not seeing her car, he'd think she was gone and leave. She waited and waited.

He didn't leave though. Instead, he started banging on her door and yelling her name. Unless she wanted him to wake half the neighborhood, she had no choice.

She opened the door, stepped out, and closed it behind her. She wouldn't let him get any ideas about coming inside. Her gaze locked with his.

He hadn't changed a bit since they began dating. His hair styled the same, faded. He wore a pair of khakis, a collared-shirt, and smelled like the cologne she bought him for their first anniversary, one he said he didn't like, which meant he only wore it after a break-up.

"Yes."

He smiled. "Hey, babe."

"What are you doing here? I told you I don't want you here."

He just stood there, not saying anything just staring at her, blankly. He did that a lot, every time he came back after a break up with the exception of the first three. She supposed after the third time since she'd forgiven him before, he figured he didn't have to waste time making promises he had no intention of keeping. It was infuriating because he made it impossible to know whether he'd heard her, didn't know what to say, was thinking of something to say, or had gone deaf.

The longer he stayed there, the hotter her cheeks got, the lower that heat crept down her face and neck. "*Well*?"

"I think…we should go out for coffee or something…"

Really? That was all he had to say?

She kept her face blank. "I don't."

"Come on, it'll be—"

"You *had* me for three years. For three years, you kept *breaking up* with me. It's over now. It's been over for five months. Your decision, the same decision you made repeatedly over the course of *three years*. Now, you have to stick with it."

She turned halfway before he gripped her elbow. Turning back, she started, "Let…"

Anger so deep flowed around her pinning her to the spot. She shifted her stare, moving it behind Mitchell.

There, heading her way, up the walkway, up the porch steps, Dodge, jaw clamped and clenched, eyes glaring and deadpanned on Mitchell. He grabbed Mitchell by the bicep and ripped him away. Mitchell stumbled back simultaneously releasing her. Dodge came to a stop directly in front of her so she only saw his wide, broad back.

"Who the fuck—" Mitchell started.

"Cullen. Get inside Lex's."

Oh God. She looked to her right. Cullen stood on her porch just a few feet from them. How she hadn't noticed him before, she didn't know.

Wearing a black skully and white tee, Cullen *smiled* at her, walked past her, opened her door, and disappeared inside.

One disaster adverted, on to the next.

She swiveled, grabbed Dodge's arm, and attempted to pull him aside. When he didn't budge, she released him then sidestepped until she stood beside him. "I'll handle—"

He didn't look her way, his gaze hard and on her ex. He growled, "Lex," in a stern tone she knew well, she used it on her students except Dodge's was scary.

"Who the fuck are you?"

"None of your fuckin' business. Now, I think Lex told you to leave." He took a step in Mitchell's direction, lifted his chin toward the street, and snarled, "Leave."

At this point, despite the fact that they both managed to infuriate her that early on a Saturday morning, she took them in. The difference between the two, vast. Dodge stood taller, wider, his muscles defined. Arched brows, dark, rich disheveled hair matching his eyes. His face had strong, clean lines, stubble covered his chin and cheeks. She had to pick two words to describe him, they'd be rugged, striking. Next to him, Mitchell with his faded light brown hair, hazel eyes, and clean-shaven face looked simple, *plain.*

She had no clue what she'd seen in him in the first place. Not that it was all about looks, but she put up with so much of Mitchell's crap, why? He'd never been a great conversationalist. He only ever wanted to do what he wanted to do, and he broke up with her repeatedly.

Mitchell's gaze sliced to her. "You know this clown?"

For some reason, she felt the need to defend Dodge. "He's not—"

"Got to the count of three before I throw your ass outta here myself."

Oh God. Dodge, no longer furious, now, livid, body rigid yet vibrating with anger. He didn't seem like the type of man who made idle threats, and Mitchell could be boneheaded when he wanted something. If she didn't stop this, her new neighbors would catch a show. What would they think? She knew one thing; she'd be humiliated.

She grabbed Dodge's arm, her nails biting into his thick bicep, and tugged. "Dodge," she said firmly. Though honest, she didn't think that tone would work, not with him.

The muscle in Dodge's jaw jumped.

Mitchell, oblivious to how much angrier Dodge had gotten, looked to her and went on, "We have to talk, Lex."

"*One*." Dodge, tone deadly, leaned in to Mitchell.

Yikes. She needed to do something, quick.

She shot a glare at Mitchell. "You need to leave."

"We need to—"

"*Two*." Dodge.

"There's *nothing* to talk about."

"We need—"

Dodge advanced. Stupidly, she jumped in front of him between him and Mitchell. Dodge bumped in to her. She staggered. His arm circled her waist, steadying her. Then he lifted her off her feet, shifted, and set her to his side, keeping his arm around her, tucking her body against his. Warmth, his, spread over her, all around her. He smelled nice, no, fantastic.

Mitchell took a step back, looking to her. "We'll talk."

Dodge took three steps until he stood inches from Mitchell. In doing this, he didn't release her but took her with him. Fingers gripping her hip, he angled her partially behind him. "You *won't* talk to her. You step foot on this street, I'll know. You step foot at the school, I'll know. You come into Wadden, I'll fuckin' know. Then you and me are gonna have a serious fuckin' talk."

Mitchell clenched his jaw, shook his head, and met her gaze. "This thug? Really?"

She didn't respond and wouldn't. Let Mitchell think whatever he wanted. A part of her wanted him to think she'd moved on so he'd finally let her be.

Mitchell walked away, got into his car, and drove off.

She released a breath and met Dodge's stare. "You didn't have to do that. I could've handled him."

"He touched you."

"We dated on and off for three years. It wasn't the first time he touched me."

He flinched. The arm around her tautened. He leaned in to her. His face so close now, his breaths heated her skin. "He *touched* you."

Staring deep into his dark eyes, she knew she hadn't been wrong in thinking he was the most gorgeous man alive. Being that close proved it. But she couldn't think of that then, she had to focus.

She swallowed. "I said—"

"Is this the first time he touched you when you didn't want him to?"

"What difference does it make?"

He leaned farther in to her. Face millimeters from hers, his expression went feral. "Asked you a question, Lex."

As scary as he looked, she wouldn't back down. She lifted a brow. "And I asked you a question, Dodge."

He released a heavy breath like she'd frustrated him when *he'd* frustrated her. "I asked first."

"I asked second."

His mouth tightened, the sides twitching. After

what seemed like an endless moment, he smiled, drew his upper body away without releasing her, and rubbed the palm of his hand over his face. “Serious here, Lex. Stop being funny.”

Amused, was he? It was beyond her what he found comical.

“I’m not trying to be funny, Dodge.”

Eyes softening, he unwrapped his arm from around her, grabbed her hands, and held them tightly in his. “He touch you before when you didn’t want to be touched?”

The way he gripped her hands, the way he looked at her, and the pleading tone he used made her give in.

She bit her bottom lip. “I don’t think so.”

He quirked a brow. “You don’t think so?”

“Honestly, I can’t remember.”

His eyes darkened. Her gaze shot to his throat, watching it work as he swallowed. “It ever hurt when he touch you?”

Was that the reason for that question? He thought Mitchell had hurt her?

Her chest clenched, but she managed to admit, “Never.”

He nodded but hesitated before he let go of her hands. “You have more of those peanut butter cookies?”

He must’ve had some of the cookies she’d given Cullen to take home and liked them.

She nodded.

He grinned.

She strode inside her house. Cullen sat on her couch staring at the TV, off at the moment. “Hey Cul. You can turn it on if you want.”

Cullen smiled, grabbed the remote sitting on the coffee table, and turned on her flat screen. Dodge closed the door behind her. She walked into the kitchen. Facing the stove, she grabbed a navy platter, opened her blue jar, and set several cookies on the platter. While she did, she thought about *everything*.

She had her dream home but was alone, and she was tired of the loneliness, tired of dealing with jerks. She'd had boyfriends, a lot of them considering she started dating at sixteen. Not one of them was worth much, not one of them was a real man, the kind who took care of you, respected you even if he didn't love you. This was the reason she made the decision to stop looking, stop dating. All she ever wanted was a family, one of her own. Giving up on men meant giving up on the family she had in mind.

Thinking this, she couldn't stop tears from welling in her eyes. She moved quickly. Escaping into the hallway, she opened the door to her garage, closed it behind her, and let the tears slide down her cheeks.

"Lex?"

Hearing his voice just feet away, she wiped her face, took a deep breath, and faced him. She didn't look directly at him, knowing looking into his dark eyes, she wouldn't be able to hold the tears back.

"You okay?"

She nodded. "Fine."

"He hurt you?"

God, yes. A lot, but not the way he thought. She'd already told him this.

Getting ahold of her tears, her gaze shot to his. "I answered that."

"You lie?"

"No."

"I can kick his ass."

She laughed, shaking her head. "Don't worry about it. Thanks for…what you did."

She could handle Mitchell, but Dodge stepping in meant maybe Mitchell would think twice about showing up again. She didn't think she had the energy to deal with him.

"Don't mention it."

Her eyes watered again, but she held his stare.

"Did he scare you?"

"No."

"Talk to me."

She couldn't. She did, she'd cry, a lot. She didn't cry in front of anyone, not if she could help it.

His face warmed. "Talk to me."

She shook her head.

"You talk to me, I won't kick his ass."

Bargaining for information? He looked serious then proved just how serious the next instant.

"That's a promise. I got a kid, so I don't break promises."

She wouldn't be held responsible for Dodge kicking Mitchell's butt meaning she didn't have a choice. Though Mitchell kind of deserved it, Cullen didn't need his father in jail for assault.

She took a deep breath, released it, and blurted, "Men always disappoint me." She shook her head. "Not all men…just the ones I date."

His brows shot up. "You're fuckin' shitting me."

That phrase, he said it often. She never understood why people used it, but Dodge saying it the way he did and how often he did brought a small smile to her lips, one she tried to hide.

"It always starts good. Then they cheat or lose interest or want space or a slew of other reasons."

He clenched his jaw. "That asshole cheated?" His voice thick, rough.

She shook her head. "Not that I know of, but we dated for three years on and off because he needed space, a lot of it over the course of those three years."

He reared back. "He fucked around during those breaks?"

She raised a brow. "Why do you think he wanted the break in the first place?"

Dodge looked down at his boots and mumbled, "Fuckin' idiot." After a brief moment, he lifted his head. "Why'd you keep taking him back?"

The million-dollar question. An easy one.

"Because I loved him."

At least, at first she did. After a while, with how often he broke up with her, she started to resent him. Even then, she stuck around. It wasn't until he ended them five months ago that she realized she didn't love him, not the way she used to, not the way she should because of everything he'd put her through. When she realized that, she made plans.

"You *loved* him?"

"I've given up, remember?" She forced a smile. "Don't get me wrong, I know there're good ones. My dad's a great one. He married my mom forty years ago and has never strayed. Tim's a good one too. I know just by the way he looks at my sister."

His eyes darkened. What she saw in the depths took her breath. Sadness, defeat…like he felt hers.

"A woman like you can have any man you want.

You're picking the wrong ones."

She had picked the wrong men repeatedly, but she had no idea why he'd say a woman like her could have any man she wanted considering he seemed disgusted with her. Maybe he'd just said it to make her feel better. Coming from him, it would've helped except she couldn't forget the way he looked at her, twice now.

"And that's why I've given up. I'm done dating. I'm done looking. I put my life on hold for him for years. Now, I'm doing what I want, when I want. Maybe I'll never know what it's like to fall in love with someone who loves me, but I can still have other things I've always wanted. I can have a beautiful home. I can have a baby—"

Eyes widening, he shook his head. "You're going to have a baby alone?"

Yes. Definitely. She wouldn't miss out on being a mom.

She nodded. "Women do it all the time. You're raising Cullen alone. Why can't I?"

He released a breath then paused for a moment. "You can… It's just… You're young. You got time."

"I'll be thirty soon."

"You got time, Lex."

She shrugged and looked to his left toward a stack of boxes with clothes she no longer wanted she meant to give to charity. "Not as much as I'd like."

She didn't say that time wouldn't matter. Men disappointed her, every time.

"Fuck it," he mumbled.

She met his stare. His eyes dark and determined. In an instant, he closed the distance between them. His hand went to her cheek, the other rested on the small of her back pressing her to him. Her chest collided with his, and then, his lips hit hers, and his tongue swept inside her mouth.

A goner.

With one kiss, he proved he could kiss amazingly. She would've never thought a biker, her rough-around-the-edges, unfriendly neighbor who seemed to hate her guts, could kiss soft and slow and intensely. Proof, there was more to him than that handsome face, more than his vulgarity, much more than his tough guy persona. Maybe she was right to want him.

When he pulled away after one hell of an amazing kiss, he stayed close, lips grazing hers, body against hers. His hand at her cheek trailed up, glided through her hair then around the back of her neck.

It took her a while to compose herself, to concentrate hard to remember why she should be upset.

"What you said…" she whispered. "Before you kissed me, what did you mean?"

His brows quirked. "You want to talk about that now?"

She nodded.

His gaze strayed from her eyes and dropped to her mouth. After a moment, he cocked his head. "What did I say?"

"You said 'eff it.' Did you mean, 'Screw it. It's been a long time. She'll do' or—'"

His brows shot up, body moving away slightly, but his arms stayed around her. "Fuck, are you serious?"

She swallowed. "Yes."

He laughed. Again, she had no idea why. She didn't get his sense of humor at all.

"Babe, I did *not* mean *that*." Pausing a moment,

still chuckling, he looked behind her.

"I don't know why this is amusing."

Eyes smiling, he met her gaze. "It's hilarious, Lex."

"Maybe if you filled me in, I could make that decision on my own."

"I said 'fuck it.' Then I kissed you. That doesn't mean 'you'll do.' It means fuck the fact you hate me, fuck the reasons I shouldn't make a move, fuck the reasons this would complicate shit for you, for me, and for Cul."

She jerked, couldn't help it. A natural reaction to hearing what he said. "I hate you?"

"Not your fault, I contributed to that by being a dick."

"But I disgust you."

Yes, that came out of her mouth.

Releasing her, his eyes widened, jaw dropped. "Why the fuck would you think that?" He shouted this.

Had she imagined that look on his face? No. She hadn't.

"The way you looked at me the other day…" She bit the side of her lip. "And the first time you saw me."

His jaw hardened, eyes narrowed. "You shitting me?" He spoke even louder.

"No," she whispered hoping he'd start too. She didn't want Cullen to hear this conversation.

He shook his head and cursed under his breath. "Lex, the first time I saw you I thought you were the most beautiful woman I'd ever seen, and I've seen a lot of beautiful women."

Oh God. The most attractive man on the face of the earth thought she was beautiful?

Her lips parted. "*What*?"

"You heard me."

"But the way you looked at me—"

"Like I thought you were hot and wanted to fuck you? Like I was pissed I wasn't inside you then and there?"

Oh God. Still, so vulgar. Face flaming, her body shuddered. Why did it turn her on? Focus. He wanted *her*?

"No, it was like you were—"

Eyes narrowing, he shook his head and snapped, "Don't say disgusted."

"Repulsed."

He snaked his arm around her waist, grasped the back of her neck, and leaned in to her. "Don't say that shit either, *ever again*, Lex."

When he spoke again, his voice had lowered an octave. "Don't you remember me saying a man would have to be blind and stupid not to find you attractive?"

She did, but he confused her. He looked at her like she disgusted him. Then he insulted her then said something sweet then acted like a jerk. A long shot, but she tried to reason.

"If you wanted me, why did you insult me?"

"I know I was a dick, but—"

"You said my house was masculine and—"

He released her, putting distance between them, and barked, "You shitting me?"

She closed her eyes tightly. "Again, no."

"I said that as a compliment, Lex. I meant that a man wouldn't mind living in your house 'cause it's not covered in flowers and pink and bullshit like that."

She shook her head. "It didn't sound like that. At

all. Then when I said I made cookies from scratch, you acted like you found that hard to believe."

He drew closer. "It *is* hard to believe, babe. You're hot, got good taste, and make cookies like that?"

She then pointed out, "You were mean."

He nodded. "I was a dick a couple of times. I apologized twice. Everything else, I think you misunderstood."

Had she?

"Are you done?"

Nowhere near. There was more, but he still stood close and that kiss was fresh on her mind, so she nodded.

He closed the small distance between them, grasped the back of her neck, and slid his hand down her spine. Wrapping the other around her waist, he rested them both on her lower back pressing her body to his. This time, he whispered against her lips, "Can I kiss you again, Lex?"

"Please."

He did, but before then, she caught him smiling.

Chapter Nine

Dodge now knew not only was she a beautiful, smart woman who baked the best cookies he'd ever tasted, but she kissed phenomenally.

That morning kissing her had been the last thing on his mind. He peered out his living room window and spotted that douche there again. He couldn't have forgotten him if he tried—her ex. Knowing why the guy was there, he carried Cullen across the street without so much as a thought. On her lawn, that ass wipe grabbed her. He set Cullen on his feet, finished closing the distance between them, ripped the douche away from her, and positioned himself between her and her ex. He didn't know why she let that shit slide, but she had. Then she looked pissed at him instead of at her ex. Now, his lips were pressed to hers, and her tongue was in his mouth, so what had happened was no longer on his mind.

She moaned soft and sweet, and he felt it in his dick. Hands on her lower back, her stomach firm against his hard shaft, he groaned and instinctively grinded in to her. She became almost desperate then. Her nipples puckered against him through the thin fabric of her shirt. Her arms around his neck, she clutched him, digging her nails into the skin on his back.

Fuck, she taunted him. She kept doing shit like

that, he'd lose his mind and take her right there. He couldn't do that, not now. He tried to stop, but then, she lapped her tongue against his again and he lost the will.

He dove into her mouth faster, harder, deeper. His hand moved to cup her cheek. He lowered the other until he rested it on her plump ass.

She tore her lips from his, arching her back. "Oh…"

He took the chance trailing his mouth down her neck, licking, sucking her. When her body quaked, he smiled against her skin.

She released him, planted her hands against his chest, and pushed. "Stop."

Shit.

Rock hard, turned on, but he let her go immediately. Arms falling to his sides, he took a step back. Because it'd been so long for him, his mind went there. Maybe he'd been too rough, or it'd been too much, too soon.

Before he'd married, he bedded taps, women who parted their legs because he wore a cut and expected nothing in return. Even Lilliam, his wife, had been one. With Lex, he was out of his element. He'd never dated, didn't even know how, and a woman like Lex dated, expected that. Fact, making out with her hot and heavy in her garage was probably not something she wanted or did. Not that he thought her a virgin, but he hadn't even taken her out on a date.

He ran a hand through his hair. "Sorry."

Her cheeks flushed, lips swollen, making her even more beautiful. "Don't be. I…"

He kept his distance, not trusting himself to keep his hands off her. "What?"

"It's just…I—" She shook her head. "—Don't know your name."

Not hesitating a split second, he gave her what she asked. "Dave Roth."

A soft smile spread across her lips.

Fucking gorgeous.

"Dave Roth, you're a very good kisser."

He grinned. "Alexa Millen, so are you."

She looked away. Her brows creased.

He tried to think of something to say to put her at ease. The harder he tried, the worse it got until he couldn't think of anything to say to change the subject.

That uncomfortable silence stretched until he saw her gaze draw behind him.

"Hey, Cul."

He looked over his shoulder. At the entrance to the garage stood his son.

"Lex. Park."

Right, they'd planned on heading to the park. Cul had just invited Lex. Turned out even his kid had more game than he did. Thank God his brothers weren't around. He'd never hear the end of this one.

"Good idea, Cul." He faced her. "You down for a trip to the park with us?"

Her eyes fell from his. She hesitated a while, making him think she didn't want to go but didn't want to say no to Cul.

"Please."

Her head shot up, stare locked on Cul, who'd spoken, only then did she smile and agree. "Cookies, first?"

He spared a glance at Cul in time to see his boy grin and nod.

****

Her stomach turned. Lex fought to ignore it and folded her hands into each other to stop from fidgeting. No denying she felt out of sorts. Not only because the most attractive man on the face of the earth kissed her twice and those kisses had been astounding. Not just because she was tagging along on a father-son outing, but also because after those kisses, around the time a man would ask her out and make plans, he just stood there and stared. In that silence, she started doubting everything and continued to even as she sat in his SUV on the way to the park.

At first, she thought he regretted kissing her. The reason was beyond her since he'd told her she was beautiful and that he was attracted to her. Besides, how could he regret a kiss like that? Maybe he didn't think the kiss had been amazing. Maybe he'd just said she was a good kisser because she'd said he was. She was thinking too much, overanalyzing, yet with him, it was impossible not to. The man was an anomaly; she never knew what to expect.

Dodge parked in a lot by the playground located on the backside of the elementary school near an open field. The ride over had been filled with just the low hum of the engine of Dodge's SUV and the radio. Her doubts made her discomfort grow to the point she avoided looking his way. As she pulled open her door and hopped down, she caught sight of Dodge rounding the back. He parted the door for Cullen, who'd already unbuckled himself from his car seat. Cullen hopped off and dashed ahead of them.

Dodge walked beside her and steered them toward one of the benches. "Thanks for coming along."

Sparing a glance his way, still avoiding his gaze, she mumbled, "No problem though I feel like I'm intruding on a father-son outing."

"We get father-son time all the time. It's nice to have a woman around."

She looked at him and caught him shaking his head and running his hand through his dark hair. They reached the bench. She took a seat. He sat beside her, close enough his thigh touched hers.

"Not just any woman… You. It's nice to have you around."

What he said and the way his voice sounded made her snap her head to him. Back ramrod straight, jaw tight, his dark eyes boring into her. He cleared his throat then swallowed thickly.

Oh God. Was he…nervous?

Releasing a breath, she chuckled.

He cocked his head and quirked a brow. "That funny to you?"

She shook her head. "No, I just… Can I be honest?"

He nodded stiffly. "Would appreciate if you were."

"We kissed, and then, you didn't say anything. I thought…" She bit her tongue so she wouldn't say it. It'd make her sound insecure.

"You thought…"

Darn it. She had to admit it now, didn't she? Her and her big mouth.

She pressed her lips together then blurted, "I thought maybe you were re-thinking having kissed me."

He smiled. "Since you're being honest, I'll be honest. You'll figure it out on your own either way, and I think it'll save us some more misunderstandings."

His gaze trailed away from her for a moment, checking on Cullen, whom she spotted trying to swing with his feet planted on the seat.

He met her stare again. “I’m no Casanova. I’m the complete opposite. It sucks to have to admit especially to a woman I want to get to know, but it’s true.”

Her brows furrowed. “You mean you’re not good with women…like it’s hard for you to pick one up?”

He nodded.

The most attractive man couldn’t pick up a woman? Not likely.

“That’s how I got my name, Dodge, ’cause women see me coming and they dodge for cover.”

Um. Wow. She giggled.

He looked down at his boots when his cheeks reddened.

She shouldn’t have laughed! It was brave to admit something that obviously embarrassed him.

She immediately slapped her hand over her mouth. “I’m sorry. I didn’t mean to laugh. It’s just…”

His gaze shot to her.

“It’s hard to believe. I mean you’re…”

He grinned. “Go on. I’m what?”

“Handsome.”

Smirking, he cocked a brow. “You think?”

“Everyone thinks.”

The flush on his cheeks deepened. It made her think the man had never been complimented. Geez. What type of woman was Cullen’s mother? And if he couldn’t get women, then how had he impregnated one?

She swallowed. “So women dodge you, how do you have a son?”

He released a loaded breath. “You sure you want to

talk about that shit now?"

She did and couldn't help it. She wanted to know. Had Cullen's mother left him? Why would a woman leave a man as attractive as him? Why would a woman leave her son too? Maybe he hadn't treated her right. Maybe Lex had been wrong to assume he loved Cullen's mother. Maybe he hadn't. Maybe she hadn't wanted to leave, but life had other plans. Maybe she hadn't left at all. Maybe he'd kicked her out though this didn't explain why she never saw her son. The possibilities were endless. But it was his life. He should share it when and if he wanted.

She shrugged. "You don't have to say. Besides, I think I know enough."

He cocked his head. "Have you heard shit 'round town?"

No, she hadn't. She hadn't asked around about him either.

She shook her head. "I've lived across the street for three weeks, and I haven't seen her. As a woman, I can't envision going a day without my child. I don't have kids of my own, but still…"

His eyes darkened. "She wanted something from me. When she got it, she decided she didn't want it anymore. And by 'it,' I don't mean Cul. To her, he was just a means to an end."

She heard the heartbreak in his voice, saw it in his eyes. Whether that was because he loved her and lost her or because the woman had never loved their son, Lex didn't know. But Lex now knew, whoever she was, she wasn't a good mother.

Devastating.

All of it.

Especially for Cullen, a beautiful, dark-haired boy who didn't have a mom. Lex couldn't picture her life without hers. At least Cullen had Dodge.

She didn't know what to say, didn't know what to do either. She knew nothing she said or did would undo that hurt, but on impulse, she placed her hand on his forearm. His stare shot to her hand. Then he met her eyes and smiled. When she returned the smile, he grabbed her hand, tightened his fingers around it, set it on his thigh, and didn't let go. They sat side by side, hand in hand talking about nothing as deep: her job, his, her family, Cullen, and so on. A great conversation, despite the cursing, it flowed easily because he was easy to talk to. She hoped to him she was too.

An hour later, on their way back to Dodge's car, her phone buzzed. She nabbed it from her back pocket and saw her sister's name flash on the screen.

Yikes. She'd forgotten. She'd called her sister last night and told her she planned to visit meaning her sister had been waiting for her all morning.

She spared Dodge a glance. "Sorry, I have to take this." She slid her finger across the screen and brought the phone to her ear. "Hey."

"Just wondering when you'd be gracing us with your presence," her sister teased. "I wanted to grab a bite when you got here, but I don't know if I'll be able to hold out."

"You should definitely not wait for me. I… Something came up—"

"Don't tell me you're not coming!" Meg, doing her dramatic bit, yelled.

"I'm going. I'm just going to be a while."

"How long?"

She swallowed. "Should be there in an hour, okay?"

"You haven't left?"

She bit the side of her lip. "Something came up."

"Fine," her sister pouted. "I'm eating without you."

Smiling, she hung up.

Dodge opened the car door for her. "Everything all right?"

"Yeah." She climbed in. "Just my sister, Meg. I told her I'd visit today, and it slipped my mind."

He nodded and closed the door. Opening the back door, he helped Cullen inside, strapped him in his car seat then climbed into the driver's side and turned on the ignition. "I'll drop you off then."

She smiled. "That'd be great."

A short drive later, he parked in front of her house and got out of his SUV. She said goodbye to Cullen. Then Dodge walked her to her door.

Once there, she faced him. "Had fun. Thanks, and thanks again for what you did."

He grinned. "Not a problem, Lex. See you around."

He waited until she opened her front door and walked inside before he turned and strode back to his car.

He hadn't tried to kiss her or hug her. He hadn't even reached for her hand. Why? Hard to tell like everything regarding him, and yet, she couldn't help but feel disappointed.

Inside, she grabbed her duffle with a change of clothes, got into her car, and drove to San Francisco, completely forgetting to eat.

Chapter Ten

"So this biker, who's an asshole, kissed you, and that's the reason you forgot you were coming over?"

Lex sat on the opposite end of her sister's big, brown, leather sectional with her feet tucked under her and a glass of wine in hand. She'd just told her what happened that morning and filled her in with every interaction she'd had with Dodge since moving into her house. Usually, she shared everything with her sister. About Dodge, she kept quiet until now. Her excuse, her big sister was overprotective, and Lex didn't want her showing up in Wadden and screaming at him, which Meg totally would do.

"He's not."

She felt the need to defend him even though he could be a real big one when he wanted.

Meg leaned forward, placed her mug of tea on the coffee table, pulled her blonde, curly locks behind her, and then quirked a brow. "So he's *that* good a kisser?"

She hadn't stuck up for him because he was a good kisser though she couldn't deny he was a fantastic kisser. Fact was she'd seen different sides to him, and that morning, she'd seen a side that softened her. He'd intervened when Mitchell grabbed her, thinking she needed to be protected, something no other man had ever done for her.

"I love you."

With saying that, Lex knew what would come—complete and brutal honesty. Sometimes, this "honesty" hurt, but Lex never held it against Meg because her sister only meant well.

"You've lost hope of finding the right guy, and I know why. I've seen you cry for every one of these assholes, and it kills me that a wonderful woman like you, my *beautiful* baby sister, can't find a half-decent guy. It's not your fault. Never did I think that guy Lex is dating is trouble or that guy is going to break her heart. They all seemed normal, down-to-earth, good guys. Then, they hurt you. Even with Mitchell, the first time he came back with his many apologies, I *believed* him. Tim didn't, but that's beside the point."

Meg shook her head. "Now, I have to say this biker has heartbreak written all over him. You *have* to realize that. I mean you've already been at the end of his nasty attitude for no apparent reason. What do you think will happen when you get involved and it doesn't work out?"

Lex couldn't argue that logic. The odds were stacked against Dodge. Not because he was a biker and cursed too much, but because he'd been a jerk more than once.

Meg looked away for a split second and took a deep breath. "You only live once, right?" She shrugged. "True. From your description, he's all bad-boy hotness and a great kisser. But, and I hate to bring this up, have you considered that if this ends bad, you'd still live across the street?"

A knot formed in the pit of her stomach.

"I thought you didn't want to move ever again because this is the *perfect* house. Please realize I'm pointing this out even though I'd love for you to leave your house and come back to San Fran to be near me."

She smiled a soft, sad smile. Her sister was right and had just proved again she had her best interests at heart.

Meg released a heavy breath. "You've always been cautious in relationships, and I feel like you aren't doing that with this guy. Don't just go for the wrong guy because you're anxious about turning thirty and not being married with two plus kids."

Her gaze flew from her sister's face to her lap.

Was that true? Had she gotten so desperate she was ignoring all the signs, the reasons why getting involved with Dodge was a disaster waiting to happen?

"Do whatever you want. I'll support you either way. I just don't want you to get your heart broken again, especially by a guy like this."

Meg's honesty, this time around, made Lex feel like an idiot. She had every reason to be guarded, yet after one great morning with Dodge, she let herself get excited and hope. While she listened to her sister, that faded. Then it crashed and burned when she realized her sister forgot to mention someone very important—Cullen. He'd grown fond of her and vice versa. She and Dodge didn't work out, Cullen would get hurt.

Before she bought her home, she'd made a decision, one she planned to stick to. She was done with men. If she happened to meet the right guy, she'd take a chance, but whether or not that happened, she'd have a family of her own.

"I can tell by the look on your face what I said sunk. Sorry to burst your bubble."

Her head shot up, stare meeting her sister's. She

shook her head. "No, it's… You're right. I guess I got carried away. I just never felt…"

She couldn't say it. She wouldn't. This wasn't a fairy tale. This was life. Life was hard, unpredictable, and happy endings weren't guaranteed. What she felt was just a trick of the mind, her wanting to believe because he made her feel things she'd never felt, he was different from the rest.

She shrugged. "So how's work?"

****

Lex spent the night with Meg and Tim in San Francisco. In an effort to avoid Dodge, she spent Sunday with them too. She didn't start her drive home until after nine that night. Getting home an hour later, she parked in her garage. Inside, she turned on as few lights as possible, unpacked, showered, and headed to bed. As she lay awake in bed, she realized she'd gone through all that trouble to avoid him for nothing.

Dodge wasn't interested in a relationship. He'd defended, complimented, and kissed her, but he didn't want her. A man who wanted to get involved with a woman made plans or at the very least asked for a way to reach her. He hadn't done either. Granted, he'd called her once, but from the garage, the same number Em called her from. She doubted he'd saved her number. If he had, he hadn't gotten in touch, hadn't made plans.

Realizing this didn't stop her from avoiding him the rest of the week, running errands, staying at school late, not going outside at all. She did it for self-preservation. Deep down, she was terrified one look at him and she'd forget the reasons she had to stay away.

****

Dodge swore things between them had changed, swore she'd come home, walk across the street, and knock on his door. Had it happened that way, he would've dragged her inside, kissed her, and then made them dinner. He had it planned out.

Saturday, he'd gone grocery shopping with Cullen, bought steaks, rice, beans, and kept watch outside all day, waiting for her. Around four, she hadn't arrived, but so sure any minute she would, he started making dinner. Hours passed. At seven, he served Cullen, not eating himself, still sure she'd come. Nine o'clock rolled around, he read Cullen a bedtime story, then tucked him in and concluded Lex had decided to spend the night at her sister's. He went to bed, woke, and looked out his windows too many times to count hoping to see her pull onto her drive. All day he waited and watched. A repeat of the day before, she never showed. After Cullen fell asleep that night, he started to wonder and worry.

She should've been home when the following day, a Monday, she had to work. He noticed she left for school at seven. It probably took her at least an hour to eat and get ready before that, and so, something had to have happened. She could've been in a wreck or maybe her sister had. He started kicking his own ass then. He hadn't asked for her number. She was in trouble or hurt, and he had no way to reach her, no way to help her. If Cullen hadn't already fallen asleep, he'd drive to the garage and look up her number in their system, if only he'd thought about it before, if only he'd saved her number when he'd had the chance.

His stomach knotted and stayed tight for a half hour. That half hour, he put serious thought into loading

Cullen in his car and driving to the garage to look up her number. Then he heard a car. He jumped off the bed, strode to his bedroom window, and parted the blinds. Spotting her car and her driving down the lane, up her drive, and into her garage, he sighed in relief, the knot in his stomach loosening.

He waited for her lights to go on. They never did like she walked through her house in total darkness. Not even the light in her room went on. Even then, he thought she'd come knock on his door, and he waited an hour before he gave up and headed for bed, deciding she hadn't because she figured Cullen was asleep. In no time, he knocked out, pleased with the thought he'd see her the following day.

The next morning, he woke at six, looked outside, and saw her leaving for work, an hour earlier than usual. Even then, he gave her the benefit of the doubt, convinced himself she had to get to school earlier for whatever reason.

That night, he couldn't deny it. He watched her house all early evening and didn't see her car pull in, didn't see her outside on her porch swing reading. She didn't come over. Every so often, like clockwork, he checked. He wanted to blame that on Cullen since his boy kept asking for her, but that'd be a lie. He did it because he'd started getting the impression she was avoiding him.

In between checking for her, he managed to make dinner and eat. A while later, he supervised Cullen in the bath, read him a bedtime story, and tucked him in. In his room, he looked out his window and knew what he thought was in fact true. She was avoiding him. She'd finally arrived. Her living room light was on, and still, she hadn't come over.

She had a change of heart, he understood. She was her own woman, her own hero, and made her own decisions. The least she could do—tell him. Avoiding him like they were teenagers was fucked. He had the urge to go over there, bang on her door, and make her explain. How he managed not to as pissed as he was, he'd never know. In the end, he made the right call. He couldn't let her know how much he cared, so he let it lie.

The rest of the week, he looked out his windows too often, but he never even caught a glimpse of her. She never got home earlier than seven, and when home, she parked in her garage and never went outside. He didn't know how her mailbox didn't overflow and figured she had at least a week's worth of trash in her house somewhere, since the town collected the garbage Thursday mornings and her bin hadn't been on the street.

All that trouble just to dodge him infuriated him more. Raising a kid, especially alone, taught him patience. He had lots of it, but she wore his thin. Any moment he'd snap, and he knew for that reason alone, he needed to stop looking out his windows, stop noticing shit, stop trying to catch a glimpse of her. He just couldn't.

Now, Friday evening, he sat watching TV and heard a car out front. Like a fiend needing a fix, he dashed to the window in the living room, looked out, and spotted Classy, Trig's old lady, parked in Lex's drive. He saw *Lex* for the first time since Monday morning.

She looked beautiful. Her long, strawberry locks

styled in curls wearing a pair of skin-tight jeans, a green shirt exposing cleavage, and high "fuck-me" heels. Dressed for a night out. Without him.

Fuck.

The full force of his anger hit him square in the chest, fury like he'd never felt. He figured any moment he'd turn green and destroy everything. Instead, he took a deep breath, stepped away from the window, and headed to his fridge for a beer.

An hour later, with Cullen fast asleep, he sat on his leather couch aimlessly flipping channels when his cell, on top of the coffee table, rang. He looked to it and wasn't surprised to read "Hash" on the screen. The brother called him at least once a week, told him to get a sitter, and party with them.

He needed to. It had been a long time, but he just couldn't. Ever since Cul's mother left, he felt guilty leaving him. Even before, he hardly left Cul. It got to a point where he couldn't trust Lilliam with her own son. The only break he got—when one of the old ladies offered to sit.

He reached for his phone, nabbed it, and answered. "Not tonight."

"I'm guessin' you done with the librarian?"

Pathetic, he never got started, but he couldn't bring himself to admit it.

"You done, you let me know 'cause I'm gonna make a move."

Hash, dark-haired, around his stature but thinner like her ex, fucked everything in sight, and he fucked multiple women at the same time. It was his thing. In fact, Dodge had never seen him with just one.

A woman like Lex wouldn't go for Hash. She

wanted family and kids bad enough she was willing to have a kid on her own.

He shook his head. "Brother, think you're getting ahead of yourself. She isn't—"

"Don't underestimate me. I throw good game. She's had a few drinks, and she's lookin' fuckin' hot wearing the tightest jeans known to man. The woman's got the nicest ass I've ever seen."

He clenched his jaw. His fingers, of their own accord, tightened around his phone.

Hash talking about her like that fucked with him. It shouldn't. What Hash said was true. She had a nice ass, and she wasn't his and didn't want him. Besides, she wouldn't go for Hash. No fucking way.

"She'd go for me."

Dodge heard the smile in Hash's voice and what he hoped was over confidence.

"I know it. Them women that look all innocent love bad boys, and every woman has had at least one one-nighter, right? I could be hers."

He saw red, adrenaline pumping, blood pressure skyrocketing. He shot to his feet. "Stay. The. Fuck. Away. From. Her. You hear me, Hash? You stay the fuck away, or I'll fuckin' beat the living shit out of you. I'm not playing, brother. She's *mine*."

He never lost his cool, even in fights. For so long, the only person who could make him snap was his mother. She died years ago, and he thought he'd been free of losing his shit. Then Lilliam came along. She had a knack for it too. Every day, he was pissed off and lashing out. She did it because she got a kick out of making his life hell, making him miserable. Now, for the first time, his brother made him flip, and it was not lost on him that it was because of a woman.

Women always fucked with him.

He gave Hash two seconds to respond. When his brother didn't, he yelled, "You fuckin' hear *me*?"

Hash chuckled. "I hear you, brother."

"Where is she?"

"The bar."

Only one bar in Wadden. That meant it was packed, the only place to pick up women, get drunk, meet people, a free-for-all.

"You keep your eyes on her until I get there. You do *not* let anyone get near. Got me?"

Hash chuckled. "Got you, Dodge."

He hung up, called Beef, one of the prospects, and told him he needed him at his house in five minutes. In four, he parted his door to Beef. "Cul's asleep. Stay here. Watch him."

Beef's eyes widened. "Dodge, don't think I'm the guy—"

Fucking hilarious. A former Marine who served four tours in Iraq was scared of watching a kid sleep? Right then, Dodge was too pissed to laugh or bust his balls.

"You're a prospect. That means you do what I say. Right now, I need *you* to sit on my couch while my kid sleeps."

"What if—"

"He's three. He wakes, you tell him I'll be back soon, to go back to sleep. That doesn't work, you let him watch TV until he passes out." He took a step toward him and lowered his voice. "No matter what, he wakes, you fuckin' call me. Do. Not. Disappoint. Me. You disappoint me, there'll be *severe* consequences.

Yeah?"

The guy looked like he'd puke, and it had nothing to do with the threat he made. He'd been in dangerous situations with Beef before. The vet hadn't even flinched.

He moved out of the way. When Beef strode inside, he locked the front door and headed farther inside his home.

At the mouth of the hall leading to the garage, he turned and locked gazes with Beef. "Watch TV to kill time. Do. Not. Fuck. Up." Then he turned and strode away.

Chapter Eleven

"Oh *shit*!"

Lex turned to Allie, sitting beside her, who'd shrunk in her seat.

She was at the local bar with not just Allie and Em but a couple of others she'd just met, Lynn and Mia. Lex had never been to the place, but it was big. High-top tables circled the large bar positioned in the middle of the room. Booths lined three walls. Those walls fixed with shelves. Arranged on them, beer bottles. The pub was crowded, but they'd managed to find an eight-seater booth toward the back near a small dance floor and a series of pool tables.

Em, Lynn, and Mia, sitting across she and Allie, spun toward where Allie had aimed her stare.

"Shit is right." Mia, a petit brunette with curves and spunk, was already a favorite of Lex's.

"Oh God, Wild's going to be so mad at me," Lynn, the total opposite of Mia, a soft-spoken blonde, mumbled and faced Mia. "I told you we'd get caught!"

Allie sipped her beer. "I can't believe it. It's Friday. They aren't supposed to be here."

Lex shifted to look where the others had. Way too many people, probably in violation of the fire code, she couldn't see who they were talking about. "Who?"

"Hash, Skim, and Rake." Em lifted her chin toward the back side of the bar. "See, over there."

With those names, she assumed they belonged to the club since the bikers she'd met went by nicknames. She looked again and finally spotted the trio. Not hard to miss now. They wore leather jackets cut off at the sleeves with the club's name and emblem. Everyone, with the exception of several scantily dressed women, seemed to be giving them room.

Still at a loss, Lex looked between the women and took a chance asking, "So what's the problem?"

Mia sipped her drink. "They don't know we're here."

She arched a brow. Too many questions running through her mind, she went with the first that slipped out. "They?"

Em took a pull of her beer. "Our men slash husbands slash 'old men' don't know we're here."

She took a sip of wine. "Old men?"

"You're exclusive with a biker, you're his old lady and he's your old man."

Her brows furrowed. She looked at each of them for a split second and realized aloud, "Wait. You're all with—"

"Yep." Mia smirked. "I'm married to Stone, and Lynn's married to Wild. You already know Allie's married to Trig, and Em's married to Ripper."

Allie shifted toward her. "We're missing Tiff. She's married to Cuss. The only reason she isn't here is that they just had a baby."

Why had Allie included her with this group? Not that she minded, at all. The women were nice and funny. Lex had been having a blast. It's just they obviously had something major in common, why invite someone who didn't? She'd never ask any one of them this though, primarily because she was glad Allie had asked her to come along. They talked, shared, and gossiped, just a little, while they drank and laughed. She'd leave that night feeling like she'd made four new friends.

"Why don't they know you're here?"

Lynn shook her head. "Because they wouldn't let us come if they knew."

Her eyes widened. She couldn't help feeling a little alarmed, a fact heard in her voice. "What? Why?"

Mia rolled her eyes. "Because we agreed to marry bikers."

Bikers didn't let their women go out? Really? Why, and why would any woman put up with that?

Allie turned fully to her. "They're a tad overprotective. If you were married, you could see why your husband wouldn't want you in a place like this without him, right?"

Lex's gaze flew from the bar that lay in the center of the room to several pool tables assembled behind it to the high-top tables to the dance floor. People drinking, laughing, and dancing, what was the big deal?

She looked to Allie and shook her head.

"How many times has a guy or a group of them come up to us?"

Her stare shot to Em sitting directly in front of Allie. She shrugged. "A couple."

More like three. She'd counted because she'd never gotten that much attention at a bar. In fact, she'd never gotten that much attention, ever. Granted, some of the men might've found her attractive, but she was with four gorgeous women, each beautiful in her own way—Mia, the feisty and opinionated brunette; Em, the blonde bombshell with attitude; Allie, the sweet and cheerful dark-haired beauty; and Lynn, the quiet and sweet green-eyed blonde.

"How many times has the waitress come over with drinks we didn't buy?" Em continued her line of questioning.

She bit her bottom lip and released it. "Four." Finally, Lex understood, but still. She found it pertinent to point out, "Every guy was turned away, and the drinks returned."

"That's the thing about bikers." Mia grinned. "When they're serious about you, you're considered theirs. They don't share what's theirs. They don't want anyone looking at what's theirs. A guy coming up to us, a guy trying to buy us drinks is just out of the question."

"That's insane."

As Lex said it, a knot formed in the pit of her stomach because she realized something—no one had ever felt that way about her. When she was in a relationship, she'd never had the urge to go anywhere without him, unless she was spending girl time with her sister, but she did because whoever she was dating did meaning she'd spent more than a few nights at a bar with her sister, Tim, and a group of friends.

"I feel the same," Lynn said softly, looking down at her drink. "I don't want anyone looking at Wild. I don't want any woman going up to him anywhere."

Em placed her hand over Lynn's. "He'd turn her down in a heartbeat."

Lex looked between the two, feeling like she'd missed something.

Allie grabbed a chip sitting in a bowl in the center

of the table, popped it in her mouth, chewed, and swallowed. "You think they've spotted us?"

Mia cocked her head. "They spotted us the moment they walked in, and you can bet your ass our men will be here in minutes."

"Great." Em lifted her brows and grinned, looking like she wanted Ripper to show up.

Why? Lex had no clue. She did not want Ripper to show. He was scary. Then again, Lex had seen Em handle him. The blonde had nothing to worry about.

"I totally do *not* need this right now." Lynn closed her eyes and shook her head. "We don't need this right now."

Mia draped an arm around Lynn's shoulders. "You stick up for yourself. Remind him *you* have every reason to be upset, and *you* needed space with your girls. And if that doesn't work, remember that angry sex is the best sex."

Angry sex? Lex had never had angry sex, and she wasn't sure she wanted to. Even so, Lynn smiled, so she didn't share this.

Allie's eyes glimmered. "We should make bets to see who'll be the first and second to get here."

Lex had two options seeing as she'd only met Ripper at the garage and Trig, Della's uncle and Allie's husband, the first week of school when he'd picked up Della.

She smiled. "I'm in. Ripper first, then Trig." She shrugged then added to Mia and Lynn. "I haven't met yours, so I can't say."

Mia grinned. "Rip then Wild."

Allie's eyes narrowed, a smile playing at her lips. "Rip then Wild."

Lynn smiled shakily. "Trig then Stone."

They all looked to Em.

"Wild then Stone."

A few minutes later, Em slammed the palm of her hand against the table. "*Ha,* I was right."

Lex looked to her right and spotted a biker, one she'd never seen before, but no doubt he was headed for them and angry. Jaw clenched, eyes narrowed, his hair was a light shade of brown. He wore a leather vest, black tee, and jeans. In his hand, he held a helmet against the side of his thigh. The closer he got, the easier it became to differentiate which side of the table he aimed his gaze at though this fact didn't help her distinguish who this biker belonged to since both Mia and Lynn sat opposite her.

Before she knew it, the biker stood at the front of their booth, his gaze deadlocked on Lynn. "*Babe.*" A growl, a terrifying one.

Lynn didn't look his way.

The next instant, he planted a hand beside the bowl of chips and leaned onto the large table. Lynn sat between Mia and Em. Still, Wild, so tall, managed to get inches from Lynn's face. "*Babe,*" he barked.

Finally, she met his stare. "Wild."

He flinched and straightened. "Come. We'll talk at home."

Lynn lifted her chin, holding his gaze. "We'll talk at home, but I'll go home when I want."

His eyes, a deep brown color, widened. Then it happened so fast, but Lex swore she saw pain streak his face before he blanketed it. Enough to know, she should excuse herself. None of them should watch, but she couldn't manage it. She couldn't even manage tearing her gaze away.

He shook his head. "Can't leave without you. You *know* this."

Tears welled in Lynn's eyes. "I don't know anything, not anymore."

Oh God. What had he done?

Lex's heart went out to Lynn. She didn't think she'd ever met a woman so sweet and nice. She slanted her head, crossed her arms over her chest, and glared at Wild.

"You know I fuckin' love you, babe. You *know* I'd never do anything to hurt you." Emotion dripped from every word he said.

Hearing it, Lex believed him, so she knew Lynn had to as well. Turning her head, she peered at Lynn just in time to watch a couple of tears drift down her cheeks, something Wild hadn't missed because even from her peripheral, Lex noticed his body lock. Em wrapped her arm around Lynn and whispered in her ear.

Lynn wiped her face and met Wild's gaze. "If you'll excuse me, ladies, I should go."

Wild expelled a breath. With it, the tension lining his body melted. Mia stood allowing Lynn to slide out and stand. The minute she stood, Wild snaked his arms around Lynn and buried his face in her neck. Lynn planted her hands against his shoulders, hesitating for a moment until he whispered something in her ear. Then Lynn hooked her arms around him even as her body trembled.

Like watching their happy ending.

Feeling the prick of tears in the back of her eyes, Lex blamed it on the wine. She didn't want to think of what it meant otherwise.

"*Lex*."

She stilled, yet her heart raced. *Oh God*. No. This couldn't happen, not to her. It could *not*! She shut her eyes tightly and convinced herself she'd imagined his voice.

"*Lex!*" Closer this time and louder.

Oh God. Her stomach turned. Sitting at the opening of the booth, she turned and opened her eyes.

Dodge stood a foot away, looking too beautiful to be real. His dark hair in disarray, stubble-covered jaw locked, too gorgeous dark eyes glaring, body stiff yet vibrating with rage. He wore his usual, a tee spread tight across his chest, his leather vest over it, and his thick legs encased in jeans.

Why had he come? And why hadn't anyone given her a heads-up? Then again, like her, they'd probably been too enthralled with Lynn and Wild.

"You want to have it out here in front of your new crew, or you want to go outside?"

What the hell they had to "have it out" about, she had no idea. She'd effectively avoided him all week, and it couldn't be about that. He made it clear he wasn't interested, which became more and more apparent as the days went by without a single word from him. Not that she cared. That was a lie, but one she'd tried to convince herself of all week.

"Are you gonna answer me or are you just gonna sit there staring."

Oh no, she *wouldn't* let him humiliate her in front of her new friends. She twisted back around, facing the table. "I'll be right back." Every single one of her new friends—except for Lynn who was still in Wild's arms—tried, unsuccessfully, to hide a smile.

She ignored this, grabbed her clutch, shifted, and met his gaze. He cocked his head to the side and smirked. She stood. He grasped her free hand and hauled her across the bar quickly. A miracle she didn't fall in her heels.

Out the wooden front doors to the bar, he walked until they were out of earshot from the scattered people at the entrance, released her hand, and faced her. "I'm gonna take you home. Then you're gonna explain why the fuck you've been avoiding me."

Her jaw dropped. They could've discussed that any day that week or he could've waited until she was home. Why did he have to ruin girls' night, and why the hell did he assume she'd let him take her anywhere?

"I haven't."

"Don't fuckin' lie."

She bit the side of her lip, hard. "Fine. I have, but that doesn't make a difference. You *aren't* taking me home. It's girls' night, and I'm having fun."

He leaned in to her.

Her breath hitched. She fought to ignore it and prayed he hadn't noticed.

"*No.*"

No? No, what? What had they been talking about?

His brows furrowed. "No, you aren't gonna have any more fun. Girls' night is over, so I'm taking you home."

Her eyes widened then narrowed. "I'm sorry to break this to you, but you can't tell me what to do."

"I can and I just fuckin' did."

She took a deep breath. "It's girls' night."

"Just said it, but I'll say it again 'cause you need to clue the fuck in. Girls' night just ended."

In an effort to keep her cool, she squeezed the hand holding her clutch. "No, it didn't—"

"*Babe*, girls' night is fuckin' *over*." His arm shot out in the direction of the bar. "You see Wild taking Lynn? Trig will show too, and then Rip will. After that, Stone. Maybe not in that order, but they'll show. They'll be pissed, and they'll take their old ladies home. You want to catch the show?"

She didn't know either of them or their husbands well enough to know whether he was right. But Allie, Lynn, Mia, and Em had agreed. Even so, she didn't want to go anywhere with him, *couldn't* go anywhere with him, and so, she decided to go for another tactic.

"You can't make me leave."

He leaned in to her, forcing her to angle her head farther back to meet his eyes. Then he taunted, "Wanna bet?"

A thrill shot through her. Proof, and the reason she couldn't let him take her anywhere. Somehow, despite the fact that her heart beat too fast, she managed not to sound affected. She hoped she looked unaffected too.

Taking a step back, she lifted her chin. "I'm *not* letting you take me home. I'm not doing *anything* you say."

He smirked. "You don't leave with me now, I'm gonna follow you inside. On the way there, I'm gonna catch all these drunks who want to get in your pants, look at your ass, which is just gonna piss me off more. I'll fuckin' manage to wait until you're at your table, then…"

He took a deliberate step toward her. So close, his chest grazed hers. "I'm gonna kiss you. When I do, I'm not stopping. You'll love it so much, you're not gonna be able to stop me, and I'm *not* stopping, means I'll take that shit all the fuckin' way. Right there."

Hearing it, seeing it in her mind, her breaths quickened. She swallowed, hating she was so weak she wanted him to do that.

God, her sister had been right. She was so desperate she was going for the wrong man. No, maybe it was something else, an intense and primal attraction, the kind that happened once in a lifetime. Did he feel it too?

Realizing she hadn't taken a breath for a while, she did and took another step back. "You're insane." She was too, for hoping.

"Insane means I do anything to get what I want, then yeah, I'm fuckin' insane." He hooked an arm around her waist, hauled her toward him, and held her tight against him.

Her hands went to his chest to stop him, one still holding her clutch. She pushed. He didn't budge. He did lean deliberately slow toward her. His mouth a millimeter from hers, she had no choice.

"Fine. I'll go with you."

Going was her best option. When he took her home, she'd tell him why she'd avoided him and especially why the two of them getting together was a bad idea. Of course, that'd only work if he didn't kiss her. If he kissed her, all bets were off. So her plan—she had to keep him away. She'd find a way to do this. She had to.

He hesitated for a moment before he released her.

"I have to say bye."

She spun and made it halfway around when his fingers gripped her wrist. He tugged, turning her to him again.

"You hear what I said before, Lex, or are you deaf?"

She clenched her jaw and fisted her free hand. Then the anger burning inside her spilled. "For an entire month, I sat in my beautiful house *alone*. That is, in between the times I got house visits from *you being a jerk*. I'm *very* angry with you for ruining the first fun night I've had since moving here."

Her face flushed with each word. That heat crept down her neck and chest. "I've agreed to leave with you, but I'm not happy about it. I'm *not* anyone you can boss or control. I were you, I'd tread *very* carefully because quite frankly, I've had it with your insults, your cursing, your caveman tactics. Bottom line…"

She tore her wrist from his grasp and shoved a pointed finger in his face. "I've had it with *you*."

A muscle in his jaw twitched. He grabbed her wrist, pulled her hand away from his face, and squeezed. "I could control you, *babe*, you'd be sitting on my face."

Holy… A shiver snaked through her, one she couldn't hide. She tried to disguise it by turning away, taking a deep breath, and heading toward the bar. He released her wrist only to grab her hand. She didn't fight him on this. That thrill made her heart race so much she felt dizzy. It wasn't under control yet. Unfortunately, that meant fainting at his feet was a possibility.

Walking to the booth where they'd been seated, she spotted Trig sitting next to Allie. Lex couldn't see Trig's face, but Allie looked to be in deep conversation, probably explaining herself. Mia was right where she'd been when Lex left, sitting in the booth. Stone stood beside her with his arms crossed over his massive chest. Mia's gaze darted away, ignoring him. Em and Ripper stood a few feet away, and they were making out hot and heavy. Lynn and Wild were nowhere to be seen.

"Can we go now?"

She jumped hearing his voice so close and faced him. "Yes."

No point in waiting. Allie, Em, and Mia were clearly busy, and she wouldn't interrupt.

Dodge laced his fingers through hers as he led her out of the packed bar. While she followed, she drew her phone out of her clutch and texted Allie, telling her Dodge would give her a ride home, not to worry.

Outside, Dodge let go of her hand, grabbed her clutch, and stored it in a saddlebag. Then he climbed onto his Harley. She hesitated for a second, wanting to admire it, a beast of black and chrome and absolutely gorgeous.

"Don't be scared."

Her gaze shot to his. "I'm not. I've ridden a bike before."

Brows furrowing, his eyes flared. "You've ridden a bike?"

"Yes."

His face went hard, jaw locking, back straightening stiffly. "Yeah?"

How that could possibly upset him, she had no clue.

"*Yes,*" she repeated, almost out of patience.

"You dated a biker?"

Why did he have to jump to conclusions? She could've ridden a friend's bike. Her brother-in-law could've taken her for a ride or her father.

"No."

His expression softened. "So your dad's?"

God, why did it matter? Either way, she didn't think she had a choice but to respond since she had the feeling he'd keep asking.

"No, it was this guy I dated."

That hard look came again. "So you *dated* a biker?"

So infuriating, all the time, and she'd had enough, so she snapped, "No, I dated a guy who had a bike. I did *not* date a biker."

His eyes flared again. He clenched his jaw before he barked, "Christ, everything that comes out of your mouth makes me wanna bust a gut laughing or bend you over my knee."

Another thrill, her legs shook making her stumble. Third time that night. She couldn't believe it. She was not into spanking, angry sex, or rough sex, never had been. Then again, a man's vulgarity had never turned her on either.

Her jaw dropped, eyes nearly popping out of their sockets. "I can't believe you just said that to—"

In seconds, he climbed off his bike and closed the distance between them. Standing inches from her, he clutched the back of her neck, snaked his other arm around her waist, and yanked her to him until her chest collided with his. Then his lips slammed onto hers and his tongue swept inside her mouth.

She could've pushed him away, could've screamed until he released her. She didn't do any of it because the most beautiful man in the world kissed her and like every other time, it was mind-blowing.

Instead, her hands, locked between his chest and hers, gripped him. As he dove into her mouth for the third time, she moaned then relaxed in his arms, surrendering completely.

At that moment, he could've done whatever he wanted. Luckily, one of them was thinking clearly.

He drew away. When her eyes parted and met his, he smirked. "Found a way to shut you up."

God, why did she want him to do that again and again? Why wasn't she mad anymore? Not fair. No man should have that much power over her. No *one* should.

"Come on, Lex. It's late."

His hand, at her neck, skated across her back then down her arm. He grasped her hand and tugged her forward. At his bike, he hopped on and held out his hand. Her stomach fluttered, not just because she was about to ride a Harley but especially because she had an excuse to press up against him. Grasping his hand, she placed one foot on the peg and swung her other leg over. Her butt landed on the seat, her chest firm against his back. Once he released her hand, she wrapped her arms around his waist and held on tight, so it was hard not to notice. The man had to be in his thirties, early thirties, and still, he had abs, defined and sculpted to the degree she felt them while he sat and over his shirt.

Insane.

He drove off. She forced herself to focus on the feel of the wind blowing against her, the sound of the echoing engine between her legs, and not on the man she held on to.

Impossible.

The ride was great, but it wasn't just about the

wind, the engine vibrating, the road. It was about him. He made it about him every chance he had when he placed a hand over hers. He didn't say a word as if with the action alone he said all he needed to, and he smelled of leather and something else that was all man and all him. Before she knew it, she pressed her cheek against his back.

It ended too soon.

He pulled up to his house, and she heard his garage door opening, her fantasy ride with the most attractive man she'd ever met ended, and reality sunk in.

Her plan, she had a plan, and she had to stick to it.

Driving into the garage, he cut the engine. Immediately, she hopped off. How she managed to do it as quickly in a pair of five-inch heels without falling flat on her face, she'd never know. The thought gone realizing she stood in his garage. She scanned it. Messy, but most garages were. Except for a couple of boxes stacked in a corner, his was littered with tools and bike and car parts, which explained why grease stains covered most of the concrete floor. Finishing her perusal, she met his gaze. His stare skimmed her face like he was evaluating her reaction. When he didn't say anything, she did.

"What?"

He cocked his chin. "Nothing to say?"

What did he want her to say? Give him a compliment? It was just a garage.

Her gaze flew from the scattered tools to the boxes back to him. "What do you expect me to say?"

He shrugged. "That it's messy or dirty. That I shouldn't have tools out with a three-year-old. Something along those lines."

"Well, it's messy, but that's not something you tell anyone when you go into their home for the first time. Besides, everyone's garage is messy. As far as the tools…" She released a breath. "…I'm sure you've warned Cullen about messing with them, and as you brought to my attention when we met, how you raise your child is none of my business."

His eyes widened just a bit then darkened, assessing her, drawing conclusions about her from what she said.

Yikes. Had he just tested her? Whether or not she passed, she didn't know from the intense look spattered on his face. Not that it mattered. She had a plan and had to stick to it.

"We can talk inside."

Alone in a house at night with him? Not good.

She bit her lip. "I don't know if that's a good idea—"

"We're talking inside, Lex. No other option 'cause I got a prospect scared half to death in there watching my sleeping kid."

A prospect? She didn't know what that meant. Reluctantly, she nodded. He handed her her clutch, walked toward a door leading inside his home, and pressed a button beside it. As the garage door slid closed, he opened the door and held it open for her. She headed toward him, strode through, and found herself in a hallway. He grabbed her hand and led her down the hall ending in a large room.

Like her home, his was open concept. From where she stood, the kitchen, dining room, family room, and living room were visible, but his main living area was easily twice the size of hers. The walls were a pale gray. Toward the front of the home, the formal living room had a beautiful white stone fireplace. In front of it, an old suede beige couch and not much else. Toward the back end were the family room, dining area, and kitchen. A large, leather sectional sat in the middle of the room, a coffee table, and a flat screen TV; surprising, hers was bigger. The kitchen, just a tad larger than hers, had dark cabinets, stainless steel appliances, an island, and a breakfast nook at the far end. Between the kitchen and family room, an empty area where a dining room table should go. Large windows and a set of sliding glass doors gave a clear view of the spacious backyard. Directly in front of her, a hallway, which she assumed led to the bedrooms.

As she took all this in, a man looking rattled came to stand in front of Dodge.

"Did he wake?"

The man shook his head.

"You worried for nothing. Go have a drink. Looks like you need it."

The man nodded then left quickly and without saying a word.

Dodge released a breath and chuckled to himself. Afterward, he turned to her. "Want something to drink?"

She shook her head.

"Let me check on Cul. Be back." He strode down the hallway directly in front of her, disappeared through a door on the left, and reappeared a moment later.

His gaze on her, forcing her to look away. Reaching her, he grabbed her hand and led her to the back of the house through a sliding glass door to the backyard. He had a beautiful dark wood deck. A couple of steps led down to the grass. No pool, but plenty of room for one. Off to the right on the deck, a seating area. To the left, a large grill. They took a right.

He waited for her to sit before he removed a sound monitor from his back pocket, placed it beside him, and sat directly in front of her pinning her with his stare. "So…"

She quirked a brow. "So?"

"Giving you the chance to explain yourself."

What the… She wouldn't sit there and be scolded.

She stood. "I do *not* have to explain *anything* to you. I do *not* have to explain *myself* to *you*."

He reared back, eyes widening. Then he stood and grabbed her elbow preventing her from turning away. "Maybe you don't, but I thought you were going to tell me why you've been avoiding me like we agreed."

Right, that's what he meant. Why had she taken such offense? The way he phrased it?

He let go of her, sat, rested his elbows on his thighs, and leaned in to them.

Releasing a breath, she took a seat, set her clutch next to her, and looked down at her lap. "I don't think it's a good idea for us to see each other."

"Yeah, I got that from you avoiding me. I want to know why." He straightened and drew one hand through his hair, something she noticed through her peripheral. "And when you tell me, I'd appreciate it if you'd look me in the face."

She lifted her head, eyes meeting his gorgeous dark ones. Already she found herself wavering. "We'd never work."

His jaw hardened. "'Cause I'm not like that douche you gave three years of your life to? You're right. I'm nothing like him. A man good with words to get you to take him back after he fucked you over repeatedly, that isn't me. I'm not good at expressing how I feel, but I promise you, I'd show you. I'd show you every day. And if I had you and fell for you, I'd never let you go, not 'cause I needed space to fuck around, not for anything. And if I had you and shit went south, I'd be a decent human. I'd end it and let you move on with your life."

He was right. Mitchell was good with words, with lies. She fell for them, and even when he stopped making promises, he didn't stop making her believe they had a future, that he loved her. But Dodge was also very wrong. He was good with words, good enough she was losing her resolve. Everything he said…beautiful. If only it were true. If only she knew how to tell.

She couldn't fall again, couldn't fail again. She had a plan, had to stick to it, but right then, she couldn't remember her well-thought-out and logical reasons. What had her sister said?

She looked away forcing herself to focus. After a moment, she met his gaze. "You don't know me. We don't know each other. There's just attraction, lust. This ends badly, we'd be stuck living across the street from one another."

He moved closer and enclosed her hands in his. "This isn't lust, Lex. Whatever it is, it isn't that. Attraction, fuck yeah. You feel it half as much as me, you couldn't deny us a chance to see where this goes."

Closing her eyes, she shook her head. "Cullen."

"He likes you."

She parted her lids and met his stare. "This ends, he gets hurt."

"We end, I'd never tell him he can't see someone he likes who's good to him."

So he said now, what later?

She swallowed. "You've already hurt me, and you can't guarantee you won't do it again."

Releasing her hands to cup her cheeks, he leaned a fraction of an inch closer. "I never hurt you on purpose, Lex. I was pissed, and I let my temper get the better of me. You do it too." He smirked. "I'm okay with you taking shit out on me."

"I don't—"

All she managed. The next instant, he slammed his lips against hers, and the little will she had left vanished.

His hands at her cheeks trailed down her neck then around her back, every touch heating her, feeding her attraction. She moaned and without meaning to pulled away from his lips. Immediately, he slid his mouth down her cheek and neck. She hooked her arms around his shoulders then drew away searching and meeting his lips again.

He thrust his tongue inside kissing her roughly, almost desperately. It spurred her. Heat pooled in her core, another moan escaping her lips. The next instant, he gripped her hips, hauled her up, standing along with her, never losing her mouth, and repositioned her on his lap over the length of him. His hands slid to her lower back and under her shirt.

All happening too fast. If she didn't stop him soon, they'd be past the point of return. Jumping into bed with someone was reckless and stupid, but with him, she couldn't stop. Because with him, it felt different, an insatiable need that grew and grew with each flick of his tongue, with each touch.

His hands now at her hips, he slipped them to the side of her ribs and pushed her away. Tearing his mouth from hers, he rested his forehead against hers.

She whimpered at the loss.

"Gotta breathe, Lex."

Pulse beating hard and fast at the base of her neck, she breathed deep.

"Need to take it slow."

No. They shouldn't take it anywhere. The reasons why beyond her now. His fault. He was a damned good kisser. She could've been shot and burned and chances were she wouldn't have noticed with his lips against hers.

She needed to decide now. To do that, she tore her gaze from his. Concentrate and simplify the problem. What would she regret more: getting her heart broken or never knowing what they could have even if it didn't last?

His brow furrowed. "You want to take it slow, right?"

She met his dark eyes.

God, so handsome, the strong clean lines of his face, his stubble-covered cheeks and chin, his full thick lips.

"I…" What had he asked? Yikes.

"Lex?"

"Hmm?"

He chuckled. "What're you thinking about so hard?"

No way in hell she'd admit she forgot what he asked.

She swallowed. "Nothing."

"So? You wanna take it slow, or should I pick up where I left off?"

She wanted to, but they really shouldn't…for all their sakes.

She bit her bottom lip. "Slow."

He smiled. "Spend the day with us tomorrow."

Oh God. Was she doing this?

Her stomach fluttered. She closed her eyes and let herself feel excited from just that simple invitation. Parting her lids, she smiled. "Okay."

There, her answer. She'd caved. Right then, his eyes on hers, a smile playing at his lips after that amazing kiss, it felt right.

"Nine too early?"

She shook her head. "I'll be over at nine."

"We'll be over at nine."

She lifted a brow. "I *can* walk across the street."

He looked about to argue. Instead, he smirked and nodded.

"It's late. I should go."

He nodded again and released her. She stood and grasped her clutch. He followed, grabbing the sound monitor and tucking it in his back pocket. Then he gripped her hand and tugged her inside. When they reached the front door, he opened it and allowed her out first.

"Stay. I can walk myself."

"Know you can, Lex."

"You know what I mean. You don't have to bother."

"I want to be bothered."

Her stomach fluttered. "Fine, but tomorrow—"

"Tomorrow, you can walk over to us alone."

He led her across the street to her door. There, he faced her, planted a hand on her lower back, pressed a soft kiss to her lips, and drew away. "Can't be more than a peck 'cause it's more than that, I might forget Cul's alone."

Yes, she was glad she'd caved.

She smiled. "Good night."

"Tomorrow. Nine. Don't forget. Don't disappear. You do." His gaze heated. "I'll find you."

She shook her head. "Is that supposed to scare me?"

"Quit playing, and get inside."

"Good night, Dodge."

"Night, Lex."

She opened her door, strode inside, and closed and locked it behind her. In minutes, she lay flat on her back in bed, replaying the last hour in her head. A great hour. Right then and there, she felt she'd made the right choice. How she'd feel tomorrow or a week from now, she didn't know, but she'd find out eventually. She wouldn't worry until then. She'd only live once and all that.

She shifted her head to her right and spotted her alarm clock on the nightstand. Seven past midnight. Maybe turning thirty wouldn't be so bad.

Chapter Twelve

Dodge barely slept thinking about her. At six, he dragged himself out of bed, usual for him since that was the time Cul woke. Amped the fuck up he'd get to see her in just hours, he hadn't been able to hold back and told his son Lex would spend the day with them. Cul had been thrilled.

In hindsight, that might've been a bad idea considering every half hour on the dot, Cullen looked to him and said, "Lex?" He'd told him seven times Lex would be there soon. Six of those times, he believed it, but now, it was nine thirty and still, no Lex.

He couldn't help but wonder if she'd changed her mind. After all, she'd done it once before, and last night, he had to convince her to give them a chance and he'd only done that by kissing her.

Not wanting to get too anxious waiting, that morning he hadn't looked out his windows. But now, he had no choice.

Walking to the closest window, he pulled the blinds aside and peeked out. In her drive, not one but two cars were parked. None of them hers.

His chest clenched. Impossible to ignore, impossible not to be pissed, not to think about anything but the fact that she was doing it again—avoiding him.

He fisted his hands, closed his eyes, and breathed deep to fight the anger burning his gut.

Not telling him to his face was fucked. Not showing up and not bothering to call to make some excuse was fucked too. He was a man, a biker, so he'd deal, but what about Cullen? Hadn't she thought it'd break his heart not showing? She could fuck with him all she wanted. Every woman did, so fuck it, but hurt his kid?

Fuck, no.

Part of it didn't make sense. She'd been worried about them because she didn't want Cullen to get hurt should they not last.

He knew what he should do—leave her be. She didn't want him. Fine. Cullen would get over it. It seemed women fucked Cullen over too. He was just like his dad in that. Though he hated his son had to learn that lesson, he couldn't protect him from everything.

"Lex?"

He looked at his boy, brow creased, eyes wide, biting the side of his lip.

Fuck that. He had to do something.

He ground his teeth. "Cul. Come."

Cullen stood from his position on the couch and walked to him, not missing his gruff tone. Dodge grabbed his hand and keys then walked out of his house. Striding across the street, he knocked on her door, not giving a flying fuck who was visiting her. He'd say what he had to say.

The door swung open, and his gaze landed on a woman who looked like Lex. Around the same age, her facial features similar, same lips and nose, but her eyes were green instead of blue and her hair was an ash blond instead of that strawberry color he loved so much. Pretty, but nowhere near Lex's beauty.

Her eyes narrowed. She smiled a knowing smile. "You must be Dodge."

Lex's sister, and it seemed Lex had talked about him, not anything good.

Cullen wrapped his arm around his leg and moved behind him, his face now pressed to his hamstring. He nodded. Before he spoke, footsteps echoed.

The door parted wider, and Lex appeared. Her eyes widened in a way he knew she was trying to communicate something, something he didn't get. She spared her sister a glance and whispered, "Be nice."

He swung his gaze from her beautifully made-up face—though he preferred it without, it was still gorgeous—to the rest of her, wearing a pair of jeans, a blue loose shirt, a yellow headband, and necklace. Her shoes, a pair of flats, were yellow too.

"Hi, Cullen."

Cul peeked from behind him and smiled. "Lex."

She stepped forward, glided her fingers from the top of Cullen's head through his hair and then rested her hand on the back of his neck. "Sorry I was late. I'm so glad you came to get me."

She angled herself toward him. Her eyes locked on his, and she whispered, "Had no idea they were coming."

"Why wouldn't we come? It's your birthday. We always spend our birthdays together."

Birthday?

Shit.

Unbelievable.

Looking sheepish, she lifted a brow. "Surprise?"

He threw his head back and burst out laughing.

When he recovered, he slanted his head down. “Heard that, Cul? It’s Lex’s birthday. What do we say?”

Cullen released him, launched himself at Lex, circling his arms tight around her hips.

Her hands went around his back. She smiled. “Thank you so much, Cul.”

“What’s going on out there?”

The door parted fully, and a woman came to view. An older version, a cross between Lex and her sister. Their mother, no doubt.

Her stare slid from Cullen to Lex to him. She smiled wide. “I don’t believe we’ve met. I’m Patricia, Lex’s mom. You can call me Patty.” She extended her hand.

He shook it. “Nice to meet you. I’m Dodge, and this is Cullen, my son.”

He didn’t think it possible, but she smiled wider. Her eyes went to Cullen. “A handsome boy.” Then she spared glances at each of her daughters. “Girls, we don’t keep company out on the porch. Let them in.”

Her mother turned and walked inside. Her sister hesitated then followed.

Lex’s eyes widened. She drew closer and whispered, “You don’t have to.”

He grinned. “It’s fine.”

More than fine, getting to meet her mother and sister was great. He’d win them over. Cullen would no doubt help because Cullen was a great kid who loved Lex, and Dodge would get to know more about Lex, which considering they were starting something was fantastic.

Lex grabbed his arm, nails digging into his bicep tightly. Then eyes wide, brow wrinkling, she shook her head. “You don’t understand—”

“Alexa, do *not* leave your gentleman waiting out there.”

Lex rolled her eyes, the cutest shit he’d ever seen, but she obliged, spinning and heading inside. Cullen grabbed Lex’s hand walking side by side with her. He followed behind. They strode toward the back of the house where two men stood talking loudly. One familiar, Dodge had seen him not so long ago hugging Lex. Probably close to his age, maybe a little older, tall, built, and he had dark hair. The other was older, also tall and physically fit with ash blond hair like Lex’s sister but graying. His eyes were ice blue like Lex’s.

The voices died abruptly. Then both males shifted their heads to them.

“Dad, Tim, this is Dodge and Cullen.” Lex, her hand still in Cul’s, turned partially to him. “Dodge, Cul, meet my dad, Aaron, and my brother-in-law, Meg’s husband, Tim.”

Aaron, Lex’s dad, looked to Cullen first. “Hey, there, bud. I see you like my Lex.”

Cullen smiled and nodded.

Aaron’s gaze then moved to Dodge. “Peculiar name.”

Dodge extended his hand and nodded. “Good to meet you.”

Aaron shook his hand but didn’t return the sentiment.

Then again, Dodge hadn’t expected him to. He didn’t know what it was like to have a daughter, but he imagined having a pretty one like Lex would suck. A man wearing a cut knocking on her door at nine thirty on a Saturday morning would suck more. He wasn’t a bad guy, never played women, but he wasn't the type of man any father wanted for his little girl. From experience, he knew a father wanted the best for his kid, and he was a biker who worked at a garage. A woman like Lex could have any man she wanted, a guy like her sister's husband, clean-cut wearing a polo.

Tim extended his hand. "Good to meet you."

He took it and shook. "Good to meet you."

Tim's gaze moved from him to Cullen. "Cullen, right? How old are you?"

Cullen looked up to Tim but didn't respond.

"He's shy." Lex slid her free hand from the side of Cullen's head to the back, threading her fingers through his hair.

Warmth slithered up his chest then spread leaving no part of him untouched. Second time she'd done that that morning and they hadn't been together longer than ten minutes. He loved it, loved when she touched his boy lovingly, kind of like a mother would. His mother had never done that. Cullen's hadn't either, and Cul loved it too. He knew just by the way his boy leaned in to Lex's touch, grabbed hold of her, and refused to let go.

"And he's three. Right, Cul?"

Cullen nodded.

Meg smiled. "Looks more about five. You're tall."

Cullen looked to her and shrugged, smiling shyly.

Meg, not hiding a smirk, looked at Lex. "Seems we've interrupted your plans, sis."

Lex's head shot toward her sister. Her eyes narrowed.

"Stop it, you two." Patty stood in the kitchen turned away from them, but she said this loud and clear in that same admonishing tone she'd used before.

"We weren't starting—"

Patty spun and strode around the bamboo top island toward them with a tray of cookies, pinning Lex's sister with a warning stare. "Yes, you were, Megan. Now, drop it. We have company."

She set the tray on the coffee table, walked the short distance to Lex, and smiled. "Alexa, you have guests. What do you do when you have guests?"

Lex turned her flushed face to his. Her eyes wide, again trying to tell him something he still didn't get. "Can I get you and Cullen something to drink?"

He bit the side of his mouth so he wouldn't laugh. Grinning, he agreed and offered to help mainly because maybe then she'd finally tell him what she tried to without words, twice.

She walked toward the kitchen with Cullen, still holding onto her like a lifeline. He followed behind.

She opened the fridge and then whispered, "You should go."

His brows shot up. He had to keep from yelling to her back. "Why?"

She spun on her heel, facing him. "Because my family's here. They're…they're just…family, you know."

No, he didn't. Growing up, his family sucked. He had Cullen now and the club, but that was different. The club was family but one he picked. Cullen was his kid, and they may be a family but not one like hers.

She released a sigh and took a step toward him, leaving the fridge parted. "You know…family." Shaking her head, she dropped her voice another octave. "They're going to share embarrassing stories.

My mom's going to continue to badger me to get you this and get you that and make sure you're comfortable because you're my *guest.* Because you're my *gentleman,* she'll insist I serve you drinks and food before I even serve myself because she thinks it's still the fifties. My sister's going to ask you a billion questions, prying into your life to find out if you're worth my time. Tim won't say anything, but he'll support Meg because she's his wife and he loves her. My dad will be the epitome of the strong and silent type until he gets you alone then…"

She leaned in to him. "He'll give you 'the talk.'"

He'd seen women be a lot of things, manipulative bitches, nags, you name it, but he'd never seen a woman throw a hissy fit until now. And fuck him, but it was hilarious and cute. Maybe because she was so beautiful, maybe because he thought she was hilarious, maybe because it was her and not anyone else, he didn't care the why.

He tried his hardest not to laugh and did this by clearing his throat. "First, you can get me drinks, serve my food, and keep me comfortable, I'll never complain about that."

Her lips parted.

"Your sister can ask what she wants. I'll respond when I want. Tim can support his woman, and I won't hold it against him. Your dad can give me 'the talk.' Never heard one before, so I'm curious. They can tell all the stories they want; I'll love every minute of getting to know you better."

Her brows quirked.

"I finally convinced you to hang out with me. Cul's been bouncing off the walls since I told him this morning, so today were any other day, we wouldn't leave. Fact that it's your birthday means there's no way in fuckin' hell, we're leaving 'cause there's no way we're missing your birthday."

Her eyes warmed. "That's sweet," she whispered. "Even with the cursing."

He couldn't help it then. He laughed loud and continued to as he sidestepped past her, grabbed the gallon of milk from the fridge, and set it on the island.

"Where're your cups?" He turned to look her way, still standing in front of the open fridge. His boy pressed to her side, grinning.

She smiled then laughed.

He knew her family watched them, probably wondering what they found funny. He didn't care. It seemed she didn't either. Her smiling gaze glued to him, a stunning grin in place.

Chapter Thirteen

"What the *hell* was that?"

From her porch, Lex heard but barely, her stare riveted to Dodge's broad back. "What?"

"*That*?"

Dodge opened his front door and let Cullen inside before following behind. She lost sight of them. Still, she had to tear her gaze away before meeting her sister's narrowed eyes. "What?"

"*That*." Meg pointed in the direction of Dodge's house.

"It's Dodge."

Her sister's jaw dropped. "What the hell did he do to you?"

What could he have possibly done to her? He spent the day with her and her family. They barely had a minute alone.

She lifted both brows. "Nothing."

"What did he say to you?"

Her cheeks flamed. "None of your business."

"It must've been mind-blowing considering you've been staring at him, oblivious to me standing here talking to you. You couldn't even look at me until he closed his front door."

"I'm not oblivious—"

Meg cocked her head. "Oh, no? Okay, what did I ask you?"

Yikes. She had no clue. "I forgot."

"You didn't forget. You weren't listening to me. I asked you three times, and you didn't hear me because you're in la-la land because he said who knows what." Meg crossed her arms over her chest. "Tell me you haven't slept with him, Lex."

Tim strode out her front door and onto the porch looking between the two.

"Let's talk about this inside." She walked past Tim into her home.

Dropping her arms to her sides, Meg followed close behind and didn't wait for Tim to close the front door before she persisted. "Tell me you didn't sleep—"

"I haven't slept with him."

"Then?"

"Then what?"

"You know what. What the hell happened? Two days ago, you told me you were avoiding him. This morning, he shows. Clearly, you two had plans."

She sighed. "It's a long story."

"Well, you better start," Meg snapped loudly.

"Babe, please, relax. Lex's a grown woman. She can—"

Meg turned to her husband. "I'm her sister. I've never lied to her. I don't plan to start now, and she better not start lying to me either."

Meg was overreacting. It was who she was and what she did. It seemed the pregnancy and her raging hormones weren't helping.

Knowing this, Lex released a breath and calmly explained, "It happened yesterday."

Meg sliced her stare to her. "What did?"

"I decided I'm going to take a chance on him, on

us."

"You decided first, you weren't." Meg shook her head. "Come on. I mean he was an asshole more than once and has heartbreak written all over him. What did he do to convince you?"

She'd never been good at lying, so she had to shut this conversation down, quick. Frankly, she couldn't tell Meg how he'd changed her mind. It'd make her dislike him more.

"We had a talk last night and came to an agreement—"

"That you're going to put your heart on a platter so he can chop it up?"

"I don't know if that'll happen. Considering my relationship history, probably, but I'll never know until I try. I've never felt like this toward anyone, so I'm going to take a chance. Maybe I'll regret it. Like you said, he's been a jerk to me. The fact of the matter is I'll regret not knowing more than I'll regret getting my heart broken." She shrugged. "If that happens, I'll have to move, and you may get your wish anyway."

Meg's shoulders slumped. Some of the tension lining her body melted. She didn't say anything though, but from the contemplative look on her face, she thought on it.

"He looks like the wrong guy for you."

Lex's gaze flew to Tim, who'd spoken. He went on.

"But looks can be deceiving, and he has a kid, a kid he obviously cares about. Motorcycle club or not, I don't think he'd be inviting you into their lives if he wasn't serious about you."

Her face softened. She looked back at her sister.

"He's not your type."

She smirked, thinking once upon a time Tim hadn't been Meg's type either. "It seemed that worked for you, so I'm following in your footsteps, sis."

Finally, Meg smiled.

After saying their goodbyes, Meg and Tim left. Her mother and father had left minutes before Dodge and Cullen took off. They'd rented a car and were headed to Napa for a few days before flying home to Florida.

It'd been a long day, her thirtieth birthday. She'd been dreading it, but she couldn't be upset about how it turned out. Surprise visit from her mother, father, sister, and Tim, who for all intents and purposes was the brother she never had, on the day she and Dodge were having their first date (sort of), it could've been disastrous.

She loved her family, but they shared too many embarrassing stories, too many being five. Throughout the day, her mother pestered her to get Dodge this and that. Luckily, they had lunch at a restaurant, so she had an hour reprieve. Her sister interrogated him, repeatedly. Her mother scolded her sister, thankfully on her side. Her father had been quiet as she expected. She stayed close to Dodge, so she didn't think her dad had "the talk" with him. Dodge handled it all superbly, and she knew he hadn't minded. His comment to her right before heading to his house clued her in on that fact. Thinking of it then made her smile.

She took longer than she anticipated and she'd take a little more.

****

Dodge's phone, tucked in his back pocket, vibrated. Finally. She took her sweet-assed time. He tugged it out and answered it on his way to the front door.

"Hey."

She sounded good on the phone, but she sounded better in person.

He opened his door. Phone pressed to her ear, a smile on her lips. He then took in the rest of her. She'd changed, her shirt at least, now wearing a white blouse. She shouldn't have. He didn't really care what she wore, and it meant she would've been there sooner.

He grabbed her hand, hauled her inside, ended the call, and slipped his phone into his back pocket. A second after closing the door, he released her hand, grabbed her hip, circled his other arm around her back, and pressed her against him. Only then, he maneuvered her so her back lay flat against the wall, and he kissed her deep.

Damn, she could kiss. It got him so heated he forgot everything. He couldn't forget, couldn't rush this, couldn't give her a reason to run.

Sliding his hands to her face, he cupped her cheeks and drew away. Her eyes glassy, breaths shallow, hands clutching his shirt. Seemed he got her heated too.

He smiled. "Happy birthday, Lex."

"You're not mad I didn't tell you."

He dropped his hands, resting them around her waist, and shrugged. "Naw. I get it."

She grinned.

"Had fun today. Your folks are good people."

Her brows creased. "You had fun?"

He nodded. "Yeah."

"They're good people. What're your parents like?"

He shook his head. "Nothing like yours."

He didn't know whether he should share so early on what fuck-ups his parents were, but he figured it was only fair since he met her whole family.

"Dad left when I was a kid. Part of me couldn't blame him, wished he took me 'cause Mom was…"

How to describe what his mother was?

He swallowed. "Difficult."

Her eyes grew soft. "Like she…"

"She was never happy. Always bitching about this or that. Always nagging Dad. When he left, she started with me. Turned eighteen and got the fuck out. I'd do my son duty and called her every now and then, visited her for her birthday, Mother's Day. She died a few years ago."

She bit the side of her lip, leaned in to him, circled her arms tight around his waist, and rested her cheek against his chest. "I'm sorry."

Fuck, that felt good. He learned something new about her. She was sweet.

Arms around her, he squeezed and shook his head, deciding in that instant he'd tell her the rest too. "Then I met Cul's mother, knocked her up. Did the right thing and married her. Turned out, she was just like my mom. I'd known that, I wouldn't've married her."

She drew away. Her eyes wide, she asked, "How long were you dating before—"

"We weren't."

"Oh…so it was like a one-night—"

"No, we were fuckin'."

He left out the fact that he hadn't known they were fucking exclusively. Lilliam, a tap, fucked his brothers too. Lex should know, but he didn't know how she'd take that information and thought it was too soon to share then.

She nodded and looked away. "So you never loved her?"

He shook his head.

Her eyes rounded. "I see."

He had no idea why, but the way she said it sounded ominous. At that moment, he'd give anything to know what ran through her mind.

"How long has it been since—"

"A year."

She reared back. "Cullen hasn't seen his mother for a year?"

"He's seen her a couple of times. It's been months since the last time though."

Looking pensive, she nodded. Again, her gaze fell from his.

Maybe he shouldn't have told her this. Obviously, she was thinking hard on it and not sharing what she thought.

His life was complicated. She knew he was a single dad, but he didn't think she'd realized until then how uninvolved Cullen's mother was. Their relationship became serious, Lex would be the closest thing to a mother Cullen had. She wanted kids, but did she want to raise one who wasn't hers? Not to mention, a woman with a family like hers, realizing he'd never had one could be a turn off. Maybe he'd overanalyzed.

"You okay?"

Her stare shot to his. "Yeah, why?"

"A lot of info I just handed you. None of it pretty. I can tell you're thinking about something hard."

"Yeah, it's just…I didn't realize Cullen hadn't seen his mother for so long. I figured she wasn't a very good one. You know being absent and all, but I just—" She shrugged. "—Feel awful for him." She smiled softly. "Thank God he has you."

He had a feeling that wasn't all, so he waited for her to go on.

"You said she wanted something from you and got it, and when she got it, she didn't want it anymore. You were talking about getting married, right?"

Not just married but status within the club. Lilliam wanted to be an old lady. She went about getting that in a fucked-up way, bringing a life into the world she had no intention of caring for, no intention of loving. He wanted to hate her because of that especially but also because when she had what she wanted, she didn't appreciate it, respect it, fight to keep it. Maybe in her messed-up head, she thought being an old lady meant she could do whatever she wanted whenever she wanted. Maybe she thought he'd never dump her. Maybe when she got what she wanted, she didn't want it anymore.

He didn't know, didn't care. He was done with her. He'd moved on. Still, he couldn't hate her because without her, he'd never have his boy and he loved Cullen more than anything in the world.

He wouldn't say any of this to Lex though. Too much shit. Too soon to share.

Instead, he nodded. "Yeah."

"And you feel like she tricked you in to getting married when she got pregnant?"

He nodded again.

"You realize just because she was pregnant, you didn't have to marry her, right?"

Yeah, he did, but he couldn't let his kid's mother

sleep with multiple brothers a night. He especially couldn't let his kid see that, and the only way she'd agreed to stop—if he married her. This, again, he couldn't say.

"My son deserved to be born having a mom and a dad. Marrying her meant she lived with me, and that meant my kid lived with me too."

This was also true and another reason he married her.

She nodded.

"Heavy talk."

She smiled, got on the tips of her toes, and slanted her head, reaching for his lips. He obliged. Leaning in to her, he claimed her mouth, kissing her as deep as she'd kissed him.

She felt so fucking good pressed against him, her fingers in his hair, her tongue in his mouth. Lex was hot, only expected, but it'd been so long for him, he was about to lose control. She wanted to take them slow, so he forced himself to tear his lips from hers.

When his lids parted, her brows drew together, looking gorgeous, lips swollen, cheeks flushed, and panting. "You should go, Lex, before I take you."

She smiled. "I should, but I don't want to."

He didn't want her to either. With the simple admission, his cock jerked, eyes flared.

She laughed. "Cute."

Lifting a brow, he shot back, "Blue balls are cute and funny to you?"

She laughed harder and slapped her hand over her mouth. "Sorry, I forgot Cullen's asleep."

Shaking his head, he grinned. "It's okay. He's a heavy sleeper, and…" He nabbed the sound monitor he'd tucked in his back pocket, showing it to her.

Cullen was kind of old for one, considering when Cullen woke, his boy went straight to his room anyway, but he felt better with it on in case he was outside when Cullen woke, or Cullen had a bad dream and woke crying. Being the sole caregiver since Cul had been born made him prepare for any circumstance, always.

Her gaze heated. "Good to know. You know, for future reference."

Lex naked in his bed. Could she be quiet? Shit. He should *not* think about that. Pointless now, anyway, she wanted to take it slow. Hopefully, for his sake, a fast kind of slow.

"Lex, you keep saying shit like that, you're gonna end up in my bed sooner than you'd like."

She shrugged. "Oh, well."

He grinned. "You're asking for it, babe."

She smiled and pressed her lips to his. When she drew away, he let her.

He slid his hand up her spine. "Tomorrow, the club's having a cookout. Come with us. Meet the brothers."

Her smile widened. "Sounds like fun. Should I bring anything?"

"Nope. First time, you're the guest. Next time, you want to plan it out with the old ladies, you can. Yeah?"

"Okay."

He grabbed her hand, pulled her away from the wall then walked her across the street. At her front door, he kissed her and wished her a good night. He waited until she closed and locked her door before he strode back to his house.

That night, he fell asleep grinning.

Chapter Fourteen

What a week. It started Sunday, the day after her birthday.

Lex agreed to go with Dodge and Cullen to the club cookout. Honest, she was thrilled he asked her, but that didn't mean she wasn't nervous. First, because she'd meet his "brothers." She'd met a few of them and had been to the garage, but going as his date was different. Second, she didn't know what to expect at a motorcycle club cookout.

She didn't know much about motorcycle clubs except what she'd seen portrayed in films and TV shows, and of course, she'd heard of infamous motorcycle gangs. None of it was good. She didn't think Dodge, a single father to a beautiful three-year-old, was wrapped up in anything illegal, but still, there was a possibility. If she had a kid to support, there wasn't a single thing she wouldn't do for him or her. Besides, the bikers she'd met were rough-around-the-edges, men who looked like they could be living on the wrong side of the law. Then again, she'd met the wives of some of these so-called bikers; these women were classy, sweet, and vivacious. Not one of them looked like the type of woman who'd associate with bikers, especially if those bikers happened to involve themselves in criminal activity. Still, Lex knew better than anyone when a woman fell for someone, she blinded herself to certain things. It happened to men too.

Dodge picked her up early that morning. She went with an open mind and comforted herself with the thought that luckily, Dodge and Cullen weren't the only ones she'd know there. They arrived a little after ten when Dodge pulled up to the back side of the mechanic shop, which sat on a large piece of property. The garage itself was bigger than she imagined, something she realized when Dodge drove around and beside it. The backlot was enormous. Most of it covered in grass, a few trees scattered and a swing set with a slide and monkey bars. Close to the back door, an area covered in concrete. At one end, a series of picnic tables and a large grill. At the other, a basketball court.

Walking with Dodge to her left and Cullen to her right, his hand in hers, they strode past the fence into the lot.

Those scattered around looked toward them and yelled, "Happy birthday!"

She stilled then woodenly snapped her head Dodge's way.

His stare on her, he winked and grinned. He then looked to the crowd. "Double birthday celebration today. Lex's was yesterday."

Oh God. Her face heated. "It's your birthday?" A whisper, barely.

He hooked his arm around her neck and tugged her so they stood face to face, her chest plastered against his. Such an intimate action and he did it in front of his club and son. It should've felt awkward. They'd only been dating a day. Then again, technically, they still hadn't been on a typical date. But it didn't feel that way. It made her breath hitch, made warmth spread through her and settle in her gut.

"Yeah, it is, Lex, and you can't be mad 'cause I didn't tell you 'cause you didn't tell me either."

What were the odds? One in a million?

He had a point. She couldn't do anything but smile and whisper, "Happy birthday."

She then slanted her head, gaze seeking Cullen. A wide grin on his face, not in the least looking bothered by her proximity to his father.

Dodge introduced her to his brothers. Early on, he stuck by her until a brother, Hash, called him away. She didn't mind. Allie neared, grabbed her hand, and led her toward a picnic table. She sat with her, Mia, Em, and Lynn. They introduced her to Tiffany, who had a beautiful baby boy in her arms. Lex, sipping wine out of a red plastic cup, watched Cullen play with Bree and Della on the swing set and talked with the ladies.

A while later, Dodge, a beer and a fresh cup of wine in hand, sat beside her. He handed her the wine and told her he was going to play basketball. She and the old ladies watched them play a very brutal version of it.

At lunchtime, she grabbed a plate and served Cullen a burger, mac and cheese, and mashed potatoes. As she reached for a spoon, she felt the heat of a body behind her, an arm wrapping around her middle, and a face in her neck.

Not a moment later, his deep voice. "Lex."

She stilled. Heart racing, her breaths grew shallow. Stupidly, she couldn't say anything but, "Hmm…"

"Don't be shy. Get all the food you want. There's plenty."

She smiled. “I see. This isn’t for me though. It’s for Cullen.”

His arm around her waist spasmed, squeezing her almost too tight. Then he released her, gripped one hip, and spun her. The white shirt he’d changed into after the game slightly sweaty. Perspiration beaded on his brow, his hair moist and slicked back in a messy way like he’d run his hand through it. Even so, he looked good, handsome. In the sea of bikers, of whom most were attractive despite the tattoos and piercings, Dodge stood out.

Brows drawing together, his voice thick when he asked, “You get my boy food before you get yourself something?”

She’d just said that. She bit back the urge to tease him with a sarcastic comment. “Yes.”

His gaze softened. Then something flashed across his face, an emotion. She didn’t know what it was but knew it wasn’t bad. He swallowed and nodded. “Burger?”

She couldn’t believe he asked. Having dated a myriad of men, never had one gone through the trouble of serving *her* food even though she’d done it for them countless times.

She nodded.

“Sit by Cul. I’ll be there in a few.” He placed a peck on her lips, surprising her more.

While they spent the day together yesterday, he hadn’t been affectionate. She thought it was because of Cullen, but now, it seemed he’d done it as a consideration to her since they’d been with her family.

She released a breath and headed toward one of the picnic tables. As promised, Dodge joined her and

Cullen a few minutes later with two plates of food, one for her and one for himself.

After lunch, Dodge gave her a tour of the inside of what he called the compound. In actuality, it was connected to the garage. He explained the club spent most of their time there. Each of the brothers had his own room. Some lived there permanently.

A few hours later, they headed home. Cullen fell asleep in his car seat, so she kissed his forehead goodbye, and per Dodge's request, she waited for him to put Cullen in bed. Then he walked her home. At her front door, he kissed her deep.

Throughout the day, while he'd been affectionate in small ways, he hadn't kissed her like that, so she'd waited for that kiss the whole day. She'd thought after waiting for it so long, it wouldn't have lived up to the hype, but it surpassed, making her wonder if he was that skilled with his mouth what else he could do.

Naturally, she hadn't wanted to let him go. She'd wanted to invite him in, let him have his way with her. Not like her at all. She'd never been one to sleep with a guy on the first, second, or even third date, but not her fault. It was *him*. He made her that way.

She didn't know how she did it. But when he drew away, her breaths heavy, heart racing, mind a jumbled mess, she wished him goodnight, went inside, and closed and locked the door behind her. Despite her wobbly legs, she didn't trip. Not the perfect ending to the great day she had, the perfect ending would've been letting him in and having her way with him but still a great end.

Lex woke Monday intent on finishing her day at school and heading to the mall. She had to get Dodge something for his birthday. She still didn't know what but figured browsing the stores, she'd get an idea. Dodge hadn't gotten her anything, but he had put up with her family, and for that, in itself, he deserved a medal. She decided spur of the moment, she'd get Cullen something too.

Midday Monday while her students were at lunch, she received a delivery—two dozen, long-stemmed, white, yellow, and red roses. Absolutely stunning. Grabbing the card, she flipped it open.

Happy Birthday.

Cullen & Dodge.

Her lips parted. She stared at the note wild-eyed coming to grips with the fact that a biker, not just any biker but Dodge, had bought her flowers.

Again, something she never expected him to do, but it had less to do with the fact that he was a biker and more to do with the fact that she couldn't remember the last time a man she was dating bought her flowers.

After snapping out of the haze and coming to her senses, she pulled open the bottom drawer of her desk and snatched her phone out of her purse. She slid her finger across the screen, clicked on his contact, and brought the phone to her ear. The call went unanswered. She hated checking voicemails, so instead of leaving a message, she hung up and set her phone on top of her desk.

Not five minutes later, her phone buzzed. She drew her gaze away from the stunning bouquet of roses, picked it up, and held it to her ear.

"Lex."

"Dodge." His name came out breathless. Then she realized she must have been interrupting his workday.

"Sorry to bother—"

"You're not bothering me."

Smiling, she released a breath. "I wanted to thank you for the flowers."

She heard his smile over the phone. "No pink."

"Um…what?"

"You'll notice there's no pink."

She noticed the colors but didn't know what he meant to tell her.

"I know you don't like pink."

She liked it just fine. She just didn't like it on her walls or floors or used as a theme to decorate anything unless it was a little girl's room, but she wore pink and liked flowers in every color. She didn't want to share this since he sounded so proud to have remembered this fact. Although at the time she thought he'd insulted her, knowing him a little better now, she realized she'd been wrong. She'd also thought she disgusted him and knew now it was *not* the case. Every time they kissed, she felt how badly he wanted her.

Even so, because they were embarking on something new and she didn't want to lie or omit anything, she found herself saying, "For future reference, women like flowers in all colors, even pink."

"Women in general or you?"

She hesitated a spilt second. "I like pink flowers though I like the fact that you remembered how much I hate my pink bathroom more."

"Better than any other color?"

"No. I like a variety the best. Roses and tulips are my favorites."

"Variety on just flowers, right?"

She laughed. "Nope, I *love* variety."

"Lex," he *growled.*

"Not what you're thinking, *Dodge*."

"So we did good?"

We. She loved he did that, never forgetting he had a son, almost like he wasn't complete without Cul.

"You both did great. Thanks, again."

"You busy tonight?"

Last night, he hadn't made plans to see her again, and she worried when he would. Not that he had to so soon, they had just spent two full days together. She knew men liked their alone time, the reason why the fact that he asked to see her for the third day in a row thrilled her.

Unable to hide her smile, she didn't bother. "I have an errand to run, but I should be home by six."

"Dinner. Our place?"

She grinned. "Should I bring anything?"

"Just you."

"Okay."

"And Lex?"

"Yes?"

"Next time I don't answer, leave a message."

"Oh, so I'm interrupting you? You didn't have to call back so soon. It could've waited—"

"Not what I meant, Lex. I meant it'd be nice to hear your voice even if it's recorded."

Her stomach fluttered. She sounded shaky when she said, "O-okay."

He chuckled. "See you soon. Bye."

"Bye."

She ended the call and looked at the clock at the far end of her classroom. Late to pick up her class at lunch, she left her phone in her top drawer and headed for the cafeteria. Returning with her class in tow, the art teacher, Miss Clark waited for them. After the students settled and she handed the reins to Miss Clark, she sat at her desk and instinctively, maybe because she wanted to relive that conversation, checked her phone. A new text message. She unlocked her phone and read it.

Like talking to you midday.

She responded, *Me too.*

Instantly, another text. *Can't wait to see you tonight.*

She hesitated then. Quite frankly, she couldn't wait to see him either, but she was scared to admit as much. In the past, it hadn't worked well. Then before she changed her mind, she typed and sent her message.

Can't wait to see Cul tonight.

A second later, *WTF?*

She giggled to herself and responded. *Can't wait to see you too.*

Someone's gonna get a spanking.

She felt her cheeks flush. *Try it and see.*

Immediately, he responded, *I will.*

A second later, another text came in: *Now I gotta find a way to get back to work with a hard on.*

Her eyes bulged. *Cannot believe you just told me that.*

Everything about you turns me on including just thinking about spanking you.

A shiver snaked through her body. Again, she typed and sent a message before she changed her mind. Maybe she'd come to regret it, but she didn't want to bring past hurts and concerns into a new relationship.

Ditto.

Instantly, another message. *Fuck me.*

Then another. *Love to spend all afternoon texting you but gotta get back so stop teasing.*

She wasn't. Though she didn't feel the need to spank him, she got a thrill every time he mentioned doing it to her. She didn't say any of this since he had to get back to work and so did she.

Instead, she typed and sent: *See you and Cullen tonight. XOXO.*

She spent the rest of the day staring at the clock in her classroom willing the hours to pass. After work, she headed to the mall, bought Dodge a couple of shirts and Cullen a football. She'd seen him with his friend throwing one around. At home, she showered and dressed before she headed over.

She strode in with the nicely wrapped presents, her gaze swinging from the beaming smile on Cul's face to Dodge.

His stare on the bags in her hand. He clenched his jaw, rubbed the back of his neck, his Adam's apple bobbing before he cleared his throat. "Thanks."

It sounded forced enough to make her wonder why, but he didn't say anything until a few hours later.

After tucking Cullen into bed, he entered the kitchen, not hiding his narrowed eyes, and closed the distance between them. "You shouldn't've spent money—"

"It was your birthday."

He stopped a couple of feet away and released a breath. "Fine, but it wasn't Cullen's."

He had a point, and she hadn't asked if she could buy Cullen something either. She didn't know what rules they had. While she'd been growing up, her parents preferred to save money for their college funds, so they never got fancy toys unless it was a special occasion, either birthdays or Christmas. This worked to her and Meg's benefit since while in college, they hadn't had to pay a dime out of pocket or get loans. What if Dodge disciplined Cul for whatever reason and she showed with a toy?

"It wasn't expensive." Impulsively, she defended then shook her head. "But I see that I should've asked you before buying him anything. I will from now on."

He cocked his head, arching a brow. "From now on, you'll ask me to buy my son stuff with your money?"

She didn't know why he had the habit of repeating what she said. Usually, it didn't bother her. Then, it did since she'd done something wrong.

She swallowed. "That's what I said."

He stared at her a long while, eyes intense, burning, and sad. She didn't know why, but that sadness she felt sear her chest.

Swallowing, she asked, "What's wrong?"

He dropped his head and ran a hand through his hair. Finally, he met her gaze. "You want to buy him something here and there, that's fine, Lex."

Not what she expected him to say. That gloomy look in his eyes, the expression on his face, a mixture of emotions, hadn't faded.

"Just don't spend a lot of money."

She nodded. "Is everything…all right?"

He released a breath. "Yeah, Lex."

No, not okay. She *knew*, and she wouldn't let something as silly as her buying Cul a gift ruin his mood.

She grabbed hold of his hand. "Listen, if you don't want me buying him things, I understand. I won't take offense. I prom—"

"It's not that." He took a step toward her and cupped her cheek. His gaze roamed her face, but he didn't say anything for a while. "She didn't work, but she spent money, maxed out all my cards. Always had something new on." He shook his head. "But she never bought him a single thing."

Oh God. That was just…horrible. Her sister wasn't even in her second trimester, and she'd already ordered her niece or nephew a couple of unisex onesies and bibs.

"I'm sorry."

Lex wanted to say more. She just didn't know what to say to make him feel better. She also knew there were times nothing anyone said could make someone feel better and figured this could be one of those times.

He traced her lips with his thumb. "Me too."

Hoping to lighten the mood, she smiled and said, "So you're hinting I can spoil him all I want?"

He smirked. "Don't spend too much, Lex."

Then he claimed her mouth. They kissed until she was close to giving in to him and instead pulled away. He walked her home and pecked her lips before she headed inside.

Tuesday, he texted her early. *Good morning, Lex.*

During lunch, she invited him and Cullen over for dinner. Fourth day in a row, she didn't know if he wanted to but figured if he couldn't make it, she'd make dinner for them another night. He texted not a minute later agreeing. That night, she made steaks, mac and cheese, and green beans. Both seemed to like it.

After, they watched TV together. When Cullen fell asleep on her couch, Dodge grabbed her hand, helping her stand, led her down the hall, into the garage, and kissed her. They made out until she again drew away. Hard, but she managed it by reminding herself Cul slept a room away.

Wednesday, again, he texted her early wishing her a good morning. The whole workday, she waited for another text. When four o'clock rolled around without, she made plans to take a yoga class. She'd been meaning to get back into a workout routine and hadn't yet. At five, she went home, changed clothes, and helplessly looked across the street. His SUV wasn't parked in the drive. Her stomach clenched. She fought to ignore it reminding herself they'd seen each other the last four days in a row.

She then drove to class. Just before it started, she checked her phone. No text. After the one-hour session, she grabbed her bag, found her phone, and looked to the screen, probably the hundredth time that day. Still, no text. That tightening in her stomach strengthened. She ignored it.

At half past six, she pulled onto her drive, her gaze flying to the porch steps where he sat resting his elbows on his knees, head up, staring straight at her. Smiling, she turned off her car, opened her door, stepped out, and belatedly realized with his expression impassive and his jaw locked, he didn't look excited to see her.

A sinking feeling settled in the pit of her stomach. She closed the distance between them on a jog. "Did something happen to Cullen?"

His eyes widened. He shook his head. "He's next door."

She wiped her forehead with the back of her hand. "Oh, okay."

He raked his gaze from the top of her head to her feet and back up again, that same look on his face that made her think she disgusted him. Then his eyes hardened.

"Why—"

He stood, towering over her. "What the fuck you wearing, Lex?"

She angled her head up to hold his eyes. "Um…" She glanced down at herself, taking in her black and neon green high-waisted leggings, matching top, a sports bra, and jacket.

"You *can't* wear shit like that."

Her lips parted. Um… What?

So maybe she didn't have the perfect body. She wasn't thin. She had a butt and boobs, but she wasn't fat! She could wear leggings. She wasn't one to show much. Technically, she wasn't wearing a shirt, only a sports bra, but she wore high-waisted leggings, so she showed barely an inch of her stomach. The leggings were tight, but that's what women wore to yoga. Besides, no hiding her butt. It was big. She wore a light jacket over and only took it off for class. It was ridiculous and maddening he thought she couldn't or shouldn't wear something because she didn't have the perfect body.

"*This* is what everyone wears to yoga and I was at yoga. I'm sorry I don't have the perfect body, but I'm still entitled to wear what I want."

His jaw dropped. Then he clenched it tight. "What. The. Fuck?"

She had no idea what he meant, and so, she didn't

respond. She did cross her arms over her chest.

He dragged his hand through his hair. “Did I say you didn’t have the perfect body, *babe*?”

“You didn’t have to. It was implied.”

“The only thing I *implied* was what I fuckin’ said. You didn’t get it, so I’ll repeat. You *can’t* wear shit like that.”

Since he’d raised his voice, she thought it pertinent to take the conversation elsewhere.

“Let’s talk inside.”

She walked past him, unlocked her door, strode in, hung her bag on the coat rack then took off her jacket, hanging it too. When she turned and faced him, his eyes went feral. His whole face flamed in anger. About what, she had no clue.

He sliced his stare from her chest to her legs then back to her face. “I’ll fuckin’ repeat. You *cannot* wear shit like that.”

“I’ll repeat. I’m sorry I don’t have the perfect body, but I’m entitled to wear what I want.”

“You got the *perfect* body, a body I don’t want anyone looking at ’cause it’s *mine* and I haven’t seen it.”

Her lips parted for a completely different reason this time. Stomach fluttering, her breaths grew shallow.

“I’ve seen you wear all types of shit, Lex. You look hot in everything, even the loose shit you wear to school. I get why you do it, but *this*…” His gaze shot from the top of her head to her toes. “You wearing tight as shit, your stomach showing, I’m seeing you like this after getting a call from Dash who saw you before I did?”

He jerked his head side to side. “Fuck *no*, babe.

Fuck. *No*. You're *mine*. I haven't seen you like this. Why the hell should anyone else get to?"

God, such a caveman! Why did it make her feel special? Like he cared? Why did it turn her on?

She had to get a grip. Waiting on her doorstep, ready to scold her about something she did unknowingly, something as stupid as his friend seeing her in yoga attire and calling and telling him about it was not okay. Anyway, he had no right to tell her what to wear.

She swallowed and tried to even out her rapid breaths. "I was at yoga." She motioned to her outfit. "This is what everyone wears at yoga."

He leaned in to her. "Wear something *else*."

Her eyes widened. "*No*. I'm a grown woman. I wear what—"

In an instant, his arm circled her waist. He shoved her against the length of him and dug his hips into her. On her stomach, she felt him, all of him and gasped. Then he gripped the back of her head and slammed his lips onto hers, silencing her. Her mouth opened of its own accord, tongue slipped out searching for his. He found hers first, kissed her with brute force, and to her surprise, it spurred her. Wrapping her arms around his neck, nails digging into his hair, she kissed him just as forcefully.

His hand at the back of her waist trailed up to the top of her leggings. He tugged them and sunk his hand inside. Then he gripped her butt hard and rubbed himself against her. Her head snapped back. Losing hold of his lips, she let out a moan. Then his mouth slid to her neck biting lightly, teasing, taunting.

Her nipples puckered against his chest as his other

hand glided from the back of her neck to her front. He grabbed the bottom of her sports bra and yanked it up. He pinched her nipple, cupped her breast, and dropped his head. The warmth of his mouth heated her there.

"Beautiful, Lex." He sucked her deep, his stubble making the plethora of sensations mind-blogging.

She should stop him, but all she could do was cry out, "Oh God…" With her hand at the back of his neck, she held him against her as she lifted her leg, wrapped it around him, and instinctively rubbed herself against him.

He tore himself away and groaned. Then he was at her mouth again kissing her deep.

"Please…" Somehow, she managed it. "Stop."

He released her so quickly she stumbled. His hands went to her waist to steady her, yet he kept his distance. Breaths rapid, jaw clenched, he let her waist go and fisted his hands. She knew what she wanted to say but needed to catch her breath.

"You…" Because his stare fell to her chest, she readjusted her sports bra and finished, "…Can't tell me what to wear."

Gaze snapping to her face, his hands went to his head. He dragged his fingers through his dark hair. The muscle in his jaw twitched. "Fine."

Her eyes widened. She won the argument? That fast?

He smirked. "You get home after whatever the fuck it is you're wearing shit like that for and give me a kiss like that one, fine."

Still catching her breath, she nodded.

"Now seeing as how I gotta fix *this*—" He pointed to his hardness. "—Before my balls burst, I'll catch you later."

She saw him and Cullen an hour later. He brought food. They ate together. Then he and Cullen left.

Thursday, she woke and found a text. *Working late today. Be home around seven. You good to eat with us then?*

She replied, *I'll make dinner.*

She did. After dinner and after Cullen fell asleep, they got carried away. Their make-out session lasted a good half hour. Again, she stopped him. Before he left, he asked her to dinner the following night, just the two of them. Naturally, she barely slept.

Chapter Fifteen

Lex realized, belatedly, she'd been a nervous mess all day for no reason.

She'd debated what to wear since last night, but once he told her they'd ride his bike, she knew dressing up was out of the question. That didn't mean she didn't try to look her best. Wearing a pair of dark-wash, skinny jeans, a fitted, white blouse, and over it, a black, leather jacket, she finished the look with a white and black scarf and a pair of flats, and though she knew her hair would be a mess after their ride anyway, it didn't stop her from styling it.

At seven on the dot, Dodge knocked on her door. She parted it and knew she hadn't gone through the trouble for nothing.

Dodge's gaze slid from the top of her head to her feet. Then he met her stare and his heated. The next instant, he circled an arm around her back and buried the other hand in her hair. Holding the back of her neck, he moved toward her. Lips an inch from hers, his body close but not touching. "Debating whether I should kiss you."

She swallowed. "You should kiss me."

"I kiss you, we're staying in, Lex. You ready for that?"

A shudder ran through her.

His eyes widened. Then he grinned a gorgeous,

wide grin. “So what’s it gonna be?”

“I want to go for a ride.” She wouldn’t know it until later, but she’d used the rest of her willpower with those words.

He nodded but stayed close, holding her close. He released her lower back to tuck a strand of her hair behind her ear then rested his hand on her hip. “You look beautiful, Lex.”

“I would’ve dressed up, but we’re going for a ride, so it didn’t make sense.”

“Like you just like this. Simple, no pretense. Not too much makeup so I can see some of your freckles.”

Oh God! No woman wanted to look simple! Wait, he could see her freckles?

She covered her nose. “I thought I’d concealed them.”

He chuckled, gliding his hand from the back of her neck to cup her face. “Babe, you hear what I said? Said I like them. First time I saw you, you didn’t have a shred of makeup on and you still looked like a million bucks.”

She relaxed a little. “Simple?”

“Yeah, I like simple.”

He must’ve read the look on her face since not a moment later, with his hand at her hip, he pushed her fully against him and pressed his forehead to hers. “And by simple, I don’t mean plain, babe. I like the idea that when you take off your makeup, you’ll look the same. Don’t like fake nails, lashes, hair, tits, ass. I like real. You’re real. I’ve seen you without makeup, and you’re beautiful. You like dressing up, dress up. Just don’t wear too much shit on your face, yeah?”

“Okay.”

He smiled and placed a light kiss on her lips before he led her out of her house, grabbed her keys, and locked her door.

"Where's Cul?"

"Sleeping over his friend Levi's house."

"Oh."

She wanted to see him, say hi, but she wouldn't interrupt his sleepover for that.

Dodge drove her to an Italian restaurant, *Anthony's,* a casual place with great food. She loved it. The best part though, their conversation. She told him how she grew up everywhere and nowhere, a military brat, how she went to college in San Francisco to be close to Meg and stayed there until recently when she finally summoned the courage to move on from her last relationship. He listened to everything she said and asked questions in between. Later, he told her about himself. He grew up in New Mexico. He never went to college; instead, he moved out of his home, worked for a year, saved enough to buy a bike then rode around the US taking jobs where he could, leaving when he wanted. He'd spent years on the road when he stopped in Wadden, found the club, and decided to prospect.

They ended their dinner with a slice of chocolate cake they shared. Then they rode home.

At the steps leading to her door, she faced him and realized that's the moment she should've been nervous about. Scanning his handsome face, before she thought it through, she asked, "Do you want to come in?"

He grinned. "Yeah, Lex, I do."

Unlocking her door, parting it, and striding through, she took off her jacket and scarf. "Do you want a beer?"

"If you got."

He headed to the couch. She walked to the kitchen, grabbed a beer for him and a glass of wine for herself then closed the distance between them, handed him his drink, and sat close beside him. He tilted his head back, taking a deep pull, allowing her to take a sip of hers before he grabbed her glass and placed it along with his bottle on her coffee table.

The next instant, he cupped the back of her head, threading his fingers in her hair, and claimed her lips, giving her one of those kisses she loved, deep and intense. There was something new to it, something desperate.

She kissed him back deeper as his hands skated down her back, crushing her to him, and trailed down her sides. He grasped her hips, lifting her up and over him so she straddled his lap. There, she felt the length of him. Instantly, she was drenched, so wet she swore he felt her soak through her jeans and his.

Then she lost conscious thought, all thought. All she did was feel. Feel his hand at her back wrap around her hair and tug, baring her neck. Feel his mouth hit her there a moment later. Feel him lick his way down her chest over her shirt. Feel him tug her shirt down, bra and all, and close his mouth over her nipple, tongue circling, sucking, and biting lightly.

She shivered and heard herself say, "Bedroom."

He snapped his head up, that beautiful sensation he created, gone. Eyes meeting hers, his jaw went hard. He swallowed. "You sure?"

She nodded.

Not a moment later, he cupped her butt and stood. She tightened her arms around his neck and wrapped her legs around his waist. Then he moved, out of the living room, down the hall, and into her room quickly. The entire time, his lips glued to hers.

He didn't hesitate. The minute he reached her bed, he tossed her on it. Standing in front of her, he unbuttoned her jeans and ripped them off, leaving her in her black, lace thong.

Then he dove, tongue first, kissing and licking from her thighs up to her stomach. When she arched her back, he snaked an arm under, helped her to a sitting position, and removed her blouse and bra. After, he tightened his arm around her waist, lifting her bottom slightly to remove her thong.

He paused, and as his gaze raked every inch of her he gripped her thighs and trailed his hands up her legs and hips to her waist and breasts slowly.

Finally, he met her stare. His eyes dark, hungry, heated.

Wanting to touch him, kiss him, anything, she reached for him. He released her, grabbed her behind the knees, and yanked forward. She fell onto her back. A second later, she felt him moving between her legs. His tongue hit her clit, rubbing, licking, sucking as he drove his fingers inside her. Devouring her so intensely, as her scream pierced the air, she gripped her comforter, arched off the bed, and trembled uncontrollably. She came in a minute flat, but he didn't stop. He fed, and it went on and on.

Mind-blowing.

Earth-shattering.

Life-changing.

As the haze lifted and her heart continued hammering hard and fast, she fought to catch her breath and focus.

He planted his face against her stomach and pressed his lips to her skin. “Fuck, Lex. You didn’t even make me work for it coming so fast. I’d only just gotten started.”

It had been too fast though it’d lasted and had been amazing. Lifting her head, she caught his stare and cupped the back of his head. In that instant, something came over her. She couldn’t explain it, but it drove her to do something she’d never done.

Sliding her hands to his face, she sat up. He straightened with her. She released his cheeks and reached for his jeans, unbuttoning them as she pressed her lips to his and kissed him. Bold and forward, possibly too forward, but she wanted him so bad she didn’t care.

“Lex…”

She kept kissing him even as she lowered his jeans and boxers and freed him.

“Babe, we don’t…”

She wrapped her hand around him and stroked him. Warm, big, and thick, she barely managed to wrap her fingers around him.

His whole body vibrated, eyes flared. “Fuckin’ shit, babe.”

She stood. He moved back allowing her to do so. Then she dropped to her knees in front of him and holding onto the base, she placed her lips on the rim. Eyeing him through her lashes, the muscles in his shoulders tense, breaths coming out his gasps, he’d never looked so handsome. She took him deep, once, twice then listening to the sounds of his moans, she lost count; she got lost in enjoying him.

Suddenly, he grabbed her shoulders, yanked her away, and simultaneously took a step back. His jaw hardened. Through clenched teeth, he groaned. "Gotta stop, Lex."

Then he closed the distance he forced, gripped her under the arms, lifted her in one swift movement, and dropped her on the bed. Her back hit the mattress. He stood between her legs, cock pulsing, so close. Her whole body shook in anticipation, but he didn't move. She slid toward him, getting closer, then wrapped her legs around him. Still, nothing.

What was he waiting for? She needed him. Now.

He reached behind him, pulled out a condom, unwrapped it, and rolled it on.

Yikes. She forgot about protection?

She didn't have time to worry about what it meant. A moment later, she felt him pushing inside. His gaze searing her, the deeper he dove, the harder the corded muscles on his neck clamped tight.

Once buried deep, he released a ragged breath.

Feeling full, completely, of him, and he felt magnificent, better than anything she'd felt in her life. Only natural, at that moment, she wanted to stay that way.

Chapter Sixteen

Fuck.

Dodge would blow before he even got started. He held back, but it was hard. It'd been too long, but it wasn't that. Lex did this shit to him, turned him into a horny teenager.

He didn't want to hurt her. She was tight, almost too much. He'd only just sunk inside, but he couldn't help it. He needed to go faster, deeper, and he didn't know if she could handle it.

Ice blue eyes on him, cheeks rosy, that strawberry-colored hair of hers a mess around her.

Beautiful.

No, he couldn't stare at her. He looked at her, he'd lose control. He couldn't lose it and give it to her hard. He'd scare her, possibly even hurt her.

He pulled out and must've hesitated too long because she lifted her hips, sinking him deeper. He groaned.

"Faster," she breathed.

He drew out then thrust faster.

"Harder."

He slid out then plunged harder.

"You won't break me. Take me."

He grabbed her hips so the back of her knees rested in the crook of his elbows then pulled out and drove faster, harder, deeper.

He didn't stop.

He fucked her because she asked him to, and he didn't stop because honest to God, just looking at her, hearing her making those sounds was enough to make him come.

Throwing her legs over his shoulders, he gripped her hips tighter and sunk deeper. She screamed. Her face flushed so pretty. He didn't know how he did it, but he held back, made it last.

When he couldn't hold it anymore, he pressed his thumb against her clit. She came undone. Body vibrating, her moans so loud he felt them pierce his chest.

It was stunning.

She was exquisite.

Not a moment later, she sat up. He lost the connection right before he'd been about to blow. The next instant, she grabbed his cut roughly, tugged him onto the bed, and climbed on top.

Her tits in his face, he met her gaze. She smiled, grabbed his shaft, positioning it at her entrance, and sunk herself into him, burying deep.

She rode him, hard and fast. So good, dizzying. In no time, she had him right where he'd been before, so close, fighting to make it last.

She screamed and moaned, hair falling against him, tits rubbing against his chest, looking wild, striking. As he watched her, he put his hands at her hips and met her thrusts. Before he came, she did again, milking the shit out of him. This time, her arms went around his neck, holding him to her even as she continued riding him.

"Dave…"

The scent of her, the feel of her arms around him,

maybe, too, the way she said his name threw him over. Finally, he came hard and for a long ass time. He couldn't do anything but give in to it completely, feel the power of it.

Aftershocks of that potent release flowing through him, he wrapped his arms around her waist, rested his head on her shoulder, and caught his breath, thinking about what just happened, what she'd just handed him.

He hadn't still held her, he would've thought he'd dreamt it. He fantasized about her a lot and when he did, she asked for it hard and fast and she screamed. He had his share of women: most were taps, some one-nighters, none were women like Lex, but that was beside the point. He knew what he liked and what he didn't. One of the things he liked—the woman to shout and moan and show him how much she loved what he gave her. Their first time and Lex gave him all that and some.

He'd never thought Lex would be like that. For one, she was a beautiful, smart, educated woman who taught kids for a living, came from a good home, baked and cooked, and loved his kid. Being phenomenal in bed, giving him exactly what he wanted and more was just too good to be true, proving he'd been right about her—she was perfect, absolutely perfect for him.

"Dodge?"

He lifted his head, met her stare, and grinned. "Lex."

She returned his smile.

"I know I gotta clean up, but don't think I can move."

She giggled and hesitated a moment before she unwrapped her arms from his neck and moved off him.

Then she grabbed a blanket on the foot of her bed and draped it over herself. “You can shower if you like.”

“Rather keep the smell of you on me.”

No truer words.

He stood, realizing he was practically still dressed. His boots on his feet, pants and boxers at his ankles. He took off his boots, walked out of his pants and boxers then strode bare-assed to her bathroom where he got rid of the spent condom. In her room, he took off his cut and shirt, draping them over her armoire. He nabbed his boxers, donned them, and headed for the bed where Lex sat, looking like she hadn’t moved. Her eyes on him.

“You’re staying?”

He cocked his head. “You mind?”

She smiled big and bright and shook her head. Then she moved to allow him to pull the comforter off the bed. She slid in. He followed, snaked his arms around her, and dragged her toward him as he lay back.

When she settled against him, he asked, “You sleep naked?”

“No.”

He grabbed the blanket she held over herself, ripped it away, and covered her with the quilt. “You do tonight.”

Her hand over his heart, she pressed her cheek to his chest. “Just for you. Just tonight.”

Burying his face in her hair, he kissed the top of her head. “Night, Lex.”

“Night, Dodge.”

****

Lex woke with a start. It happened sometimes. She had no idea why.

The moment she woke, she realized she was alone.

Awaking up alone was the norm for her, but she shouldn't be then. She fell asleep with Dodge after having the best sex of her life.

She hadn't been with many men, but she had experience. She knew the average time a man could go and what the first time was like with someone new, and Dodge blew both of those out of the water. She had her first orgasm while having sex. In actuality, two.

Then Dodge cleaned up and went to bed beside her. But now, she'd woken alone. Chances were he wasn't in her bathroom since the light was off. Sitting up in bed, her gaze snapped to where he'd left his jeans and boots on her floor then to where he'd draped his cut and shirt. No longer there.

A man left in the middle of the night, the night a woman first had sex with him, it meant one thing. He got what he wanted and didn't want it again.

She wanted to believe the week they'd spent together meant something to him. Him meeting her parents, her meeting his brothers, spending so much time with his son, their first date, their insanely phenomenal first time, even their first fight meant something to her. Not the fight, per se, but the way it ended, definitely.

Her stomach rolled and soured.

Her sister had been right. She was desperate. She gave him a chance and let herself think one week, although they'd done a lot that one week, meant more than it should.

Her throat clogged. Tears rushed her. She took a deep breath and promised herself she wouldn't cry. Standing, she grabbed her nighty from under her pillow, donned it, and headed out of her room and down the hall. In her living room, she walked toward her door and locked it. He hadn't considered her safety leaving her door unlocked.

She swallowed, forced herself not to look outside, strode into her kitchen, poured herself a glass of water, and took a long gulp.

A loud bang sounded on her door. It came so suddenly, startled, she dropped the glass. It hit the floor and shattered. Something she'd have to pick up later.

She walked carefully around the glass. Then another bang echoed. She rushed and felt a prick on the bottom of her foot. Ignoring it, she continued toward the door and opened it.

Brow furrowed, jaw clamped tight, dark gaze pinning her. Dodge ran a hand through his messy hair. "Lex, tell me there's a good reason why you locked me out."

She couldn't do a thing but stare.

He shook his head. "I'm gone for not ten minutes and you lock me out?"

After another silent moment, one she spent scanning his face, his eyes hardened and narrowed. "Are you gonna explain?"

She found herself blurting, "I thought you left."

He reared back. "After what we did, you thought I left?"

What was she supposed to think? She woke up, and he was gone. Still, he said it like it was absurd. Instead of answering him, she nodded.

His eyes widened. Then his expression softened. He moved, closing the distance between them and cupping her cheek. "Do I look stupid to you?" He shook his head and chuckled. "Don't answer that."

She smiled.

He wiped the grin off his face. “A man’s gotta be a stupid fuck to leave you after that, Lex.” Drawing a strand of her hair away from her face, he pressed a soft kiss to her lips. “A man’s a stupid fuck he leaves a woman who goes wild like that for him.”

Her smile widened, cheeks flushed. “Sorry, I kind of lost control—”

“Don’t ever apologize for that.” He drifted an arm down her back and wrapped it around her waist, tucking her to his side. He closed and locked the door then turned fully to her. “Was putting my bike away.”

Oh God, and she thought he’d left? That made her look bad in one of the worst ways, *insecure*. “Sorry…I just—”

He quirked a brow. “Sorry?”

She didn’t know what to say.

“Lex, I know you’ve been hurt, but you gotta trust me. I know I messed up with you in the beginning, but we’re starting new. I don’t want to keep having these discussions.”

So it troubled him to assure her?

She looked away from him to gather her thoughts. “You don’t want to keep having these discussions?”

He nodded.

She pulled away. “Then don’t.”

His brows furrowed.

“You don’t want to trouble yourself with these discussions, then don’t. You know where the door is.” She spun on her heel then felt his hand grasp her upper arm.

He turned her. Surprising, he didn’t look angry. When he spoke, he didn’t sound it either. “I explained this to you, Lex. That conversation we had about me and women?"

How women dodged him? What did that have to do with this?

"That's happening now. I said something to get you pissed, but, babe, I didn't mean it in a bad way. It's no trouble for me to tell you that I care about you, to show you, but I don't want you to keep thinking that I don't. I don't want you to think I'm like all those assholes you dated who hurt you. I'm nothing like them."

Right. Good thing he explained.

She closed her eyes tightly, feeling nothing but warmth spreading through her chest. "You didn't say that," she heard herself say in a small voice. "You said, and I quote, 'I don't want to keep having these discussions.'"

"I know I don't explain shit right sometimes, Lex, so knowing that, you should ask then let me explain. I do and you're still pissed, then I probably deserve it. Just give me a chance to clarify before you get pissed."

She nodded.

He pressed his lips to hers for a quick kiss. "Let's get to bed."

"I…um…have to clean up."

Releasing her, he quirked a brow. She strode toward the kitchen, but she didn't make it two steps before she felt the heat of his arm circle her waist and his chest press tight against her back. He lifted her off the floor, walked to the counter, and settled her on it.

"What—"

"You hurt herself." He grabbed her left foot and lifted it to his face. Dropping it, he did the same with the other. His finger then skimmed her heel. “It hurt?”

She shook her head.

“You got something to clean it with?”

“In my bathroom. I can—”

“Go, I’ll take care of this.”

“You don’t know where I keep my rags.”

He straightened and smirked. “Where do you keep your rags?”

She smiled. “The drawer to the right of the sink.”

“Now I know.” Placing his hands on her hips, he lifted her off the counter, strode a distance away from the broken glass, and set her on her feet. “Go on. I’ll be in bed in a few.”

Turning toward her room, she took three steps before he called her name. She looked over her shoulder.

“Like the nighty, but when I get in bed, I want you naked, like before.”

A shiver skated down her back. She rushed past her room, into her bathroom, cleaned the cut, took off her nighty, and climbed into bed.

Not five minutes later, he appeared at the door. He held her stare for a moment too long then walked toward her slowly. En route, he took off his boots then clothes. The way he did it, taking his time as he undressed, meant she got a good look at him, something she hadn’t had the chance to do before. Tall, big, and chiseled, not in an overly obvious way, in the way anyone could tell he worked out but didn’t obsess about it. His arms, chest, abs, legs, all of him… Just beautiful.

“Like what you see, Lex?”

Her gaze still on his abs, she nodded.

He laughed, making her snap her stare to his

handsome face. "You aren't the only one, babe."

She smiled. "You ready for bed? I'm exhausted."

His eyes narrowed playfully. He smirked. "Not yet. I'm gonna make you come a couple more times."

"So sure of yourself?"

He got into bed directly in front of her, grabbed her hips, and roughly yanked her to him then covered her with his massive body.

The suddenness of it startled and thrilled her. She let out a squeal.

When he positioned himself right between her legs, she wrapped them around him, bringing him closer, and felt him lengthen against her. Jaw clenched, his expression grew intense. She meant to tease him some more, but that hungry look stopped her.

"Are you gonna go wild for me again?"

Breaths growing shallow, she nodded though she didn't know for sure since she hadn't planned it before.

He kissed her.

Then he did more.

To her delight and his, she went wild.

Much like the first time, she couldn't have helped it.

Before she slid into a deep sleep, her chest tucked against his side, his arm around her holding her close, he buried his face in her hair and whispered, "Sweet dreams, my wild woman."

Chapter Seventeen

Lex had started to believe she'd do just about anything if it made Dodge happy.

They spent much of the last few weeks together. Not just her and him, but Cullen too. In fact, they hadn't been on a typical date since their first two weeks ago.

He worked. She worked. After work, he cooked, she did, or they ordered in. When he made the meal, they ate at his house, and when she did, they had dinner at hers. Sometimes, the nights he cooked, she made dessert. Usually, she baked cookies, but once, she'd made brownies and another time, a chocolate cake. Leftovers, Dodge took to the garage, which he later told her the brothers devoured five minutes after he walked in. The nights he cooked, if she made dessert, Cullen helped her. Other times, she read to him while Dodge finished dinner. Sometimes, Cullen watched TV or played in the kitchen with his toys. This happened when it was too late to play outside with his friends. The nights she made dinner, Cullen lounged at her house so did Dodge. Every night, she ended up at their place since Cullen's bedtime was nine. After Cullen fell asleep, she and Dodge spent time alone.

Not only hadn't they been on a date, but they hadn't left Cullen with a sitter and Cullen hadn't had sleepovers either. Technically, they hadn't been alone.

Cullen asleep in a room nearby didn't count. At first, it made her uneasy because after Cullen went to bed, Dodge made his move. From experience, he touched her, she lost logical thought and rationale.

The first night he tried had been the Saturday after their first date. They'd spent the day together and ordered pizza for dinner. After eating, they sat around the television and watched a cartoon with Cullen. Dodge sat pressed up against her right side, his arm draped around her shoulders, Cullen to her left. When Cul started to get tired, he laid, placing his head on her lap. She couldn't help herself then, so she ran her fingers through his dark, thick hair mindlessly.

"You can stop that, Lex. He's out."

She turned her head, meeting his eyes, and read something in his gaze. He carried Cullen into his room and tucked him in. Only when Dodge rejoined her did she realize what that look meant—gratitude.

He grabbed her hand, tugged her up and off the couch, and led her into his bedroom. A huge master with a dark wood sleigh bed and matching furniture, the navy bedspread similar to the color on her living room accent wall. The room was masculine and not just because clothes littered the floor. It was a mixture of everything, the furniture, the comforter, the messiness, and hard not to notice, there was no décor. No picture frames on his nightstand, no artwork on the walls, no candles scattered around the room, no vases on his armoire.

She took this in and met his stare. He released her hand and crossed his arms over his chest. She knew by the way he scanned her face he was waiting for her reaction.

"It's big."

A slow smile spread across his lips. "That's all?"

"It's masculine."

He chuckled, uncrossed his arms, and lifted a brow. "Lex, you come in my bedroom for the first time, a room that looks like a disaster to me so I know to you, it looks worse, and all you gotta say is that it's big and masculine?"

"There's no point in saying it's a mess because I think you know it is. Beside the fact, it's rude." She inched closer to him. "It's my first time in here, and it's not my place to say."

"You're mine, so it *is* your place to say."

He had a point. They were embarking on something new, and it was best to be honest.

She shrugged. "Maybe you're right."

"So what else do you have to say?"

She released a breath. "I don't know why I have to say something you already know. I'd be nagging then."

His smile widened. "And you don't nag?"

She grinned. "I try not to."

Slowly and purposefully, he closed the distance between them, planted his mouth against hers, and snaked his arms around her waist. She hooked hers around his neck. As she did, he skated one hand up her spine to grip the back of her neck and deepen the kiss.

Need consumed her. That easy, that fast.

She drew away before she got completely lost. Fighting to catch her breath, her eyes met his. He drew his brows together.

"We can't. Cullen's—"

"Passed out, babe." A second later, his lips slanted over hers. He tightened his arms around her waist, plastering her body to his.

Sliding her hands to his chest, she pushed. She only managed to get a millimeter between them, just enough to speak. “We can’t. What if he wakes up or—”

“You gotta be quiet, babe, or you’ll wake Cul.”

She didn’t have time to process that before his mouth covered hers again. When she did, she giggled.

Pulling away on his own, he smirked. “What’s so funny?”

“I’m serious. He doesn’t know we’re together. What if he catches us—”

He released a sigh. “First, he knows more than you think, Lex. We’ve been spending a lot of time together. He’s three, but he isn’t stupid. He may not say much, but he’s always watching, and I’ve seen him looking our way when I sit next to you or grab your hand.”

She hadn’t noticed that. They hadn’t been together long, but around Cullen, Dodge was never overtly affectionate.

“Last, I locked the door, so he isn’t gonna catch us doing anything but being in my room.”

She hadn’t noticed he’d locked the door. Then again, she’d been preoccupied.

“I know you get loud and trust me, babe, I fuckin’ love that, but I think for our sake ’cause Cul’s asleep, you can be quiet, right?”

She hoped so since he was very much right. If she couldn’t be quiet, then they’d never have sex. She didn’t want that. Honestly, she didn’t think she could go weeks waiting until Cullen had a sleepover.

“I don’t know if I can.”

He grinned. “How about I find creative ways to cover your mouth if you get too loud?”

She didn't know why, had never done it before, but she wanted him to do that. A full body shiver snaked through her making her legs quake. Her body pressed to his, he felt it and took it as a cue.

The next moment, he drove his tongue into her mouth, slid his hands between them, and unbuckled her jeans.

He took her on his bed, him on top, hard and fast, almost desperate. The whole time, he kept his mouth glued to hers. She came undone, moaning softly into his mouth as she did. Before the aftershocks fully faded, he pulled away, gripped her right hip, and flipped her on her stomach. Then grabbing both hips, he lifted her butt off the bed and thrust into her from behind, his balls slamming hard against her clit. She snapped her head back and let out a deep moan.

Instantly, he removed one hand from her hip to wrap around her middle, sliding it swiftly up her chest until it rested between her breasts and he'd grabbed hold of her shoulder. He lifted her upper body. On her knees, her back pressed to his chest, the cool air hit her nipples. She shivered, a whimper escaping her lips.

He covered her mouth with his other hand. His fingers dug into her cheek as he buried his face in her neck. Against her skin, he said, "Fuck me, Lex. Hearing that one moan, almost shot my load."

She was helpless, and yet, despite her position, she felt *in control* and turned on beyond belief. It could be what he said, the way he sounded, how his breaths heated the skin on her neck, or how his whole body shook with restraint. Maybe a combination of all four.

"I hate it, but you gotta stay quiet. Okay?" His voice gruff.

Her chest heaved as she caught her breath. Still, he held his hand over her mouth. Nothing she could do but nod.

He waited what seemed like forever. Maybe to torture her, maybe to make it last longer, she had no clue. What she knew—the whole time she prayed he'd put her out of her misery. When he didn't, she rubbed herself against him. One hand gripped his thigh; with the other, she reached for her clit.

"Fuck me. Are you…" He dug his fingers into her jaw and groaned against her neck. "Are you touching yourself?"

She nodded.

"Fuck."

He pulled out and thrust inside. Hard. After that, he didn't stop, but he did place his hand over hers and worked her as she worked herself.

She came a minute later.

A minute after that, he did.

Only then did he uncover her mouth.

After, he slid out, collapsed beside her, hooked his arms around her, and hauled her until her chest lay pressed against his. "Thought I was gonna die waiting to see if we'd woken Cul."

She had too except she hadn't known that's what he'd been doing.

He cupped her cheek. "You do that to me."

She smiled.

After falling asleep on his chest, she woke around midnight and headed home. Dodge didn't argue, but he did walk her home.

The next night, they had dinner at her place. Later, they headed across the street to Dodge and Cullen's.

She read to Cullen, per his request, for a half hour before Dodge told Cul he needed to bathe and head for bed. She graded some papers in the meantime. After Cullen fell asleep, Dodge grabbed her hand, tugged her off the couch, and led her into his room. Again, she worried about waking Cul. Dodge assured her Cul had passed out. After two mind-blowing orgasms, she fell asleep beside him. Hours later, she woke, and Dodge walked her home. Now, it was somewhat of a routine. They still tried to be quiet, but she was less worried about waking Cul.

In between this routine, she started some of her own. Twice a week, she stayed at school until six grading papers, revamping her corkboards, and writing lesson plans. Decorating the classroom for obvious reasons had to be done while she was at school. The rest though she did at school because she knew if Dodge and Cullen were home, she wouldn't get anything done. Not their fault but hers.

Everything had been smooth sailing, not only remarkable but unbelievable. It'd only been three weeks since they started dating, but they spent a portion of every one of those days together, which made it feel like they'd been dating for a few months instead of just twenty-one days. Usually, by date twenty-one, she'd already spotted several negative qualities in her partner. Granted with Dodge, she spotted those before they started dating since he'd been a jerk on more than one occasion, but in the last twenty-one days, with the exception of him disliking her workout attire and picking a fight, everything had been great.

It wasn't just about the sex either. Sex with Dodge was the best, but there was more. He didn't just cook for her, and she didn't just make them dinner. She cooked; he stayed in the kitchen with her and vice versa. They talked about their day. They joked and laughed a lot so it felt like they were not just lovers but friends. Several times while she read to Cullen, she spared a glance at him and noticed him watching them with a soft look in his eyes and a smile on his lips, that same expression of gratitude on his face.

She loved that, loved spending time with him, talking to him, loved when he was affectionate. Mostly, she loved seeing him smiling and laughing, looking carefree. He shared some of his life, so she knew he hadn't had much of that. And she loved, *loved* Cullen. All these feelings grew by the day, more so as she got closer to Cullen and Dodge. They were becoming a staple in her life.

Case in point, Thursday night, she offered to watch Cullen. While Cullen slept, she had two mind-blowing orgasms. Dodge had one, which she hoped was mind-blowing. They lay facing each other, still naked, cuddled close. Her head rested on his arm. His arm wrapped around her neck, hand buried in her hair, the other on her hip.

He pressed a kiss to her forehead. "Gotta work Saturday. I work Saturdays once a month. The brothers, we take turns so no one has to work every Saturday."

"I'll watch Cul."

He stilled, not breathing, not speaking, not for a while. She kept her stare on him and waited.

He slid his hand from her hip to tuck her hair behind her ear. His eyes warmed. "Lex, I wasn't asking you—"

"I know."

He hesitated then released a breath. “I know you care about Cul, but you don’t have to watch him. You can go to yoga or grade papers or chill with Allie or whatever you want. You deserve the day off instead of having—”

Putting an elbow on the mattress, she pulled herself up and kissed him. “I’m offering because I want to.”

“I don’t want you feeling obligated ’cause I gotta kid, you gotta start—”

“I don’t feel obligated to do anything. I promise. I like kids, and I love Cullen. He’s sweet.”

Not a lie. It took her hours to realize she loved him.

“Babe, I know he’s sweet to you, but you gotta have noticed he’s a typical boy. He plays rough, and he’s always coming up with ways to get himself hurt.”

She tore her stare from his and thought out loud, “Are you worried he’ll get hurt while he’s with me? I have experience—”

He shook his head. “Fuck, no.” He said it in a way she believed him instantly. “I’m worried I’m gonna get home, and you’ll be too tired for me.” Then he broke out in a smile.

She laughed. “So I’ll watch him?”

He nodded. “’Course, Lex. He’ll be stoked when I tell him tomorrow.”

Saturday morning, as Dodge headed for work, she and Cullen went to the mall. Friday, she’d looked up places to go with a three-year-old. That’s how she discovered the kids’ gym at the local mall. She could’ve taken him to the park, but she wanted to do something out of the ordinary. At the massive place filled with bounce houses and video games, Cullen had a blast.

On their way out, they walked by a kid’s clothing

store. Her gaze flew to the large signs that read, "sale" in big, bold, red letters. Cul's hand in hers, she led them inside. In seconds, she realized it wasn't just any sale but a massive one. Every item had been marked down fifty to seventy percent. Needless to say, she couldn't help herself. She bought her new niece or nephew a couple of unisex onesies, and for Cullen, she purchased four superhero tee shirts and two pairs of jeans. No doubt, he liked the tees since he nodded excitedly when she picked them out. She asked him about the jeans, but he shrugged. She got them anyway, having noticed some of his were worn.

They walked out of the store, one of her hands still in Cullen's, the other holding a bag with the store's logo.

"My baby!"

She turned to look but didn't manage it. Cullen squeezed her hand almost painfully only to release it, launch himself behind her, and circle both arms around her waist in a death grip.

She shifted, angling herself awkwardly trying to meet his gaze. She then dropped the bag at her feet and planted a hand on his shoulder. "Cul, what's—"

"Who the fuck are you?"

Her head snapped to the woman standing too close, a tall blonde wearing a jean mini skirt, a cleavage baring pink shirt, and five-inch heels. Attractive definitely, but she'd twisted her face in a nasty way, not to mention she dressed like she wanted the wrong kind of attention.

Lex didn't know her nor did she know why she felt the need to curse at her in a public place in front of a child and a multitude of others. Believing the woman had to be mistaken and not wanting to cause a bigger scene, Lex asked, “Excuse me?”

Those steely gray eyes narrowed. “Who. The. Fuck. Are. You?”

Lex took a deep breath and a step back carefully so she didn’t knock over Cul. “I’m no one who knows you, so if you’ll excuse—”

“I’m *his* mother.”

Cullen’s hold on her tightened.

Damn it. The blonde was his mother *and* Dodge’s ex.

Lex didn’t have time to let that sink. She had a feeling what’d come next wouldn’t be pleasant for her and especially for Cullen. Lex didn’t know Dodge’s ex, but she knew Cullen had only seen his mother a couple of times in the last year, and she knew what she’d just witnessed. The woman was foul-mouthed in front of her son, a son who acted like he feared her.

Her stomach hollowed out even as her pulse spiked. Lex didn’t let it show, keeping calm and her voice level. “I’m Alexa. I’m—”

“The woman who’s fucking *my husband*.”

A blow, a physical one. Her heart squeezed, body flinched.

Was Dodge still married? He told her… What had he told her? Why had she assumed they were divorced?

She swallowed thickly but kept her face blank. “You’re separated.”

“He’s seeing you, is he? Or you mean he’s fucking you and using you to watch *my* son? Don’t get too comfortable. We’ve *separated* before. He *always* comes back because I’m *his wife* and the *mother* of his son.”

For a split second, her face fell. Harder to hide this

time. The fact of the matter, Lex didn't know if the woman lied.

The blonde moved to her side, gaze shooting to Cullen. "Let's go." Then she reached for him.

Face pressed against her, Cullen whimpered, and his small body trembled.

Lex wrapped one arm behind her, resting it against Cullen's back, gripped his hands at her stomach with the other, and angled her body, blocking Cullen from sight. She stepped back from his mother, again carefully, taking Cullen with her. "He was left in my care. If you want to see your son, you'll have to speak to his father."

The woman's eyes widened. "*You* don't want me to do that. The minute I talk to him, he'll come crawling back to *me*."

Her chest clenched painfully. She ignored it, lifted her chin, and shot back instantly, "Not one thing you say will make me release him."

She hadn't lied. She didn't care what else Cullen's mother said, no way she'd let Cullen go with her. The woman may be his mother, but he was terrified. If Lex had to, she'd fight her tooth and nail.

"Listen, you fucking bitch, I'm taking my son!"

"What's going on here?"

Lex looked to the man standing beside them, the mall security.

"She won't give me my son!"

Several people stopped and stared.

Lex's face flamed. Not that it mattered, she was so angry, it was already beet red. Addressing the security, she spoke. "His father left him in my care. If she wants—"

"I'm his wife and the mother. She's just his skanky mistress!"

More people stopped, more stared.

All of Lex's instincts screamed for her to defend herself. She wasn't a pushover or a coward, and she didn't want people in their small town believing anything Cullen's mother screamed. Worse, she didn't want Cullen to hear it. But she couldn't say anything. For one, she didn't know if they were lies. Second and most importantly, she couldn't react. Whether true or not, Cullen's mother was trying to get a rise out of her. Matters would escalate. The one most affected—Cullen. He needed her to keep her cool.

The security crossed his arms over his chest. "Call the father. He can come deal with you two."

Without losing sight of Cullen's mother, Lex released his hands at her stomach to pull her phone out of her back pocket. Then she dialed and waited.

Chapter Eighteen

His phone rang. Dodge plucked it out of his pocket, read Lex's name on the screen, and smiled.

He loved she was so predictable. He loved it more it didn't bore the shit out of him. He told her he'd work morning and be off by lunch. Noon on the dot, he bet money she'd called to find out what he wanted for lunch. She did that shit all the time. During the week, she called him at lunch and asked what he wanted for dinner. Every other day, he had to tell her he'd make dinner; otherwise, she'd cook for him and Cul and make dessert too. He didn't watch it, he'd gain fifty pounds by year end. When they ate at her place, she set the table with fancy-assed cloth napkins and a matching tablecloth like they were special or some shit. It was the little things she did she probably thought he didn't notice. She pitched in without him asking to, sometimes even after he told her not to. Case in point, he had to work and she insisted on watching Cul.

They hadn't been together long, only a few weeks, but she made getting up in the morning easier with just knowing he'd see her. It wasn't about him knowing two to three times a week he didn't have to cook or about knowing his house would be a little less of a mess in between when he paid a cleaning service. It was that even if he was cooking, she'd be right by him telling him about her day, her students, the other teachers, making him laugh and making him feel carefree. Doing all that, she also made him feel like he wasn't alone raising a kid on his own, and it didn't hurt that she was beautiful, smart, good to him, and especially, good to his boy.

He had his brothers, the club, but not one of them knew what it was like to be a single father to a three-year-old, not one of them was raising a kid on his own. His brothers helped him always, but they weren't Lex, a woman, unbelievable in bed, always wanting him, always smiling, talking to him about nothing and everything, making him laugh, and reading to his boy.

He was a man who hadn't known much joy in his life. Thinking about it then, it was the first time he felt truly happy, and a big part of that was that his boy was happy too. So with a smile on his face, he answered his phone.

"I'm down for whatever my woman and son want to eat, babe."

She didn't respond, but in the background, a spine-curling shrill rang out.

"Let me talk to him, now!"

Dodge couldn't forget that voice. He tried and failed. Hearing it, it still didn't sink in because he *couldn't* be hearing that voice when he and his boy just found their happy.

"I need you to come to the mall."

Lex, but not the Lex he knew, *his* Lex. This Lex was someone else, her voice dull and stiff, nothing about it lighthearted.

His stomach rolled.

"I said gimme the fuckin' phone!"

He flinched, actually cringed at hearing it again.

"We're by the food court entrance."

"I said—"

"Ma'am, you need to step away from her." This, a man said.

Then he heard Lex again. "Did you hear me?"

"Yeah, be there in a few." Before he hung up, he'd walked halfway to his car.

He locked gazes with Hash and Rake, a few feet away sitting astride their bikes shooting the breeze. "Need both of you. Get in."

Unlocking his SUV, his brothers didn't question him. They hopped in. When he drove away, he explained. By the silence that ensued, he knew they knew how bad the situation was and how much worse it could get.

Cullen's mother wasn't just a class A nag but a manipulative bitch who got off on fucking with people's lives. She fucked with Rip and Em's first, the reason why Bree grew up without her dad for close to five years. Then she fucked with Trig. When Trig told her to fuck off, she fucked him then proceeded to fuck with not only him but their son until he wised up and kicked her out. She fucked with people by lying, cheating, and manipulating. He had no clue how long she'd been spewing shit to Lex but knew she had because that's what she did. Hopefully, Lex didn't believe her. He had a feeling she did though. The sound of Lex's voice, clue enough, so he moved on to hoping Lex let him explain before she decided anything.

Arriving, he illegally parked at the entrance and left the keys in the ignition, knowing either Rake or Hash would move his car. Then he dashed inside.

He spotted them right away. Cullen, his arms tight

around Lex's hips, his face planted against her. Both of them faced away from him. Lilliam stood in front of them, not two feet away. A mall security guard stood beside them.

He saw Lilliam, and still, he couldn't believe it. It'd been months. Last he heard, she'd moved to Santa Rosa.

The next instant, she proved he wasn't stuck in some nightmare. Lilliam grabbed Cul's arm and yanked. Cul let out a terrified scream. Lex moved quickly, turning her body, *shielding* Cul, protecting him from his own mother. The security said something Dodge didn't hear because blood rushed to his head making it pound.

He sprinted and latched onto Lilliam's wrist, fingers tightening hard enough he pried her away from Cul. His voice thick, deadly, when he said, "You touch my boy again, we're gonna have bigger problems."

Her eyes widened. When she recovered, she took two steps toward him and pressed her breasts against him.

He balked, releasing her and backing away. Not something he could help or control. She disgusted him. It hadn't always been that way. At one point, he thought she was real pretty. She'd been a tap, gave good head, and he had her and continued to have her. Then he knocked her up, married her, and *really* got to know her. After that, she became the ugliest woman he'd ever met, not physically, but where it counted, on the inside. Not that it mattered, after having Lex, knowing Lex, no one compared.

The mall security cocked his head. "You got this?"

He spared a glance at him and nodded.

The man shot Lilliam a nasty glare before he walked away. After seeing what he had, Dodge couldn't blame the guy. No one would.

He shifted toward Lex and Cul. He looked to Cul, face now buried against Lex's stomach. She had one arm tight around him, the other in his hair. Luckily, he got there in time, got Lilliam away before she physically hurt his boy, and now Lex held him, comforted him. All of it meant Cul would be fine.

His gaze shot to Lex. Her silky, long hair loose around her face, barely any makeup, her expression blank. Still beautiful. She didn't meet his stare, but he realized her eyes were blank too.

His stomach soured. Despite this, he lifted his chin toward Hash, standing several feet behind her and Cul. "Hash's taking you to the compound."

"My car's here."

"Hash'll drive it. Take you both to the compound."

She nodded. That blank stare still hadn't met his. Hash walked to her and Cul, picked up a bag at their feet. Holding Cul against her, she then turned and walked away without another word. Dodge watched them go. Before his boy strode out of the mall, Cullen looked over his shoulder at him. His son's face blotchy and red.

His chest squeezing painfully, anguish so deep he knew it'd never fade, a mixture of regret and guilt. He'd done this, kept his mother around longer than he should've, hoping, praying she'd change. She never did, never would.

He clenched his jaw to fight that ache and sliced his gaze to Lilliam. All it took for his body to pulse with rage. "You ever touch my kid like that again,

I'll—"

She took a step toward him. Her hand went to his chest. "Baby—"

He caught her wrist, shoved it away, and took a step back. "Don't fuckin' play games, woman. I don't mean shit to you. Never have, never will. Can't say I'm surprised considering your own kid doesn't mean shit to you."

Her eyes widened, jaw dropped.

Playing more games. No surprise there.

"I can't believe—"

"You grabbed him hard enough you made your son cry? Are you proud he's scared of you? Are you proud he's shaking and—"

Her eyes rounded. She shook her head. "I—"

"And now you're blind?" His arm shot out. "No one here is. Every-fuckin'-one saw it."

Her eyes flashed. Face twisted, lip curled.

There, that was the woman he knew.

"I don't know what you're talking about."

He fisted his hands. "What'd you tell her?"

Her eyes narrowed. "I don't know what you're talking about."

"I know you told her something to fuck with her 'cause that's what you do. You fuck with people. There's no low for you 'cause you even fuck with your own kid. Now I wanna know—"

She smirked. "I didn't have to say anything—"

Getting nowhere and he wouldn't get anywhere, not until he spoke to Lex. He had to get this shit over with.

"Stop delaying the inevitable."

She cocked her head. "Umm? What?"

Now playing stupid. Sometimes, he wished she was a man just so he could beat the shit out of her.

He took a step toward her and in a low, lethal voice said, "Stop stalling the divorce."

"Oh, sweetheart, you know you don't mean that. You know eventually you'll get tired of your whore. We'll work this out, and we'll be a family again," she said this loud enough the nosy people who weren't already huddled around them stopped and stared.

This was all a game to her. She liked attention, any type she could get, but she only got the bad kind. She used her own son to do it even hurt him in the process.

"She's *not* a whore. You *are*. Married you 'cause you tricked me and got pregnant. Married and you were still whoring around. Now, I got a real woman, a woman my son, the one you aren't mother enough for, the one you couldn't care less about, *loves*."

Her face fell, eyes watered.

Finally. Something sunk. Maybe not. Maybe she thought with tears she'd soften him.

"You're smart." He jabbed a finger at her. "You'll stop delaying the divorce. I've been patient with you, but you've worn that patience thin. Now, you fucked with my son for the last time, so my patience is *gone*."

He then turned and stormed off.

****

"It's okay, sweetheart."

Cullen had passed out a minute after he lay down next to her on the bed in Dodge's room at the compound. Cuddled close, his head resting on her shoulder, face turned toward her. One arm around him, she continued to glide her fingers through his hair. Still, she repeated it, kept at it trying to soothe him as he slept. Maybe, subconsciously, she was trying to soothe herself too.

They'd been escorted by Hash to Dodge's room. After she and Cul entered and Hash closed the door, he stayed outside probably to make sure she didn't leave. She knew this since she heard him on his phone outside. She should've told him not to waste his time. No way she'd leave without talking to Dodge first, and she'd never leave Cullen alone, period. She didn't tell him. Instead, she lay beside Cul, wrapped her arm around him, threaded her fingers through his hair repeatedly and whispered to him.

Her mind wouldn't give her a break. A part of her couldn't believe what had happened.

Dodge had never said anything half positive about Cullen's mother. Yes, there were two sides to every story, but maybe Dodge had nothing good to say because there was nothing good to say. An absent mother, one who terrified her son and used force to get him to do what she wanted, hurting him in the process… Troubling and frightening, for Cul especially.

The woman said things about Dodge, things Lex didn't want to believe. Dodge being married, for one. If true, she didn't know if she'd forgive him for not telling her. They'd been dating a short period, but that's the type of information a person disclosed on the first or second date. Had he thought she wouldn't find out? She may be the newcomer in a small town, but eventually, she would've and she had in the worst possible way. Cullen's mother made a complete fool of her at the mall. By mid-week, the whole town would know the new kindergarten teacher was someone's mistress.

Maybe they were divorced. Maybe Cullen's mother

lied, and Lex worried for nothing.

Either way, Dodge had a history with this woman. He said he'd never loved her, but she was the mother of his child, nothing would change that. Maybe that was enough for him. Maybe because of that, he'd take her back.

Her chest clenched, a deep ache sliced through her.

No surprise. The last few weeks had been amazing. She adored Cullen, and Dodge was close to perfect, if he hadn't lied about being married, that is.

The door parted. Her back faced it so she couldn't see who opened it but had a feeling it was Dodge. She had a choice, pretend to sleep or get this over with. Putting it off would only postpone the inevitable. They had to talk. Both had a decision to make.

Turning her head toward the door, she caught his gaze. She barely got a look at him before. Now, she saw he still wore jeans and a work shirt, a black tee with the garage's name and logo in white, bold letters across the chest. Both his shirt and jeans stained with grease.

She tore her stare from his and slowly maneuvered away from Cullen. Standing, she grabbed the blanket at the foot of the bed and tucked it around him. Then she closed the distance between Dodge and herself, the whole time avoiding his eyes. He moved making way for her to exit the room. He closed the door behind her, gripped her hand, and tugged her down the hall. Parting a door, he pulled her in, closed and locked it then released her hand, allowing her to take several steps inside. She looked around the spotless room. A picture sat on the armoire. She recognized the woman in it, Allie. She was laughing, her head turned looking at a man who wasn't her husband, but he was grinning big and wide too. She'd met him at the cookout but couldn't remember his name.

Dodge came to stand in front of her. "That's Army, Allie's brother."

That made sense. She noticed the resemblance, same colored hair and eyes. "He's neat."

"Yeah, Army was in the military. Guess it stuck. Though Trig was too and he isn't. He isn't a mess like most of us, but he isn't a clean freak either."

She quit stalling and finally met his gaze. She wished she hadn't though. Looking at him, she got lost in his too handsome, too rugged face. Strong square jaw, stubble marring it, dark arched brows, big, dark eyes snaring her.

"I gotta know what Lilliam told you, Lex, so I can explain."

Now the woman had a name. Only one thing she needed to know.

She swallowed. "Are you still married?"

His face hardened a moment before he dropped his head. After a long pause, he met her stare again. "Yeah."

He didn't have to say it. She knew from the look in his eyes. It said something he was man enough to admit it, but it didn't change facts.

Married, and he hadn't bothered to tell her.

As many times as she'd been hurt, she never got good at hiding it. Instantly, her chest tightened painfully making her eyes water.

His expression morphed. Something close to the ache she felt flashed across his face. She caught it briefly before her gaze fell from his. She didn't let herself think about how *he* felt.

She knew in her bones what he'd say next, a lousy excuse. Just like the rest of them. They lied and cheated and *wounded her*. She trusted every one of them. In the end, she had to force herself to walk away.

Why? Why did this always happen to her? This time was worse because she let herself believe Dodge was different, because she had the best three weeks of her life and now it was over, and especially, because she'd lose Cullen too.

"We've been separated for more than a year now, but technically, I'm still married—"

And there it was—his excuse.

Heat suffused her body. She narrowed her eyes. "*Don't!*" The strength she used to say that one word startled even her.

It affected him too, making his eyes widen, his frame rear back.

"Don't *bother*."

He swallowed.

"If I didn't know what you were going to say, I could guess, and it doesn't matter. It's just an excuse, and it'll be bull." She spun, headed for the door.

He grabbed her arm, forcing her to turn. Her stare flew behind him and landed on the neatly made bed. Then she shut her eyes hating she didn't have to look at him to remember he was handsome, hating more she let herself believe in him, in them.

She tried to snatch her arm out of his grasp. He tightened his grip.

God, why didn't he just let her go? Why make her lose it in front of him? Why not let her walk away with her pride intact?

"I filed for divorce more than a year ago, when we

separated. Court served her a month after I filed. There's a six-month waiting period in California. That's not why it's taken so long. She won't sign the papers. Her lawyer keeps asking for more time. Judge keeps granting it. Don't know exactly what she wants except to fuck with me 'cause she gets off on fuckin' with people. She maxed out all my cards buying herself shit, and she knows she left me in debt, so I doubt it's money she thinks she can get."

He said it all and with emotion, so she couldn't help it. She parted her eyes and met his big, beautiful ones, identical to Cullen's.

"I hadn't pushed her to stop stalling 'cause there's nothing she won't do to fuck with me. She's a shit mother, doesn't want to be one, doesn't give a crap about Cul, but out of spite, she'll try to take him from me 'cause she knows fucking with him is the biggest and best way to fuck with me. I didn't want to do anything to make her *even think* about doing that 'cause I *can't* let her take him."

Cullen with a woman who terrified him? God no, no, no. Her heart clenched. She blinked again and again hoping her eyes would dry.

"Don't care about her hurting me, Lex. I care about her hurting Cul…"

He needed to stop, needed to let her go. She didn't want to hear it, didn't want to know. It wouldn't change the fact that he hadn't told her something so important.

His eyes watered, voice heartbreaking when he said, "He doesn't talk."

Oh God. Her throat clogged, stomach rolled. Without blinking, thick tears drifted down her cheeks.

"Not like he should."

She bit her lip, hard.

"He used to say things, used to be vocal like kids are. Sometimes it was words, sometimes it was gibberish, but it was normal. Over time, he just—" He swallowed and shook his head. "—Stopped. I've been taking him to a speech therapist. He won't say anything to him either, but I know in my gut it has something to do with *her*."

Oh God. Thick tears streamed down her cheeks. She swallowed a sob.

She wanted to look away from the anguish in his expression. It broke her heart as sure as it broke his to admit it, but she couldn't. Her eyes on his, she felt it with him and he didn't have to feel it alone, didn't have to fight tears alone. She wanted to give him that at least.

He released her arm and dragged a hand through his hair. "It's my fault. I fucked up. I kept her around hoping she'd change. She never did, never will."

He blamed himself? How could he? She didn't. She couldn't. No one would. He'd done what he'd thought best for his son. She would've done the same.

Pressing the palm of her hand to his stomach, her voice choked up when she said, "It's not your fault."

He cupped her cheeks, wiping her tears with his thumbs. Then he just stared at her, not saying anything, just waiting.

Should she stay or go?

She didn't know. He'd lied and a lie was a lie.

She closed her eyes tightly then parted them and met his. "You should've told me."

He released her and shoved his hands in his pockets. "You're me, would you have?" He shook his head. "Don't know about you, Lex, but for me, these past few weeks have been amazing. You with us… Fuckin' amazing. I've heard Cul say your name more than anything else he's said his whole life. This makes me happy. I get home and see you, and you're happy making us dinner or trying to help me make dinner and making dessert. This makes me happy. We don't do much, and still, we have fun."

He shrugged. "At least, I know Cul and me do. We're happy, with you. There's no fighting, no nagging, no Cul crying his eyes out, or hiding out in his room. Just us having a good time doing nothing big. I tell you Cullen's mother's a bitch who lives to fuck with people, there's a chance you hit the road before we even got a good start 'cause honest to God, Lex, what you saw today is nothing."

He swallowed. "Before I put Cul in daycare, at least three times a week, I'd get home from work and he'd be in his room crying. She'd be in ours with headphones on listening to music. My kid's crying 'cause he's shit or he's wet or hungry, and she's *ignoring* him. Every time I asked her about it, she said that she'd just checked him and he was fine. That shit lasted too long, *months*."

"Stop…" She shut her eyes and shook her head. "Please. Stop."

"You can't handle me telling you this now, how do you think you would've handled knowing this weeks ago before we had anything good?"

He had a point, a good point. Still.

Hands grasping her biceps, he pulled her close and leaned in to her. His body warm, lips an inch away. "Didn't think it mattered, Lex. Technically, I'm married, but her and me have been separated for more than a year. Before that, our marriage wasn't good. It was never good, and everyone in this town knows that."

She nodded.

"What else did she say to you?"

How did he know? Well, she supposed he knew her.

"Gotta tell me, Lex. Gotta give me the chance to explain. Don't let shit eat at you."

She tore her gaze from his, staring down at his chest, and bit the side of her lip. "She wanted to take Cul. I told her if she wanted to see her son, she had to talk to you. She said if she talked to you, you'd go crawling back to her because you always do."

She met his eyes in time to see them flare. Jaw clenched, his whole body strung tight. Looking so angry, he looked scary. He let her go and took two steps away, putting distance between them.

"That's what she does. She fucks with people's lives by lying. She made Em think Rip was fuckin' around on her. Em, pregnant with Bree, leaves Rip. For years, they were apart, years Rip wondered why Em left, years Bree didn't have her father."

Her eyes widened. What? Happy, not-afraid-of-anyone, completely-in-love-with-Ripper Em left him? Because of Lilliam?

"What I told you about her and me isn't even scratching the surface. Ask anyone. Ask everyone."

She didn't want to believe this about Cullen's mother, yet she couldn't deny what she'd seen. What Dodge told her she could easily verify by talking to Em. Besides, he had a point. Some things were not meant to be shared so soon. Unfortunately, she ran into his ex before he'd told her. It didn't make it okay, but it made it explicable. Most importantly, he was right about something else too. The past three weeks had been the absolute best. She was happy too, with them, because of them, and she didn't want to let them go.

The knot in the center of her chest loosened. She parted her mouth to speak but didn't manage it before a knock sounded on the door.

"Fuck."

Dodge sidestepped past her. She turned. He swung the door open a second later, his body relaxing. Lex couldn't see who stood there since Dodge's big frame covered the doorway.

"Hey, Cul. You okay?"

She didn't hear a response. Then again, with Cul, that was never a given. He must be starved though. Past one, they had breakfast at seven.

Moving beside Dodge, she smiled at Cul. "Must be hungry, huh?"

Cullen grinned and nodded.

"Right." Dodge nodded. "Where do you want to eat?"

Brows wrinkling, Cullen looked between the two and shrugged.

"I think I know what my boy wants. Burgers, right?"

Cullen broke out in a smile and nodded.

"And fries?"

Cullen's smile widened, nodding again.

"Give your old man a hug first, and then, we'll go get some grub."

Cullen launched himself at his father, wrapping his arms around him tightly. Dodge returned the hug. One hand stayed on Cullen's back, the other moved through his hair and ended resting on the back of his head. Cullen pulled away to tilt his head back and peer at his father.

"My boy's getting stronger."

Cullen smirked.

"You know I love you, right?"

Her heart clenched in her chest.

Knowing his father said something important, Cullen's smile faded. He nodded.

"More than anything. Before anything and anyone."

Warmth spread through her.

Cullen's big eyes widened and watered before he looked down, pressed his forehead against his father's stomach, and nodded again.

"Right, your old man's done being soft."

Cullen's head shot up, a soft smile spreading across his face. "Lex. Come."

"Don't know if Lex—"

They weren't done talking, but she wanted Dodge to know she made her decision and she did by saying, "I love burgers and fries."

Dodge turned his upper body her way. His eyes softened. Then he grinned a beautiful, lop-sided grin.

****

"Dave…"

Nothing better than when she moaned his name.

Lex arched her back, her tits rubbed against his chest. "Please…"

Fuck that, nothing was better than when she moaned and begged.

Laying over her, he pulled out then slid into her soft, slow.

He liked it fast and hard and rough, but for a while that day, he thought he'd lose her, so he'd take her slow, enjoy her, sear the memory of her in his brain.

"Oh…Please…"

Her legs around his waist tightened. She grinded against him.

Wrong again. That was better. Her moaning, begging, and rubbing against him beat everything.

She tightened her arms around him, digging her nails into his back. "I'm going…"

He knew then she was close, so he gave it to her how she wanted it, how she liked it. Hard, fast, he pounded into her.

It took seconds. Then she was gone, her moans rising, her body shuddering, her pussy milking him. So good, not a moment later, with his hands in her thick hair as he stared at her beautiful face, he blew.

After, he collapsed on top of her. Holding his weight on his elbows, he buried his face in her neck and let the scent of her fill him as her pants at his throat heated him. With her arms around his neck, she squeezed him.

Fucking perfect.

The way she smelled.

The way she felt.

The way she acted like she didn't want to let him go.

"I'm happy too."

He lifted his head and caught her gaze. "Yeah?"

She smiled and nodded. "Yes."

He grinned, thinking maybe he'd been wrong again. Maybe hearing her say that was better than anything else.

"I'm glad, Lex."

He shifted to lay on his back beside her. When she moved, turning to him, he wrapped his arm around her. She rested her head on his shoulder and kicked her leg over his.

"Do you want to go to the beach tomorrow?"

Spending the day with his woman and his kid, Lex in a bikini, soaking up the sun, Cullen playing in the sand while he had a beer?

Nothing better than that.

He angled his head to her. "Fuck, yeah."

She lifted her head, rested her chin against her hand on his chest, and narrowed her eyes. "Must you curse?"

"It was necessary."

"Cursing is never *necessary*."

"It's a form of expression, babe. To show you how much I love the idea of spending the day with my woman and my kid at the beach, I needed to say 'fuck' before I said 'yeah.'"

She stared him down for minutes without saying a word then giggled. He had no idea what she found funny but figured that counted as making her laugh.

He was more than good with that.

Chapter Nineteen

Lex heard the door but wasn't sure if it was part of her dream, so she ignored it.

"Lex?"

She cracked her eyes open.

Cullen, wearing his favorite superhero pajamas, stood just beside the bed. His hair a disheveled mess, big, brown eyes curious and wide staring into hers. She knew why.

Sun shining through the blinds, she lay in bed with his father. Not wanting something like this to happen, she always left before morning. She and Dodge had been dating for three months, but considering Dodge was still married to Lilliam, she thought it was too soon for Cul to find out about them.

She explained this to Dodge and also mentioned that when the time came, Dodge should sit down with his son and explain. Dodge didn't agree. He thought there was no point in telling Cullen something he already knew. Anytime she mentioned it, he repeated the fact that Cullen was not stupid and knew very well they were an item. To her, this was unlikely. Yes, they spent a lot of time together, but Cullen was just three and they were never overtly affectionate in front of Cullen, per her request, one Dodge fought her on. They held hands, something Cullen couldn't have missed, but they didn't kiss though Dodge found times when Cullen wasn't looking to steal kisses, run his hand down her spine and backside, and so on.

Last night, after an activity-filled Saturday and a quickie, she'd dozed off. In fact, she couldn't remember putting on clothes.

Her face flamed. She pressed her hand against her stomach.

Thank God. Cotton, probably one of Dodge's shirts.

Lex sat in bed and looked down. As she'd thought, one of Dodge's many Harley shirts. Her gaze flew to Cullen.

Something was wrong. She'd gotten good at figuring that out by his expression. Right then, he held his hands together in front of him, curiosity in his stare but also a little…fear. Eyes round, brows drawn, frown in place, almost pleading.

She threw her legs off the bed. "Is something wrong, sweetheart?"

He nodded.

"What is it?"

He looked to the bed then met her stare and pointed at her. "Sleep."

Yikes. How badly she wished Dodge had spoken to him about them before then. Both their faults. He didn't think he had to and she thought it was too soon.

"Yes, I slept here with your dad. We're…"

Cullen shook his head. "Bad doream."

She tilted her head to the side. "Oh, you had a bad dream."

He nodded.

Then she assumed aloud, "And when you have a bad dream, you sleep here with your dad?"

He nodded again.

She held out her hand. "Come here. I'll let you sleep with your dad."

He shook his head. "Want you."

Two simple words and an emotion too beautiful to fully express rushed her bringing tears to her eyes. She swallowed and nodded.

He climbed into bed and lay down between Dodge and her. As soon as she did, he circled his arm around her waist, pressed his face against her chest, and burrowed in to her.

She fell asleep with her hand in his messy hair.

****

Where the fuck was Lex? He didn't feel her, which meant she woke in the middle of the night and left. He finally caught her on a night she'd been too tired and took advantage—letting her fall asleep and not waking her. But she must've left. If she were there, she'd be hard-pressed against him.

Shit.

He cracked his eyes open, turned to look at the pillow next to his, and spotted her sound asleep. Facing him, strawberry hair sprawled above her, her arm tight around…

Shit.

Cullen lay beside Lex, facing her. He must've had a bad dream and climbed into bed. Cullen did that on occasion. Dodge didn't mind it. One of the pluses of being a dad and something else he could give his boy so he did. Right then though he couldn't help feeling jealous. His boy chose Lex over him? Then again, he couldn't blame him. He was in Cul's shoes, he would've picked Lex too. So beautiful, those curves, all warm and always smiling.

He grinned. Maybe Lex would stop telling him when the time came, he had to explain shit to Cul. He knew his boy. Cul knew about them, had known for a while.

Slowly, so he wouldn't wake them, he sat up in bed. His old mattress creaked. Cullen turned to him. His eyes open wide like he'd been up for a while. For that, Dodge couldn't blame him either. She smelled nice. He would've stayed in bed too.

He smiled. "Morning, Cul."

Cul grinned.

"Are you gonna get up with your old man, or are you gonna stay in bed with Lex?"

Cul didn't say a word but gave him a look, one that said, "You'd do the same if you were me."

Hell yeah. His son knew him well.

He fought not to laugh. "Come. Let Lex sleep."

Cul shifted away. Amazing, his whole life, Dodge had never seen him do anything so carefully. The kid was all boy, rough and tough. Everything he did, he did with brute force, force that'd surprise anyone a three-year-old had though it was necessary to point out he was big for his age. And yet for Lex, he made an effort proving his boy was a good kid and especially, thoughtful.

He pulled himself out of bed. Cul did too. They exited the room together. He headed straight for the kitchen, coffee on his mind. Cul strode into the living room. No doubt, toys were on his.

****

Slowly, the haze lifted. Lex stretched her arms over her head and parted her eyes. Not her room, not her bed and it was empty, unlike the last time she'd woken.

Sitting up quickly, she hopped off the bed and headed for the bathroom. Since she didn't know how much time she had, she quickly ran her fingers through her hair, rinsed her mouth with Dodge's mouthwash, and patted her cheeks lightly for some color. Striding into the room, she found her clothes and dressed. Once semi-presentable, she walked out, down the hall, and into the living room. Cullen, sitting on the floor playing with a car track, looked up and smiled her way.

"Morning, Cul. How'd you sleep?"

His smile widened.

Not a moment later, a set of arms circled her waist. Dodge buried his face in her neck. His stubble against her skin making her shiver. Then he pressed a wet kiss to her pulse.

Cullen's gaze still on them, so with her smile in place, she whispered, "Dodge."

He chuckled, the warmth of his breaths heating her. "He knows, babe. Told you this." He loosened his hold around her.

She faced him simultaneously putting distance between them. "You should talk to him about it," she whispered. "I know he's smart, but he's just a kid. He must be confused."

Dodge held her stare for a moment.

While he did, she realized something. Cul was his son, not hers. She had no say in how he handled him. When they'd met, Dodge made this clear, something she hadn't thought about while she'd continued to insist he talk to Cullen about them until then.

She took a step back, mumbling, "Sorry—"

He caught her wrists and held her in place. His

brows furrowed. "Sorry?"

"Yes. It's not my place to say—"

Without losing hold of her eyes, he shook his head. "It *is*. You and me, we're together, so it *is* your place to say."

Her chest warmed. "Really?"

Gaze softening, he released one of her wrists to cup her cheek. "Yeah, Lex, really."

God, he trusted her that much? They hadn't been together long. Wasn't it too soon? Her feelings for him had grown exponentially over the course of that short period. In fact, she'd fallen for him but had no idea if he felt the same, so she hadn't said the words.

"That means…" She hesitated trying to find a way to express herself without saying too much. "…So much."

Lame, she knew but hadn't known what else to say.

He grinned. "Hey, Cul?" For a moment longer, he held her stare before looking to Cullen. When he did, she turned and did too. "We gotta talk."

He glided his hand from her wrist to her hand, tugged her toward the couch, and sat. Grabbing her hips, he lugged her to sit beside him and slung his arm around her shoulders, holding her to his side.

No, he couldn't possibly be doing what she thought. She'd advised him to talk to Cul *alone*. Her being there defeated the purpose.

She looked to Dodge and widened her eyes hoping he understood her hint. He saw her look when he glanced in her direction. How could he not when she was burning him with her gaze? But he drew his stare to Cullen, who sat down on the coffee table in front of them.

“You know your mother and me aren’t together anymore.”

Cullen nodded.

“We’re not getting back together. We’ve been separated for a while ’cause we’re getting divorced meaning we won’t be married anymore.”

Cullen nodded.

“I’m with Lex now.”

Cullen slid his gaze to her.

Face flaming, she fought not to shrink under the scrutiny of those big, brown eyes.

A moment later, a smile spread across Cullen’s lips. Then he shifted his attention to his father.

She expelled a breath.

“You understand what I said?”

Cullen nodded.

“Are you okay with this?”

Cullen’s smile widened. He nodded again.

“Good. Breakfast’ll be ready in a few. Today, we got the cookout, yeah?”

Cullen nodded, stood, and strode to his toys.

Dodge grabbed her hand and tugged her up. He then proceeded to drag her to the kitchen.

To his back, she whispered, “I meant you should talk to him alone.”

Turning, he lifted a brow. “Why?”

“Because if I’m there, he may not be honest with you if, let’s say, he has concerns about us or doesn’t like me.”

He threw his head back and laughed.

She narrowed her eyes. “May I ask what you find amusing?”

“Lex, you shitting me?”

"My pants are on and I'm not squatting over you, so no."

His smile died, gaze heated.

That look, she knew what it meant and when he gave it to her, it made her want him too. Still, how could discussing feces turn him on?

Her lips parted.

His jaw clenched, stare raking her from top to bottom. "Picturing you with your pants down does the trick, Lex."

Her breaths grew shallow. He didn't miss it. The heat in his eyes intensified. In that instant, he knew she wanted him as badly as he wanted her. Not a thing they could do about it then.

His stare slid to her lips. He leaned in.

Planting her hands on his chest, she stopped him from nearing. "Let's get back to the topic at hand."

He leaned farther and claimed her mouth, taking what he wanted. She gave in wholeheartedly. In the back of her mind, she had a good reason why she shouldn't have, but she couldn't remember it then.

When he drew away, he smirked. "I laughed 'cause it's hilarious you'd think for a second Cul doesn't like you, that he'd have any *concerns* about you, about us."

He cocked his head. "He may not say much, Lex, but he does a lot. He always has. Even as a baby, he wouldn't stop. Never in my life had I seen him sit down and listen to anyone read him a book for longer than a couple of minutes. He's a boy. He plays rough, does everything with force, yet getting out of bed this morning, no one would've guessed it 'cause he did it so carefully and slowly just so he wouldn't wake you. He's not much for hugging his old man either, but every time he sees you, he rushes in for a hug, and he talks more around you than anyone else."

He shook his head. "So I don't need him to tell me he likes you, Lex. I know he fuckin' *loves* you."

Her throat clogged. "He told me he sleeps with you when he has bad dreams."

A soft look came over his face. "Yeah, he does that. One of the best parts about being his dad is that right there. When he does shit like that, since he doesn't often, not to anyone except you, you appreciate every minute of it."

Now, she had no idea what to say. Did he mind Cullen was more affectionate with her than him? She wouldn't hold it against him if he did. Maybe because they were both the same sex, Cullen wasn't affectionate with him as often. Still, if she had a daughter, she'd want her daughter to be affectionate with her.

He cupped her cheek and glided his thumb across her bottom lip. "I'm glad you're you, Lex."

That said it all.

It also melted her heart.

Chapter Twenty

Lex laughed, loud. As she did, she wondered about the biker called Trick.

She, Dodge, and Cullen arrived at the compound an hour ago for the club cookout. She'd been slightly nervous. Granted, she'd been to a club cookout before, but she still didn't know much about bikers and the club though Dodge had told her the club was not involved in anything illegal.

The minute they strode into the backlot, Dodge headed for the grill, his turn to cook. Lucky for her, she caught sight of Allie and Tina, Della's mother, near the playground and headed for them. Cullen dashed to the monkey bars. Not ten minutes went by, Della spilled soda on herself. Both Allie and Tina went inside with her to find her a suitable shirt. Still early, none of the other old ladies had arrived. She sat at a picnic table alone watching Cullen play for ten minutes before Trick, whom she'd met the first time she went to the garage, approached her with a couple of beers in hand and made conversation. She didn't drink beer, not ever, but she took sips of the one he brought her and thanked him. The conversation consisted mostly of him talking.

Trick was younger than her, mid-twenties, dark, longish, curly hair tied in a ponytail at the base of his neck. His eyes dark, like Dodge's, like Cullen's but not as expressive. From what she'd seen for the past fifteen minutes, they'd only shown her a couple of expressions: humor and mischief.

A talker or better said, a storyteller, he told stories in a way she felt like she'd been there too. Quite a gift. It didn't hurt he was funny, and his stories were hilarious. She found herself relaxing.

A biker, an amusing one, and he seemed like a nice guy who'd gone out of his way to talk to her and keep her company. It made her think the rest of the members of Hell Ryders could be just as nice or funny. She relaxed further, that nervous energy finally fading.

As she took another sip of beer, Trick grabbed his and stood. "See your new crew's here, so I'll leave you be." He lifted his chin behind her.

She looked over her shoulder catching sight of Lynn, Mia, and Em.

"Nice talking to you, Lex, though I guess you didn't do any talking, only laughing."

She smiled. "Thanks for the laughs."

He nodded and strode toward the compound.

Em, Lynn, and Mia joined her, Mia and Lynn sitting across from her and Em. Immediately, they started making plans for another girls' night.

"It needs to be somewhere we won't get caught." Mia took a deep pull of beer. "Out of Wadden. Anywhere."

"If we don't want to get caught, we should have girls' night at one of our houses. You know, make what we tell our men the truth."

Mia's eyes nearly popped out of their sockets. "That takes the whole fun out of it."

Lynn shook her head.

Em shrugged and smiled. "Mia has a point."

Lynn and Mia's gazes lifted. Then Mia's brows furrowed. Lynn's eyes widened.

"What. The. Fuck?" A half growl, half yell.

That voice, one she knew.

She twisted her head, snapped it up, and met his eyes. The man standing there, she knew too, intimately, but then and there, he was a stranger.

Angry. No, beyond it, and the fury transformed *him*, made him someone she didn't know. Body stiff and tense, demeanor and manner hard. Brows scrunched tight, cheeks covered in stubble flamed, lips thinned, jaw clenched.

Her mouth parted as her heart pounded furiously inside her chest. Dumbfounded, not knowing why he was incensed and why he'd aimed that rage at her, she didn't say anything.

They hadn't been there more than an hour. During that hour, she'd sat in the same spot watching Cullen and socializing.

The last few months had been almost perfect. They grew closer, comfortable with each other. They were good. No, great. Twice, they'd been to the beach. Once, they drove to San Francisco to visit her sister and Tim. Since the day she ran into Cullen's mother, they hadn't fought, argued, or had a misunderstanding.

Yet there he stood, that narrowed gaze pinning her while he yelled at her in front of her friends, in front of his brothers.

"You talk to me when I'm fuckin' talking to you."

She jolted, pressed the palm of her hand to her stomach, and shifted in her seat so she fully faced him. Taking a moment to recover, she kept her voice low. "What's wrong?"

His eyes turned to slits. “I asked you a question.”

What had he asked? She couldn’t remember.

She swallowed. “Just calm down—”

“*Fuck. Calm.* Answer the fuckin’ question.”

She felt the heat of everyone’s eyes on them, felt her face flame. Still, she hesitated trying to find a way to calm him. Maybe because she was so shocked and confused. Maybe because she wanted to salvage what they had.

She released a ragged breath before she pressed the palms of her shaking hands against her thighs and stood. “I don’t know why you’re mad, but we can talk about this in private—”

He leaned in, forcing her to tilt back. Then he reached behind her, grabbed a bottle, and launched it. She didn’t see what it hit but heard it shatter. Her nerves wound tight, the sound made her flinch.

Still, she didn’t lose hold of his eyes. She held them in complete disbelief and scared. *He* terrified *her*, the same man who a couple of hours ago cupped her cheek so tenderly and melted her heart. She had to get away. Taking a step behind her, she bumped in to the bench.

He took a step forward and leaned in to her, so his hard eyes were all she saw. “You gonna fuckin’ answer me?”

“I don’t know—”

“No!”

She angled her head to the sound. Cullen, chin lifted defiantly, pushed his way between his father and her, making Dodge take several steps backward.

So many people around and the one who stood up for her—a three-year-old? Not that she blamed anyone for minding their business, getting in the middle of a couple's argument was asking for trouble. Still, Cullen was just a boy, and he felt the *need* to protect *her*.

Her chest compressed, the ache it caused, crippling. A rush of emotion clogged her throat. In that single moment that seemed suspended in time, the magnitude of the love she had for Cullen slammed in to her.

Dodge's jaw twitched. He slanted his head, eyes shooting to Cullen. "Inside."

Cullen didn't move, not a muscle. As seconds ticked, the look on Dodge's face grew more furious, a rage she wouldn't let him unleash on Cul.

She planted a hand on Cul's shoulder. Hesitantly, as if he didn't want to lose sight of his father, he angled his head to meet her stare.

"Sweetheart, I'm okay. Go inside. I'll see you after I'm done talking to your dad, okay?"

He scanned her face.

"I'm fine. I'll be in soon."

Lynn stepped forward, standing to her left, and grabbed hold of Cullen's hand. "Cul, come on. Let's go."

Finally, Cullen nodded. He also glared at his father but then strode toward the compound with Lynn. Once the door into the compound shut behind Lynn and Cullen, Dodge spoke again.

"And now, you're turning my kid against me. Fucking fantastic. I think I finally found a good woman and she's a manipulative, loose bitch like the rest of them."

Audible gasps sounded.

Her jaw dropped. Heart squeezed; pain radiated out

of her chest to her limbs leaving no part unmarked.

Head spinning, it hit her she didn't recognize this man because she *didn't know* this man. She fooled herself thinking she did. Exceptionally stupid and reckless considering after three years, she hadn't known Mitchell. Further, she knew Dodge could be harsh, and still, she let herself believe. Worst judgment call she'd made in her life, and yet, she didn't regret it because of Cullen, the beautiful boy she loved who'd stood up to his jerk father to defend her.

She was any other woman, she'd lose her cool and create a bigger scene than Dodge had. He deserved worse, but she was smart enough to know if she responded now, even if to defend herself, he'd hurl more undeserving, hurtful insults her way. She knew when to cut her losses and it was time to do that.

"I should go," she said, surprising herself with how strong her voice sounded. She hoped and prayed it'd stay that way until alone.

"I'll drive you."

A hand grasped her elbow. Lex shifted looking to her right. Em stood there glaring at Dodge. Mia stood to Em's other side. She, too, shooting daggers his way.

A small weight lifted. At least, she'd made friends, good friends she wouldn't lose.

She released a breath. "Thanks, Em. I appreciate it."

"Just like that? You're gonna fuckin' go?"

She snapped her head his way. For a single moment, she let herself feel a little bit of anger so she could say what she had to without bursting in to tears. "You've made your opinion of me clear."

She scanned the lot. She'd felt their eyes, but now,

she knew everyone was looking their way. Then she met his stare. "To *everyone*. I don't know what you expect me to do."

With those last words, she sidestepped him and walked away. She didn't look back, not once.

The moment she opened the door leading into the compound, Cullen's body slammed in to her. Instantly, she snaked her arms around him. When she drew away, she knelt in front of him and clasped his hands in hers. "You and I will *always* be friends, Cul."

She didn't have to say that his father and she were over, but Cullen understood.

His chest rose and fell quickly. Then his chin trembled, and his beautiful, dark eyes watered.

Mind-numbing.

Heartbreaking.

Gut-wrenching.

She released his hands to cup his face. "Always, Cul. We're neighbors and friends. Anytime you like, you can come over, and I'll make you cookies and read to you, okay?"

A tear slipped out and skidded down his face.

She wiped it away, threaded her fingers through his thick hair, leaned in, and pressed a kiss to his forehead. "Love you, Cul. *Always*."

To her disbelief, he whispered, "L-love you."

She held his gaze, forced a smile, and prayed with every ounce of hope, she wouldn't lose him. Heart pounding, eyes searing, anguish slicing her insides apart, she walked away from him.

It was the hardest thing she'd ever had to do.

****

Lex pushed open the door to her house after a

mostly quiet car ride. Mostly because Em tried to advise her, tried to get her to talk, and offered to be there if she needed to vent. Lex liked Em, liked the old ladies and wanted to keep them as friends, but she wanted them to know too, and made it clear to Em, that she and Dodge were over. After, she thanked Em, offered her a smile, one she knew was sad, stepped out of the car, and walked onto her porch.

Inside her home, she locked the door, leaned against it, and stared blankly at her hardwood floors thinking she was glad she hadn't started demo on her pink bathroom. She spent so much time with Dodge and Cullen, she hadn't put time in to deciding on a contractor. The bathroom was untouched and dated, but as a working bathroom, she'd sell her home much faster.

She hated to move but didn't think she had another choice. No way she'd let him continue to demean her and no doubt with her living across the street, he'd do that every chance he had.

Hurt, hopeless, and humiliated, a rush of emotion overwhelmed her. She held her own for as long as she could, refusing to blink until she couldn't see through the tears welling her eyes. After that first wave, no stopping them. The dam broke.

Lex didn't let herself cry for long. She wiped her face, packed a bag, and drove, having no idea where she'd go but knowing she had to get away.

Chapter Twenty-One

Dodge watched Lex walk away until she was out of sight. Then he dropped his head, kicked a rock, and ran his hands through his hair. Heart pounding loud and hard against his ribs, body vibrating, he stood frozen staring at the ground, feeling the heat of everyone's eyes, not giving a fuck about anything except his kid who was no doubt devastated by the turn of events.

Lifting his head, he caught Mia's glare. He clenched his jaw and without thinking better of it, barked, "You got something to say, say it."

Mia took two steps toward him. "I don't think anyone needs to tell you what you did to Lex is fucked."

"That's none of your fuckin' business, Mia."

She quirked a brow. "*You* made it everyone's business, Dodge."

Fuck women. They only saw what they wanted to see.

"*She* made it everyone's business."

Mia crossed her arms over her chest.

He cocked his head and quirked a brow. "Missed that?" Clamping his jaw shut, he then spit, "Ask. Trick."

"You gettin' in my woman's face?"

He twisted his upper body and caught Stone's hard gaze.

No one fucked with Mia; her old man defended her no matter what. Considering Mia always had something to say, Stone stepped in a lot.

He fisted his hands, his nails bit into his palms. "No, brother, your woman's getting in mine." Then because he didn't need any more problems, he walked away.

Dodge entered the compound with one thought on his mind, his boy. He combed the place, yelling Cullen's name. It took a while, a good fifteen minutes before he found him and only because of Lynn, who'd told him Cul was hiding under the desk in the surveillance room, a room Cul knew he shouldn't be in.

Dodge strode inside. His gaze, not on the desk, series of monitors, computer, chair, but on his kid. Cul had his thighs pressed to his chest, arms wrapped around his legs, and his head bent and resting on his knees.

He closed the distance between them and squatted. "I know you're upset, but we're gonna be fine, yeah?"

Cullen didn't look up, didn't respond.

"Dodge."

He looked over his shoulder.

Trick, the last brother he wanted to see, stood at the entrance to the room. "Gotta talk."

He closed his eyes and grinded his teeth. "I'm busy." He shifted back toward Cul, but before he made it, he heard Trick again.

"Can't wait."

Turning back around, he glared.

Trick took this as a chance to explain. "You told Mia I had something to do with you getting pissed at Lex?"

The brother had the nerve to play it like nothing happened? Lex was beautiful, but was she worth losing his brother, his club?

Dodge's jaw went hard. He stood, fully turned to Trick, and strode toward him. Trick moved but not fast enough. Dodge bumped in to his shoulder on his way out. When he heard the door close, he faced him.

Trick raised his hands, palms out. "You gotta problem—"

"Nope." He jerked his head side to side. "I don't gotta problem 'cause I just got rid of *my* problem. She's free now to be yours."

Trick, eyes widening, dropped his hands and reared back. "What the *fuck*?"

He clenched his jaw so hard it ached. "I saw you, *brother*. I saw you with *her*."

"A lot of people saw us seeing as we were sitting at a picnic table outside. Yet you're pissed saying you and Lex are over, and Mia's all up in my shit saying I had something to do with it. I got no clue what's going on, but I hear you and Lex have been spending a lot of time together and that you and Cul are happy, so I'm asking again, what the fuck I gotta do with this shit?"

Trick took a step in his direction. "You wanted shot of her, and you're using me as an excuse? I got your back, brother, like always, but you gotta let me in on that so I don't look like it's news to me when Mia and the rest of the old ladies come asking."

He took a menacing step. "This isn't a joke, Trick. This is *my* life—"

Trick shook his head. "You saw us *talking*. She was sitting alone looking tense. I get that and I get why. I knew you were busy at the grill. I thought I'd do you a solid and make her feel welcome. I went over to her with a beer, told her some stories so she'd loosen up, relax, and hopefully realize we're all just people despite the cuts. That's all I did, talk. She barely said a word."

Trick shrugged. "I did something else, you tell me now."

His gut clenched. "She was…"

Trick lifted a brow. "She was?"

He swallowed. "Laughing…and I—" It'd pissed him off, bad, and he'd reacted the worst possible way, but all she'd done was laugh. He just assumed.

Shit.

His face flamed, stomach rolled.

Trick shook his head. "We were just talking. She wasn't flirting or anything like that, brother. Honest."

He dropped his head and dragged a hand through his hair, swallowing the bile rising in the back of his throat. "I know."

Then and there, he did. Lex wasn't that type of woman. He'd just gotten so jealous. That jealousy quickly turned to something else—anger so much of it, he hadn't been able to think straight. He'd never felt that in his life and he never imagined he'd feel it because of a woman.

"I just fuckin' lost it."

"She isn't Lilliam. You know that, right?"

He nodded. "Lilliam deserved it and *never*, not once did I lose my shit with her. I lost it with her for other reasons but not for this." He shook his head. "With Lex, no reason to and I fuckin' lost it."

"'Cause you care."

Obvious. Still, he found the need to point out, "I cared about Lilliam too."

"You cared 'cause she's the mother of your kid, and you didn't want your kid seeing her being a tap, but you didn't care about her."

Trick made a point, and yet, Trick didn't know Lilliam like he did. Even when she got what she wanted—married him, a brother—she never gave him anything to like. He tried to make it work, tried to make her happy. She just wasn't. He couldn't do anything right, ever. She was manipulative and cruel too. No other way to explain why she didn't give a shit about their boy, why she got off on hitting on his brothers in front of him. By the point she started doing it, he knew nothing he did or said would make her stop, make her change, make her give three fucks about him, but he kept her around because he wanted his boy to have his mother, because he prayed she'd wake up one day and give a shit about Cullen.

Yet Lex wasn't Lilliam. He hadn't known her long, but he knew this.

The magnitude of how bad he messed up hit him full-force. Shit feeling knowing he'd fucked up something good. Worse, knowing he hurt someone he cared about for no reason.

He had to fix it. He just didn't know if he could. The deed was done. He had a kid and a nasty soon-to-be ex-wife, and what he'd done was fucked. Lex cared about him. He knew that, but they'd been dating for a few months. They were at a point where it could easily end, and both of them could go their separate ways. Besides, a beautiful woman like her could have any man she wanted. How to convince her to forgive him and give him another shot?

He had no clue, but he had to try.

He sidestepped past Trick, strode into the room, and crouched at the desk in front of Cullen. His boy hadn't moved.

"I fucked up, Cul, with Lex, with you too."

Cullen's head snapped up. When he met his red-eyed gaze, Dodge swore his heart split in two.

He extended his hand, reaching for his boy. Cul flinched away, stopping him in his tracks. It hurt, but he didn't let it show. He did there was a chance Cul would feel bad about it, and he didn't want that. He deserved it anyway.

"I'm gonna fix it. I promise you I won't let you lose Lex."

Looking away, he released a pained breath before he once again met his eyes. "I'm proud of you, Cul. I always am, but today, I'm prouder than I've ever been 'cause you stood up for someone you love and took care of her. That makes a good man a great one. You aren't a man yet just a kid, but one day you'll be one. It's good you start learning now."

Cullen's face softened, not much, but enough Dodge knew his son understood.

He stood, turned, exited the room, and found Lynn standing just outside.

She bit the side of her lip. "Is he okay?"

"He will be. Gotta ask—"

She smiled. "Don't worry, go. I'll watch Cul."

He nodded, thanked her, hopped in his SUV, and headed for Lex's house. He hadn't been slow about it either, but when he arrived, she was gone. Only one place she'd go.

An hour later, he checked parking spaces outside her sister's townhouse in San Francisco. Lex's car wasn't there meaning she wasn't either, but he had a feeling she'd show eventually because Lex and her sister were tight, so he parallel parked at the end of the block and waited.

The first hour flew by, thinking about what he'd say and how he'd say it. By the end of the second hour, he was out of sorts, a mess of nerves and truth be told, worried. She wasn't home or at her sister's, and he had no clue where she could've gone. He hadn't bothered to call her because he didn't think she'd answer. As he thought this, he spotted her car turning onto the street. He watched her parallel park, exit her car, duffle bag and purse in hand, and watched her go inside her sister's place. Then he forced himself to wait a full ten minutes before he followed.

Taking a deep breath, he knocked.

The door parted.

Face blotchy, eyes swollen and red, makeup smeared, and still, she looked stunning.

His stomach soured.

Her eyes widened then narrowed. "W-what are you doing here?"

"You weren't home. Figured you were with your sister."

She crossed her arms over her chest. "Right. It doesn't matter—"

"I need to talk to you."

"You did plenty of talking earlier."

He had, and she hadn't said a word, not even to defend herself. The shame of what he'd done choked him, but the need to fix what he'd destroyed overrode it.

"I fucked up. I know I did. Just let me make it up to

you—"

"No."

He'd been so sure she'd hear him out. Maybe that's really what he'd been doing those hours he'd waited, convincing himself she'd listen, that she'd forgive him.

He squeezed his eyes shut then parted them. "You're not even gonna let me explain?"

"What difference would it make?"

"We've had months of happy, Lex. Don't know about you, but I've had months of *perfect* and I've never treated you like that, never wanted to, never even dreamed of it. Don't you want to know why?"

It'd buy him time, he hoped.

After a long pause, she released a breath. "Fine. Explain."

He looked around. "Out here?"

She nodded.

She'd listen, but she'd made up her mind. She was done with him, with them. He'd had a chance, she would've let him in. He knew this because he knew her. She liked her privacy, and right then, she didn't care about making a scene because in her mind, after that day, he'd never show there again.

No choice, he *had* to convince her, an added pressure he didn't need.

Heart racing, he swallowed thickly. "I'm sorry. I was out of line. It's not your fault. You didn't do anything wrong, but I saw you with Trick. He was talking, and you were laughing a lot and…" He shook his head. "I got jealous, and I fuckin' lost it."

She let her head fall slightly, gaze drifting behind him. Her expression softened so subtlety if he hadn't known her well, he would've missed it.

His chance, the one he needed to break through.

"Cullen's mother came on to my brothers. She did it all the time and she did it to rile me. It never worked 'cause I didn't care. That's not what you did, but 'cause it's you, 'cause I care about you, I got jealous and pissed."

Her stare shot to his and narrowed. "So you're saying that technically, this isn't your fault because the woman you impregnated and married flirted with your friends to get your attention because she knew you didn't care about her?"

"I—"

She tilted her head. "This is supposed to make me feel better?"

"I'm trying to explain why I acted—"

"Like an asshole?"

He reared back. She never cussed. He did a lot and on a weekly basis, she explained why he shouldn't.

"Except your explanation makes you look like a bigger *asshole*. The poor woman you knocked up and married, just so you could say you did the right thing, knew you didn't care about her, so she flirted with your friends to get you to show her some kind of emotion, some kind of affection. If she went to those lengths, I can only sympathize with *her.*"

That sounded fucked. Had she twisted it? Kind of because Lilliam did more than flirt, and Lilliam didn't want him to care about her. She just wanted to fuck with him because she lived to fuck with people.

"You don't know the whole story. I can explain—"

"I know she's a bitch now. I know she doesn't care about her son. She never sees Cullen and the last time she saw him, she terrified him. But I also know there're two sides to every story. From the bits and pieces you've told me, I see faults with both."

That didn't mean his wasn't the right one.

He shook his head and repeated, "Lex, you don't know the whole story. I can explain. I promise—"

"You're right. I don't. I also don't care to know it either. You *humiliated* me in front of your *brothers*, in front of the few *friends* I managed to make for *no reason*. I can say this since you were upset about something your *wife* did and not me. By doing this, you forced me to walk away from Cullen who was in tears. A million apologies couldn't repair what you did to me because not everything can be mended with apologies."

His chest clenched. Pain radiated out of his middle and spread.

No, that he couldn't accept. There had to be a way to get her back.

She shook her head. "Besides, you're a grown man. There's no changing a grown man. If I forgave you, what you did to me today would just be the beginning."

He shook his head. "No, Lex, I—"

"This is it for me and you. I ask that you keep your word and let me see Cullen because I, for one, do *not* want to lose him."

Dead serious, there'd be no convincing her. He just couldn't accept it. The pain burning his insides wouldn't let him let her go.

He took a step toward her, cupped her cheek, snaked an arm around her waist, hauled her against him, and held her there. Her ice blue eyes widened. She planted her hands against his chest and pushed.

He leaned in to her, grazing his lips against hers. Then he drew away just enough to meet her eyes. "*You* and *me* aren't done, Lex. We're just beginning. I'm gonna give you space. Then we're gonna sit down and talk. I'll explain everything to you. After, you're gonna kiss me, and then, you're gonna fuck me."

Her breath hitched.

He let her go, turned, and walked away.

Nursing the ache in the center of his chest, Dodge drove home thinking about her and the vow he made. He'd give her two weeks tops because he didn't think he could go more.

Chapter Twenty-Two

On his living room couch, Dodge sat with Lex, one arm slung around her shoulders, another on her thigh. She shifted, throwing a leg over and straddling him. Grinning, he cupped her ass and inhaled. Smelling her perfume, he slid a hand up her spine. Chest pressed to his, she hooked her arms around his shoulders and buried her face in his neck.

With her beautifully thick hair in his face and her lips against his pulse, she whispered, "Missed you so much."

His arms, snug around her waist, tightened on instinct. "Not letting you go again, Lex. Not ever."

She giggled, lifted her head, and met his stare. When she did, her smile died, yet her expression softened. "Do you love me, Dave?"

He grinned. "You know how I feel about you."

She smiled.

"Do you love me, Lex?"

Her eyes watered. Before she responded, she faded away.

****

His eyes snapped open with a start.

Shit. Same dream. Now three times in one week. More like a nightmare, every time he woke before she said the words. He didn't know if he loved her, but he wanted her to love him.

Since their fight, he'd barely seen her. He kept his word, giving her space, letting Cul go to her house whenever he wanted, almost as if they shared custody. A drastic change from before, and he hated every second of it.

He'd been counting down. In four days, he'd walk across the street and convince her to give him another shot. He didn't know exactly what he'd say, but he wasn't worried about that, not yet since he still had several days to think on it.

Lying on his back, he caught sight of the red and blue lights flashing through the blinds illuminating his dark room.

Peering at his nightstand, he spotted his alarm clock, two a.m. He sat up in bed, strode to his window, and parted the blinds.

Cops.

Across the street.

At Lex's.

His stomach knotted.

He rushed into Cul's room, wrapped an arm under his butt, another around his neck, lifted him, and draped him across his chest. In the living room, he grabbed his keys, unlocked the door, and walked out. Crossing the street and rounding the police cruiser, he spotted her standing in front of two cops.

Wearing a robe and slippers, face fresh and makeup less, her hair loose looking like she'd styled it even though he knew she must've just woken. Stunning, yet within all that beauty, he saw it. Eyes guarded, hands clasped together yet unsteady.

Her head came up. Her eyes met his and widened.

The uniformed cops, backs to Dodge, turned and

faced him. One of them, the taller of the two, late twenties with a crew cut held his hand up, stopping him from nearing. “Can I help you?”

Dodge sliced his gaze to him. “Yeah, you can let me get to my woman.”

The cop faced Lex for confirmation.

Lex spared a glance at the cop, met Dodge’s gaze, and whispered, “What’re you doing here?”

“You okay?” He asked though he knew the answer. She wasn’t. Far from it.

“I’m fine.”

She lied and she knew he knew she had. He saw it on her face. He also knew she expected what he did next.

Not knowing what she’d do when he reached her or if she’d push him away, he closed the distance between them. A step away, she pressed her cold hand to his bare stomach. Because of that simple, possibly insignificant touch, he did what came natural.

He wrapped his empty arm around her back and brought her close. With her face planted on his chest and her body against his, he trailed his hand up her back until he buried it in her hair. Then he pressed a kiss to the top of her head. “You’re not.”

She shook her head.

“What happened?”

Pulling away, she slanted her head to meet his eyes. “My back door… There was a loud crash. I—”

He squeezed the back of her neck. “Someone came in?”

She shook her head. “Just a rock.”

“Do you know anyone who’d do something like this?”

Dodge turned to face the cop who spoke, the shorter of the two, his nameplate read, Marks. Lex shifted too. He kept his arm around her, tucking her against his side.

"No."

"It was intentional, Miss Millen. Now, we need to determine if it was a random act or if whoever did this has a vendetta against you?"

"No." She shook her head. "No one would want to scare me or…"

The way her voice trailed off made Dodge angle his head down and to his side to look at her, but he couldn't read the expression on her face.

She lifted her head, stare seeking and finding his. "You should put Cul down. He needs his rest."

He cocked his head. "You gonna tell me what you just realized when I get back."

Her gaze fell. She hadn't planned to, and now, she was thinking whether she should. When her stare met his again, she nodded a firm nod. She might still be pissed at him, but she wouldn't lie.

He clutched her lightly before he released her, rushed across the street, and lay Cul in bed. When he tucked him in tightly, Cul mumbled incoherently but didn't wake. Dodge hadn't expected him to. His boy had always been a heavy sleeper.

On his way out, he grabbed the sound monitor and buried it in his pocket. Back outside and nearing Lex and the cops, he heard the taller cop ask, "How many calls?"

She shrugged. "A couple a day for a week."

Shit. Not good. Someone was fucking with her, with *his* Lex.

Ignoring the bile rising in the back of his throat, Dodge wrapped an arm around her and brought her close. Her front plastered against his side, she spared a glance at him then met the taller cop's gaze. Dodge took that chance to glance at his name, Johnson.

"Anyone you can think of who'd do this to you?"

She hesitated and shook her head. "No. I don't—"

"Her ex."

She jerked against him, angling her head to his face.

He met her gaze for a split second then peered at the cops. "They've been off for a while, but he wants her back. A few months ago, he came by. When he didn't get the welcome he wanted, I stepped in."

Johnson's eyes narrowed. "Meaning."

"Meaning I pulled him away and told him to get lost."

The shorter cop shifted his feet. "So there wasn't a physical altercation?"

"She told him to get lost. He didn't and thought he'd grab her to make his point. I saw it, stepped in, pulled him away then told him to get lost. It didn't get more physical than that."

She shook her head. "I don't think he had anything to do with this."

All gazes turned to Lex.

He tightened his arm around her, pressing her snugger against him, and cupped her cheek with his other hand. "Think he would, Lex."

"I've known him a long time. He isn't the type."

He cocked his head. "You know the type?"

He didn't think she did, but if she did, he wanted to know who and when.

"No, but I know the type of man he is. If something becomes too hard, he walks away. You stepped in, and he walked away. He hasn't even called."

A fucking idiot. A man had Lex, he did everything and anything to keep her. Dodge fucked it up too but not because he wanted anyone else, and he wouldn't stop trying to win her back.

He released her cheek and looked to the cops. "Everyone likes Lex. He's the only one with motive."

"His name," Marks asked.

"Mitchell Adam Upton. He's 32, lives in San Francisco." She then recited his phone number by heart.

Dodge's arm around her involuntarily tautened. He thought it'd been subtle, but Johnson's stare trailed to his arm then shot to his face.

"If you think of anyone else, please give me a call Miss Millen." Marks handed her a card. "You should stay somewhere else until you repair that door, and you should think about getting an alarm." The cop turned, headed for his car.

Johnson handed Lex a card and held her eyes for a moment before he, too, walked away.

When they climbed into their patrol car, Dodge hauled her to his chest. "Let's get your stuff. You're staying with us tonight."

He thought for sure she'd argue. He'd fight back. No way he'd let her stay alone. But she didn't, and he knew she hadn't forgiven him because just the day before, she couldn't even look at him. Her not fighting meant she was terrified. Shit circumstance but it was a chance, so he'd take it.

Grabbing her hand, he strode toward her house, entering first. He caught sight of the mess in her living room, mostly shattered glass and the rock that did the damage. He asked her to wait while he checked the house front to back.

Spotting some large boxes in the garage, he carried them inside, placed them in front of the broken door, blocking entry. She followed him as he did this, insisting she help. He refused. After, he moved her beige couch in front of the boxes to hold them in place. It wouldn't keep anyone out, not like a door, but at least her house wouldn't be open to the elements.

He then grabbed her hand and strode to the mouth of the hall leading to the bedrooms. "I'll board that up for you tomorrow. Get what you need and anything valuable you have too."

She nodded and dropped her head slightly, looking behind him. "Can you…come with me?" Her voice quaked, asking like it pained her to. Because she had to ask him or because she hated to ask anyone, he didn't know.

He went without a word. Reaching her door, he stopped, waited, and watched while she packed. When she finished, he took the duffle bag from her, grabbed her hand, walked her out of her house, locked the door, and crossed the street to his.

He pulled her inside, not letting her think twice about it, locked the front door, and headed down the hall. He stopped by Cul's room and found him asleep like he expected since he hadn't heard a sound through the monitor. He then strode to his room. Once inside, he dropped Lex's bag on the floor and led her to bed.

"Take the bed. I'll sleep on the couch."

He went to turn but didn't make it halfway around before she gripped his hand. He stilled and faced her.

"Don't go," she whispered. Setting her other hand on his stomach, she leaned up to him.

It wasn't right. She was vulnerable. Scared and shaken, she wasn't thinking straight, but fuck, she initiated it. It made him a dick, but it had been more than a week without her lips, her smile, *her*, so he couldn't fight the pull.

He leaned down just enough so she reached him. The instant he did, her arm hooked around his neck, and she pressed her lips to his.

The sweetest kiss. He'd never been kissed like that, never kissed anyone like that, but he took what she gave him and gave it back.

He didn't want to pull away, let go, but he knew he kept at it, he'd take them all the way and that was not just wrong but fucked. She'd wake up regretting what they did, hating herself and him too.

He thought it'd be harder to tear himself away, but remembering she wasn't herself, he managed it. Still, so close, he could taste her.

Her ice blue eyes watered. "Stay with me."

For the same reasons, he shouldn't, but like with the kiss, he couldn't say no.

He nodded and watched as she removed her robe leaving her in a nighty and lay in bed on her back. He walked around the bed, set the sound monitor on the nightstand, and laid beside her, thinking he wouldn't get a wink of sleep with her so close.

She shifted to face him. "Someone's been calling me."

He knew this. Still, it comforted him she said it directly to him.

He looked at her but didn't shift because he wasn't

sure he could stop himself from reaching for her. "When it start?"

"A week ago."

He nodded. "You don't know anyone it could be?"

"No."

"I know it's hard, but you gotta trust that we're gonna find who's doing this and stop it."

Her brows creased. "You mean the police?"

No, he didn't. He meant the club, but he couldn't get in to it then. It was late, and most importantly, it was club business, and she wasn't his. He didn't want to answer and lie, so he did something else.

Lifting himself slightly, he grabbed the back of her head, leaned toward her, and pressed a kiss to her forehead. "Night, Lex."

She wrapped her arm around his waist. When he settled on his back, she moved to him, tucking her body against his and resting her head on his shoulder. "Missed you so much."

A weight lifted. He couldn't have helped himself then. He faced her, snaked his arm around her waist, and tucked her against him. Then staring straight into her eyes in his dark room, lying in his bed, he vowed silently, "*Not letting you go again, Lex. Not ever.*"

Just like his dream.

He held her close, half asleep himself when he heard, "I love you, Dodge."

A beautiful ache sliced through his gut, up his chest, and settled in the back of his throat. He couldn't believe it, so he drew away slightly and scanned her face.

Eyes closed, a soft smile on her lips. Asleep, but she said it.

He leaned in, grinned against her hair, and muttered, "Fuck, Lex." He kept that smile in place while he drew away and closed his eyes. In no time, he fell asleep.

Chapter Twenty-Three

The bed creaked. Her bed never squeaked, so she cracked open her eyes and spotted him. Cullen sat on the edge of the bed, his hair a beautiful mess.

He grinned wide. “Lex.”

It took her a few seconds, but she realized where she was and why. All of that explained why Cul would be there too.

Looking at his sweet face, the magnitude of the mistake she made hit her full force, a mistake that’d hurt him the most. She had no clue how to fix it, but for the moment, it could wait.

“Did you have a bad dream, sweetheart?”

He shook his head.

Dodge appeared at the door leading into the room. She planted a hand on the bed and straightened while simultaneously pulling the blanket draped over her to her chin.

His eyes warmed. “Coffee’s ready. There’s a clean towel for you in the bathroom. You want a cup or a shower first?”

“I… What time is it?”

“Six-thirty.”

She nodded. “Shower.”

He transferred his gaze to his son. “Come, Cul. Let’s get you ready.”

Cul hesitated until she got out of bed. When she

did, he snaked his arms around her waist. She wrapped hers around his back.

Lifting his head to meet her stare, he smiled. “Morning.”

A new word. She smiled, slid her hand across his cheek then threaded her fingers through his hair. “Good morning, sweetheart.”

He released her and turned toward his father. Dodge closed the bedroom door on their way out. She showered, dressed, and rummaged through her bag, realizing she’d forgotten to pack her makeup. Grabbing her duffle, she walked to the living room, smiled when she spotted Cul, and headed toward the kitchen.

Dodge stood hip leaning against the counter, his hand around a mug of coffee, another cup beside him. “Made you a cup.”

Thoughtful. Then again, she expected nothing less. The months they’d been together, he’d been all that and more.

“Thanks.” She neared, stopped next to him, angled toward the counter, grabbed the mug, brought it to her lips, and took a sip. Looking into her coffee, steam hitting her face, she blurted, “Last night doesn’t change anything.”

He turned his body to her. The heat of his eyes burned.

She slanted her head and met his gaze. “You shouldn’t have let Cul see me either,” she whispered. “He’s going to think we’re together.”

Eyes narrowing, he lifted a brow. “We aren’t together?”

She shook her head. “No.”

“So last night?”

"Last night, I was…" She couldn't admit it, how terrified she'd been, and so, she didn't. "I made an unwise decision."

"I get you were scared. I get you were vulnerable. It's why I didn't fuck you when you were clearly giving me the vibe, Lex. You *kissed* me. You asked me to *stay*. You *cuddled* with me. You told me—"

Her face flamed. She shut her eyes tightly, set her mug on the counter, and parted her lids. "I know. I'm sorry. I shouldn't have done any of that. It's just…"

His jaw clamped tight.

He had a right to be mad. He wanted her back, and she'd led him on.

She swallowed. "I feel horrible. I shouldn't have stayed, asked you to spend the night with me, hold you, or say what I did. Being terrified is not a good excuse, but—"

He arched a brow. "So you lied?"

She wanted to lie then, knew she should, but holding his piercing stare, she couldn't.

She shook her head. "I didn't lie. Of course, I've missed you, but it doesn't change what happened. It doesn't change my decision."

He looked away. The muscle in his jaw twitched.

"I really am sorry, especially because of Cul."

When his gaze met hers again, some of the anger had melted. "Told him the lock on your back door broke and it wasn't safe, so you stayed the night."

She expelled a breath. "Oh, so he doesn't think we're—"

He shrugged. "Don't know. Suppose he'll figure it out."

How he handled his son wasn't her business, not

anymore, but she cared, so she'd say what she had to. She hoped it wouldn't anger him since it seemed he was handling their break up and the fact that she hadn't changed her mind about them better, than her anyway.

"Don't you think you should talk to him about it? I don't want him to think we're together—"

He smirked. "No point. When I get you back, I'll have to explain shit to him again."

Her lips parted, eyes widened, and she whispered, "I told you I'm not—"

"If you're right, then you have no business telling me what to do with my kid." He leaned in to her. A breath away, the proximity making her breath hitch. "But I think you're wrong. That's why I'm listening to you tell me what to do with my kid. That's why I'm not gonna sit down with him and tell him we aren't together 'cause when you get over this shit fight, you'll be mine again and I'll have to sit down with him and explain shit again. No point in getting him involved in our tiffs."

Her breaths coming out in spurts, she shook her head. "This isn't a tiff. We're broken up."

He cocked his head. "Lex, you got a wild hair about that now, but you're lying to yourself. Last night proved it. You came to *me*. I mean something to you, much more than you're willing to admit."

Her eyes nearly bulged out of their sockets.

He was so right and so wrong. He meant something to her, but she couldn't take him back, not after what he'd done.

She shook her head. "I didn't go to you. You came to me."

"I saw the cops outside. I went to you. I told them

you're mine, and you didn't deny it. Then *you* touched me. Then *you* let me hold you. Then *you* stayed over. Then *you* kissed me. Then *you* asked me to sleep beside you. Then *you* told me—"

God, she was starting to hate admitting he was right, even to herself. She had no excuse except the fact that she'd been scared and weak and hadn't wanted to be alone. No, that was a lie. It's not that she hadn't wanted to be alone; it's that she wanted to be with *him*.

She planted a hand on her hip. "You're infuriating."

He had the gall to smirk. Moving away slightly, he took a sip of his coffee. "So you're gonna hang with Cul here tonight?"

Hadn't he just heard a word she said?

She kept her cool but raised a brow in question. "Why would I do that?"

"You got someone to fix your back door and install an alarm already?"

Damn it. She forgot about that. His fault.

She grabbed her mug and took a sip of coffee before she responded. "No, I'll have to stay in a hotel for the time being."

"There aren't any hotels in town, Lex. You'd be driving to Santa Rosa about half an hour away. That's gas money and whatever the hotel costs. Spending that is dipping into your pink bathroom fund."

She knew this, but… "I don't have another choice."

She wouldn't impose on the lives of her new friends and staying with Dodge was out of the question. She trusted him not to take advantage but didn't trust herself.

"Yeah, you do. I'll fix your door. I'll have a brother install an alarm. Tomorrow, it'll be ready. You can stay here until then. You stay in my room, and I'll take the couch."

Nice, sweet even.

She shook her head. "I can't."

He shrugged. "Okay. Spend your money."

For a man who claimed he *would* get her back, he gave up too easily. Why did that make her want to ball her eyes out?

She took a deep breath. "I have to go."

"No makeup today?"

He noticed. No surprise there. When she wore it, he told her she didn't need it. She missed that. She missed a lot more too.

She swallowed. "I left it at home. I have to go get it."

He placed his coffee on the counter. "I'll go with you."

"I can—"

His eyes narrowed. "Back door stayed broken all night, Lex. You wanna go in there alone, that's great, but I'm *not* letting you, so make it easy for the both of us, yeah?"

She forgot about that too but wouldn't let him know.

He and Cullen walked her across the street. He grabbed her keys, unlocked her door, and proceeded to check her house while she and Cullen waited on her porch. When he gave her the go-ahead, she went in, grabbed her makeup, and strode outside. Then he locked the door and handed her the keys. She kissed Cullen goodbye, thanked Dodge, and drove away without looking back.

****

Hands shaking, pulse spiking, Lex gritted her teeth. "What're you doing here?"

She meant to go on, tell him to take a hike, but she caught sight of Cullen sprinting toward her, so she shut her mouth and softened her expression.

Dodge, saved from her wrath by his son, grinned.

That morning only a half hour after arriving at school, Lex realized she should've packed a bag, saving her the trouble of going home before heading to a hotel for the night. During lunch, she'd been busy. She scheduled a repairman to fix her door the following morning and booked a room. After school, she drove home to pack a bag. Imagine her surprise finding several bikes on her drive and her door wide open.

Dodge. It had to be. Then she remembered he'd locked her door that morning.

Parking behind the series of bikes, she removed her keys from the ignition and checked. Her house key was gone.

Incredible! She hopped out of her car in a haze just as he stepped out of her house. Barely containing her fury, she closed the distance between them and asked what he was doing there. Almost as if he planned it, Cullen rushed her, crashed in to her, and wrapped his arms around her.

Schooling her temper, she snaked her arms around Cullen.

He looked up at her. A smudge of dirt on his cheek, a wide smile on his beautifully flushed face. "Lex."

The tension lining her body melted. She ran her hand through his thick, dark hair and smiled. "Hey, sweetheart. Did you have a good day?"

He nodded.

"Head on in. I'll be inside in just a second to get you a snack."

She followed Cullen with her gaze. She then sliced it to Dodge, wearing that same grin.

The gall!

She narrowed her eyes. "You are *unbelievable*. I can't believe you stole my key. I can't believe you—"

He lifted his hands. "Shh, Lex, babe, you should be thanking me."

Shushing her!

Her face flamed. "You have ten seconds to get out of my house and off my property before I call the police."

Thick dark brows drawing together, he reared back and wiped the smile off his face. "Come on, babe, you don't mean that."

She did, very, very much. To prove it, she pulled her phone out of her purse and began dialing.

He snatched it away. "Listen. I took your key, yeah, but I did it to fix your door so you wouldn't have to stay at a hotel."

Thoughtful, but it didn't make what he did right or legal.

She fisted her hands. "So you fixed my door, is that supposed to make breaking into my house okay?"

"I didn't break in. I used your key."

She took a step toward him. "A key you *stole*."

"I borrowed it. I didn't steal it. I was gonna give it back."

"Taking without permission *is* stealing."

He clenched his jaw.

Getting angry? Good. She was livid.

He released a heavy breath and with just that, the anger faded. He extended his hand, handing her her phone. “All right, Lex. You wanna call the cops, get me arrested ’cause I took your key to save you the trouble of staying at a hotel, spending money, and ’cause I wanted to make you safe, whatever. Do it.”

Why didn’t he understand? It was wrong, a violation of her privacy, and illegal.

“Just so you know, I could’ve gotten into your house through that broken back door and didn’t do it ’cause I didn’t wanna fuck up anything in those boxes or your couch.”

Oh God. Oh God!

“I had to do it again, I would ’cause I gotta keep you safe. It’s my job to keep my woman safe.”

Hadn’t they just had this conversation? If she were a cartoon, this is when her head would explode.

Instead, she snatched her phone from his hand. “I’m *not* your anything!” Her voice rose, sounding hysterical and sort of panicked.

“Lex, it was just a fight. My fault. I apologized. I gave you space. Now, you gotta let it go.”

She fisted her hands, the one around her phone squeezing it, and let out an irritated sigh. “Give. Me. My. Key. Then get off my property.”

A howl of laughter erupted. Snapping her stare behind Dodge, she spotted Hash and Army. The heat on her face trailed down her neck and chest. She dropped her head and swallowed as the memory of the last time she’d seen them resurfaced, the day Dodge humiliated her.

“Told you this shit wouldn’t work.” Army

chuckled. “Women get pissy about their privacy, brother.”

She angled her head, looking their way, and bit her tongue so she wouldn’t point out that men got “pissy” about their privacy too.

Dodge, looking over his shoulder, sniped, “What the fuck would you know, Army?”

“I got a sister.”

Hash smirked. “’Sides it doesn’t take a genius.”

A muscle in Dodge’s jaw twitched as he took a step toward them.

Hash laughed. “Don’t get pissed ’cause we’re right. Told you this wasn’t the way to get on your woman’s good graces.”

“I didn’t ask for your fuckin’ advice,” Dodge snarled.

“Maybe you should’ve…” Hash’s voice trailed off when Army stepped in front of Hash and said something she didn’t hear, thankfully, since it defused the tension between Dodge and Hash. The last thing she needed on the day her ex stole her key and broke into her house—her ex fighting with one of his friends on her front porch.

Taking her chance to get away, she sidestepped past Dodge and managed two steps before he grabbed her upper arm and came close to her back. She felt the heat of him then stupidly took a breath and smelled the cologne he always wore, a scent she loved because it reminded her of him.

“We gotta talk.”

She spun toward him, the suddenness making him release her. “You wanted to do something for me, so you steal my key, break into my house, get your friends, the same ones you humiliated me in front of barely two weeks ago, to help you? Classic."

She paused for a moment letting that sink. "I've said what I needed to say, Dodge. There's nothing else for me to say, and there's nothing else I want to hear from you, not even a goodbye."

He dropped his head and released a sigh. After an endless moment, he met her gaze. "You wanna throw that in my face now?" He arched a brow. "You sure? Take a good look at what you're doing, Lex, in front of my brothers and the whole fuckin' neighborhood."

It wasn't the same, yet it kind of was. She'd seen the bikes, knew his brothers were inside. Her neighbors were milling around, per usual, watching their kids play, taking out the trash, getting their mail, or just getting home from work. She wasn't being loud, in fact, quite the opposite. Since Cullen was inside, she'd kept her voice low. She hadn't insulted him or disrespected him, but it was clear to anyone who cared to look she was angry with him. She meant to point all of this out, but before she managed to, he spoke.

"Don't worry. We'll be outta your hair in no time."

He turned, took three steps then stopped and faced her. "You think I humiliated you, but the truth is I humiliated myself. Everyone knew I was outta line. Everyone knew you didn't deserve the shit I dished out. Everyone knows I'm eating my words now and trying my goddamned hardest to get you back." With those last words, he spun and walked away.

She stood there staring at where he'd been trying to forget the last bit of what he'd said. Then she headed inside, ate some cookies with Cullen, and read to him.

Chapter Twenty-Four

The sound jolted Lex awake. Continuous, loud, smashing like she was inside a glass jar being beaten with a crowbar. It went on for what seemed like forever.

She shot up in bed, clutched her blanket to her chest, and stayed frozen long after the sounds died.

Then loud banging.

She moved knowing she'd stalled long enough and couldn't waste more time. First, she had to call police and manage to do it before whoever was pounding on her door knocked it down.

Shame that at that moment, for the life of her, she couldn't remember where she left her cell phone. Checking her nightstand, she spotted it, picked it up, and dialed 9-1-1.

She spoke to the operator giving her the address, telling her what happened, mentioning someone was at her door, banging. After she managed that, the pounding still hadn't stopped. The operator advised her to stay in her room and keep her on the line.

Heart slamming hard against her ribs, hands trembling, it went quiet.

"Lex! Lex!"

Dodge. She closed her eyes tightly as the breath rushed out of her.

"It's… It's my…neighbor."

"Where?" the 9-1-1 operator asked.

"At the door."

"Ma'am, stay in your room. Wait for police."

The operator could say that since she didn't know Dodge. He'd knock her door down. Besides, it was *Dodge*—Dodge who broke into her house, recruited his brothers to help install a hurricane-proof sliding glass door and then refused to take money for it, the same man who showed on her doorstep the day after insisting one of his brothers install an alarm system in her house. She had to open the door, not just because of those reasons but because she *needed* him right then.

Lex stood on shaking legs, walked out of her room, into her living room, and to her door.

"Lex! Lex!" His voice thicker, rougher, and louder.

"Ma'am, do *not* open the door. Stay away from your door."

She parted the door.

What a sight. His long body filled the doorframe, in the shadows his hair a mess. All she took in before, fortunately, his arms went around her, and he hauled her to him. Her cheek landed on his bare chest. He buried his face in her neck, and as his ragged breaths warmed her skin, his hands moved over her head, shoulders, arms then back.

"Lex, fuck me, Lex." He cupped her cheeks and tugged her away just enough to meet her face. "Baby, you okay?"

Terror. His. She read it on his too handsome face. So much of it, it was comparable to hers.

Seeing that—all it took.

Sobs tore from her throat, the strength of them making her body tremble.

The fear had built for days knowing it was only a matter of time before whoever was terrorizing her did it again, only a matter of time because the calls hadn't stopped. In fact, they were now incessant, five calls a day. She didn't answer, but a message was left, a message of someone's breaths like something out of a horror movie.

He wound his arms around her, one hand dove into her hair holding her firm against him. "Shh, Lex, babe. It's gonna be fine. You're safe. I'm gonna keep you safe."

He said it like he meant it.

He held her like he wouldn't let her go.

She needed that, so she took it, not thinking about the consequences and refusing to acknowledge she wanted no one but *him*.

He buried his face against the top of her head. "Shh, baby, I'm here."

"Don't…go…p-please…" Her plea so muffled she didn't know if he understood.

His hands came to her face again, pulling her away slightly. "Gotta calm down, Lex. Gotta talk to the cops."

Police officers were there already?

She took a breath and wiped her face.

He looked over his shoulder. "Just a sec." He met her gaze. "Get your robe."

Yes, she needed her robe.

He walked her into her house. One arm stayed behind her holding her close to his side. In her room, he released her. She grabbed her robe, donned it, stepped into a pair of flip flops, and together, they strode out of her house.

The loud noises, now clear to see, were rotten eggs, rocks, and debris sprawled around her yard, drive, and porch. Some of the rocks had hit her door, others a series of potted plants on her porch she'd purchased yesterday intending to plant that weekend to keep busy and not think about Dodge. Some of the rocks, eggs, and debris struck her windows, cracking yet not shattering two. Thankfully, she'd parked her car in the garage.

Same cops, same questions, a repeat of just days ago. In a haze, she answered their questions, the weight of her body supported by Dodge. She hadn't noticed how much until a cry sounded. Dodge nabbed the monitor from his pocket and didn't waste a minute. Instantly, he released and faced her.

She nodded. "Go."

He left, and the cops continued asking questions. Most she answered half-heartedly and therefore, poorly.

With the scare and tears, only natural, exhaustion took hold. With Dodge's arm around her, he'd been supporting her not just physically but mentally and emotionally. Added to that, she now worried about Cullen.

"Miss Millen, do you realize the severity of the situation? Someone's after you. We haven't been able to get ahold of your ex meaning we have no clue who's doing this. We don't know what they're capable of, but we know the acts are escalating."

She tore her gaze from the mess of dirt and plants on her porch to Officer Johnson. "Yes."

"But you don't know anyone who could've done this?" He asked again a question she'd answered days ago and once earlier.

"No, I don't. I don't think my ex is capable of this. There's no one in my life that would do this." She swallowed. "I'm a kindergarten teacher. I don't party, smoke, or use drugs. I'm not the type of person who makes enemies, and besides, I haven't been here long."

"It's not necessarily a requirement," Marks added. "People who do this kinda thing, there's no telling where you might've caught their eye. It may even be someone you don't know."

Johnson took a step toward her. "You're dating a biker from Hell Ryders Motorcycle Gang—"

"Ace," Marks cut him off and looked to her. "We know you're tired. Maybe, tomorrow you can come to the station."

She nodded. "I'd appreciate that."

Johnson handed her his card. She still had the one he gave her but didn't have the energy to tell him. She took it and thanked them. As they left, she stood there and stared at the mess on her lawn, drive, and front porch. She wouldn't get a chance to clean it until after school tomorrow, which meant the neighbors who hadn't been woken in the middle of the night would see the house she worked so hard to make into a home vandalized.

Time to go in and try to get some sleep. What if whoever had vandalized her house came back? What would she do to defend herself? She didn't even own a bat.

She turned to face her door, pressed her trembling hands against her stomach, and breathed deep. She needed strength, needed not to be afraid, needed to get some sleep, but she *couldn't* move. Her eyes watered. She closed them tightly and swallowed.

"Lex, babe."

Eyes shooting open, her hand flew to her chest.

Dodge closed the distance between them until he stood in front of her. One of his hands went to her hip. The other grasped her hand. "Didn't mean to scare you."

"Not your fault." She finally met his gaze. "Cul?"

"He's up. Had a bad dream. Told him I was with you, just outside. Didn't tell him why. He wants you to tuck him in."

Her eyes widened. "Really?"

A smile spread across his lips. "That surprises you?"

"I have to…um…lock—"

He cupped her cheek. "I'll take care of it. You go to Cul. He's waiting for you in the living room."

She nodded.

Dodge released her. She strode across the street and into his house. Inside, Cul rushed her and wrapped his arms around her. She hugged him too, and together, they headed into his room. When he lay in bed, she sat on the edge and sang to him softly.

In no time, he fell asleep. When she stood and turned, Dodge waited for her by the door. She walked to him. He moved making way for her to stride out. Then he closed Cul's door, grabbed her hand, and led her into his room.

She took off her robe and climbed into bed. She didn't have to ask him to stay. He got into bed, rolled to his side, and faced her. When she turned to him, his arm went around her waist, hauling her close.

He pressed his lips to her forehead. "Your phone's in the living room."

Her phone? She couldn't remember giving it to him.

Staring at the corded muscles in his neck, she mumbled, "Thanks." Then her mind drifted thinking too much, about it all. Helplessly, tears rushed her. Fighting them, she swallowed. "Can't do this anymore. I'm not strong enough."

His finger went under her chin, lifting it until her eyes hit his. "Yeah, you are, Lex. You don't need a hero. You're your own hero."

She had told him that. Now, it seemed so long ago.

Truth was she wasn't, not then, not now.

She'd spent her life savings on a house, moved away from her sister and friends for this dream, and someone wanted to ruin it. She didn't know what to do, how to make it stop, or where to go.

Who would want to hurt her this way? What could she have possibly done to deserve this?

One thing she knew, she couldn't fight this on her own.

"Right now, I'm not. Right now, I need to be saved."

A soft smile spread across his face. "I'll save you."

"You can't. You have Cul."

No truer words. His number one priority was keeping Cullen safe. No matter what Officer Johnson implied, whoever was terrorizing her was after *her*. It had nothing to do with the club. If something happened to Cul because of her…

The breath froze in the back of her throat. Her hands went to his chest. She pushed, sat up, and turned. "I shouldn't—"

He snaked his arm around her waist and hauled her

until he'd pressed her back against his chest. Then he buried his face in the crook of her neck. "You're right where you need to be."

"Being here will put you both—"

"You gotta trust me when I say nothing's gonna happen to Cul. Nothing's gonna happen to me, and nothing's gonna happen to you."

She looked over her shoulder. "If that's what you really think, then you're in denial. My house was vandalized twice in a week. The calls are coming more frequently too. I'm…"

She didn't think she had to say what he could clearly see.

He released a breath then relaxed. "You don't gotta be scared. I'm here. I'll keep you safe. You let me, I'll get the club to find out who's doing this, and we'll make them stop. No one'll ever hurt you again, Lex."

The day after he broke into her house to fix her back door, he'd showed on her doorstep and asked to borrow her key so one of his brothers could install an alarm system. She'd not only vehemently refused, she'd also told him if he cared about her at all, he'd promise to stay out of her life and keep the club out of her business too. He had promised, but she knew it'd cost him by the torn and ravished look on his face. In all honesty, she didn't think the club could help her anyway so it didn't matter, but she'd made him promise because she needed him to keep his distance. She feared if he didn't, she'd lose her will and take him back.

"What?"

He dropped his head and pressed a kiss to her shoulder blade. "It's late. We should sleep."

He didn't explain, but he had a point. She was dead

on her feet. The past several nights she'd barely slept so afraid of every sound, even the smallest waking her. Tonight, she should take advantage. With Dodge, she'd sleep soundlessly.

She did just that.

****

Warmth, so much of it, Lex didn't want to move. She burrowed in to that heat. Skin against her chest, arms, legs, and cheek, she parted her eyes.

A broad, muscular back…Dodge's. She was cuddled against his back, her arm tight around his waist, one of her legs tangled between his.

Darn it. She should've kept her eyes shut, should've pretended to sleep so she could enjoy him a little longer, enjoy the fact that she slept soundlessly for the first time in days. Now, she couldn't stay in bed, couldn't forget why she needed to pull away, couldn't ignore what happened last night, couldn't overlook she made another mistake, the same she'd made days ago.

She promised she'd cut all contact, promised she'd figure out her predicament all on her own, and promised she wouldn't go running back to him because she was scared.

What had she done?

Just. That.

Granted, he'd gone to her, as expected considering someone had vandalized her house in the middle of the night. But she ended up in bed with him, tucked tightly against his back, so it seemed her unconscious mind didn't keep promises either.

Only one thing to do—get away.

Ever so slowly, she shifted backward and managed an inch before he grasped the arm she had circling his waist. A moment later, he flipped to face her and hooked his arm around her back.

He grinned. "Morning, Lex. How'd you sleep?"

She swallowed. "We should talk—"

His smile faded, his eyes narrowed before he repeated, "How'd you sleep, Lex?"

"I know it's my fault, but—"

"How. Did. You. Sleep?"

She hesitated before finally saying, "Fine."

"That's a lie, Lex. You slept like a baby. Didn't move all night except when I pulled away. I pulled away 'cause I figured you'd wake and pull the same shit on me, and when I pulled away, *you* came to me. Even dead asleep, you came to *me*."

She dropped her chin, losing hold of his eyes. "Fine. I slept great. It doesn't change—"

He trailed his hand up her spine and grabbed the back of her neck. His thumb resting on her jaw, he angled her head, forcing her to look at him. "I've been patient. Two weeks, I've waited for you. You're more stubborn than I thought and you're not gonna let this go, so I'm gonna be just as stubborn."

This didn't sound good.

"You say we're done. I say we're not. Last night, again, you showed me we aren't over, so *we are not done,* nowhere near it."

She swallowed. "Dodge, we are."

He leaned in to her. "We're not."

She attempted to tilt back, but his arm slipped from the back of her neck to her waist. "Let me go."

His jaw hardened. "Say we're together."

Her eyes widened. "I can't say that because we are *not*."

"We are, babe."

"*We* aren't anything, Dave."

"We are *everything*."

Her chest seized wanting that to be true, hating it wasn't. She ignored the ache as best she could. "We are *not*."

"We are."

Planting her hands on his chest, she shoved.

His arm tightened around her. He didn't speak, just kept staring at her. His deep, dark, beautiful eyes burning her, owning her, searing her.

Her pulse raced, mind blanked. She shut her eyes and forced herself to focus. "You can't make me change my mind."

"I can and I will. I'll keep you in this bed just like this all fuckin' day, all night, forever until you admit I mean something to you, that *we* mean something to you."

She cracked her eyes open. "Of course, you and Cullen mean something to me—"

"Not '*we*' me and Cul, babe, '*we*' me and you. What we have, you want, but you're scared I'm gonna hurt you again, so you're not giving me a chance. That's bullshit and cowardly and you, Lex, are no coward."

No use in arguing when he was absolutely right about one thing. With the other, he was dead wrong.

Eyes filling with tears, her voice wavered. "I am a coward. I sat in bed last night shaking while some jerk vandalized my house. I couldn't move. *I* forgot where I put my phone, and it was right next to m-me."

In that instant, his face and eyes softened. He slid his hand up and down her back soothingly. "You aren't a coward, Lex. You got every right to be scared, and I already told you I won't let anything happen to you. I'm gonna take care of you."

"You'll just be putting yourself and Cul in danger."

"Babe, please, listen to me. I got this."

She believed him, but she couldn't let him handle anything for her. It'd just encourage him.

She shook her head. "Don't—"

"I'm gonna handle this, then we can move on, 'kay?"

God, this again?

She gritted her teeth. "We are not together—"

The fire in his eyes came again. With the arm around her, he squeezed her. "We are."

"Are *not*."

His jaw clenched. "We. Are."

They'd go on forever, she knew. In sheer exasperation and since she had to get to work, she expelled a breath. "Fine. We're together. We're one of those couples who never have sex."

He scoffed. "That'll make two for two."

She quirked a brow.

"Before you, it'd been years since I got laid."

Why?

He leaned in to her, lips grazing hers. "*Years*. I can hold out. As long as you're not seeing anyone else, fuckin' anyone else, I'm good. When it's not working for me anymore, I'll let you know and we'll both go our separate ways. But for now, you said it. You can't take it back. We're together. You're *mine*. You don't flirt, don't date. You're *taken*." His stare shot to her mouth as he raked his thumb against her bottom lip.

Gaze scanning his handsome face, she shook her

head. “Wait, what do you mean you hadn’t had sex for years before me? You were married. You *are* married.”

His stare shot back to hers. “*Separated* for more than a year now, Lex, and the two and a half years we were married and not separated, we never had sex.”

Again, what? Why?

“W-why didn’t you…”

“Speak up, *babe*.”

God, he could be a jerk!

“Why didn’t you just cheat?”

His eyes widened then narrowed. “’Cause I was married and I took a vow. I didn’t love her, but I respected her as the mother of my kid. I wouldn’t cheat on the mother of my kid, no matter how big a bitch she is. Besides, she’s a horrible mother. I knew eventually it’d end, and I couldn’t give her ammunition to take my kid.”

That made perfect sense. Her thoughts drifted back to what he said before. He was fine with not having sex with her as long as she wasn’t with anyone else. So he’d have her any way he could get her?

Her stomach knotted, an uneasy feeling settling in her gut. “You’re okay with being in a relationship with me and not having sex?”

“That’s what I said.”

Her chest warmed. She shut her eyes fighting to ignore it.

“And Lex, you know what this means, right?”

She snapped open her eyes. “What?”

“It means we’re a couple, a real couple, so that promise you made me make you—that I stay out of your life—is null and void. I handle shit for you. I take care of you. We do shit every other couple does like before. You come over. I go over there. We go out on dates. We may not have sex, but you're mine in *every other way*. Everyone will know *you* belong to *me*."

Not a good idea. She'd never get over him, just fall deeper, but she didn't have another choice. He wouldn't take no for an answer.

She swallowed past the lump in her throat and nodded. Then he let her go, turned, threw his feet over the edge of the bed, and stood.

"Does this mean you're not going to be with anyone else either?"

He stilled.

She hadn't meant to ask, wasn't thinking straight, and it slipped, proving how much she cared.

Finally, he faced her and smiled. "Didn't cheat on my kid's mother. Some could say she had it coming, so there's no way I'd cheat on you, Lex."

Relief swept through her. She didn't move though. Still thinking about what he said and what it meant, she couldn't.

"Need me to get you a change of clothes?"

She sat up in bed. "What?"

"You didn't bring any clothes last night. Do you need me to run over and grab you some?"

Would he? Seriously? Just so she wouldn't have to walk across the street in her robe? So thoughtful.

"Um, I… Do you mind?"

He smiled. He had a great smile, one of the things she missed the most. "I'm asking you means I don't mind."

She smiled too. "You wouldn't know what to get."

"Makeup, clothes, a thong and bra, shoes, what else?"

She laughed, the first time in too long. “Okay. I’ll make it easier for you.” She made him a list with instructions where to find each item.

While he went across the street, she got out of bed and made coffee.

Chapter Twenty-Five

Lex caught Cullen's gaze from across the hall and smiled. He grinned, released Allie's hand, and rushed her dodging people as he did. A moment later, his small body slammed in to hers. She'd prepared for the impact but still had to take a step back to steady herself.
His arms around her, hers around him, he looked up.

"Hey, sweetheart. How are you?"

A beautiful smile lit his face. "Lex."

Dodge texted her earlier that day and told her he had to work late then asked if she wanted to "chill with Cul." His words, not hers. She needed to clean her yard desperately, but she wouldn't pass up a chance to spend time with Cullen. Her yard would have to wait. No hiding the vandalism, so what was a couple of hours more?

She spent the day purposefully thinking about the vandalism to avoid thinking about the fact that she and Dodge were a couple again. The way it'd played out made her feel like an idiot. Though in her defense, never in a million years had she thought a man, a tough biker especially, would agree to be in a relationship with a woman and not get rewarded for it, the reward being sex. She tried to trick him, but he agreed without the slightest hesitation, and it made her rethink everything.

A man who agreed to that kind of arrangement *had*

to truly care for the woman, right? Did this mean she should forgive him? Did it mean she'd overreacted when she'd ended them? Did he deserve a second chance?

She didn't know. She did know he was right about one thing. She was afraid of getting hurt *again*.

Lex had been hurt a lot, true. She'd forgiven a lot, also true, but this was Dodge and he was unlike anyone else she'd dated. She always believed it wasn't possible to fall for someone so fast, but she had. When he'd humiliated her, it *wrecked* her. It had only been a few months, but it felt a thousand times worse than the many times Mitchell dumped her.

"Weead me, please."

Read me, please. Three words in a row.

Her heart squeezed; warmth spread through her chest, an array of emotions: excitement, love, and most shocking, *pride*.

Trying to get a handle on herself, she hugged him tight, bent over, and pressed a kiss to his forehead. When she straightened, she met Allie's gaze, standing a few feet away. Della stood beside her.

"Hey." Allie wrinkled her brows. "Are you okay?"

God, she'd noticed her watery eyes.

She nodded. "Yeah, fine."

Since Dodge's outburst at the cookout, Allie had reached out to her. All the women had. In fact, last Saturday, they—with the exception of Tiffany who was at home with her newborn—had met for lunch.

"Girls' night soon?"

"Wouldn't miss it."

"Got to go, but I'll call you."

She nodded. After the rest of her students were

picked up, she tidied her classroom. Cullen played with a car toy he'd brought. She then graded a few papers and read Cullen a book. Belatedly, she realized she didn't have a snack for Cul. He was big for his age, and at times, it seemed he had the appetite of a grown man, so she decided to go home. She didn't want Cullen to see the mess on her yard, granted he may have seen it that morning, but Cullen had to eat.

She packed, locked up, and with Cul's hand in hers, she walked outside. Parked behind her car, she spotted a police cruiser.

Right. She'd agreed to go to the station. Though she supposed it didn't matter since Officer Johnson who emerged from the car decided to pay her a visit instead.

"Good afternoon, Miss Millen."

"Alexa."

"Ace."

"I know I said I'd go to the station today, but as you can see…" She glanced down at Cul. "I'm unable to."

He jerked his head. "You realize you're in—"

She looked down at Cullen. "Honey, do you want to listen to some music?"

Cullen tilted his head back. Before he responded, she pulled her phone and earphones out of her purse, helped Cul put them on, and played music.

Only then did she address Officer Johnson. "It may seem like I'm in denial about just how potentially dangerous my situation is—"

"What it seems is that you're not interested in our investigation because your man and his gang are investigating, so then your man and his gang can administer *their* form of payback. I guess that works for some people, but I'm an officer of the law, Miss Millen. I stand by the law. I don't condone revenge or payback or make excuses for vigilantes. Like every other criminal, they're breaking the law. Our system may fail sometimes, but it's the best we've got. The day we start following Hell Ryders' moral code is the day this country and the world will go to shit."

She swallowed, mind scrambling trying to process everything he said. So much information, all new to her.

"This, that's happening to you… We don't have leads. For the life of me, I can't figure out who'd do this to a woman like you. It doesn't make sense. Add a motorcycle gang to the equation and it makes perfect sense. You mess with enough people, someone's gonna mess with you back, and Hell Ryders has been messing with people for a long time."

What? She was still at vigilantes and the club… Damn it! Could her life get any more complicated?

Her lips parted wanting to say something, anything. Nothing came out.

"You want to follow the law, you know where to come. You want to play by their rules…" He shrugged. "It's your decision. Though I will say, a woman like you should be far away from that."

Officer Johnson climbed into his cruiser and drove away. She unlocked her car and helped Cullen into his car seat. After Dodge texted her and she agreed to watch Cullen that afternoon, Dodge stopped by the school and installed it in her car. How he got into her car, she didn't know. She hadn't even known he'd dropped it off until he texted her and told her he'd already installed it.

She drove to her house going over everything Officer Johnson said. The minute she pulled onto her drive, she scanned her lawn. Spotless. The potted flowers and dirt picked up; she assumed thrown out. The front of her house, door, and windows cleaned, two replaced. She lowered her window. The smell of rotten eggs was gone too.

Seeing this, it made perfect sense why Dodge had to work late. She thought it had been a ploy to get on her good side, letting her spend time with Cullen while he wasn't around. Now, she knew better, and she didn't like what it meant. He took time off work, enlisted the help of several people—no way he hadn't considering the mess that had been there before—to clean her lawn and replace her windows. He managed this in the span of eight hours. Why had he done it? To help her out? So she wouldn't have to?

Resting her forehead against the steering wheel, she released a breath and tried to convince herself she hated what he'd done. She failed because she loved it. She just hated it made her soften. He was so good at that. Maybe it wasn't about him being good at it. Maybe it was about her being in love and weak.

"Lex?"

She lifted her head and unbuckled her seat belt. "Yeah, honey."

Exiting her car, keys in hand, she helped Cullen out and headed up her front steps. Inside, she busied herself making chocolate chip cookies, Cullen's favorite, and not thinking about Dodge.

Chapter Twenty-Six

"So what's the deal with your girl? She yours—"

One look from Dodge and Hash shut his mouth though his brother never wiped that shit-eating grin off his face.

Dodge was in no mood to deal with him. He'd barely slept and spent the better part of his day cleaning the mess at Lex's house. Not to mention, he had to find out who was fucking with her. The faster, the better because he couldn't stomach even the thought of Lex scared and in tears. She'd finally agreed to be his. That meant the promise she made him make her—that he stay out of her life—was null and void, so he could now enlist the help of his club to find out who was messing with her and make whoever it was stop.

Prez, surrounded by the brothers, stood at the head of the table in the room they held club meetings. "Know what you want."

Not surprising, Dodge didn't know how, but Prez knew it all. They lived in a small town; word about what happened at Lex's could've gotten around to him easily, but there were plenty of instances where that wasn't the case.

Prez inclined his head toward Hash. "To get what you want, you gotta answer that question."

Dodge reared back, gaze raking the room, his brothers, all waiting to hear what he said. Not one did what he should've, jumped in on his behalf. Instead, they had a question as if whatever he said would change the fact that he was part of the club, a brother, and deserved nothing but their full support. He'd been with them for years, given them nothing less.

Adrenaline shot through his veins making his heart race. The tension in the air heightened. Then he barked, "Are you all shitting me?"

Dash, his VP, shook his head. "Don't make this more complicated than it needs to be."

He took a step toward Dash. "Then why are *you*?"

"We're not, but we're clean. We don't know anything 'bout her, what she's involved—"

"She's a kindergarten teacher."

"Listen, brother." Bud, standing to his left, crossed his arms over his chest. "She's not from around here. We don't know who she hung out with before. We don't know what she was involved with, if she's running from something—"

Dodge couldn't do anything but repeat, "She's a teacher." Then he looked to his president and VP. Neither seemed swayed by what he said. "I know *her*."

Dash cocked his head. "You haven't known her long."

He hadn't, but he knew her, knew her down to her soul. Lex was good, sweet, kind, fucking beautiful.

So as he scanned the room, he pointed out the obvious. "It's what we do."

Mellow shook his head. "We don't."

Slick cleared his throat. "We get paid for guards and that includes extras, yeah, but we aren't cops. We don't investigate—"

He raised a brow. "No?" Sarcasm dripped his tone.

"We handled Classy's ex, Tiff's stalker then went head-to-head against a street gang for Em."

Prez's gaze hardened. "Different. On every level. We didn't investigate—"

His eyes widened. "Classy's ex?"

"I paid Doug to handle that."

He shot his head in Trig's direction and seared him with a glare. "We went guns blazing when she was kidnapped, Trig. Not long after, we did the same for Em."

Ripper took a step toward him. Bud's arm shot out and hit Ripper's chest, stopping him. Cuss tensed just as Trig said, "They're old ladies."

Dodge's jaw hardened. "We started dealing with Classy's ex before you'd claimed her."

"But she's my blood," Army, standing next to Trig, added.

"Yeah, and Lex's my old lady." He slammed the palm of his hand against his chest. "She's with me."

Rake nodded. "So she's yours?"

He skimmed the room yet again. "You brothers deaf? I just fuckin' said that." Then he met Prez's stare, waiting for a reaction, an explanation.

Finally, Prez inclined his head. "I ask her, she'll say the same?"

They had to be fucking with him. No way his club, his brothers wouldn't back him.

He fisted his hands. "Enough of this shit. I'm not playing games. Lex's—"

"You're right. This isn't a game."

His gaze sliced to Blaze, who'd spoken, then veered right back to Prez. "You ask her, she'll say the same. She's *mine*. What that has to do with her being in danger and needing us, I still have no clue."

Dash shifted his weight. "We don't know—"

"We know she's *mine*. We know she needs *us*."

"There's a new police chief and that chief doesn't give a fuck we cleaned up this town." Prez shrugged. "We wanna stay outta trouble, we gotta lay low."

Finally, he had a reason. Why it seemed he was the only one who didn't know, he had no clue. Yet the reason wasn't good enough. Then again, he'd never find a good enough reason not to protect Lex.

"Had a sit-down with the chief last week." The muscle in Prez's jaw twitched. "Today, he dropped in with a couple of new cops."

Cops keeping tabs on them? The club was clean, but not everything they did was legit. Not to mention, some of the shit they did back when the club wasn't clean could still land some of them in prison. They didn't need anyone, especially cops, snooping around. He knew this, and still, he couldn't help but feel abandoned by his club, his brothers.

He swallowed thickly. "You guys do what you gotta do. I'm gonna do what I gotta do."

"It ain't like that." Dash jerked his head. "She's yours, she's part of this club too. We're brothers; we got your back. It's as easy as that."

Prez nodded.

He swung his stare around the room meeting the gazes of his brothers. They had his back. They had Lex's. He released a breath, and that knot in his gut loosened. "Appreciate it."

****

Dodge grabbed the knob and turned it. Unlocked. Un-fuckin'-believable. Coming home to find this after the day he had pissed him off.

Would she do something to infuriate him because she wasn't set on being with him? He didn't know. But risking herself and Cul was reckless and stupid and wouldn't make him angry; it'd make him lose his shit. Maybe she wanted him to so she'd have an excuse to dump his ass.

He opened the door, strode inside, and his senses were assaulted, the unmistakable smell of freshly baked cookies mixed with perfectly seasoned meat. She'd cooked for Cul and no doubt for him too. The only woman who could get him so riled in one second then ridiculously blissful the next. She had him by the balls, could make him do just about anything, and she didn't even know it.

Striding farther into her house, he removed his cut and draped it over the couch then dropped his keys and wallet on the coffee table. Heading into the kitchen, he spotted them. She stood at the stove, turned away from him. Cullen sat on the island just behind her. His boy looked over his shoulder. When his gaze hit Cullen's, he smiled.

"Dad."

His heart squeezed in his chest.

It'd been months since his boy called him that, months since he'd called him anything.

He walked straight to him, grasped Cullen under the arms, lifted him off the stool, and hugged him tightly. "Your old man missed you." Pulling away, he set Cul on his feet. "You save me some cookies?"

Cul shook his head.

He laughed. "No?"

Cul giggled and nodded.

He lifted his head, gaze shooting to Lex, still turned away and stiff. He moved, closing the distance between them. Before he reached her, she faced him.

Her stare hit his chest for a split second before she looked away. "Hey."

He snaked his arm around her waist and tugged her to him. She planted her hands on his chest, fingers gripping his skin. Her eyes widened and rounded. Maybe she thought he'd kiss her. He had no plans to. Well, not like she thought anyway.

They were a couple, one who didn't have sex. Fine by him, for now. As long as she was his, as long as he could protect her, he didn't care because he knew soon she'd realize just how much she meant to him, she'd forgive him, and they'd move on. When she set her stipulation about sex, she hadn't mentioned kissing. Still, he wouldn't kiss her if she didn't want him to.

Leaning down, he pressed a kiss to her cheek. "Hey, Lex."

Her shallow breaths heated his skin. "Hi."

When he drew away and released her, he smiled.

Again, she didn't meet his eyes. Strange. She couldn't be pissed he'd cleaned the front of her house and yard. He'd done her a favor. They agreed to no sex, but she was his in every other way, so she had to accept him handling things for her, protecting her. Maybe it was about the money. He had two windows replaced. No, that didn't make sense. Even angry, she met his gaze head on, was never afraid to speak her mind. The way she acted like she was…scared, of him.

"Dinner's ready," she said to who, he had no clue since she hadn't looked at anyone.

He turned to his boy. "Cul, go wash your hands

and meet us at the table."

By the time he faced Lex, she stood at the other end of the kitchen pulling mac and cheese out of the oven, his and Cul's favorite. He had no idea what she did to hers, but it was the best he ever had. Just the smell had him salivating.

With Cullen out of earshot, he cleared his throat. "Lex, babe?"

She placed the mac and cheese on the counter beside the oven and without looking his way said, "Yes?"

"Is there a reason you're not looking at me?"

She removed her oven mitts and set them on the marble countertop. "We can talk about it later."

He released a breath, leaned his hip against the island, and crossed his arms over his chest. "Talk about what exactly?"

"We'll talk about it later."

He moved, closing the distance between them. Only then did her gaze finally come up. Eyes wide met his.

Yep, scared. Of him.

He clenched his jaw and fought to keep his voice level. "No, Lex, we're not talking about it later. If there's a reason you can't look at me, that's a big deal, so we're not gonna sit and eat, you not looking at me, me wondering what the fuck I did and how the hell I'm gonna fix it. We're gonna talk about it now."

"Dinner will get cold."

"I'll heat it up."

Her eyes lowered, and she whispered, "Cul's probably starving."

"Knowing Cul, he probably ate too many cookies.

Knowing you, you let him. He's fine. I'm starved, but I'll live. So are you gonna tell me what's wrong?"

"I think we should talk later."

"No, babe, we're talking about whatever it is now. The longer you take, the longer it'll take." He paused for a second, the entire time watching her closely. "So tell me."

Her brows drew together. "Tell you?"

"Yeah, tell me what I did this time."

"It's not…" She released a breath. "What does the club do?"

He kept his face blank, ignoring the roll of his stomach.

He should've been prepared, should've seen this coming. People talked, and they lived in a small town. In fact, it was a miracle she hadn't heard anything before now. He didn't need another obstacle. They had enough. Eventually, he would've told her, but now wasn't the time. First, he needed her to be his, completely his.

"So it's true? You're vigilantes?"

He had to say something, so he did. "Don't know what you heard 'cause I don't know who you've been talking to, but just so you know people tend to say a lot and most of the time it isn't true.

"I'll be honest with you. We aren't vigilantes 'cause we don't need to be anymore. Sometime ago, it was a different story. That's not the case now. The day that shit changes, I'll let you know."

"So you used to…"

"Wadden wasn't always what it is now. Those secluded mansions at the edge of town have always been there, but that new development near Main Street was not there. There was something else, and it was bad, so bad it leaked often and made the rest of town bad."

"So how did you—"

He shook his head. "Not getting into that. You and me become more, you still want to know, we'll talk. I'm being honest with you 'cause I care about you and you want to know, but that shit's long over now."

She hesitated, lowered her head, eyes falling away from his. Then she nodded and swallowed.

He hated every minute of it. He wanted her happy, laughing, and carefree like she used to be.

He turned his head and spotted Cul headed for them. "Cul, watch TV for a minute while I finish talking to Lex. Then we'll eat, yeah?"

Cullen, his too smart three-year-old, picked up the mood. Looking between the both of them, his gaze scanning Lex, he hesitated.

"Go on, sweetie. We'll be out in a few."

Cullen walked away.

"So what does the club do?"

"We got the garage. It makes good money."

Her brows shot up. "That's it?"

No. It wasn't it, and he didn't want to lie, but right then, he couldn't tell her the whole truth. When she became his, fully and completely, he would but not as things stood.

Holding her stare, he admitted part of it. "The club's got another business too. We're bodyguards."

Her eyes widened. "You're a bodyguard?"

"Those jobs bank. It's how I was able to buy a home, but most of the time, those jobs take me away, so I haven't been on a job since Cul was born."

She visibly relaxed, shoulders slumping, breath rushing out of her. Nothing had ever made him feel so good and like such a dick at the same time, knowing there was another part to the job he'd purposefully not mentioned, another part he couldn't mention because she wasn't his completely.

Her gaze went to his and held. "So you're not going to find who's doing this to me and kill him, right?"

He reared back. "You shitting me?"

She laughed. "God, I…" She shook her head, still laughing.

He knew he should tell her he'd find whoever was fucking with her and teach him a lesson before he handed the bastard over to the cops. Not telling her could bite him in the ass later, but he was just too enthralled with watching her laugh. It felt like it'd been so long since he'd seen it, heard it. The sound so beautiful, it rippled through him.

"Babe," his voice a growl. He hadn't meant it to but couldn't have helped it. The look on her face, the dinner she made for him, for his boy, made him want to do more than he could right then.

"You leave the door unlocked?"

Her laugh died. "Oh, you were on your bike. I heard you coming, so I unlocked it just before you—"

"I appreciate it. Any other time, I'd love it, but until we're in the clear, I need you to stay safe."

"We're?"

He nodded. "Yeah, you, me, Cul."

"You and Cul aren't a part—"

"We're all in this together."

Her eyes softened. "We shouldn't be."

"We are. You, me, and Cul. We're gonna get through this, yeah?"

She held his stare and nodded.

"So are you gonna keep the doors and windows locked even if you hear me coming?"

She nodded again. Then her mood shifted, she smiled. "Cul said three words in a row today."

He quirked a brow. "Yeah?"

She nodded, her smile widening.

"What he'd say?"

"He said, 'read me, please.' I know it's not much, but isn't it great? It means he's getting better, more confident. He's learning and in just a matter of months…"

The tears in her eyes made his heart clenched so tight it hurt. His boy deserved a woman like Lex for a mom. His fuck-up, his fault.

"I didn't make a big deal of it, of course, because what if he's just shy and bringing it up embarrasses him and he stops? Right?" She tucked a strand of her strawberry hair behind her ear. "I don't know if it's that he's taken a liking to books, but what if it is? What if he wants to learn to read aloud for himself?"

She tipped her head to the side. "What do you think?" A tear spilled out.

He brought his hand to her cheek and wiped it away. "I think it's just you, Lex."

Another tear trailed down. This time, she rubbed it with the back of her hand. "Stupid, I know I'm overreacting."

He cupped her cheek. "Not to me, babe."

She smiled.

He leaned in so tempted to press his lips to hers.

Instead, he lifted his head and kissed her forehead.

They ate dinner together. Conversation flowed easily. For dessert, they had chocolate chip cookies and vanilla ice cream. Nearing Cul's bedtime, he told her she should stay over. She refused. It'd been the first time in a while she'd been relaxed around him, and he hadn't wanted to mess with that, so even though he didn't want to leave her alone, he let it lie. He told her Strike would be around tomorrow to install an alarm. This time, she didn't fight him. Instead, she thanked him. Cullen hugged her tight and mumbled a "night" before Dodge leaned in to her and kissed her cheek. He waited until she closed and locked the door then headed across the street.

That night, he barely slept.

Chapter Twenty-Seven

Her phone rang.

A chill ran up her spine, Lex cringed.

With every call, her fear grew. As a defense mechanism, after the last vandalism, she began silencing her ringer. Dodge hadn't liked this since he couldn't get ahold of her. Made perfect sense, he cared and worried. He suggested they change her number. Four days ago, she had. The calls stopped for a couple of days then started again. Not wanting to worry Dodge more, she hadn't yet told him, but she'd called Officer Johnson. Around this time, she started turning off her ringer again. The only reason it wasn't—because Cullen was with her and she knew eventually Dodge would call. She hadn't wanted to miss his call and then have to lie about the reason. She wasn't a good liar. Dodge would notice. Then she'd have to tell him about the calls and the reason she hadn't told him.

She lifted her head, looking in Cullen's direction, sitting at the far end of her classroom playing with a train. Thankfully, he hadn't noticed her reaction. She pulled open the top drawer of her desk.

Smiling, she slid her finger across the screen. "Hi."

"You okay?"

"Yeah. Fine."

See. Bad liar. She never said "yeah."

"Yeah?"

She swallowed. “I’m fine.”

“When did you get a call?”

She sighed, lifted her stare to Cullen, now looking her way. “Can we talk about it later?”

“Going to you.”

“No,” she said too quickly. “I’m fine.”

“You got a call, Lex. We gotta talk about it now.”

“I’m fine. I’m working. We’ll talk about it later.”

“Right,” he growled and hung up.

Rude, but his way of venting his frustration. She’d deal.

Not ten minutes later, he strode into her classroom, jaw clenched, hands in fists at his sides.

Her gaze darted to Cullen, who hadn’t missed his father enter but kept his distance, his stare unafraid yet vigilant.

Keeping her voice level, she looked to Dodge. “I told you we’d talk about it later.”

Dodge peered at Cullen, and instantly, his eyes and demeanor softened. “Cul, come give me a hug.”

Cullen walked to his father and hugged him. When Cul pulled away, Dodge looked down at him. “Gotta talk to Lex about something important. Go play, but stay where Lex and me can see you, ’kay?”

Cul nodded and headed back to his toy. As Dodge neared, Lex dropped her pen and stood.

“You see anyone stop me coming in here?”

She shook her head. “I-I wouldn’t know.”

“Answer’s no, Lex. I know the school’s got a security guard, but he wasn’t up front. I walked right in here. No one stopped me. No one asked me where I was going. No one even saw me.”

A new hurricane-proof sliding glass door, a couple

of new windows, an alarm system, and the only reason there weren't cameras installed as well was that she argued against them until she was blue in the face, meaning Dodge had made it hard for anyone to get to her while she was home. The next best option, her work. Still, she hadn't considered it primarily because there was school security.

She swallowed. "I see your point."

"Yeah. So now are you gonna tell me when you got the call?"

"Two days ago."

He didn't say a word, just stared at her, eyes on fire, jaw clenched, face beet red. Then he turned and stormed off.

Her gut clenched then rolled.

She'd done it—gotten him so mad he'd walked away. Had she accomplished what she set out to do—convince him they should go their separate ways? Maybe, and that scared her more than the lunatic terrorizing her because exactly what she feared happened in just a week.

She'd fallen more deeply in love with Dave "Dodge" Roth. He accomplished that by simply being there for her, making it impossible for her to keep her distance. He texted her, spent his nights with her and Cul. He cooked, or she did. She read to Cul, or they watched TV together. Just like before except she refused to spend the night at his place or have him stay at hers, and he hadn't fought her on this. Aside from a few pecks on her cheek and forehead when he greeted her or said goodbye, he hadn't even kissed her, but they talked a lot about everything and anything. Whenever she felt scared, somehow he knew and comforted her.

He'd become her rock.

Naturally, then and there, it felt like her world had crumbled, so she stood frozen nursing a deep ache in the center of her chest.

When he didn't return, she took a seat intending to finish grading the stack of students' work. Instead, she stared at the pile hoping the pain inside her would fade.

Her classroom door parted. She lifted her head as Dodge strode through. It'd been at least a half hour, and it hadn't done him any good. Face impassive, but his jaw was hard, and his eyes were ominous.

He closed the distance between them. "Get your stuff. It's time to go."

She didn't argue. She wouldn't. For one, she wasn't done, but what she had to do, she could do from home. Besides, she was relieved he'd come back, and as pathetic as it was, she didn't want him to leave again. Anyway, she owed him this, right? When she was angry, he always heard her out. Sometimes, he gave in. Case in point, her yoga attire and the cameras she refused to have installed. Only fair she did the same for him.

When she nodded, his eyes widened subtly.

She turned her head. "Cul, honey?"

Cul already looking their way.

"Pick up your stuff, we're leaving."

He looked to his father then back at her and did as she asked.

She grabbed the stack of papers she meant to grade, stuffed them into a folder, carted her purse out of the bottom drawer of her desk, and stood. "Cul hasn't had a snack."

Dodge nodded.

He walked her and Cul to her car. "You got his car seat, he can ride with you."

Snatching her keys from her purse, she unlocked her car.

Dodge helped Cul inside and strapped him in. Then he shut the door, turned, and said over his shoulder, "Meet you at our house."

"Cul hasn't had a snack."

He faced her. "We have food at our place."

"But there're cookies at mine—"

"There're cookies at our place too. There just aren't any of yours."

"But he was…"

Dodge released a loaded breath.

"…Excited. I told him he could have some."

That muscle in his jaw twitched, but he nodded.

She hopped into her car and drove. In minutes, she parked in her garage and helped Cullen out of his car seat. Inside, she turned off the alarm, grabbed two cookies and apple juice, Cul's favorite, from the fridge, and set them on the counter for him.

When a knock sounded on her front door, she headed for it, looked through the peephole, and opened it.

"You look?" he asked as he strolled inside.

"Yes, of course."

Locking the door behind him, she faced him.

"No, babe, not 'of course' 'cause you've been getting calls, and *you* didn't tell me. I'm trying to protect you. You have Cul with you, for fuck's sake—"

"I reported it." This, she hoped appeased him.

He reared back. When what she said seemed to settle, much to her surprise, his body locked. "You called the cops?"

"I called Officer Johnson—"

Through gritted teeth, he said, "So you ran to that fuckin' cop who wants to fuck you, but you didn't say shit to *me*?" His voice a low growl.

She shook her head. "He doesn't—"

He leaned in to her until a breath away from her lips. "Babe, wake the hell up. That cop wants to fuck you, and you went to *him* instead of *me*." He slammed his palm against his chest. "So it looks like you want *him* looking after you instead of *me*."

God, he was jealous? Never had a man been jealous about her. Not until him. The first time, he'd insulted and humiliated her. Now, he made her feel…*worth*.

Her turn to be shocked, so stunned she couldn't put words together. All she managed to do, stand there staring at his too beautiful, angry face and let that warmth in her gut rise all the way up her throat.

She swallowed. "I didn't want you to worry any more than you already were…are. Besides, he's a cop. It's what cops do."

He pulled away slightly, face and body relaxing as he scanned her. Finally, his lips quirked up. "Lex, baby, you realize what you just said?"

Yes. She cared and said as much. She was tired of trying to convince herself otherwise, tired of fighting him, yet she didn't have to say this aloud.

"Don't worry about me. I worry about you, about Cul, about us. It's my job. I gotta protect you. You don't worry about anything but being happy."

"It's…"

He snaked his arm around her waist, tugged her

body to his, and cupped her cheek. "The club, we're a family. We take care of our own. You're with me, so you're part of this family too. We'll all look out for you, so you can't hide shit from me. We can fix this and we will, but we gotta do it together."

God, he was so close. It had been a week since he'd insisted they were together, but in that week, he'd only touched her to comfort her. Only natural that right then, the urge to get on the tips of her toes and press her lips to his overwhelmed her.

"Promise me."

What was she promising?

The hell with it.

"I promise."

Darn it. Now, she didn't know what promise to keep.

He grinned. "You promised, Lex, can't break promises, so you're not gonna hide shit from me, right?"

She smiled. "I promise I won't keep anything from you."

She wanted so badly to kiss him then. She almost did. Before she summoned the courage, he pressed a kiss to her forehead and released her.

She shifted her head. Cullen sat on a stool, a cookie in hand. His head cocked to the side, brows creased looking right at them.

"Everything okay, Cul?"

He looked between his father and her in that observant way.

She smiled assuring him.

Only then did he nod.

****

It felt like she'd just drifted to sleep when the jarring sound of her phone ringing woke her. She'd forgotten to silence it. Without thought, Lex reached to her nightstand, snatched her phone, and answered.

"Hello," she mumbled sleepily.

Nothing.

Then ragged breaths.

She shot up in bed, covered the mouthpiece of her cell with her hand, and stilled.

A moment later, a chilling, distorted voice, "I'll find a way in."

Breaths shallow, her hands trembled.

The line went dead. Dropping her phone, she jumped out of bed and flipped on her lights. Frantically, her gaze flew from the tossed comforter and blanket to the windows facing the front of her house beside her. Blue drapes still and unmoving. She snapped her head. Dark wood armoire sat in front of her, a decorative vase and a series of perfumes on it. Next to the armoire, another window. Those drapes, too, unmoving. She looked to her right, toward the small hall leading to her bathroom and closet. The lights off, the door to her bathroom parted.

Had she left a window open? The door unlocked? Had she set the alarm? What the hell should she do? Call the cops? For what? A prank call?

Her phone rang.

She let out a small, terrified wail and slapped a shaky hand over her mouth.

Deadening silence. Then it rang again.

Her heart pounded louder, drumming against her chest.

Should she pick up? Should she pack a bag and

stay at a hotel for the night? Right then, she couldn't do either. She couldn't move!

The ringing stopped. Tears threatening to spill, she took an unstable breath, almost relieved until the ringing started again and seemed like it got louder and louder. She had to make it stop.

Walking to her bed, she found her phone, nabbed it, and stared at the screen. Dodge's name flashed. She answered it and brought it to her ear.

"Lex, you okay?" His voice rough.

She released a breath and ignored the tears pricking her eyes.

"Babe, talk to me. Gotta know you're okay."

"I'm…" She swallowed. "I'm…not okay."

"I'm coming—"

"No, you can't!" Tears trekked down her cheeks. "Someone c-called. It woke me. He s-said…" Her voice broke. "He said h-he'd find a way in. What if he's outside? What if—"

"Gotta calm down, Lex."

"I'm scared. I-I'm—" Even to herself, she sounded hysterical.

"Baby, calm down. Don't hang up, but look on your phone like Strike taught you. Check to see if the alarm's still on."

She pulled the phone away from her ear. Without hanging up, she searched for the app, clicked on it, entered her passcode, and made sure her house alarm was activated. Her shaking hands made it take longer than expected. She double-checked before she brought the phone back to her ear. "It's on."

"Okay, now, are you still in your room?"

She nodded. "Y-yes."

"Stay there. Try to relax and breathe, Lex. It'll be a little while."

"For?" she asked, in part trying to get her mind elsewhere.

"Brothers are coming. They're gonna check outside your house. Then they're gonna knock on your door. I'll—"

"W-what?" She wiped her face. "I'm fine. It's nothing. You… When did you tell them?"

"While you were checking the alarm."

That fast?

She swallowed. "You shouldn't have bothered them, Dodge. It's fine. I'm fine. Everything's fine."

"It's *not* fine, Lex. Someone called you and scared the shit outta you, so you're *not* fine. You're terrified thinking someone's outside your place, and I'm across the street and I can't do shit 'cause if there's someone out there, I can't leave my boy alone means I'm *not* fuckin' fine either. My woman needs me, and I'm powerless to do shit, but wait, so nothing's *fine*."

God, how was she supposed to resist that? The man she loved worrying about her just because she'd gotten a stupid phone call, which was mind-numbingly frightening but she didn't expect anyone who wasn't in her position to understand.

Warmth spread through her chest and settled in her gut. With that, she lost her will. She couldn't resist him and she wouldn't, not anymore. He'd proved he was more than the mistake he'd made. He could hurt her again and that terrified her, but she'd take the chance on him, on them.

"Lex, you there?"

"Y-yes."

"What's wrong? You heard something?"

"No. I… Why? Did you?"

The sound of his humorless, rough chuckle came through the phone. "Naw, Lex, you were quiet a while. It's why I asked."

A second later, he spoke again. "They're here. You may hear them searching around your house, 'kay? Don't be scared."

Easier said than done. For his sake, she mumbled, "Okay."

Silence.

"Now, walk out to your living room, Lex, but carefully, yeah? Turn lights on, look around. You see anything out of the ordinary, you scream. They'll bust through the door."

Oh God. Oh God.

She pressed one shaking hand to her stomach. "But the alarm's still on. How could anyone—"

"Just being extra careful."

"Okay." Hesitantly, she walked to her bedroom door, opened it, and immediately turned on the hallway lights.

"Where are you now?"

"H-hallway." She looked around. Her master bedroom at the far end of the house, so it took a while to get to the opening leading into her living room. Luckily, she didn't have to worry about looking into the two other rooms. The doors were closed as she kept them.

At the mouth of the hall leading to the living room, she turned on the light. "Living room." Her stare moved, looking beyond the living area into the kitchen. Empty. She then swung her gaze to the front of her house to the seating area and last to her front door. On her alarm, a red light flashed signaling it was on.

She'd made such a big fuss for nothing. Still, as silly as she felt, even staring at that red blinking light, that fear didn't abate, the courage to cross the expanse of the room to her front door fleeting.

"Lex?"

"Going." She took a deep breath, ran across the room, disabled the alarm, unlocked, and opened her front door. She met Hash's gaze first.

His went to her chest then back to her face. He cleared his throat. "You okay?"

She nodded. "It's Hash," she said to Dodge, stupidly considering he probably knew.

"He's gonna bring you over to me."

"Okay." She looked at her phone briefly and ended the call. Her head snapped up realizing several others joined Hash. One she knew by name, he'd been there not long ago, Army, Allie's brother. The others she knew their faces but wasn't sure about their names. Right then, not a high priority. "Thanks for—"

"Don't mention it," one of the others said. "We take care of our own. You're with Dodge, you're part of us too."

Hearing that reminded her of something Dodge had said to her hours ago: *The club, we're a family. We take care of our own. You're with me, so you're part of this family too.* Here was proof. These men had been woken in the middle of the night because she got a prank call, and they were here for her, for Dodge.

She had the sudden urge to cry. Eyes watering, she looked down at her bare feet and nodded.

"Come." Hash turned.

She followed him down her porch steps, across her lawn, sidewalk, street, and onto Dodge's lawn. His door parted, and finally, she caught sight of him. In his usual sleep attire, shirtless with a pair of athletic shorts, his hair a mess, his gaze searing her.

She ran straight to him. His eyes widened for a split second, something she wiped out of her mind the minute she reached him. Burying her face in his chest, she snaked her arms around his waist and squeezed as hard as she could. One of his arms wrapped around her back, the other grasped the back of her neck. She inhaled, and the smell of him spread through her.

Safe.

Finally.

She held onto him for several minutes as the tension and fear left her.

His hand at the base of her neck moved, clutching her cheek and angling her face to meet his. She got on the tips of her toes, released his waist to hook her arms around his neck and tug his lips toward hers. Then she invaded his mouth.

It had been so long. She craved him so much that she surrendered completely. All she could do, cling, hold on, and pray he wouldn't let go.

He groaned. His hand, cupping her cheek, drew her away. She whimpered at the loss.

"Fuck, Lex." He swallowed. "You okay?"

She nodded.

His eyes flared. "You're barefoot and half naked."

Darn it. No denying it, and his brothers had seen her.

Her cheeks flamed.

"You hadn't just kissed me like that I might've had

to bend you over my knee."

She shot him an annoyed look even though she wasn't really.

He grinned. "Get in bed, baby. I'll be right there."

She nodded and walked away, knowing she couldn't deny for a brief moment in his arms, because of him, she forgot what had happened and how terrified she'd been.

Chapter Twenty-Eight

Dodge had never been more afraid in his life. Nope, not true. That day Lex dove in front of a car to save Cullen beat it.

Standing immobile in his house, not able to do anything while his woman was just across the street frightened half to death, sucked. It could've been worse. Someone could've broken into her house. She could've been hurt, and he wouldn't have been able to do anything but watch.

He learned his lesson. It ended tonight. He didn't give a fuck if tomorrow she woke and insisted they were nothing more than neighbors. He'd tie her to him, but no way in hell she'd be away from him more than absolutely necessary. While she was at work, he'd have a couple of brothers outside the school on the lookout. They couldn't, he'd do it himself. That meant nights she spent with him. His house or hers, he didn't care as long as her ass was beside his. It was the only way he could protect her, protect Cul. He needed them together.

Finally.

Thank fuck.

He slept practically nothing all week. With someone harassing her, now threatening her, he'd been waking up every few hours to peek out his window and check on her. That night though he hadn't yet fallen asleep when he looked out and saw her light go on. Two in the morning, he knew something was wrong, so he called her. The first call she hadn't answered, he'd grabbed his gun. He called again, and thankfully, she answered.

Shit.

That kiss got him heated. He needed to focus. Hash was looking at him, waiting.

"What'd you find?"

"Nothing. Brothers still looking around, but it's dark, probably better to look again in daylight."

He nodded. "What about the phone company?"

As soon as she told him the calls started again, he told his brothers, figuring it was a lead. When they changed her number, they listed it as private. No way anyone could've gotten it unless they worked for the phone company or bribed someone who did.

"Still lookin' into it. But the phone company's on the defensive, they're not gonna be easy to get info from. Could take a while."

He swallowed thickly. "What about the ex?"

By this point, Army, Blaze, and Strike had joined Hash on his front porch.

"Guy's not even living in San Fran anymore. Neighbors say he got a job in LA. Took off two months ago," Army said.

Meaning they were at a standstill. It seemed the only chance of finding this guy was to wait until he made his next move and catch him in the act. That wasn't good enough for Dodge. It meant Lex had to live with this shit until then, and he wanted to end this yesterday.

Strike lifted his chin. "Hate to point out the

obvious, but since you haven't mentioned it… You think maybe Lilliam's behind this?"

No, he didn't because while mind games were her thing, she didn't care about him or Cullen enough to go to the lengths this asshole was. The constant calls and vandalism were time consuming. Lilliam liked to fuck with people's lives, but she wouldn't mess with her own to do it. She lied to manipulate, but aside from that, she was a bunch of hot air.

He shook his head. "I don't think she'd do this. She doesn't give a shit about me or Cul. She doesn't give a shit about Lex with us either."

Hash cocked his head. "It didn't look like that to me."

"She ran into Lex and Cul at the mall and made a big deal about it, said shit to Lex to make her question me, to terrify her own kid, to fuck with Cul and me, but trust me, in the end, Lilliam's glad it isn't her dealing with a kid even if that kid is her own. She wanted to be part of this club. When she got what she wanted, she made it clear she didn't want it anymore."

Blaze shrugged. "Yeah, but maybe now that she's lost it, she's realized she wants it back."

Over his dead body.

He shook his head yet again. "Doesn't make sense. She doesn't want to be a mother or a wife."

Strike nodded. "Still think we should check her out."

He nodded. "We find her, I'm there. Don't think she's involved, but it doesn't hurt to check, and I gotta get her to stop stalling the divorce."

Blaze quirked a brow. "Fuck, you're still married?"

He and Blaze weren't as close as he and Hash

were, the reason Blaze had no idea.

He dipped his chin. "Her lawyer asks for extensions, judge grants it. I'm tired of it."

Army dug his hands in his pockets. "Right, brother, good night. We'll keep you in the loop if we find anything."

"Thanks for coming out."

Hash smirked, gave him a chin lift, turned, and strode away with the rest of his brothers. Dodge watched them go thinking he was lucky he had them.

****

Lex strode into Dodge's master bathroom and washed her feet with warm water and soap. After drying off, she climbed into his bed, buried her face in his pillow, inhaled his scent, and waited.

Catching sight of him at the doorway to his room, she sat up in bed. Instantly, her gaze shot to his hand. Firm in his grip, a gun. "Y-you have a gun?"

He strode into his closet and walked out a minute later. "Yeah, Lex. I got a few."

"What for?"

Walking around the other side of the bed, he sat and turned to her. "Bodyguards tend to be armed. Don't do that anymore, but I used to. When I did, I needed to be armed, so I bought several guns. I got a permit too."

He wrapped his arm around her waist, slid her close, and laid back, taking her with him. Hooking his other arm around her neck, he angled himself toward her and released her waist to cup her cheek. "You sure you okay?"

She swallowed. "Yes. I'm okay."

Amazing, but true. She wasn't scared anymore because Dodge wouldn't let anything happen to her.

Even before she decided to forgive him, she trusted him to keep her safe.

"You weren't tonight."

She shook her head. "No, I wasn't, but I'm good now."

Holding her stare, he vowed, "We're gonna find out who's doing this and make him stop."

He'd said this before. He hadn't told her how the club would make whoever was terrorizing her stop, but she believed he and the club would keep her safe. She believed this not only because Dodge had thus far done anything and everything to protect her and he was part of the club but also because she'd grown close to Allie and the other old ladies. Last night after Cullen and Dodge headed home, she'd called Allie and told her the latest—that the prank calls started again, that she hadn't told Dodge, and that when he found out, he'd been upset. Allie told her to trust Dodge, to trust the club. Then Allie went on to share something Lex would've never imagined. Allie said her ex-fiancé had kidnapped her, and that the club had rescued her. And so, Lex had no doubts, the club, because of Dodge, because she was his, would help her, help him, help them.

After a long moment, he scanned her face and pressed a kiss to her forehead. "Night, Lex."

She smiled softly, closed her eyes, and drifted to sleep easily.

****

Dodge didn't want to get up. His pillow smelled like Lex, and for a while, all it smelled like was him.

Shit.

Lex.

Sitting up, he swung his arm out beside him,

gripping the empty sheets. Then he scanned the room and dragged a hand through his hair. This time, she hadn't even tried to convince him they wouldn't work. She'd just left.

Tearing the blanket off him, he climbed out of bed, intent on hauling his ass to Lex's and bringing her back. He spared a glance at his alarm clock. Ten a.m. He hadn't slept past seven in years. Grabbing the shirt draped over his armoire, he threw it over his head and strode into the hallway, stopping in front of Cul's room. His boy wasn't there and hadn't woken him. Out of the ordinary. When Cul woke, he woke him mainly because he was hungry and he needed his old man to make his breakfast.

Nearing his living room, he heard it—the sound of Cul giggling. His chest expanded like it did every time he heard his boy laugh. He heard it so often as of late since Lex came into Cul's life, he'd thought it wouldn't affect him.

At the mouth of the hall, he spotted the back of his leather sectional. He couldn't see Cul sitting there, but he saw the mass of Lex's strawberry locks.

She and Cul burst into giggles. His gaze wandered to the TV. He thought, not for the first time, he needed to upgrade. Recognizing the movie on the screen, he smiled. Cullen's favorite, he played it over and over again, so it wasn't the first time Lex watched it with him.

"Dad!"

He moved his stare to the sofa. Cul now stood on it, his hands grasping the backrest.

"Morning, Cul. You sleep good?"

Cul nodded.

Lex stood. Her gaze on his boy when she said, "I'm going to make your dad breakfast, okay?"

Cul nodded.

"Be back." She smiled and closed the distance between them.

Inches away, she got on the tips of her toes, pressed her hands against his stomach, and slanted her head back, lips nearing his.

As of late, he'd only reached for her when he couldn't help it. Though he'd kissed her forehead and cheek a few times since their big fight, he'd never even attempted to kiss her lips, mainly because he hadn't thought she wanted him to. Right then and there, no denying she wanted him to, so he leaned down and took what she offered.

After a brief kiss, she drew away smiling. "What do you want for breakfast?"

His chest tightened. It happened every time she looked at him with her heart in her eyes. He hadn't seen that since he'd fucked up. Not that he blamed her, she was scared he'd hurt her again. It hadn't stopped him from hoping he'd earn her trust and get to see that look again, so he kept at it, talking to her, calling her, texting her, spending time with her.

This was better though. He woke one day, and there it was—that look. There she was—his Lex, unguarded, sweet, and perfect Lex.

He swallowed. "So we're good?"

She grinned. "Yes."

He arched a brow. "Because?"

"You need a because?"

No, but if there was one he wanted to know.

"I care about you. I always did." Her eyes softened.

"You were right. I was scared."

"And you're not anymore?"

She shrugged. "I am, but I trust that you wouldn't purposefully do anything to hurt me."

He cupped her cheek. "I won't, Lex. Promise."

She smiled.

He then kissed her deep, and she let him.

Chapter Twenty-Nine

Her phone rang.

Lex had come to hate when it did. Dodge noticed, of course, and stopped calling her altogether. On weekdays, he had her check-in with him during lunch, and when he wanted to get ahold of her, he texted. Sweet, then again, Dodge was thoughtful, always.

Sitting at her desk, half past three, the reason it wasn't on silent to begin with was that she was expecting a call from Allie. Her phone rang for the third time. She finally garnered the courage to open her desk drawer. Spotting the number on her caller id, she released a loaded breath. Not the call she dreaded. Those came from a private number.

"Hello."

"Miss Millen?"

"This is she."

"Ace." A pause then, "Officer Ace Johnson."

Finally. He had news. It had to be good news. At this point, any news would be good.

She straightened. "Yes, have you found any—"

"No, Alexa. We haven't, and it got me thinking. Have you had any issues with your neighbor?"

Her brows drew together. "My neighbor?"

"Yes, Dave Roth."

"He's more than my neighbor—"

"Right." His voice tight. "Have you broken up or

taken time apart recently? Have you considered it?"

Where was this coming from? And why was it police business?

She swallowed. "How is this related?"

"After the last vandalism, several neighbors reported seeing a dark sedan driving off, but no license plate, probably because it was dark. Even in a small town like this, there're hundreds of dark sedans. We've gotten nowhere meaning we've exhausted our leads. That coupled with the fact that you aren't someone disliked by anyone leads me to believe Roth could be involved."

No. No way. All Dodge had done was protect her. All his club had done was protect her.

She shook her head. "That's ridiculous—"

"It would be if he didn't have a motive, and only you can answer that. So does he, Alexa?"

No. Dodge didn't. Before she insisted on this, Officer Johnson spoke again.

"If he's losing you, he could do something to make you think you need him."

The breath whooshed out of her.

Even as she thought about it, she knew. Dodge wouldn't. He loved… No, he'd never said it, but he cared about her a lot. He *couldn't* possibly be so callous, couldn't do something so horrible to her, someone he cared about. Besides, they had an issue, but he'd always been so certain he'd get her back. Why resort to scaring her?

"Alexa, you still there?"

"I-I…yes." She cleared her throat. "I'm here."

"Has he ever been with you while you've gotten a call?"

"Yes, of course."

They spent a lot of time together, and the calls came five to six times a day.

"The first time your home was vandalized, did you tell him? Is that how he knew? What about the second time? When we showed, he was already there. Did you call him? He could've easily vandalized your house then showed before we did to make himself out to be the hero."

God, no. No, no, no. She'd seen the look on his face, read the fear. He'd been terrified for her. When she got that threatening phone call, he'd been angry he couldn't get to her. In the middle of the night, *his* club searched.

She defended him, but she couldn't deny the calls hadn't started until she insisted they go their separate ways. Another fact, she hadn't called Dodge either time her house had been vandalized. He'd shown. Granted, the second time, the vandal woke the whole neighborhood.

Thinking on this, she remembered something else. Dodge called her moments after getting that threatening call. How had he known? The caller said, "I'll find a way in." In where? Into her life?

God, Officer Johnson *could* be right. Dodge could've put this into motion, but why hadn't he stopped when she'd given in to him completely? There was another thing that bothered her. Since she'd decided to give him another chance, they hadn't yet had sex. Saturday night, she fell asleep on the couch with Cullen. Sunday, he said he needed to meet with the club. She tried to wait up but eventually fell asleep. Monday and Tuesday, he worked late and arrived after she went to bed. He hadn't left them alone though. Some of the brothers had been parked outside his house. Before he'd been insatiable and with him, so was she. Why hadn't he made the time? Was the guilt of what he was doing to her eating at him? Was the man she fell in love with capable of doing this to her?

Her stomach rolled, a painful ache in her chest making it hard to think straight. Then the room went hazy.

"If I were you, Alexa, I'd get as far away from him and his gang as possible. You want protection, I can offer you protection."

Police could, but he didn't say police. He said *he* could, and he said it so casually like he hadn't just ripped her world apart.

Yet this didn't change the fact that he could be right.

"You have my number. Call me. Anytime, Alexa." Then he hung up.

Hand clutching her phone, a sob tore from her throat. She slapped her hand over her mouth as tears streamed down her face. Grabbing her purse from the bottom drawer of her desk, she shoved her phone in it, snatched her keys, and ran out of her classroom.

Only one way to find out if Officer Johnson was right.

****

Dodge's phone buzzed. He straightened making sure he didn't slam his head under the hood of the Charger he'd been working on and plucked his cell out of his pocket.

Sparing a glance at the caller ID, he slid his thumb across the screen and brought the phone to his ear.

"Blaze."

"Don't know what the fuck happened."

His body locked; heart dropped to the pit of his stomach.

"Must've gotten another call. I asked her, but she wouldn't say. Don't get it. She's crying bad, Dodge. Not tears, she's fuckin' hysterical. All red like she'd been crying for a while."

His fingers tightened around the phone as he swallowed the bile rising in the back of his throat.

"She just got in her car and drove off. Skim's following her."

He clenched his jaw. "You let her drive like that?"

"Tried to stop her, and she got worse. Brother, don't think you understand how upset she is."

He didn't know but could imagine. Without even laying eyes on her, he *felt* it, a knot in his stomach rising up his chest, puncturing every organ along the way like he'd taken a bullet or several.

He felt at a loss. All he did was try to find who was messing with her, slacking even as a father to make this shit stop. Luckily, Lex stayed with Cul, and Cul didn't mind one bit. But Dodge had gotten nowhere. His brothers had gotten nowhere. It meant he *couldn't* make it stop. His beautiful, snappy, funny Lex, when would he get her back? When would this shit end?

"Where's she headed?"

"Thinkin' if she was home, Skim would've let you know already."

"Fuck."

He needed to find her, had to comfort her. Where would she go? Last time she'd been upset, she drove to her sister's. He hoped this time that wouldn't be the case. She had to know better than drive an hour, had to know she could go to him.

He dropped his head, stared at his boots, and dragged his hand through his hair. The worry making it so he could barely breathe.

"Skim'll keep an eye out for her."

Blood rushed to his head. "She doesn't need Skim. She needs *me*."

Hearing a whistle, he snapped his head up. Her car pulled into the lot, Skim riding his bike behind her.

"She's here. She came to me." He ended the call, tucked his phone in his back pocket while he sprinted across the garage to the parking lot.

She hadn't yet gotten out. When he neared, he knew why. She was busy wiping her face. He opened her car door. Her head shot to him.

Shit. Blaze hadn't lied. She wasn't hysterical, per se, not then, but her makeup was smeared. Her face was blotchy and red, and that redness ran all the way down her neck to her chest.

She drew the big-rimmed sunglasses resting at the top of her head down to cover her eyes.

He ignored the pain slicing through his chest and reached for her. "Baby…"

She flinched away from *him*. She'd gone to him, but it looked like she didn't want him. It *killed*, and he couldn't play it off. Gut clenching, heart tightening, he couldn't do anything but stop in his tracks.

She hadn't missed his reaction. The next instant, she mumbled a half-assed apology. "I…I'm sorry. I…" A pause, then, "We need to talk."

There it was. He meant to nod, but it was more of a swift jerk. He turned, walking inside the garage into the compound. He wanted to go into the first room he found empty, but he didn't want them interrupted, and Lex liked her privacy. She wouldn't want anyone listening or seeing her so torn up, so he went all the way up to the second floor to his room.

Holding the door open for her, she walked in. He closed it behind himself, spun, and met her gaze. She dropped her purse on his bed, lifted her sunglasses, and rested them at the top of her head, pulling her hair back partially and revealing her swollen, red-rimmed eyes. He'd seen them before, and still, he hadn't been prepared to see them again. Like a kick to the balls.

He swallowed thickly. "You get another call?"

"I n-need you to be honest with me. If you're never honest w-with me again, fine, but right now, I *need* you to be h-honest with me." Her eyes welled. "Whatever you tell me, I'll believe you b-because I *trust* you, but you have to understand that once that trust is broken, it's d-dead and there're no m-more second chances."

He shook his head. "I—"

"Did you have anything to do with this mess? The calls, the vandalism, that threatening call?"

His heart came to a stop. He heard her wrong, or he'd hallucinated. No way his woman, his sweet, beautiful Lex would think that.

He reared back. "Come again?"

She shut her eyes tightly and took a ragged breath. After a moment, she parted them. "Did y-you tell anyone to call me? Vandalize my h-house? Threaten me? Did y-you do it yourself?"

"No," he barked the word immediately.

His head throbbed, pulse spiked. Pissed at himself, at her, at the fucked shit that happened to him. That anger would've built and built, but the moment he said it, her shoulders slumped, expression transformed, remorse and relief shining through her teary eyes. He would've reached for her except not ten minutes ago she'd flinched away. Not to mention, he had no clue where they stood.

Those tears in her eyes fell and stained her face anew. "I-I'm…" Her voice cracked. Her hands went to her stomach, clutching there. "I'm sorry… It's just… I s-started thinking, and the first time my house was vandalized, you just showed. I hadn't told you about it, and then days ago, you called me right a-after I got that call and…" She hiccupped. "H-how did y-you know unless…"

Her hands, against her stomach, trembled. "And you haven't even tried to touch m-me since… All of it made me think that maybe it was possible you orchestrated this. I'm s-sorry. I just let m-myself—"

Sorry. Yeah, he knew. She believed him, but it didn't change that she thought him capable of it, proved it by asking. He just couldn't wrap his mind around how she'd come to that conclusion.

"In all that thinking you did, did you consider I have no reason to want to scare the shit outta you?"

With tears streaming steadily down her face, she swallowed visibly. "Everything started after we b-broke up, so—"

Sock to the stomach, no, to the heart.

He winced. "So you thought this was my big plan to get you back?" he screamed, not because he meant to but because what she said was so ridiculous. Did she not know him at all?

Lex wiped her face. "I'm so s-sorry." She shook

her head. "I know I-I shouldn't have b-believed it. I should've…"

He turned away, took three steps, putting distance between them, and ran his hands through his hair. Right then, he couldn't stand looking at her. Her tears, her agony, he felt it like it was his own, and it was fucking devastating.

She shouldn't have believed it? How would his sweet Lex consider it? How had her mind even gone there?

Anything he had in his power to do, he did for *her*. Move the earth, bring her the moon, turn himself inside out… He thought she knew this because every chance he had, he showed her.

Though he had to keep in mind this wasn't his Lex, this was scared-out-of-her-mind Lex who'd been fucked with for weeks. Even then, his Lex wouldn't jump to this conclusion. No, she loved him. She didn't know she said it, but she had.

He faced her and balled his hands so he wouldn't touch her. He wanted to, but he didn't know if she'd cringe again, and he couldn't take that twice in one day.

Tears continued to flow. "I've made such bad choices with m-men that it was e-easy for me to believe I h-had messed up again."

Again, she used the word "believe," instead of saying she'd jumped to conclusions. Why?

Then bam.

Just like that.

It hit him.

Livid, scorching anger, so hot, he felt the blood pumping through his veins boil. "Someone told you this. Someone made you think this, planted the seed."

Her eyes widened. “I…I…”

It’d been a guess, but now he knew.

Eyes narrowing, he took a step toward her. “Who?”

She covered her mouth with her shaking hands and shook her head.

“*Who*?”

She dropped her hands and wrapped her arms around herself. “I c-can’t. I *can’t*.”

“Who *lied* to you? Who fuckin’ made you doubt *me*?”

“Please. P-please, I’m doing it for you. I don’t want you to—”

“Who the *fuck* was it*?*”

“It doesn’t matter. I believe you! I love you!”

He stilled, heart clenching, bursting, searing.

She loved him.

She said it.

Willingly.

To him.

He knew it, but there was something about hearing her admit it when she wasn’t asleep that made it real.

No woman had ever said that to him, not even his mother. Lex was the first.

Amazing, so he stayed there staring at her, eating up that beautiful feeling, and it made him feel like a bastard, feeling so good while Lex kept crying. The tears wouldn’t stop. They flowed and flowed silently like they were part of her face.

He swallowed. “Who told you?”

The light went out of her eyes as if her heart broke through them. Instantly, her tears dried. “I’m not telling you.”

He cocked his head. “Bet I can guess?”

Lifting her chin, she held his gaze.

He made a good guess because he thought it through. Not many people didn't like him, he stayed out of trouble, but most importantly, he looked after his kid and knowing Cullen's mother, people admired that about him. Lex wouldn't believe Lilliam after last time so that left, "Officer Wants-To-Fuck-You?"

She didn't move, but her eyes changed. That hopelessness though still visible faded enough for something else to shine through—fear.

He turned, took two steps, parted the door, and strode out. She ran after him. He heard her telling him to stop, begging him to. When she clasped his elbow, he spun, tore his arm out of her grasp, turned again, and strode through the compound, through the garage. He then hopped on his bike, revved the engine, and drove away.

Before he knew it, he'd parked in front of the police station. Cutting the engine, he heard the roar of bikes. He ignored that too and strolled inside. Officer Asshole desk was in view of the entrance, their eyes locked.

He didn't make any sudden movements, didn't even close the distance between them. He knew cops, knew dickhead cops better. That asshole would construe anything as assault. He didn't need to end up in the slammer. Lex needed him. Cul needed him.

From the entrance, he said loud enough the asshole forty feet away heard, "She believes *me* 'cause she knows I'd do anything for her, 'cause she loves *me*."

Officer Asshole's gaze hardened.

Dodge glared right back. The door opened and closed behind him. He ignored it and went on. "So I'm here to let you know you were trying to win her, but *all* you did was fuck with her. That your way to protect and serve? Making a woman who's been through a fuck ton of shit the past few weeks lose her shit?"

He shook his head. "It is, you did a fantastic job, officer."

With those parting words, he turned, ignored Trick, Blaze, and Hash standing by the exit, and stormed off.

Chapter Thirty

Eyes swimming, hands shaking, the world spun. Lex couldn't see the series of cars parked in the garage, couldn't see his brothers rushing behind Dodge, but she *felt*, felt her muscles clench, her stomach roll, her heart ache.

God, oh God, what had she done? What the hell to do now? Wait for him to get arrested? Wait for his call to bail him out? No, that would never happen. That indomitable male pride of his wouldn't let him ask anything like that of her.

She should've known better than to trust that officer. She should've trusted herself, what she knew to be true, that Dodge cared about her even if now she knew he didn't love her.

That hurt the most—blurting something she couldn't have held in much longer while staring straight at him and seeing nothing. No pride, no relief, no excitement, no smile—nothing, like she'd said the simplest, most mundane thing.

She needed a break from her life. As of late, it'd become too much to handle.

Lex grabbed her keys from her back pocket where she'd tucked them, walked to her car, and hopped in. She heard her name called and ignored it. She didn't need to be babysat every second of every day, not by the brothers of the man she loved who didn't love her.

That wasn't fair to him, but at that moment, she didn't care.

She shoved the key in the ignition, and the engine rumbled to life. Backing out of the parking space, she sped off. Driving out of town, she looked in her rearview mirror. No one had followed. Whether it was because Dodge told them not to or because she lost them, she had no clue.

Lex didn't care about that either. In fact, she preferred it this way. She needed to be alone. The fact that she'd left her purse and phone in Dodge's room at the compound meant no one would call. She hadn't known where she planned to go but somehow ended up at the beach. Taking off her shoes, she walked up and down the shore alone trying not to think about anything. After watching the sun go down, she decided it was time to head home.

Not a minute after entering Wadden, a bike tailed her. At the next light, another joined and then another. She pulled onto her drive with three bikes behind her car.

Dodge sat on the steps leading to her porch, head bent, elbows on his knees. Looking up, he jumped to his feet. Before she knew it, he dragged open her door, helped her to her feet, and encased her in his strong arms.

"Baby…" His hands slithered up her back then down leaving no part untouched, unheated. Cupping her cheeks, he drew away to look into her eyes and took a deep breath. "Fuck." He kissed her deep, long, and beautifully.

When he broke the kiss, his eyes narrowed, and his big, strong hands at her cheeks squeezed. "Don't ever do that shit to me again, Lex."

She meant to tell him again that she trusted him, meant to apologize, but he didn't give her the chance.

"You realize some fuckwad is out there doing shit to scare you and making threats. We have no clue who it is, and you take off alone? We've been looking for you for hours. Couldn't find you. None of us could."

One arm snaked around her waist pressing her closer. His jaw hardened. "You have any fuckin' clue how scared outta my mind I was?"

She shook her head.

"Scared enough I was about to call the cops even knowing they can't do shit for twenty-four hours, even knowing I'd be working with Officer Wants-To-Fuck-You."

God, that made her feel good, warm.

She bit the side of her lip. "I'm fine. I just needed some alone time."

"Next time, you get your alone time in my vicinity."

She smiled. "That's not alone time, Dodge."

"Yeah, you get a room. I'll get another."

She shook her head.

He cocked his. "How about when this shit's over, we'll talk about this again?"

She nodded. "I'm glad you didn't get arrested."

"I'm not stupid, Lex. Just told him what I had to say then left."

He tugged her against him, tucking his face against her neck, and breathed deep. It lasted a while. Then he drew away, grabbed her hand, and walked her into her house. Unlocked, she figured he opened it with his key, one she gave him after the last incident when she started spending nights at his house. He'd asked her for it so he could check her house every morning and make sure no one had vandalized it or found a way in.

In the living room, he sat on her beige couch, grasped her hips, and lugged her onto his lap. "First time, your house was vandalized—"

"You don't have to explain—"

He cupped her cheek. "I'm gonna explain 'cause though I know you believe me, you and me are a team. You want to talk about something, there won't be a day when I won't give that to you."

She closed her eyes and let the warmth in her chest spread.

"First time, it was late. I woke up, saw the lights, looked out my window, realized there were cops at your place, so I rushed out to you. It's not uncommon for me to wake up once or twice in the middle of the night. Ever since Cul was a baby, I've been doing it."

He released a breath. "Second time it happened, I heard it. Everyone heard it. Days ago, when you got that call, I was still up. After that second time, I hadn't been getting much sleep. You weren't staying with me, and I was worried, so I had a hard time falling asleep at night. I'd check on you every few hours. It just so happened I was looking out when I saw your bedroom light go on."

Eyes warm, face soft, he snaked his other arm around her waist and tugged her closer. "Nothing more I want than to take you, Lex. I'd take you every hour, but I've been busy. Neglecting you and Cul and work—everything but finding the asshole who's fuckin' with you 'cause it's my job to keep you safe. I can't have you living scared. I gotta make you happy. I can do that by finding whoever's fuckin' with you."

Resting her forehead against his, her hand on his chest, she whispered, "But I need you."

She said it, and she didn't care she'd given him that. She loved him. He may not love her, but he cared a great deal and showed her just how much.

His eyes heated. "You need me, you call me. I'm there."

Her heart squeezed. "Okay."

He slid his hand from her cheek to the back of her head. "And Lex, baby, haven't said it, but I appreciate everything you do for me and especially for Cul. Watching him, taking care of him, keeping him company, I couldn't do all I've been doing if I didn't know you were there treating him like he's your own."

She shook her head. "You don't need to thank me."

"I do, babe, and I am. It's hard enough to find a good woman. A woman who loves my kid, treats him like he's hers?" He shook his head yet never lost hold of her eyes. "I thought that was impossible. Me feeling the way I do about you and you loving my boy and making him happy is a dream come true."

She smiled.

"Don't really want to talk about this now, but I think it's time."

The smile died on her lips.

"Meant to talk to you about this a while back, but shit got in the way. It's about Cul's mother."

She had time to think about it, and the fact was she didn't want to know what happened between them. That was before, and this was now. They were new, different.

She shook her head. "I don't need to—"

"Yeah, you do 'cause you have ideas about me and her and need to know the truth."

She nodded. "Okay."

He released her neck and dropped his hand to hers on his chest. "Lilliam was a tap."

Her brows furrowed. "A what?"

"A tap, a woman who hangs out at the club and—" He looked behind her and then met her eyes. "—Offers herself to us."

"You mean for—"

"Yeah, she's one of those women who doesn't mind getting fucked by a different biker every night, by several of us a night."

Oh God.

"When she told me she was pregnant, I wasn't pissed. I had reason to be. She'd been trying to get Trig to make her an old lady. When Trig found out she told Mia and Lynn he'd patch her, he stopped fuckin' her. She moved on to me. Because she was a tap, I never thought she wasn't fuckin' anyone else. As it turns out, when she started fucking me, she stopped fuckin' the rest. All part of her plan—get knocked up by a brother. Then she'd get what she wanted, become an old lady or at the very least be the mother of a kid whose father's a biker. She picked right 'cause I found out, I married her making her an old lady, exactly what she wanted."

She swallowed.

"I wasn't pissed though. I thought maybe the way it happened was the only way I'd ever be a father since I'd never been in a relationship. I always wanted to be a dad. My old man left when I was a kid, but I thought I could be someone's and I could be good at it."

He released a breath, and his hand, over hers

against his chest, fell away. "I didn't love Lilliam, but I was stupid and naïve and thought maybe if I got to know her, I'd grow to."

Her eyes widened. "You thought you could *grow* to love the woman who tricked you into marrying her?"

He chuckled humorlessly. "Yeah, I did. She was never a knockout like you. She was pretty—"

"Is."

He cupped her cheek and drew her close, resting his forehead against hers. "No, Lex. *Was*. She was pretty. Not like you. Nowhere near gorgeous. Maybe she's still pretty." He dropped his hand, moved away slightly, and shrugged. "I married her thinking she's pretty, and maybe it was stupid, but I married her hoping I got to know her, something'd grow. Maybe not love, but maybe respect, friendship, something, *anything*."

Made sense, after all, it was human nature to hope for something more, something better.

He shook his head. "I was wrong. Since she was pregnant, we married quick, and after that, I got to know her. I didn't like her as a person 'cause there was nothing to like. She bitched, nagged, yelled, picked fights for no reason, complained about everything. Then to me, she was ugly. Who she *is* tainted her looks so I didn't see pretty anymore. Still don't. I didn't think I could like her less, then Cullen was born and I started wanting to hate her."

Her eyes widened.

"Even in the beginning, he'd wake up at night crying, she'd refuse to get up and feed him. She refused to change him, bathe him. I had no idea what I was doing, but I did it all 'cause she did nothing. Granted with a baby, your first, no one knows what they're doing, but you try. And Lex, believe me when I say, I knew being a parent wasn't gonna be easy. I knew I had to pitch in, but she refused to do *anything*."

God. How could she not get up and feed her crying baby?

"I had time off work, but eventually I had to go back. I told her she had two choices, stay home and care for our son or get a job. She chose to stay home and watch Cullen. At the time, I was glad. I thought she'd bond with him."

His eyes turned pained. "Didn't happen. At least three out of the five days of the week, I'd come home and find Cullen in his room crying and her in our room with headphones on."

Her chest clenched.

"Three months of that shit, I couldn't take it anymore. I couldn't take wondering how long he'd been crying, wondering if she even took him outta that crib all day, so I put him in daycare.

"Then she spent her time spending money. She spent fifty grand, money I had to pay back trying not to sell my house, a house I bought for her and Cul and me, for the family I thought we were gonna be.

"I know what you're thinking, Lex, but regardless of the fact that I didn't love her, we could've had a good life. I would've taken care of her. I would've tried to make her happy. I *did* try to make her happy. Thing was nothing made her happy 'cause she didn't want *me*."

He pointed toward his house. "She didn't want that house I bought, which was shit but it's not shit now and it wasn't shit when Cul was born 'cause the brothers and me fixed it up before then." His voice grew thick when he said, "She didn't want *Cul*. She thought she wanted to be an old lady, but when she was one, she acted like she was still a tap, hitting on my brothers, and I *didn't* stray, not once.

"I tried and tried even after realizing she was a bitch. I gave her shit I thought she wanted: a ring, a marriage, a home. All she did was nag, bitch, and complain. While she did all that, I didn't get laid once. First 'cause she was pregnant and didn't feel up for it. I'm a man. I can't imagine what it'd be like carrying a baby, throwing up, feeling like shit, but I get that. Then she was tired she said 'cause Cullen kept her up all night even though I'm the one Cul kept up 'cause she wouldn't get up."

His hands went to her hips and squeezed. "We weren't even married a year, and I stopped trying to fuck my wife. It was pointless. I thought I hated her, not 'cause she wouldn't give it up even while she acted like she'd give it to my brothers but 'cause of the way she treated her son, *my* son.

"I realized she didn't want to be an old lady anymore. She wanted shit, expensive shit. To get expensive shit, she nagged and bitched. When that didn't work, she went out and used my credit. A new purse, new shoes, whatever the fuck… All of it costing more than I could afford. I'd stopped trying to fuck her, but I kept trying to make us work 'cause I wanted my boy to have his mother, 'cause I thought one day she'd wake the hell up and realize he was her kid too, a kid who's sweet and smart and fucking amazing."

He shook his head. "When it all became too clear I was wasting my life and Cul's childhood dealing with his bitch mother, I gave up. I told her to find somewhere else to live and filed for divorce."

Right choice. Definitely. Cullen deserved better. Dodge deserved better.

"You didn't have to tell me this so I'd hate her. I already hate her."

She did. Lilliam was so lucky to be Cullen's mother, and she treated him like he didn't matter.

A shadow of a smile crossed his lips. "Not telling you so you hate her, Lex. At one point, I thought I did, but the truth is I don't and I can't hate her 'cause she gave me Cullen and he means the world to me. I'm telling you so you know what happened between her and me so you don't think I didn't want it to work, that I didn't try."

Her brows drew together. "Why would I think—"

"The day I fucked up. I tried to explain, and you told me you understood her. I thought you should know the whole story."

He remembered that? In truth, she couldn't sympathize with any woman who came on to her husband's friends. It was *wrong* in so many ways, but he took it out on her, undeserving of it. She'd been angry and hurt and said somethings she didn't mean.

Wrapping her arms around his neck, she pressed her lips to his, pulled away, and met his stare. "I was upset. I didn't mean it. There's no excuse for what she did to you. There's no excuse for what she does to Cullen. I knew that then, but I'd come to the conclusion that I didn't want to pay for her mistakes."

His eyes darkened. "I won't hurt you again, Lex. I promise when I get that pissed, I'll walk away so I don't lose it on you. I promise I'll come back when I've calmed down some."

He'd already done it. The day he found out she hadn't told him the calls started again, he'd walked away, but he'd come back.

"I promise I'll give you and Cul everything I got, try beyond my means to make you happy."

She smiled.

"I love you, Lex."

Her heart stopped. The breath rushed out of her. "You don't have to say it just because I did."

Shaking his head, he grinned. "Why do you think I waited to tell you until now?"

"Y-you love me?"

Lifting a brow, he shot back, "Like you can't fuckin' tell?"

Could she?

Yes. Everything he did showed it, proved it.

She fought a smile then buried her face in his neck. "Now, I'm *really* glad you didn't get arrested."

He burst out laughing. His hands slipped from her hips up her back and squeezed her tight.

A knock sounded on the door. She didn't bother moving.

Dodge, though, turned his head and shouted, "You better have a good reason!"

The door parted then a sweet little voice said, "Dad? Lex?"

Drawing away, her arms fell to her lap. She twisted and smiled at Cul, rushing toward them. A second later, his small body slammed in to them. He wrapped his arms around her waist tightly and rested his head against her stomach.

She snaked an arm around his back and cupped the

back of his head. "Hey, sweetie."

He looked up at her and removed one arm from around her to rub his eye.

"It's bath time, then bedtime."

Cul met his father's gaze. "Lex tucks me."

Three words in a row. Getting better, more confident.

Her chest further warmed realizing what he'd said. Eyes watering, she swallowed her tears and drew her hand through his hair. "I'd be happy to tuck you in tonight."

She did.

After he fell asleep, she headed for the master bedroom. Not seeing Dodge, she decided to take a warm bath. While immersed, he walked in and joined her.

That night, he made love to her soft and slow. It was perfect.

Chapter Thirty-One

"Please..." Bent over the bathroom vanity, chest to counter, hands sprawled on the mirror, eyes glued to Dodge's reflection, she moaned. "Harder."

Head cast down, no doubt watching their connection, he pulled out of her, sunk himself deeper, and held still.

"Stop torturing me..."

He lifted his head, and his dark, hooded, and heated eyes met hers. Hands grasping her hips squeezed her. "You don't know shit about torture, Lex." He drew out and slammed into her.

God, so close.

He slipped a hand under her, across her stomach and chest lifting her upper body off the vanity. Then he buried his face in her neck and sucked on her lobe.

Her eyes rolled to the back of her head. "Oh..."

Releasing her, he grabbed her hips and slid out.

"No!"

He spun her to face him, grasped her butt, lifted her, and set her on the marble. His hands gripping her hips, he thrust inside.

"Oh God...please..."

"Want it?"

She nodded.

"Then fuckin' look at me."

She angled her head. Her stare hit his and held. He

thrust into her repeatedly. When she thought she couldn't take anymore, he pressed his thumb against her clit and pushed hard. Her nipples puckered, her body shuddered, and her world went hazy.

Unbelievably magnificent.

Too intense to keep quiet, to remember why she had to.

A cry tore from her throat. He released one hip and placed his big palm over her mouth. Not a second later, his shaft pulsed inside for a long while. Then he collapsed against her and wrapped his arms tight around her back.

Cheek resting against her chest, breaths heating her, he whispered, "Best I ever had."

She stilled, feeling warmth spread through her chest.

He lifted his head, chin between her breasts, locking gazes with her.

Gliding her hand through his hair, she quirked a brow and smirked. "Are you talking about me?"

He grinned. "Fuck, yeah."

****

Lex looked away from the onions she'd diced and met Cullen's gaze. "Hey, sweetie."

He smiled so bright but didn't say her name.

She hated that. He'd been saying more, true, but it'd been days since he last spoke. He knew words, and when he spoke, he did it well, pronouncing syllables correctly. He just chose not to. Why? He had the sweetest voice, so soft yet firm.

He neared, grinning wide. She knew what he wanted—food. He snacked often, amazing how it never ruined his appetite. It made her think he must starve during the week when he was in daycare.

She wiped her hands on a kitchen towel, leaned down, and cupped his cheek. “I love hearing your voice. It’s beautiful. Did you know that?”

His big, striking, brown eyes widened and welled. Chin trembling, he parted his mouth then closed it.

She waited and watched a boy so young fight tears. Why did he? Because he was a boy?

Her stomach rolled, heart clenched. She slid her thumb along his cheek. “It’s okay, sweetheart. You don’t have to say anything, but I just wanted you to know I love the sound of your voice. I love when you share things with me. I love when you smile and laugh. I love you.”

She smiled. “Another thing, it’s okay to cry. If you don’t want anyone to see you, come to me. I’ll hold you, and I promise I won’t tell anyone.” She then pressed a kiss to his forehead.

When she straightened, he wrapped his arms around her middle, hugging her tight. His body stiff while his tears wet her shirt. He didn’t cry for long, only a few minutes. The whole time, she fought not to sob.

Then he let her go and looked up. “Love you, Lex.”

Three words…

The best three words she’d ever heard.

****

Lex barely said a word all night. She talked, not so much it was annoying but enough to enjoy. Then again, maybe Dodge enjoyed it because he liked her voice, liked to hear her talk, loved her and didn’t mind listening.

He didn’t know what could’ve happened. It’d been

a regular Sunday. They went to the park in the morning and had burgers for lunch. He dropped off Lex and Cul at home while he went to the compound to talk to the brothers. When he returned and relieved Beef of duty, who'd been keeping an eye out for them, Lex had been in the kitchen cooking, Cul sitting on a stool, a series of toys on the counter in front of him along with an empty plate, one that had no doubt once held some of Lex's homemade cookies.

He kissed the top of Cul's head and closed the distance between him and Lex. By the time he got to her, she had faced him, a soft smile on her face.

"We missed you."

He grinned.

"Steaks, mashed potatoes, and green beans."

"Sounds good."

They had dinner. She'd been quiet then too, but he hadn't thought anything of it since she didn't look upset. They watched some TV with Cul. Then, too, she'd been reserved. He left to supervise Cul in the bathtub and tuck him into bed. When he walked into their bedroom, he couldn't deny it.

Wearing one of his shirts, she sat on the bed, her long legs in front of her, a book on her thighs. Her head tilted down, but her gaze was on the floor.

"Lex?"

Her head shot up, and her eyes widened like she'd been so stuck in her head she hadn't noticed he'd been standing there staring at her.

"You okay?"

She nodded. "Yeah."

He cocked his head. "Yeah?"

She smiled a sad smile, closed her book, placed it

on the nightstand, and tucked her legs under herself. “Cullen.”

Striding toward her, he took a seat on the bed in front of her.

“Today, I told him I love the sound of his voice, that I love to hear him talk. I was trying to encourage him to speak more.” Her eyes watered. “We know he can. He just…doesn’t.” She shrugged. “Then he started fighting tears, and it got me thinking.”

She released a loaded breath. “Why?”

He hated this, hated his boy rarely spoke, hated it worried Lex, hated to be so worried about his boy.

Swallowing, he shook his head lightly. “Don’t know why he doesn’t talk much, babe—”

“No, Dodge. I meant why would a three-year-old fight tears? Why does he think he can’t cry? Is it the same reason he doesn’t talk often?”

His gut twisted. He dropped his head and remembered something he’d tried to block out but never could.

“What is it?”

His gaze hit hers. With a rough voice, he admitted, “Cul had just turned two. It was a holiday, so the daycare was closed. I had to go to the compound for a meeting. I wasn’t gone for more than an hour. When I got home, from the doorstep, I heard her yelling, telling him to ‘shut the fuck up and stop fucking crying.’”

He swallowed. “I opened the door and found them in the living room. Cullen was on the floor, his hand to his knee like he’d hurt it, silent tears streaming down his face.”

Dodge had been so pissed he’d told her to find somewhere else to live, that he was done. She left but returned a week later crying fake tears, telling him how much she missed her son, and then, she said something that resonated with him. She'd said she wasn't a perfect mother, but she tried her best. She promised she'd do better. He let her stay. It didn't last long after that, but the damage was done.

Why hadn't he thought of this before now? He knew deep down Cullen not speaking had something to do with Lilliam, but he hadn't linked it to that incident. That was just one time, the one time he caught her. For all he knew, she could've spent every second he was away yelling at Cullen, telling him to shut up, to stop crying. Maybe it's why he didn't talk often, why he fought tears. Maybe he thought by doing what she wanted she'd come back. Dodge didn't think Cullen wanted his mother back, but he couldn't be sure.

Bile rose in the back of his throat.

Lex's jaw dropped. She covered her mouth with the palm of her hand. Then without blinking, tears spilled out of her eyes. "He thinks he's good when he doesn't cry."

He nodded, feeling nothing but an ache slicing open his chest. He didn't try to hide it because he knew that kind of pain couldn't be.

Lex stared at him, eyes and face soft. "He thinks if he's quiet, he's good."

His chest tightened, throat clogged making it hard to breathe. He nodded again.

She leaned in to him, hands on his cheeks, fresh tears glistening her eyes. "This isn't your fault, honey. Please, please, listen to me. Believe me. This isn't your fault."

"One day, you'll be a mom, and you'll come to

realize guilt's part of being a parent. Something bad happens, you blame you. It's just the way it is." He shook his head. "This isn't that though. This *is* my fault. I knew she was shit, and I kept her around. I—"

"Maybe you knew she wasn't the best mother, but she's still his mother. It wasn't an easy choice, but you did what you thought was right at the time."

Maybe. He knew one thing for sure. He needed to talk to Cul, not tonight though. Tomorrow. Tonight, he'd enjoy his sweet Lex, always there for him, for his boy.

Snaking his arms around her waist, he lifted her, hauled her against him then lay on his back with her sprawled on him. "So glad you moved across the street."

She smirked. "You have a poor way of showing it."

Cocking a brow, he shot back, "The sex isn't good for you, babe?"

That sadness lighting her eyes faded. Looking away, she shrugged.

He rolled, trapping her under him. "Taking that as a challenge. That means you're lucky if you get a couple of hours of sleep tonight. Don't complain. You asked for it."

He kissed her deep.

Then he made her come several times.

Each time she went wild, she told him she loved him.

****

Cul, sitting on a stool at the counter, gulped the rest of his milk, wiped his face with the back of his hand, and met his gaze.

No one could say his boy wasn't smart. Already

he'd picked up on his mood. The curious and cautious look on his face clue enough.

Dodge pulled in a deep breath then released it. "I gotta talk to you about something."

Cul hesitated for a second before he nodded.

The marble counter between them, Dodge leaned forward resting his weight on his elbows. "I told you Lex and me are together now. I told you me and your mother are getting divorced, which means we won't ever be together. We won't ever live together. I told you this, but I realized it was me talking and I should've been listening."

Cul wrinkled his brows.

"I messed up, and I'm sorry, Cul. I'm not perfect. I make mistakes. I never want you to feel like you can't talk to me. You can, anytime. I don't want you to ever be scared of telling me anything, no matter what it is. You're just a kid, so I'm gonna do my best to ask you, but if ever you need to tell me something, you can, 'kay?"

Cul nodded.

"So is there anything you want to tell me?"

Cul leaned back against the chair and shook his head.

"Anything at all you want to talk to me about? About Lex and me and your mother?"

Cul held his gaze but didn't say a word.

He tried a different tactic, simple, to the point, yes or no questions. "You like Lex?"

Cul nodded immediately.

Right, he knew that much. Easy questions first.

"You mind she's…with me? That we're together?"

Cul shook his head.

"You mind she's living with us?"

"No." A firm no, holding his father's stare, he hadn't even blinked.

"I…" He walked around the counter and plucked Cul from his seat. Moving aside the empty plate and glass, Dodge sat Cul on the marble and sat on the stool in front of him. "I love Lex. I love a lot of things about her, and one of the things I love most is the way she's with you. She worries about you, takes care of you, loves you."

Cul's eyes watered. His little face scrunched up, fighting those tears.

"I think the way things are going maybe someday she'll be part of our family."

Cul's eyes widened. He nodded swiftly. "I want."

Some of the tension lining his body melted, he smiled. "You want that?"

Cul blinked, and thick tears streamed down his face. He nodded again instantly.

Dodge reached for Cul's hands settled at either side of him on the marble and held them in his. "I want that too."

He dropped his head and stared at his lap to get the courage he needed to ask what he had to. Lifting his gaze, he met his boy's eyes. "You know 'cause things change, it doesn't mean you can't miss your mother—"

Cul's expression tightened, nostrils flared. Shaking his head, he shouted, "No!" Then he drew away, ripping his hands from under his.

"Cul—"

His chest rose and fell quickly. Breaths came out in gasps. "No! No! No miss! No want! Want Lex! I! Want! Lex!" Then he hid his face in his hands and sobbed.

Never had he heard Cul say so much. Amazing, and he couldn't enjoy it. That deep pain slicing through his gut, up his chest and throat wouldn't let him.

He hauled his boy against his chest, holding him tight. His small body trembled against his. "Shh…" Throat clogging, he rubbed his son's back. "I got you, Cul. It's okay. It's gonna be fine."

"N-nooooo, Mother! Want L-Lex…" Each word coming out higher and higher until his voice cracked.

"I know Cul, and you got her. We got her. She's not going anywhere."

"Mother, no!" Another sob tore from his throat. "Lex, yes. Lex! Lex!"

The magnitude of everything Cul said overwhelmed him. He understood that his boy didn't want his mother. Cul wanted Lex. What he didn't get was why his boy was so upset.

When the thought came, his heart sank to the pit of his stomach.

He grasped his son by the shoulders and drew him away, catching sight of his red, tear-streaked face. "Your mother ever hurt you, Cul? She hit you?"

Fresh tears welled. Cul blinked, and they ran down his face. "Mother's m-mean." He shook his head, and looking so much older than his three years, he said convinced, "She don't want me, don't love me." He wiped his face with the back of his hand. "Lex l-loves me. I know. Lex said…she loves m-me."

His chest contracted; pain rippled through his insides and spread leaving no part of him unscathed.

He wanted the best for his boy. He'd do anything and everything to give him that, and he'd never wanted him to learn that sometimes the people who were supposed to love him the most didn't.

He rested one hand on the back of Cul's neck. "Some kids don't have parents, Cul. Some only have a mom. Others only have a dad. You have me. You have Lex. You have all your uncles and aunts and the club. You have a lot. You gotta live your life thinking about all you have, not what you're missing. You don't, you'll never be happy with all you've got."

Cul sniffed and nodded. "Lex leave?"

He shook his head. "Lex isn't leaving you. She loves you. You believe me, yeah?"

Cul wiped his face. "Yeah."

Chapter Thirty-Two

Lex tucked Cul tightly in bed, stood, and turned.

"Wish you were my mom."

Her body locked. Her palm went to her chest, fingers gripping her skin. She blinked repeatedly, forcing the tears that welled instantly to dry. Then she dropped her hand and faced him.

Laying in his full-size bed, his superhero comforter over him, hair ruffled from when she'd pushed it away from his face to kiss him goodnight. His beautiful brown eyes wide awake and on hers.

The most she'd ever heard him say, and he said it slow and clearly like he wanted to make sure she understood.

Her hammering heart stilled, chest tightened. His face blurred, something she couldn't have prevented staring at him after having just heard him say what he had. With no clue of the right thing to say, she did what came naturally.

Closing the distance between them, she sat on the edge of his bed where she'd been just a moment before. She leaned in to him and hugged him tightly. Then and there, tears drifted down her face. After a long while holding him, she wiped her face, sniffed, pressed a kiss to his forehead, and drew away. Gazing into his eyes, she threaded her fingers through his hair and said the God's honest truth. "Me too, sweetheart."

Fighting tears, she stayed with him until his eyes got heavy and he fell asleep. Only then did she whisper, "Sweet dreams, honey."

She closed her eyes, breathed deep, and stood. Walking out of his room, she closed the door behind her, made a right, strode down the hallway, and took a left toward the front door.

"Lex?"

She stilled. "Yes?"

"Where're you going? You need something from home? I'll get it for you."

God, she didn't need him to be sweet. She needed him to leave her alone so she could cry her eyes out.

"No, I-I just need some time…"

That didn't come out right, but she'd make it worse if she tried to explain. Maybe this one time, he'd let it go.

"You need time?"

"Yes, space."

Damn it! Why had she said that and made it sound worse?

"You need time and space?"

She swallowed. "Yes."

"Why?" His voice gruff.

"I just…do."

He grabbed her upper arm and spun her to face him. Coward she was, she shut her eyes. She couldn't look at him. She did, she'd cave and she couldn't.

"No."

She snapped open her eyes and met his dark, angry ones. Then her gaze swept his handsome face. All it took for her will to crumble. "No?"

He leaned in to her, his breaths heating her face.

"No. I'm not giving you time or space." His voice low and rough.

"You'll keep me here when I don't want to be?"

Jaw hard, eyes narrowed, he shot back, "You want to go, you tell me why."

She could attempt to pry his fingers off her and run, but he'd chase her. No other choice.

Biting the side of her lip, she whispered, "Cul…"

His eyes widened.

Without so much as a blink, tears trailed down her face. "He told me he wished I was his mom."

He parted his mouth, shut it, and let her go. Then he balled his hands and took a step back, his pained stare never leaving hers.

"I told him I did too."

His eyes softened.

"I didn't lie."

He drew his brows together as he scanned her face. "So you want to go home 'cause he wants you to be his mom and you want to be his mom?"

She angled her head slightly, stare shooting behind him into the kitchen. The dishwasher open, the bottom rack pulled out, a series of plates and pots lay on the marble counter. "Not exactly."

"Then?"

"I'm upset and…angry. It's just so unfair." A river of tears running down her cheeks, a fruitless effort, but she wiped them away. "He's so special, and he doesn't have a mom. I don't want him to hurt. I wish I could take it away."

He released a breath. "Lex…" The next instant, his arms hooked around her, and he drew her to him. Her chest hit his. Then he rubbed his hands down her back.

After a moment, he cupped her cheeks and slanted her face to his. "He's got you."

"I'm not his mom—"

He wiped the tears from her face with his thumbs and grinned. "Are you proposing?"

Making a joke to liven her mood, he always did things like that.

She laughed.

"Okay, Lex. I'll marry you, but when we tell this story, I proposed to you, yeah?"

She laughed harder. He slid his hands across her cheeks to the back of her head and down her back. She buried her face in his chest. One of his hands glided up and came to a stop at the base of her neck.

"I know you want to marry me, know you love my kid. You're the closest thing he has to a mom. He's crazy about you, just as crazy as you are about him, so I still don't get why you want to go home."

She angled her head back to meet his eyes. "I needed to have a good cry."

He quirked a brow. "If we're gonna get married, you gotta learn to share stuff with me even if it means you'll have a good cry while doing it."

She smacked his chest playfully. "Stop messing around. I'm serious."

His eyes softened. Then he wiped the smile from his face. "I'm serious too, Lex."

Serious? No. They couldn't get married! They'd only dated a few months.

He grabbed a strand of her hair, tucked it behind her ear, and cupped her cheek. "Love you, Lex. Want you to move in officially. Want you to marry me. Want you to be Cul's mom. Want to get you pregnant and give Cul a brother or a sister."

Her heart stopped. Jaw dropping, she pointed out, "But you're still married."

"Won't be for much longer. She can't keep stalling. Judge is gonna get fed up."

Heart pounding, she whispered, "You're serious?"

"Talked to Cul this morning. He wants you with us. We want you with us, not just until you're safe but always." He pressed his forehead to hers so all she saw were his big, beautiful eyes. "It's right. I know it. Cul, you, and me, we work. We're a family. I'll sell this house. We'll move into yours. I'll buy you a ring, pay for whatever kinda wedding you want."

Everything he said made it sound like he'd put thought into this, like he had it all planned out, but it was too soon. He could get tired of her in a month or a year.

"Y-you're…crazy."

"Then be crazy with us."

Simple as that.

Us. Not just her and him, but Cullen too. She wouldn't be just Dave Roth's wife. She'd be Cullen's stepmom. She wanted that, but she was terrified. It was soon, too soon. What if this blew up in their faces hurting not just her and him but Cullen too and arguably the most?

"Okay." The word slipped from her lips before she talked herself out of it.

He grinned wide and beautiful. "That's all I get? An 'okay'?"

Smirking, she shook her head. "I love you too."

Chapter Thirty-Three

Lex looked around her classroom. Freshly decorated corkboards, done. The stack of her students' work, graded. Onto planning. The reason she loved teacher planning days: it wasn't even noon and she'd gotten so much done.

It'd been three weeks since Dodge proposed. They hadn't told a soul. This partly since he was still married. The secret was easy to keep since she didn't have a ring. It was an added cost they could avoid, so she didn't want one and told Dodge so. They met with a realtor last week, put both their houses on the market, and started looking for a home of their own. This was something they decided together, feeling the best move was to start fresh in a new house. She'd miss her house, the one she'd remodeled to her taste, but she wanted their home to represent the three of them, not just her. Besides, her home wasn't big enough since they wanted to add to their family. He made it clear he wanted more kids not just the day he'd proposed.

Two weeks ago, they lay in bed, Dodge on his back, an arm around her shoulders. Her head nestled in the crook of his arm, her leg tangled in his.

He cupped her cheek with his free hand and turned toward her, meeting her gaze. His arm around her drifted to her lower back then up to her hair. "How many kids does my wild woman want?"

She shrugged. "I always wanted three, but—"

He smirked. "But what?"

"But we already have one."

He reared back. Eyes growing intense, he scanned her face. "I meant how many do you want of your own?"

"Just because he didn't grow inside me doesn't mean he's not mine."

His brows furrowed, eyes darkened. He drifted his hand from her hair to the back of her neck and squeezed. Face softening, he smiled. "Yeah, Lex, you're right. He's yours. He claimed you, and you claimed him."

He made love to her after that soft, slow, and sweet. It melted her.

The following night, after an intensely long round of sex, they lay facing each other. One of his arms around her shoulders, another snaked around her waist. Both of her hands firm against his chest.

Catching her breath, she smiled. "How many kids do you want?"

"It's not up to me."

Eyes widening, she reared back. "It *is*. I don't want a child unless—"

"Not what I meant." He chuckled, and with the arm around her waist, he tugged her close, closing the small distance she'd forced. "I meant you're the one who has to go through being pregnant and the labor. Raising a kid isn't easy especially the first few years. It's exhausting, but I like kids. I love Cul. I know I'll love a baby that's you and me too. I could go for two even three more, but it's not something I'd push you for unless I was sure it's what you wanted."

He kissed her softly. "I never had a brother or a sister. I would've liked to, so I'd like Cul to have one. Gotta admit I like the idea of him having someone after we're gone. Think he'd like it too."

She fell asleep that night smiling.

A few days later, they lay in bed sated, her twice, the reason she'd been half asleep already when he spoke.

"How soon do you want to start?"

She slipped her hand from his stomach to his side and moved closer. "Hmm?"

"How soon do you want to start trying?"

"Trying?"

"Yeah, to make a baby."

Her eyes shot open. She shifted, lifting her head away from his chest to peer at him. "I'd like to be married first."

She wasn't overly religious or old-fashioned, but she believed certain things were meant to be done in order. To her, it was important their child was conceived after they made vows and committed their lives to one another.

"So when do you want to get married?"

The more she thought about it, and she'd thought about it a lot, the more she thought they should wait at least a year. After all, they hadn't known each other long.

"We have to wait until your divorce is—"

"Told you that's gonna happen soon, babe. Don't let that stop us from planning."

"Still, I think we should wait a while."

"Like a couple of months?"

She shook her head. "No, like a year."

Eyes widening, he lifted his head from the pillow. “A year?” After a moment, he relaxed. “Guess that’s what it takes to plan a wedding anyway, right?”

Her sister’s took a year, but Meg had a big, lavish wedding. Lex didn’t want that.

She shrugged. “I want a small wedding.”

His hand moved through her hair. “So you want to wait ’cause of something else?”

“I think it’s the smart thing to do for all of us. I mean Cul—”

“Loves you and wants you in his life, Lex. Talked to him about this.”

“And if it doesn’t work? I’ll lose you and him.”

“It’s up to me, you’re never losing me. You change your mind about me and want out, I pray you’ll always be a part of Cul’s life.” His eyes darkened. “I fucking mean that, Lex. He loves you. I want my kid happy and him happy is you being a part of his life.”

Her eyes watered. Lifting herself, she pressed a kiss to his lips. “I love you so much.” She settled beside him and fell asleep.

They hadn’t talked about babies or marriage since. Knowing Dodge, he was giving her time to think.

Her alarm sounded. Ten to noon. Since she had the habit of losing track of time while planning, she set her alarm to remind her Dodge would be over to bring lunch and eat. She organized her desk, grabbed her purse, and headed to the restroom to freshen up. Gaze on her phone, deleting emails, she strode inside.

A flash of movement. She lifted her head. Pain exploded on the side of her face. She stumbled and fell, landing on the floor with a thump.

Then everything faded away.

****

Dodge walked into her classroom with a bag of takeout in hand.

Empty.

Placing the food on her desk, he checked his watch. Ten minutes late, she knew he'd bring them lunch. He couldn't explain it, but that instant, that fast a sense of dread settled in the pit of his stomach.

Nope. No fucking way. Nothing to worry about. There hadn't been a call for a week.

It wasn't easy to shrug off the concern. He worried about her a lot. Sometimes, he couldn't get ahold of her and panicked. He needed to stop, but he couldn't, not until they found whoever was messing with her.

Tugging his phone out of his pocket, he dialed Hash, who he'd passed on his way into the school.

"Brother."

"Lex. She leave?"

"Been out here all morning. Besides when she walked in, haven't seen her. Her car's still here too."

His chest tightened. "She isn't here."

Maybe he was overreacting. Maybe he wasn't. Until he found her, he wouldn't know for sure, and he wasn't taking any chances, so he gave the order.

"Search the school."

"I'll call the brothers on my way in."

Dodge dashed out of Lex's classroom and into the room directly across from hers. Finding a woman around Lex's height with dark curly hair in it, he asked her for Lex. She said she hadn't seen Lex all morning. He mumbled his thanks then continued.

With each classroom he searched, with each step he took, and each minute that drifted, the anxiety strengthened until tension lined every muscle in his body.

Reaching the end of the hall, he came across the restrooms. Going into the men's first, he didn't think she'd be there but checked anyway and found it empty. On a sprint, he crossed the hall to the women's. The moment he entered at the far end, he spotted her, not the her he was looking for.

His gut soured then rolled. "What the fuck are you doing here?"

Lilliam, standing just outside a stall, turned, phone in hand. His gaze snapped below. Visible under the stall, four feet.

"I found them like this."

He moved so quickly, Lilliam barely had a chance to move out of the way. Reaching the stall, a man faced him. He grabbed him by the front of his shirt and dragged him out. Gaze glued to the inside of that stall, now, he saw what he couldn't before—Lex.

Lying against the toilet, the navy blue shirt she wore that morning torn down the middle, her bra hiked up to her chin, breasts in view. Her jeans unbuttoned, unzipped, and halfway down her thighs. Eyes closed, a bruise marred the top right side of her forehead, blood dripped from a wound.

Now, everything became crystal clear.

The calls and vandalism—Lilliam, her sick plan to fuck with him hurting her child in the process.

He swallowed the bile rising in the back of his throat and fought the rage building inside.

First thing, he took off his cut and draped it over Lex. Then he spun. He didn't know who the man was, didn't care. What he knew, Lex was near naked, and *that man* had been standing over her. Dodge *knew* who made it happen—Lilliam. Still, it didn't change the fact that this man made this happen too.

Dodge swung his fist into his nose. The punch connected. He heard a crack. When he lifted his arm, blood gushed out. The man fell to the ground. He pounced. He lost count how many times he landed a blow, couldn't even say if the guy started to fight him because he went into a haze. Before he knew it, someone hauled him off the man. Some of the cloud lifted. The ass lay on the ground bleeding, groaning, and whining.

He shoved away whoever held him.

Then Trig got in his face. "She needs you. You gotta keep your head."

Yes. He had Lex. He had Cul, and they *needed* him. *He* brought this down on her. *He* had to fix it, had to make amends.

Fisting his hands, feeling his knuckles burn, he took several deep breaths. Then he looked beyond Trig and spotted Hash, Army, Ripper, Strike, Mellow, Bud, Blaze… All of them—his club, his brothers—they filled the women's restroom making the place feel tiny.

His gaze stopped on Prez. "Both of them at the compound. Keep them until I deal with Lex."

He looked to Trig and Rip. "If one of your women can help with Lex while I deal with them, much appreciated."

They nodded and walked out of the restroom. He turned and headed for Lex.

Cuss stood inside the stall, a hand under her head, the other by her neck, index and middle fingers pressed there. "Pulse is good. Steady breathing. She's got a nasty bump and cut. You may wanna take her to the hospital to make sure she doesn't got a concussion."

Thank fuck.

He nodded. "I got her. You go."

Cuss nodded. "Wait for you outside."

He squatted next to Lex and slowly and carefully righted her clothes, setting her bra in place, pulling her jeans to her waist then zipping and buttoning them. He couldn't do anything about her torn shirt, so again he draped his cut over her. Placing an arm around her back, one under her knees, he lifted and carried her out.

In the hall, he looked to Blaze. "Grab her purse and phone. I spotted them on the bathroom floor."

Blaze nodded.

Dodge strode out of the school and hopped into the back of Cuss's SUV. Bud and Hash helped him load Lex, laying her stretched out in the back seat with her head on his lap. While Cuss drove to the hospital, he kept a hand under her head.

"J-June."

He snapped his head down, gaze meeting hers. Her eyes parted half-mast; a smile played at her lips.

He expelled a loaded breath and forced a smile. "What?"

"I want to get married in June."

She wouldn't want that after she knew all he brought down on her.

"Lex, babe." His throat clogged. "This shit… My fault."

Her brows creased.

"Lilliam's the one who attacked you. She's the one who's been scaring the shit out of you."

She closed her eyes and took a deep breath. "June."

He swallowed. “Baby, did you hear me?”

She parted her lids and met his stare. Eyes warm, she nodded. “June.”

Fuck him.

What he ever did to deserve her, he’d never know.

He nodded. “Next year.”

A soft smile spread across her lips. “This year.”

He’d marry her that day if he could, and he didn’t want to make her rethink her decision, but it was only fair he point out the obvious.

“That’s in two months. Is that enough time to plan?”

“I want a small beach wedding, so yes.”

He was still married, but he’d be divorced by then. He’d make sure of it because Lex wanted to get married in June, so they’d get married in June.

He grinned and pressed a kiss to her forehead. “Gotta get my wild woman a ring.”

“I told you I don’t need a ring, honey, just you and Cul…my boys.”

Her boys.

Fuck.

“Getting you a ring, Lex. You say you don’t want one, say you don’t need one. You can start bitching and complaining all you want, but it’s still gonna happen.”

He’d make it happen.

She burrowed herself against him and smiled. “Oh well, if you insist.”

He couldn’t help himself and chuckled.

The thing about his wild Lex—she could make everything, even the aftermath of dire situations, seem just perfect.

Epilogue

Lex sat with her family and friends around her at a stunningly decorated table: ivory tablecloth, gold table runner and embellishments, a towering bouquet of white roses in the center and candles spread throughout. She clutched her hands together and rested them on her lap against the most gorgeous ivory, lace wedding dress she'd ever laid eyes on.

"It was beautiful," Meg, her hand on her pregnant belly, said as tears gleamed in her eyes.

Lex smiled, reached for her sister's hand, and squeezed it. "Thanks."

Dodge and her wedding had been at the beach, but for the reception, they'd rented a picturesque, quaint hall with lots of charm: French windows and doors, a dome ceiling, and chandeliers.

Em smiled. "Absolutely stunning."

Mia took a sip of champagne. "I have no idea how you planned this wedding in two months. Seriously, you should be a wedding planner."

She laughed.

"You deserve this," Lynn whispered.

A lot had happened in the last half year. She made a big move, met the man she'd marry, fell for his handsome boy then fell for him. There was some bad in there too. She couldn't forget their big fight, when she ended them. She couldn't forget the calls and vandalism, or how much it terrified her. Despite trying her hardest, she couldn't forget being assaulted at school.

She dreamt about it repeatedly, woke up in a sweat at least once a week. She'd been seeing a therapist, and over the last month, she'd realized it had little to do with the attack and more to do with fear of what could've happened. She'd been knocked out, suffered a bump, bruise, and cut but hadn't had a concussion.

She couldn't remember what happened in between the time she was knocked out and when she woke. Her shirt had been ripped, and she'd later found out Lilliam's plan had been to take pictures of her naked with that man, post the pictures on the school bulletin board, and spread them throughout town. Lilliam wanted Dodge to think Lex had cheated on him, wanted her to lose her job, and have to move away since the other methods of tormenting her hadn't worked.

The man who took part in Lilliam's plot, Alfred Baker, happened to work for Lex's phone company and had access to private numbers, which explained how she kept receiving calls even after she'd changed her number. According to Dodge, Lilliam offered the man sexual favors in exchange for helping her.

In the end, Dodge kept his word. He'd found who'd been tormenting her. He'd made them stop. He'd saved her. The club, his brothers, helped too. Because of them, Lex had pressed charges against Lilliam and Alfred and filed for restraining orders, which had been granted. Not two weeks after the attack, Dodge's divorce was finalized. Lilliam had also given up her parental rights.

The ordeal would take time to get over, but she

wasn't worried. She had a great family and wonderful friends supporting her and a new husband who'd do just about anything for her. She also had Cullen, her *son*. Last month, she'd adopted him.

It'd been a normal school night. After she'd made dinner and they ate, she'd settled on the counter looking through a brochure with a series of centerpieces trying to decide what she wanted for their wedding. It took a half hour, but she'd narrowed it down to three. Noticing Cullen and Dodge come near, she lifted her head, gaze glued to Cul, and smiled.

He handed her a folder.

Brows quirking, she opened it and read the heading of the document: adoption papers.

Her heart expanded so much she'd thought it'd explode. She wanted it, wished it, but she hadn't thought it possible, so she settled for being his stepmom and had been more than thrilled to be. Adopting him was much, much more than that. It meant, God forbid, if anything happened between she and Dodge, Cul would still be *hers*.

Tears swimming, she moved her stare and met Cullen's. Honest to God, she hadn't thought she could even speak without bursting into blissful hysterics.

When Cul's hopeful eyes began swimming too, she couldn't hold back. She stood, knelt in front of him, and cupped his cheeks. "I'm already your mom, sweetheart."

He hooked his arms around her neck tightly. She circled hers around his back. Dodge knelt behind Cullen and snaked his arms around them both.

Holding Cul tight against her, she peered at Dodge. Then she whispered, "Thank you."

His eyes warmed.

She knew she didn't have to explain. He understood.

It'd been one of the best moments of her life.

She now knew more about the club as well. One night in bed while they lay facing each other, Dodge told her everything. Hell Ryders had once been involved in illegal activities, running guns and drugs. Years ago, the club became clean. Now, they lived off the garage and their guard services, which weren't entirely legal either since often they were paid for extras, namely manhandling men who deserved it. While this knowledge had been terrifying at first, it didn't change how she felt about Dodge or Cullen.

Arms went around her shoulders, his breath at her ear, he whispered, "Want my wife."

She smiled, grasped his hands, and stood. "If you'll excuse me, I'm needed."

Dodge tugged her to his side and walked to the middle of the room, the dancefloor. A stunning chandelier hanging above them, they slow danced for a full sixty seconds before Cul rushed them and cut in. She danced with Cullen for another minute. Then Dodge carried Cullen and wrapped his free arm around her waist. She danced the rest of the song with both her boys.

It was perfect.

****

"Fuck, babe… Lex…"

Her body spasmed then went limp.

His heart dropped. "Fuck."

No doubt now. He'd been too rough. He just needed her so bad.

They'd moved into their new place just a couple of days ago. Both so tired, trying to get everything in order and set up, when they hit the bed at night, they just cuddled. He was still beat, so was she, but they were finally unpacked. With Cul at a sleepover, they ordered pizza. He'd finished his third slice when she walked into the living room wearing a blue nighty, the sides made of mesh, stockings, and heels. All it took, one look. He prowled to her and kissed her. When her back hit the wall behind her, he started touching her.

"Don't make me wait. Please…"

Hiking up her nighty finding her bare, he freed himself and lifted her. She immediately wrapped her legs around him allowing him to dive deep.

Then she hooked her arms around his neck, buried her face against his throat, and clung to him. "Please…harder…"

He lost it. He never dreamed of being so rough with anyone, least of all her. He shouldn't have listened, should've taken it slow no matter what she said, what she claimed to want. She was so soft and delicate, and he was twice her size. He could blame it on a bunch of shit—the nighty, her whispers, it'd been days—but it didn't dissolve him of fault.

Swallowing his fear, his arm around her waist tightened. He cupped her cheek with the other. "Lex, baby? Wake up."

Her eyes cracked open. "Why'd you stop?"

"'Cause I fuckin' hurt you."

Her eyes widened. "You couldn't. Please…" She bucked her hips pressing herself against him.

He groaned, almost spilling. "Fuck, Lex. Don't. I'll lose it again." Shaking his head, he snapped, "Can't take you like that again."

"Please…" She smiled. "That was the best."

The best?

She shifted her hips again. Her lips slammed against his, kissing him deeply.

He gave it to her rough, hard, fast like she wanted it. Her body strung tight then shuddered as she moaned his name. Music to his ears. He followed, coming just a second later.

All of it—perfect.

They'd been married for a little more than a month, and still, he couldn't believe it. How he managed to snag the perfect woman, he'd never know.

After all had gone down and he'd told her who'd been fucking with her and why, she had reason to blame him, but she hadn't. To this day, she had nightmares but not nearly as often. When they came, she just wanted him to hold her, claiming he kept them away. As much as that thrilled him, it killed knowing he could've prevented it had he not underestimated his ex. One of the many reasons he woke up beside her every morning and made sure he told her he loved her and when he went to bed with her every night, he reminded her. One of the many reasons, he did whatever he could to make her happy. She wanted a beach wedding; he gave it to her. She wanted to be Cul's mom; he made it happen. She fell in love with the four-bedroom house from just looking at the pictures on the realtor's site; he bought it.

He'd continue to do what he could no matter what it cost until there was no breath left in him. It was all he could give her. It wasn't nearly as much as she deserved, but she wanted them, loved them, and showed them every chance she had.

Holding him tight, her lips inches from his. "I'm buying more sexy lingerie."

He chuckled. "It means you're gonna scare the shit out of me like that again, I rather you didn't."

Her brows drew together. "It wasn't good for you?"

"Fuckin' amazing like it always is, but I thought I'd hurt you."

She giggled. "Yeah, I think I fainted."

His eyes hardened.

"In a good way…" she added quickly. "I…um…never felt anything like that before. I thought it was over, but then it kept going. I think it just got too intense and…" She met his eyes and flushed.

Satisfying to no end, knowing she got that from him, and the way she said it like it embarrassed her, hilarious. All of it turned him on.

He smirked, shaking his head. "What am I gonna do with my wild woman?"

She grinned. "Guess it takes a wild ride."

They burst out laughing.

About the Author

J.L. Sheppard was born and raised in South Florida where she still lives with her husband and sons.

As a child, her greatest aspiration was to become a writer. She read often, kept a journal, and wrote countless poems. She attended Florida International University and graduated in 2008 with a Bachelors in Communications. During her senior year, she interned at NBC Miami, WTVJ. Following the internship, she was hired and worked in the News Department for three years.

It wasn't until 2011 that she set her heart and mind into writing her first completed novel, which was first published in January 2013.

~*~

Visit J.L. at
www.jlsheppard.com

~*~

To chat with J.L. Sheppard and other Wild Rose Press authors of erotic romance, join us at
www.groups.yahoo.com/group/thewilderroses.

Also available from
The Wild Rose Press, Inc. and major retailers.

Running Wild

Hell Ryders MC Book 1

By J.L. Sheppard

When the perfect life Alyssa Holden planned turns out to be a life of lies, she runs to her brother, the only person she can trust. She has no idea she's running straight into a world of badass bikers who live and ride by their own rules. One tatted rebel in particular calls to her wilder side, and while everything in her draws her toward him, every experience she's had with men warns her away.

Jace Warren is doing what he's done his whole life—trying to survive, making the best with what he'd been given. The only life that makes sense after the military is Hell Ryders Motorcycle Club, but the sweet innocence of his army buddy's sister promises a different life, one a man like him can only dream of. Problem is, being his MC brother's sister puts her off limits. Hard as it is, he keeps his distance. Then she kisses him, and all bets are off.

Also Available
from The Wild Rose Press, Inc.
and major retailers.

When You Close Your Eyes

By Roxanne D. Howard

Dreams are the perfect shelter for fantasies, safe havens to step inside without changing our daily lives. For Lark Braithwaite, all that is about to change. During the last six months, Lark has dreamt of a mysterious Irish lover who knows what she wants and gives her exactly what she needs. In her waking life in busy London, things aren't as ideal as her long-term relationship with her controlling fiancé Charles has hit a dry spell.

When Lark is called home to Oregon for her father's funeral, she comes face to face with the demons from her past, but she never expects to meet her dream lover in the flesh. Niall O'Hagan steps straight out of her fantasies and into her life, and the powerful connection they share rocks her foundation. Although she's dealing with the bitterness of her fiancé's betrayal and his jealousy, Niall soon stirs Lark's awareness of her superficial existence and reawakens her sexuality…and her soul.

Thank you for purchasing
this publication of The Wild Rose Press, Inc.

For questions or more
information contact us at
info@thewildrosepress.com.

The Wild Rose Press, Inc.
www.thewildrosepress.com

To visit with authors of
The Wild Rose Press, Inc.
join our yahoo loop at
http://groups.yahoo.com/group/thewildrosepress/

www.ingramcontent.com/pod-product-compliance
Lightning Source LLC
Chambersburg PA
CBHW051127030726
47504CB00004B/746
9781509225750